PREGNANT BY THE COWBOY CEO

BY
CATHERINE MANN

Published in Great Britain 2015
by Mills & Boon, an imprint of Harlequin (UK) Limited,
Eton House, 18-24 Paradise Road, Richmond, Surrey, TW9 1SR

© 2015 Catherine Mann

ISBN: 978-0-263-25269-9

51-0715

Harlequin (UK) Limited's policy is to use papers that are natural, renewable and recyclable products and made from wood grown in sustainable forests. The logging and manufacturing processes conform to the legal environmental regulations of the country of origin.

Printed and bound in Spain
by CPI, Barcelona

USA TODAY bestselling author **Catherine Mann** lives on a sunny Florida beach with her flyboy husband and their four children. With more than forty books in print in over twenty countries, she has also celebrated wins for both a RITA® Award and a Booksellers' Best Award. Catherine enjoys chatting with readers online—thanks to the wonders of the internet, which allows her to network with her laptop by the water! Contact Catherine through her website, www.catherinemann.com, find her on Facebook and Twitter (@CatherineMann1), or reach her by post at PO Box 6065, Navarre, FL 32566, USA.

To my family—my world

Prologue

Two months ago

Amie McNair had never considered a one-night stand. Until now.

A champagne fountain gurgled beside her as she stared across the ballroom full of partiers gathered to celebrate her cousin's engagement. The night had been fun so far, but too similar to so many other glittering events that she attended in her work. She'd been thinking up an excuse to leave soon so she could trade her silky dress for the comfort of cotton pajamas. The jeweled choker at her throat was a gorgeous piece, but the yellow diamond at the base of her throat felt heavy. Tight. Like a collar keeping her neck in check. She liked her longer, bohemian-style pendants.

Those mundane thoughts scattered when he entered the room.

The broad-shouldered man striding confidently through the arched entryway pulled the air from her lungs. The connection was instantaneous. She wasn't quite certain why, but she forgot all about a desire for cotton pj's or the need to tug off her necklace. Her nerve endings sat up and paid attention.

Sure, he was tall, dark and hunky. But her world was filled with commanding, powerful men—from the cowboys that worked on her family's Hidden Gem Hobby Ranch, to the executives who worked in the family's Diamonds in the Rough jewelry-design empire. This man certainly measured up, from his muscled chest in the custom-tailored tuxedo, to the black Stetson he swept from his head and passed to an attendant near the entrance.

Yes, a Stetson and a tux.

And a boldly handsome face, tanned, with a strong square jaw. A face that had been lived in. His coal-black hair had a sprinkling of silver at the temples. That hint of age shouted wisdom, resolve. *Experience.*

A shiver tingled through her, gathering in all the right places.

Yet, in spite of all that, she found herself drawn most to his eyes. Even from halfway across the ballroom she could see they were a mesmerizing mix of gold and green that shifted ever so slightly with the chandelier sparkling overhead. She'd worked with amber that color in her jewelry designs and the changeable nature of the hue fascinated her. His gaze swept over her, past, then back again.

Holding.

That shiver inside her turned into a full-fledged fire. Her hand trembled and she set aside her champagne glass, her body already drawn forward in an undeniable magnetic pull. The urge to find out more about him propelled her feet across the room in time with the live band playing a classic Patsy Cline love song. Amie walked beneath the oversize, multicolored paper lanterns that decorated the room, toward the mystery man as he angled past guests in tuxes and formal gowns.

Other women noticed him, too, some of them watching every bit as intently as she did. But his eyes stayed on her as he closed the gap one bold step at a time.

Who was he? She knew most of the guests but didn't recognize him. Still, enough people nodded in greeting to him for her to know he wasn't a party crasher.

His gaze stroked over her, his hazel eyes gliding along her body like whispery smoke, confirming the awareness was reciprocated. She let herself relish the feeling, because honest to God, the last year had drained her. The grief over her grandmother's cancer, over the impending loss of the most important person in her life was heavy. Too heavy. From tip to toe, she hurt over losing her grandmother and, knowing Gran's legacy, her company was in the process of being handed over to a new CEO. So much change. Not the way her family's business was meant to be handled.

But right now, for the first time since her grandmother had announced her terminal brain tumor, there was a distraction from that ache in her heart.

A compelling, fascinating distraction.

She stopped in front of him, only a few inches apart. The crowd was so thick around them, the hum of their conversation and the band's tune created a false bubble of privacy. He held his silence, just looking back at her with a furrowed brow. Nice to know she wasn't the only one baffled by this moment.

She certainly didn't believe in love at first sight, but she couldn't deny the chemistry, the intense attraction, the connection that felt like more than simple lust. She understood physical attraction but considered herself beyond those superficial types of relationships. After all, her mother had trotted her across pageant stage from toddler days. Hair teased. Makeup. Ruffled custom dresses and shiny tap shoes.

Amie had been judged on her appearance, her walk, her smile for longer than she could remember. She'd seen enough backstabbing beauties with a Mona Lisa smile to know that the true value of a person went much deeper than the surface. Even knowing that, she couldn't deny how much she wanted this man.

She meant to say hello or introduce herself or ask his name. Instead, she glanced at his hand. No wedding ring. No tan line. "Are you married?"

A dark eyebrow lifted in a brief flash of surprise.

"Are you?" His voice rumbled between them with a hint of twang.

Local? Not quite. But definitely from a nearby region. His voice tripped along her senses, a deep tone that shivered against her skin.

She shook her head. "I'm not married."

"Me neither," he answered simply, without touching her. "Are you seeing anyone?"

She liked that it mattered to him. That said something good about him. "No. Are you seeing anyone?"

"Only the woman in front of me."

Oh. Damn. He was good. A small smile teased the corners of his mouth.

She wasn't sure exactly who moved first, but somehow her hand was tucked in the crook of his arm and he led her to the dance floor where they moved silently, their bodies in tune, step for step, through a slower country-music classic. The thick clusters of bright paper lanterns made the room glow with a rainbow of colors.

She breathed in his scent, clean but spicy, too. Masculine. Heady. His touch warmed her where he touched her waist. Her hand.

How long had it been since she'd felt a man's hands on her?

The energy between them crackled like static along her skin. Each chord from the string band strummed her oversensitive senses. She breathed in and he breathed out. Their steps synced effortlessly, her body responding to the slightest movement of his, shadowing his steps as she fell deeper into the spell of his gaze.

The dance gave her rare moments of pleasure in a year of hellish hurt and worry. No wonder she'd been drawn to him. She needed this. And in the same way that she could follow his steps, her body anticipating his next move, she could tell that he needed this, too. It was in his eyes. In the way his hand spanned her waist.

A step and swirl later and they were in the hall, then tucked in the deserted coatroom.

Then in each other's arms.

The dim lighting cast the room in shadows as she arched up into his kiss, his arms strong around her, but loose enough she could leave if she wanted. But the last thing she wanted was to stop. Pleasure pulsed through her at the angling of his mouth over hers, the touch of his tongue to hers. The kiss went deeper, faster, spiraling out of control in the quiet of the coat closet—a seriously underutilized space since it was spring in Texas.

Still, someone could walk in, and while she wasn't an exhibitionist, the possibility of discovery added an edge to an already razor-sharp need. The muffled sounds of music and partiers wafted under the door. She pressed herself to the hard planes of his body.

His arms moved up and he cupped her face, looking at her with those intense hazel eyes. "I don't do this sort of thing, tuck into coat closets with a stranger."

She covered his mouth with her hand. "We don't need to make excuses we have no way of knowing are true. This moment just…is. I don't understand why. But we're here." She took a deep breath of courage and said, "Lock the door."

Without a word, his hand slid behind him and the lock clicked in the long closet. The simple sound unleashed her barely contained passion. She looped her arms around his neck and lost herself in the kiss again. In the feel and fantasy of this man.

Her breasts tingled and tightened into hard beads of achy need. She couldn't remember when she'd been this turned inside out. She was thirty-one years old, not nearly a virgin. But she was unable to resist the draw of this stranger. The hard length of his erection pressed against her stomach, a heavy pressure that burned right through the silky dress she wore.

She couldn't deny where this was headed or that she wanted this. Him. Now.

His mouth traveled down her neck, then along her collarbone. "Condom. In my wallet," he said, his hands grazing under her breasts. "I'll get it."

He started to ease back and she stopped him, gripping his lapels.

"Let me."

Slipping her hand into his tuxedo jacket, she let her fingers stroke across the muscled heat of his chest. This was a man, the very best kind, powerful in body and mind. She tugged his wallet from inside his jacket and considered for an instant looking for a name, ...but her thoughts were scattered by his hands over her hips, gathering her dress. She plucked out a condom packet and tossed his wallet to the floor.

His hands were back on her just as fast, roving, keeping the flame burning.

She unzipped his pants as he lifted her hem. Her gown bunched around her hips, he hitched her up onto the small corner table where the coat check would normally pass out tickets during colder months. The wood was cool against her legs and then she slid them up and around his waist as he pressed against her, into her, with a thick pressure that sent a moan rolling up her throat.

It wasn't an elegant coupling. Her need was frenzied and his matched hers. This was crazy and out of control. And perfect. She lost herself in the pleasure, her senses heightened until everything felt...more. The tangy scent of his aftershave swirled inside her with every breath. Music muffled from the other room serenaded them, syncing their bodies into the most fundamental of dances.

And then thoughts disintegrated, the pace speeding, rising, bliss swelling inside her until she bit her lip to hold back a cry of pleasure that would betray their hideaway at any moment. He skimmed down the shoulder of her dress, dipping his head to take her breast in his mouth. That warm, moist tug took away the last of her restraint. Her head falling back, she surrendered to the orgasm sparkling through her like the facets off a diamond. The hoarse low sound of his release as he thrust deeply one last time sent another shimmer through her, leaving her languid, replete.

Using a last whisper of energy, she lolled forward. Her head rested on his shoulder as she waited for her racing heart to slow. His hands glided up and down her spine, easing her back to her feet, holding her up.

He smoothed her dress into place again and pressed a kiss to her temple. "We should tal—"

She shook her head. "Please. Don't say anything." She tugged her capped sleeve back over her shoulder and skimmed along her hair, the French braid having stayed miraculously in place, right down to the jeweled flower pin she'd clipped to the end of the braid. "Let's go back out. Go to separate sides of the room. And when, or if, we meet…it will be for the first time. Let this be what it is."

A fantasy. A once-in-a-lifetime crazy encounter—and she didn't want to hear it was commonplace for him. Didn't want to think about what she'd just done. Not while her body still trembled with pleasure and her heartbeat pulsed an erratic rhythm.

She didn't wait for his answer.

Reaching behind her, she simply unlocked the door, tucking out and around. Her legs were less than steady as she made her way back to the ballroom, and the sound of his footsteps close behind her didn't help. Was he following her? Was he going to insist or make a scene?

A mix of anticipation and dread made her chest tight with nerves.

The cool blast of the air conditioner in the hall rushed over her heated skin, goose bumps rising along her arms. The band still played, having picked up the speed with vintage Johnny Cash.

And before she could clear her head, she realized her grandmother had blocked her path. Mariah McNair looked regal but frail as she clutched her cane.

The tangy scent of masculine aftershave teased Amie's nose. Was it wafting from him behind her? Or just clinging to her body to remind her of what she'd done?

Her grandmother gripped the cane in a hand bearing sparkling jeweled rings. One of them was an amethyst heart Amie had designed as a teenager. With her other hand, Mariah took hers in a cool grasp, her skin paper thin and covered with bruises from IVs. Despite her frailty, Mariah's grip was firm, confident. "Amie, dear, I was just looking for you to introduce you. But I see you and Preston have met."

Foreboding iced out residual passion. "Preston?"

Her brain worked overtime to make the pieces fit any other way but the one she feared.

Yet the magnetic, compelling man she'd just given herself to in a coat closet stepped around her, his eyebrows now pinched together as he whispered, "Amie?"

Her stomach dropped as if she'd just fallen down an elevator shaft. Dawning realization robbed her of speech, her mouth bone dry.

Her grandmother squeezed Amie's hand as she smiled at Preston.

"I'm so glad you've had a chance to get to know our new CEO." Mariah extended her hand to the man. "Welcome to the Hidden Gem Ranch."

One

Two Months Later

Preston Armstrong was not a fan of weddings. Not even when he'd been the groom. Since his divorce ten years ago, he was even less entertained by overpriced ceremonial gatherings. He considered himself a practical businessman. That mind-set had taken him from a poor childhood to the top of the corporate ladder.

So, attending a marriage ceremony and seeing Amie McNair front and center of attention as a bridesmaid took his irritation to a whole deeper level—even now at the reception. Especially given that she'd ignored him for the past two months.

And most especially since she looked sexy as hell in a peach-colored bridesmaid's dress. Weren't those gowns supposed to be ugly, hated by bridal attendants around the world? But then, beautiful Amie with her luscious curves and confidence could probably make a burlap sack look sexy as hell. She'd won all those beauty-pageant titles for a reason.

Although he thought she was more alluring now with her at-ease boho look than the old runway-glitz photos that still periodically showed up in the social pages. Even her signature-designed coral teardrop earrings and necklace held his attention. Particularly the way that pendant nestled between the swell of her breasts.

He tipped his aged bourbon back, the sounds of the reception wrapping around him as he put in his required appearance at the McNair wedding event. He glanced at his watch, figuring he had to put in another half hour before he could check out and head back to the office. It was quiet there at night. He got more work done.

If Amie would talk to him alone for five damn minutes, he could reassure her that the closet encounter would never have happened if he'd known who she was. From the horrified expression on her face when her grandmother introduced them, clearly Amie didn't want anything to do with him either.

Business and pleasure should be kept separate. Always.

He didn't have the time or patience for awkwardness. He was confident. In charge. But that had all changed the minute he'd looked across the social function and saw a woman who'd flipped his world upside down.

This whole wedding week had gone to a new level of uncomfortable, to say the least. Being around Amie at work, they could keep things professional, if tense. It wasn't easy with all those thoughts of their explosive encounter hammering through his memory, but he managed to keep his boardroom calm intact.

However, the parties this week reminded him too much of that night he'd met her at the newlyweds' engagement shindig.

He'd meant it when he'd told her that impulsive encounter wasn't the norm for him. While he wasn't a monk, impetuous sex with strangers had never been his style. He'd spent a large part of his adult life married and monogamous. Then after his divorce, affairs had been careful, sensual but civil, with no long-term expectations.

He had affairs. Not hookups. And he sure as hell didn't have anonymous sex with a woman more than a decade younger than him.

Until Amie. Nothing about her followed a familiar pattern for him.

Keeping his hands to himself today was an exercise in torture, just as at work. Hints of her sucker punched his libido. The soft scent of her perfume lingering in his office after a meeting. The heat of her as she stood near him in a crowded elevator. And the list went on since she worked in the same building, her role as a renowned gemologist crucial to some of the most popular Diamonds in the Rough jewelry lines.

Up on the small stage in the oversize barn, the country band returned from their break, taking their place again and picking up instruments. Although to call it a barn didn't do the space justice. The reception was being held at the McNairs' hobby ranch, Hidden Gem, so the place was high end rustic, just like the company jewels.

Gold chandeliers and puffs of white flowers dangled

from the rough-hewn rafters. Strings of lights criss-crossed the ceiling, creating a starlit-night atmosphere. Bouquets of baby's breath and roses tied with burlap bows on the tables made him recall his earlier thought about Amie classing up a burlap sack. The inside had been transformed into rustic elegance, with gold chairs and white tulle draped throughout.

At the entry table next to the leather guestbook, seating cards were tied to horseshoes that had the bride's and groom's names engraved along with the wedding date. A cowbell hung on a brass hook with a sign that stated, Ring for a Kiss.

Good God. He wanted out of here. He knocked back the rest of the bourbon.

Amie's cousin Stone McNair, the former CEO of Diamonds in the Rough, was the groom, and there was no doubt he believed in all this forever, happily-ever-after nonsense as he twirled his blonde bride around on the dance floor.

At least the ceremony in the chapel had been brief. One bridesmaid and one groomsman—Amie and her twin brother, Alex. Amie's dark brown hair was loose, in thick spiral curls that made him want to tug just to see what she would do.

To hell with standing around. He might as well confront the awkwardness. It wasn't as if she could run away from him here.

He set aside the cut-crystal glass and strode through the crowd, a who's who list of Texas rich and famous. Just like that night two months ago, he made his way to her, this time determined for closure rather than a start of something.

Getting her semi-alone here shouldn't be too tough.

The exclusive venue had plenty of dark corners arranged for privacy so guests could visit and catch up.

He stopped behind her, smiling over her shoulder at the mayor. "I'm sorry to interrupt, but Miss McNair promised me this dance."

Amie gasped, her mouth opening to protest. But Preston took her hand and pulled her onto the dance floor before she could speak. He hauled her out in front of the small chamber orchestra, moving quickly before the stunned expression could melt from her elegant face. Before a closed, frosty one took its place. He'd watched that transformation too often over the last eight weeks and it was time to put an end to it.

He slid an arm around her and drew her close, those dark brown curls brushing him. "You look lovely tonight. Especially for being stuck in a bridesmaid's dress."

"It would have been nice to be asked if I wanted to dance. What are you doing?"

"Dancing with the groom's cousin. A perfectly acceptable move, nothing to draw attention to us. Unless you cause a scene out here in front of your whole family, our business acquaintances and some mighty prominent politicians."

Which he definitely did not want her to do. Then, he would have to let her go. And he liked the feel of her in his arms again too much to have her walk away yet.

"Fine," she conceded, blue eyes predictably turning to ice as she spoke. "Let's dance for appearances. Gran's always saying it's good for the company if we show a unified front."

Oh, he had her here for more than appearances and business. He was going to find a way to get past her cold shoulder. He couldn't stop the attraction, and chances were slim to none that he would be able to act on it. But he could damn well do something to disperse the tension between them.

He hoped.

Preston sidestepped another couple and swept her to a less crowded corner of the dance floor, mindful of the security guards posted around the perimeter of the event. "It's quite a party tonight. Congratulations to your cousin and his bride on their nuptials."

If Stone hadn't given up his role as CEO of Diamonds in the Rough, Preston wouldn't have been here. And the job was damn important to him. His job was all he had after the crash and burn of his personal life.

She smiled tightly, her body stiff and unyielding in his arms. "We do have all the tools for a first-rate wedding at our disposal."

The bride's thirty-thousand-dollar tiara had been custom designed for the event; in fact, a delicately understated piece that Amie had worked on personally for weeks. The tiara alone had created industry buzz and media coverage alike, a key piece in the company's new bridal collection.

"Do you realize this is the first time we've spoken about anything other than business?" He respected her work ethic, and discovering that admirable trait about her made this all the more difficult. Unlike her father, she was more than a figurehead. Amie contributed immeasurably to the company, so Preston crossed her path. Often.

She angled closer and for an instant he thought maybe… his pulse sped. His gaze dropped to her mouth. To her lips, parted.

And then, too soon, her breath teased against his

neck as she whispered, "I just want to make it clear, we won't be heading for the coat closet tonight."

There was no mistaking her determination. Too bad her method for delivering the news had him ready to sweep her off her feet and back to the cabin he'd reserved on the property for the night.

"I'm quite clear on that after your big chill these past two months." His hand twitched against her waist, the memory of her satiny skin still burned in his memory. "I'm just glad to know you're finally willing to acknowledge it happened."

"Of course it happened," she hissed between pearly-white teeth. "I was very much there."

The brush of her body against his was sweet torture. "I remember well."

Shadows shifted through her sky blue eyes. "Did you know who I was that night?"

Her words slowed his feet, stunning him. He picked up the dance pace again and asked, "Is that what you've thought all this time? That I played you on purpose?"

"Forget I said anything." She pulled back. "It doesn't matter now."

He strengthened his hold. "Not that you would believe me regardless of what I say. Although it was more than clear you didn't know who I was, and if you had, that night wouldn't have happened." He touched her face lightly. "And that would have been a damn shame."

They stood so close, their mouths only a couple of inches apart. He remembered how good she tasted—and how complicated that had made things for them the past couple of months. Having an affair with her would be a bad idea, given he was her boss and she was the granddaughter of the major stockholder.

But God, he was tempted.

So was she. He could see it in her jewel-blue eyes and the way she swayed toward him an instant before she stepped back.

Grasping his wrists, she pulled his arms from her. "I'm not sure what spurred you to reminisce right now since you don't seem to be the type to get sentimental at weddings. But now is not the time or the place for this discussion."

His eyebrows rose in surprise. "You're willing to talk then? Later?"

She held up a hand. "Talk. Only. I mean that."

"Let's step outside—"

"No. Not here. Not tonight."

He reached for her, sensing already she was just putting him off again. "Amie, if this is another stall tactic—"

"We'll have our secretaries check our calendars and schedule a lunch next week. Okay? Is that specific enough for you? Now, I need to check on my grandmother." She spun away in a swirl of peach silk.

Standing in the middle of the dance floor, he watched her walk away, the sway of her hips and those million-dollar legs peeking through a slit in the dress. Stepping off the dance floor, he wondered what the hell he hoped to gain in a conversation with her. An affair, given their work connection, was a bad idea, but he wasn't in the market for anything long term. Not again.

He charged back to the bar for another bourbon on the rocks, ignoring a waiter's offering of the evening's signature beverage, a Mouton Rothschild favored by the couple. Tonight, bourbon would do just fine. Marriage hadn't worked out well for him. At all. Just ask his ex.

He was too absorbed with work, too much of a loner. After all, a boss couldn't party with his subordinates, which put a serious dent in any kind of social life. He wanted to say that's what had made him so susceptible to Amie that first night, but he knew it was more than that. He was a man of control. Calm. Yet, the second he'd seen Amie, he'd claimed her with that first look in an explosive chemistry that went beyond any he'd experienced before, even with his ex-wife.

No wonder his marriage had failed early on. He'd made a fortune and in the end it hadn't made a bit of difference when things mattered most.

Rather than subject their daughter to a divorce, he and his wife had tried to hold it together for their child. But theirs had become a marriage in name only. Eventually, his ex had found someone else. She'd told Preston her new love would at least be around, which was better for Leslie than an absentee father. He'd bought into that, feeling guilty as hell and incapable of giving his child what she needed.

He'd replayed that decision a million times over, wondering if he'd fought harder for his marriage, for his child, if life could have turned out differently. Guilt piled on top of more guilt.

His baby girl had flown out of control during her teen years. Drugs, alcohol, sex. He'd tried grounding her, taking away her car, her allowance. He'd planned to take a vacation week to spend time with her, let her pick the vacation spot. She'd turned him down.

He should have persisted. He'd thought about it. Then it was too late.

Leslie ran off with her boyfriend the day after graduation, seventeen years old, pregnant. She'd ignored all offers of help and advice, determined to put her parents and the lifestyle she hated behind her. She hadn't cared about wealth or private jets. Hadn't wanted her own driver or a massive home. She'd even snubbed a doctor's care.

She and her baby boy had died seven months into the pregnancy. Premature delivery. Something with the placenta presenting first. His daughter, Leslie, bled to death. The baby lived for two days before dying.

The Armstrong portfolio was worth billions and his daughter and grandson had died from lack of prenatal care because she hated him that much. So much, she wouldn't take a penny or the most basic advice from him.

Some days the senselessness of it made it nearly impossible to hold back the rage.

The pain.

His child. Gone.

His ex blamed him. Damn it all, but he blamed himself, too.

So he put one foot in front of the other and existed.

Until that moment he'd seen Amie McNair. What was it about her? He wasn't the type to fall for a pretty face. But she was more than that. Not that he'd known as much that night. He'd just looked into her eyes and he'd seen…

Something that scared the hell out of him. Something worth going back for.

A risk he couldn't take again.

Pushing her grandmother's wheelchair down the hall to the family quarters, Amie took comfort from the ever-present scent of oak and pine that permeated the main lodge at Hidden Gem Ranch. The family wing could be accessed privately from the outside, but tonight, she'd taken the easier path through the lobby, waving to the night desk clerk on duty.

Now, as they passed through double doors that required a pass code, Amie could still barely breathe after how close she'd come to kissing Preston right there on the dance floor in front of everyone. She did not need people gossiping about the two of them. Especially not now. Damn him for rattling her. She needed to keep a cool head for her grandmother's sake.

Amie had never been known for her restraint.

She'd been sorely tempted to steal one more passionate moment with him before the inevitable conversation he'd insisted on having. But then her stomach had started churning and she'd made the excuse about secretaries and calendars before bolting.

Throwing up on his shoes would have been the worst way to tell him their night in the coat closet had created a baby.

Somehow, in spite of the condom, she was undeniably pregnant. She hadn't been with anyone else in six months, so there was no question about the paternity. She needed to tell him soon and agree on a plan before she shared the news with her grandmother.

Amie glanced down at her grandmother's gray head, her body frail from cancer, her once-long hair now short, just beginning to grow back from the latest round of treatments and surgeries that had only delayed the inevitable. "You overextended yourself this week, Gran."

Amie backed into her grandmother's suite of rooms, a decorative set of cattle horns on the door, an old joke of Gran's from her days in the corporate boardroom when a competitor had called her bullheaded. Gran had proudly taken to displaying this set on the front of her chauffeur-driven vehicle. These days, they resided on her door, still a reminder of her strength.

"Of course I did." Gran reached back to pat Amie's fingers on the handle, hand trembling. "I would rather die a day or two earlier than miss making the most of my grandson's wedding festivities."

"Well, that's blunt." Amie maneuvered the chair along a Persian rug, past a long leather sofa, the fireplace roaring with a warm blaze despite the summer temperature outside. Her grandmother appreciated the ambience and didn't mind the extra warmth in her more frail condition.

"You're one to talk considering you are just like me, stubborn as hell."

"I'll take that as a compliment, thank you very much."

Gran would be happy about the baby, no question. But Amie worried about the future because there was no way the critically ill woman would live long enough to see her great-grandchild's face. Amie couldn't bear to add more concerns. Beyond making her final days peaceful, stress was also a danger to her already fragile health. Amie needed to get her life together and develop a plan regarding Preston's role in their child's life. In this much, at least, she could be like her grandmother. Strong. Driven.

Calculating.

As the wheelchair rolled to a stop, Mariah folded her hands in her lap again. The bedroom was at once familiar and alien with its soaring high ceilings in rustic woodwork, supported by exposed beams in a darker wood. A two-tiered cast-iron chandelier hung over the living area, casting a warm glow, with lights that looked like gently flickering candles. Two wingback chairs bracketed the stone fireplace where she'd shared secrets and hot chocolate with her grandmother. But now there were additions to the place—a wheeled hospital cart of medical supplies and a leather recliner where the night nurse usually kept watch.

No doubt, Gran's caregiver would report in as soon as Amie sent her a text.

"Can I help you get settled? Bring you anything before I call for the nurse?" She took out her phone but wanted to stay. Wanted to visit the way they used to, never caring how late the hour.

Her eyes burned as she blinked away unexpected tears.

Her grandmother gestured for her to sit. "Amie, I've lived a full life. Of course I would have liked to have more, or at the very least live these last days in full health. But I'm making the most of the time I have left. I've seen one grandson married and have hopes the other grandson will be settled soon."

Ouch. No mention of her granddaughter. Just that Stone was married, and Alex had found the perfect woman. She swallowed hard.

"Alex and Nina are happy, and her son, Cody, is precious." She was happy for Alex. Her twin's joy was her joy.

"It's good to see a child here in the house again. I've missed the laughter of a little one."

Did her grandmother know? Was she hinting for an admission or just referencing Cody? Shooting to her feet, she turned away to hide any telltale expressions on her face. Amie picked up the pewter pitcher on the bedside table and refilled her grandmother's water glass, unable to pull her eyes away from the photo of her grandparents on their wedding day. "You should turn in early and conserve your strength for the family breakfast tomorrow."

"I'm resting now and my strength isn't going to return," she said with a dry laugh. She sipped her water, cleared her throat and continued, "I don't have to sleep to relax. Let's talk."

"About what?" Her skin prickled. She sat on the chaise at the end of the four-poster bed that had been converted into a queen-size hospital bed. Unwilling to think about that—and how hard life had become for her beloved grandmother, Amie bent to breathe in the delicate scent of lilies of the valley in a big bunch on the nightstand.

Gran set aside her glass of water. "Stone and Alex have both passed their test to assure me they can handle their share of the inheritance, that they can carry on the McNair tradition in the spirit I would wish."

Her cousin Stone had surprised them all by stepping down as CEO of Diamonds in the Rough and developing his nearby land. He'd started an equine therapy camp for children with special needs. Her twin brother, Alex, had gained their grandmother's trust to keep running the Hidden Gem Ranch and opened up parts of the facility for Stone's camp.

"Ah, so now you get to the reason for this conversation." She sagged back, clutching a decorative pillow protectively. "What do you have cooked up for me?"

"You don't need to look so worried." A smile lighting her sapphire-blue eyes, Gran smoothed her grandmother-of-the-groom turquoise satin dress, the hem heavy with silver embroidery that mimicked a Diamonds in the Rough necklace she favored.

"Of course I'm worried. And more than a little curious. You saved my test for last for a reason, I'm sure.

I assume that's because my challenge is the most difficult. Or I'm the most difficult to deal with." A bitter memory from her past seeped in. "Mom always coveted that slot to perform last in a pageant to keep me foremost in the judges' minds. After the bar had been raised as high as possible, she figured I would know how well I had to perform to win."

Like the year her mother had changed Amie's baton-twirling act into a fire-throwing stunt—just half an hour before Amie took the stage—since another girl had done a great baton act. Amie would have never guessed her mother could find a way to light the ends of her batons on fire in thirty minutes. But with Mc-Nair wealth and a helpful hotel concierge, anything was possible for a demanding pageant mother. Amie hadn't burned down the building or set herself on fire, but she hadn't won and she'd been scared as hell.

Gran's smile faded and sympathy filled her eyes. "The test I have in mind isn't like your mother making you compete in all those beauty pageants."

"Isn't it?" Amie said bitterly, then felt guilty right away. It wasn't her grandmother's fault. "Never mind. Forget I said that. I know you're not like Bayleigh... You love me, so whatever you're doing must be for a reason."

"Your mother loves you, dear, she's just..."

"Self-absorbed." There was no denying the truth. "I've acknowledged that and moved on. I'm an adult and I accept responsibility for my own feelings."

Gran tipped her head to the side. "You say that, but until this moment, I never realized this test would make you feel as if my love is conditional...like your mother's."

"Does that mean I'm off the hook with my challenge?

You'll fire Preston and put me in charge?" she asked, only half joking.

"Oh dear, you always did have a great sense of humor," Gran said affectionately. "This isn't about my love for you. Love isn't about money. You have millions with your trust fund and personal earnings. This is about figuring out where you best fit professionally in the business."

"What if I do like Stone and decide to build my own future?" She just wished there was something else she wanted to do, but she lived and breathed to work at Diamonds in the Rough.

Or at least she had until Preston showed up and took away the job she'd hoped for as her own.

"That's your choice. But keep in mind Stone still took his test because he knew that would put my mind at ease. These requests of mine are because I love you and I want the best for you."

Amie sighed, exhaustion stealing through her. "I do know that, Gran."

Her grandmother's shoulders braced. "This week Preston Armstrong is traveling in support of the unveiling of our new line. I want you to go with him."

She waited for the rest and…nothing. "That's it?" Amie asked, incredulous. "That's my test?"

"Yes, be civil. Don't cause a scene. Truly show the world that we're a unified force, even away from the office, and stockholders will be reassured."

"A week on the road with no scenes." She'd kept her distance from him for two months, she could do so for longer.

"That's all."

"You're letting me off rather easy," she conceded,

hoping she could finish up some design work on the trip since she'd been working night and day on a secret collection—a labor of love that she worried wasn't right for Diamonds in the Rough.

"I don't think so." Her grandmother shook her head. "Not considering the cold shoulder you've given him these past couple of months."

She could have sworn she'd kept that from her grandmother. Mariah wasn't at the office often at all. Amie had imagined—hoped—her chilly reception would be perceived as businesslike.

She'd guessed wrong. "I apologize if you think I haven't been receptive to your new CEO. I thought I was simply being professional."

"Don't try that innocent act with me," Gran snorted. "You won't even stay in the same room with him unless forced by a meeting. I'm not sure what your differences are and I don't need to know. We are very lucky to have lured him away from his job in Oklahoma. It was a big sell convincing him this job would increase his corporate appeal as a man of serious net worth and business importance. I do not want to lose him at Diamonds in the Rough, as our stocks continue to rise since we announced he was taking the helm."

"Rising at the expense of firing some of our most loyal, long-serving middle management," she reminded her grandmother.

"And I can see you're still bitter about that decision to consolidate here and expand other offices."

Amie pressed her lips together to keep from arguing with her grandmother, something that would only stress her out since clearly this battle was already lost.

Gran nodded wearily. "Reconcile with him. Because,

like it or not, he is the CEO, and if having you there up-
sets the flow of business, well, I can't have that."

The full weight of her grandmother's words sunk in.
"Are you threatening to fire me?"

And just as troubling, what did Preston have to do
with this? Had he been pressuring Gran to nudge her
out of the company? Or to find another angle to wran-
gle his way into her bed?

His approach tonight might not have been coinci-
dental. He could have set this whole thing up, damn
him. Anger fired hotter inside her, almost a welcome
relief after the frustrated passion, fear for her child—
and grief for Gran.

"Let's not borrow trouble. Focus on the week and learn
to forge a friendship with Preston."

Friendship? With the father of her child from a one-
night stand? And how was he going to react to the news
of the baby? Gran's request might not even be possible.
"What if Preston doesn't agree? Or if he's antagonistic?"

Her grandmother smiled with a narrow-eyed determination Amie recognized well. "Then you'll just have
to win him over. Because, like it or not, your days of
avoiding him are done."

Two

Hands jammed in his tuxedo pockets, Preston strode away from the barn to the resort cabin where he planned to spend the night. Most of the guests were either staying in the main lodge or in one of the bungalows scattered around the property.

He'd done his duty at the reception, put in an appearance. With luck, he could pull out his laptop and log some extra hours preparing for his upcoming business trip. He would try to numb his mind and body against the attraction. Just being near Amie at the wedding had desire pumping through him. He needed to come up with some kind of plan to work with her without this eating them both alive, but damned if he knew which way to turn. For now, burying himself in reports and numbers would have to do.

The reception was still going strong in the towering barn, music and conversation swelling out into the night. The lodge itself held two wings, one for family suites and the other for guests. Then the cabins offered larger, more private space, farther away from the din of the ongoing party.

A movement from the family quarters snagged his attention, a shadowy figure charging across a first-floor veranda. The moonlight cast a glow, illuminating the unmistakable silhouette of... Amie. She paused at the railing, scanning the grounds. She was looking for him—that was clear the second her gaze landed on him.

Her shoulders went back, her breasts straining at the strapless dress, teardrop earrings brushing her bare shoulders. She flicked her long hair over her shoulder, her eyes narrowing. She stomped down the porch steps, hem of her bridesmaid's gown in her fists and hitched to her knees so she could storm closer all the faster. Something had lit her fuse. He wanted her attention back on him anyway.

He stopped in his tracks and waited. Anticipation pumped through him. Even mad, she was incredible, a sight not to be missed. Besides, there was something about knowing he got under her skin this much. That he'd put all that spark and fire inside her.

She stopped in front of him under the shade of a sprawling oak strung with white lights. Her breasts rose and fell rapidly, enticingly. "Are you responsible for this?"

Responsible for what? He could hardly think with her so close, her heaving breasts nearly brushing his chest. He would only need to move one step closer. "You'll need to narrow that down for me."

"You said on the dance floor that we need to talk soon." She jabbed him in the chest with one finger.

He grabbed her finger. "And you said our secretaries need to set up a lunch next week."

"Did you know that couldn't possibly happen? Did you pressure my grandmother into making me travel with you around the country this week?"

He dropped her hand. He didn't know what the hell she was talking about. He was heading out for a week to launch a new line for Diamonds in the Rough, but he'd made no plans to take her along. Apparently she thought otherwise for some reason.

Still, that didn't explain her angry reaction. They'd worked together for two months. Why was she so upset about this trip? He was missing something and he wasn't sure what.

But he intended to find out. "Why would I go out of my way to insist on that?"

"For a week of repeats of our encounter in the coat closet two months ago."

Righteous indignation steamed through him. "Have I pressured you in any way that would make you assume that I would disregard your wishes? Because I take the issue of sexual harassment in the workplace damn seriously."

"No, you haven't done anything inappropriate," she acquiesced, chewing her full bottom lip. "But you sounded determined tonight. I just had to know if you're manipulating me behind the scenes as well."

Unable to resist taunting her, he stepped closer, letting his gaze linger on her mouth as their bodies brushed. "Should I have?"

A light flashed in the night sky and an appreciative

murmur went up from a crowd gathered on the western lawn. The fireworks show had started to celebrate the nuptials.

"Quit twisting my words around." She tipped her face toward him without backing down, her creamy skin lit by the purple-and-white lights sparking overhead. "I don't like being played, that's all."

He swept a stray lock of silky dark hair over her shoulder, his knuckles skimming her soft skin, the teardrop earring cool across the top of his hand. "I take this to mean we're going on a business trip together this week."

The crowd watching fireworks cheered as a series of pops and bangs ended in a giant red heart burning into the cloudless Texas sky.

Her eyebrows pinched together, her gaze never wavering to watch the display. "You really don't know about my grandmother's plan for us?"

Gently, he gripped her shoulders and turned her so she could see the bright red heart before it faded. While she watched, he leaned closer to speak into her ear.

"I have no reason to lie to you." In fact, he just wanted to open a dialogue with her so they could figure out how to work together—or resume the affair. He couldn't help but wonder if part of the reason they kept sparking off each other was that they hadn't let all that attraction run its course. "It's been tough breaking through your walls these past two months, but I wouldn't go to someone else to take care of that problem for me. And I certainly wouldn't worry a terminally ill person with my concerns."

She turned to face him again, giving him a clipped nod, some of the tension easing from her while the orchestra played a Mozart piece timed to coordinate with the explosions in the air.

He leaned back against the tree trunk and jammed his hands into his pockets and away from temptation. "Now catch me up to speed about what's going on with this business trip, since it appears to involve us both and Diamonds in the Rough."

"My grandmother has insisted that I accompany you for the unveiling of the new line to reassure the stockholders that the McNairs fully endorse your leadership." Sighing, she perched a hand on her hip.

Preston's gaze fell to her waist, the dips and curves of her so damn alluring his mouth watered. "That's a sound business decision on her part. What's the problem?"

He didn't understand why she was so upset. She'd worked hard on the new line, had invested a lot of time and creative energy toward putting it together. She deserved to see the first public reactions to her work.

But she shook her head. Visibly upset.

"The problem is… She's an amazing woman and I just want to do what she needs." She blinked back tears, making her blue eyes shine in the reflected light from the soaring roman candles in a multicolored display. That sheen in her gaze made him want to hold her.

"Amie?" He resisted the urge to reach for her, half certain she would bolt. "Losing someone you love is not easy. I'm sorry about your grandmother's illness."

"Me, too." She swiped her wrist over her eyes, smudging mascara. "So we're traveling together this week for the unveiling tour. Just the two of us."

"Apparently so." He wondered what her grandmother was up to with this last-minute idea and why she hadn't discussed it with him first. "To Los Angeles, New York City and Atlanta. It may be for the best. We have to figure out how to work together without all this tension."

He had sensed that Amie was working on a private project these last few weeks and he wondered why she hadn't shared any details. That kind of closed-off creativity didn't benefit the larger company. He needed her communicating more.

Had that been Mariah McNair's intent, to smooth the business waters before she passed away? It wasn't such an odd wish. The woman did live, eat and breathe the business, even from her sickbed.

Amie crossed her arms over her chest, her breasts pushing even harder against the fabric. "We've been doing fine so far at the office."

"Are you serious?" These had been some of the most tense workweeks in his life. He'd never had personnel problems—until now. Until her.

"Has my work performance been in any way substandard?"

"Of course not," he admitted, not mentioning the way she'd retreated to her office for long periods at a time with her door closed. "But it would help workplace morale if you didn't act like you want me dead."

Her shoulders sagged, her eyes softening. "I do not want you dead."

"Then how exactly do you want me?" He stepped closer, his eyes falling to her mouth, to her full lips. Amie McNair had a way of knocking the props out from under him by just walking into a room, and he was damn tired of tap dancing around the subject. He was too old for games.

The fireworks on the lawn churned faster, shot after

shot popping and exploding, sending showers of sparks into the night sky. The fireworks reflected in Amie's eyes as she stepped back, expression iced over again. "If we're going to be away for a week, I should start packing."

Turning, she marched across the grass, her beautiful body illuminated by white lights in the sky that turned on and off, on and off.

Just like Amie herself.

Amie was exhausted to her toes. Not just from the wedding but from the shocking talk with her grandmother to the confrontation with Preston.

She was truly going to spend a week alone with him.

Closing her bedroom door, she finally let her guard down. Kneeling, she held out her hands for her cats, a gray tabby in her lap, a Siamese at her feet, both hers, and Mariah's two Persians as well. Yes, she was just shy of a crazy-cat-lady starter kit, but her furbabies brought her comfort. With a final stroke along each feline's arched back, she stood. She'd loved growing up on a farm with animals all around, even if her room was far from rustic, a jewel box of a space, from the strands of multicolored glass beads around her bed, to the stained-glass insets in the high windows above her reading area.

Walking out of her shoes, she reached behind her to unzip the bridesmaid's dress. She shimmied it down and kicked it aside. She sagged to sit on the edge of her bed. She flopped back on the bed, the silk of her camisole and tap pants soft against her skin still tingling from Preston's touch. Damn it, she hated losing her composure. And to lose it twice in one night?

Her hand slid over her stomach. No baby bump yet, but soon more than just her breasts would be swelling. And her hormones were out of control, leaving her tearful most of the time and nauseated the rest of the time. Her figure would soon be evident to everyone. No more pageant jokes about her size.

She'd been the first runner-up in the Miss Texas pageant over a decade ago, reportedly the first beauty competition she'd lost since her mother had teased up her hair and sent Amie tap-dancing out on the stage at four years old. She'd "Good Ship Lollipopped" her way through puberty into bikinis and spray tans. Her mama had lived for her daughter's wins.

She didn't even want to think about her parents' reaction to her pregnancy.

There wasn't anything she could do about it tonight and she truly was exhausted. No matter how much she slept, her body demanded more. She reached on the bedside table for her mouth guard by the phone. Tension had made her grind her teeth at night since she was seventeen and entered higher-stakes pageants.

She'd already seen a doctor to confirm and start prenatal vitamins. The appointment had been scary and exciting at the same time. Preston deserved the opportunity to be a part of his child's life from the start—if he wanted. She would have to tell him about the baby this week. It wasn't fair to wait any longer. This was his child too. She would just have to find the right time. His reaction would also have a lot to do with how she presented the news to the rest of her family.

If only she knew him better, knew how he would react, how he would want to proceed. She was capable and prepared to take care of the baby herself. But she didn't want her child to live with a father's rejection.

She squeezed her eyes shut and buried her face in her pillow, wishing she could will herself to sleep faster.

The phone rang on her bedside table, jarring her. Was something wrong with her grandmother?

Flinging back the covers, she grabbed the receiver and pulled out her mouth guard. "Hello?"

"Amie?" her twin brother's voice filled her ear. "Are you okay?"

"Of course." She tugged the covers back up again. "Why do you ask?"

"You left the reception before it was over. That isn't like you."

They always had been in tune with each other's moods. Her brother wasn't normally a chatty person, so for him to call, he must sense something was up. But she wasn't ready to tell him. It wouldn't be fair to tell anyone before Preston.

"Gran was tired, so I took her back to her room, then I decided to slip out. I did see the fireworks display though. It was a beautiful touch." No way was she telling him about Gran's test. He would worry, wonder— question. "I hope you don't mind that I left the hosting duties to you."

"Of course I don't mind. We're family. You've been carrying more than your fair share of the McNair face time for Hidden Gem business this past year. The reception was winding down by the time you left. Mother and Father were in their element entertaining anyway."

"They do like to play the head-of-the-family role."

Their parents lived off a trust fund, tightly managed by Gran's lawyers. Their cousin Stone's mother also lived off her trust fund, working to stay clean after multiple stints in drug rehab. Leaving the bulk of her estate to her grandchildren was a huge vote of confidence from Gran that Amie didn't take lightly. Her grandmother's respect meant everything to her.

Amie was determined to do better by her own child than her stage mom, Bayleigh. Without question, Mariah was the better role model.

Amie tucked the phone more securely under her neck. "Was there anything else?"

"What was up with you and Armstrong on the dance floor? Any progress getting along better with the new boss? He's really not such a bad guy. We had a good time playing cards at the bachelor party."

"Have you been talking to Gran?" she asked suspiciously.

"No, I just got to know him better with all the wedding parties this week. We talked some."

"Talked about what?"

He laughed softly. "You sound nervous."

The twin bond was sure a pain in the butt sometimes. "I'm not nervous. I'm just exhausted." Really exhausted. She'd never been as tired in her life as she'd been the past few weeks. "Good night, Alex. Love you." She hung up the phone and resisted the urge to pull the covers over her head.

Someone was going to guess soon and her secret would be out. She needed to control the telling.

Sunday morning, Preston waited beside the limo, outside the Hidden Gem Ranch. It wasn't like Amie to be late. Ever. She was always one of the first at work and last to leave. But she'd kept him out here hanging around for over twenty minutes.

He definitely wasn't accustomed to anyone making him wait. Maybe she was playing a mind game?

The door to her quarters opened and she backed out onto the veranda, her curvy bottom wriggling as she juggled her purse and some kind of bag. Turning, she faced him and started forward, wearing turquoise high heels, pencil jeans and a flowy white shirt with multiple strands of signature McNair necklaces. The long loops of her necklaces drew his eyes down her body, hinting at the curves that lay beneath the shirt.

As always, he braced for the fact she damn near took his breath away.

His eyes fell to the little pink leopard-print carrier that wobbled back and forth to the side as something fuzzy and shadowy moved around inside. He frowned. "I thought you said you were packing clothes? Not live-stock."

Stopping in front of him, she lifted up the frilly carrier. "Clearly this isn't large enough for a horse. I sent my bags ahead to the airport. This is one of my carry-ons. It may come as a surprise to you, but I do not travel light."

He opened the limo door for her. "You're one of those types that takes a cute little dog everywhere."

"Don't let my cat hear you call him a dog. He hates that." She slid into the long leather seat.

"You travel with a *cat*?" He dropped into the seat across from her and stared at the carrier beside her. This woman never failed to surprise him in every way possible.

"Are you saying cats miss their humans less than dogs?"

"No—" he chose his words carefully "—cats are more independent. More easily left on their own."

"Well, I won't be leaving this one." Her chin tipped. "If you have a problem with that, you can be the one to call off the trip." She flashed a thin smile at him. "Could you possibly be allergic?"

Was that her plan? To get him to bail? It would take a lot more than a feline to make that happen. Still, he couldn't help digging. "I am not allergic to cats—or dogs, for that matter. But surely someone on the staff can handle that. You have other pets."

"This one is special." She unzipped the top and the fluffy Siamese's head popped out. The cat yawned and stared at Preston with blue eyes just as intense as Amie's. "He's old and has diabetes. He needs his injections."

Guilt kinked his neck. "I'm sorry for leaping to conclusions." He shook his head. "But I have to confess, I still don't get it. You have the money for fancy pet sitting, including injections. So you need his company? Don't you have two or three other or a dozen other cats? There are varying accounts around the office of how many. How did you pick which one to bring?"

"Four. Just four," she said tightly. "My other three cats are staying with Gran. But I only trust Johanna with this one since she's a vet tech, and as you know, she is on her honeymoon. Other than her, there's no one I trust to administer the medication who's also familiar to Roscoe—"

"Roscoe? I thought your family named all people and animals after gems." Her brother was actually Alexandrite and she was Amethyst. Even their horses had gemstone names.

"My grandmother and my parents did that with the names. I don't. Trust me, learning to write Amethyst in preschool wasn't easy. So, this is Roscoe. It fits." She smoothed a hand over his head. "I know I could hire some high-end pet sitter for him, but his diabetes gets worse when he's stressed, and when he misses me, he stresses."

"We can't have that happening." He scratched a furry ear and the cat erupted into a low, humming purr.

"This is not a joke," she snapped, hugging the carrier closer. "I couldn't bear it if he passed away while I was gone. I'm important to him and he's important to me."

He rested his hand on her knee. "I'm not laughing at you. I'm just wondering if the cat is going to need jewelry for the galas too."

"Ha-ha. I'm not taking him to work with me." Her gaze flicked to his hand and she chewed her bottom lip. "Just traveling and keeping him in my suite."

"You genuinely seem to care." And that made her all the more attractive somehow.

"I do." She lifted his hand from her knee, but the flush on her neck showed she wasn't unaffected. "Now, can we get going? The plane is waiting."

He let the air crackle between them for an instant before signaling the driver. It was going to be an interesting—and tempting—week.

Three

Amie buckled her cat's carrier into the seat beside her on the luxury jet, larger than the McNair family's plane, with more space for the lengthy travel planned for the week. Plush leather seats. A semicircular sofa around a dining table, with a galley kitchen off to the side. Even a small shower and sleeping area curtained off.

Other than a pilot behind the bulkhead wall, she was alone with Preston for all of the flights. Day and night. She sagged back in the leather recliner, the sounds of Preston across the row tempting her to look. Just sitting in the limo with him had been tempting. That's why she had strengthened her defenses. She had to. What would this week—even the past two months—have been like if she wasn't pregnant? Would she have eventually fallen under the spell of the sexy, brooding CEO in spite of the fact he ran the company she'd once hoped to head?

Unlikely once the pink slips had started being handed out to employees. Sure, he was getting results, but she still wasn't convinced his way was the best way. Maybe she could use this week to find out his future plans for the company. And if they involved more of his hatchet style of leadership? She hoped to persuade him to find a compromise that didn't gut the heart of the family business.

She jammed earbuds in to prevent further conversation and closed her eyes against the morning nausea. She *felt* Preston settle in his seat. Instinctively, she reached for the volume control, pressed the button and tried to lose herself in the music. Anything to dull her interest in the man sitting across from her. She kept her eyes shut, and tried her best to relax her jaw. To be natural and unconcerned even though her nerves were raw.

This was really happening. She'd wondered how she would tell him about the baby and now it was clear that conversation would have to happen this week. At the end of their travels, because if she told him sooner, the rest of the trip would be impossible to withstand. She had to use this time to find common ground, a peace of sorts before telling the rest of the family.

Easier said than done.

He was an arrogant man. A fair boss, but distant. Cool. She wanted and needed more in her life. She'd been left with no choice in her distant parents. But she'd seen her grandparents' marriage and the way they loved their family unconditionally. She would settle for nothing less for herself or her child.

The plane taxied and took off smoothly. Amie thought she might just get away with listening to her favorite folk music all the way until lunch. And if he lost himself in work, maybe she could pull out some of her own sketches for the collection she hadn't shared with anyone else. Ideas were buzzing in her head for the snake-themed coils she'd designed, the patterns of their markings inspiring interlocking pieces for multicolored chains in precious metal. They were more urban and sophisticated than the rustic luxury items that were the company cornerstone, potential crossover items into a younger, more international market while staying true to her roots.

She hadn't shared them because what if they ventured too far off the mark? Weren't as good as she hoped? She didn't think she'd get sacked for stepping outside the design aesthetic, although with Preston at the helm…who knew? Her bigger concern was that she'd spent time designing pieces that would never be made. The artist in her mourned that.

Then she felt a gentle tug on an earbud. A sideways glance revealed Preston with the earpiece dangling between his fingers.

His face was open, receptive. "Now that we're settled for the trip, do you want to tell me why you've gone out of your way to ignore me since that night in the coat closet?"

Leave it to a man—and a billionaire CEO at that—to be direct.

"We work together. It isn't wise to pursue a personal relationship." The sight of him in a black suit and leather cowboy boots threatened to take her breath away even now. She had continued to want him over the past two months. That was part of the problem.

All that male arrogance and remorseless reorganization hadn't done nearly enough to make her body stop wanting him.

"Amie, clearly we have to find a less antagonistic way to be in the same room." He draped the earbud over her armrest, just a hairsbreadth away from her arm. "I assume that's why your grandmother sent us on this outing, to keep drama out of the workplace."

"Drama?" She plucked the other earbud out and resisted the urge to toss something at his head. "Are you calling me a drama queen? I am a professional in every way at the office. You're the one who thinks I'm plotting your death."

"Okay, we've agreed you don't want to tie concrete blocks to my ankles and throw me in the Trinity River, but you're still a professional dripping ice every time I walk into the room." He leaned on his armrest, coming closer and pinning her with a laser gaze. "I wouldn't put up with this from any employee, male or female, no matter who they're related to. I find nepotism to be abhorrent, in fact."

Nepotism? The word seared her. She worked twice as hard as anyone else to prove otherwise and still she couldn't catch a break. If she didn't love the family company so much, she would have left long ago. "I apologize if I've been less than cordial or in any way taken advantage of my family connections."

"There's that ice I was talking about. Combined with a beauty pageant answer—carefully worded."

She smiled tightly, irritated and turned on—and scared. "Well, you're the one asking for world peace."

"Just a cease-fire."

"I want that, too." She needed it. For their child's sake. "I'm just not sure how. This probably sounds strange after what we did two months ago, but I really don't know you."

The steel in his gaze lightened. He leaned back in his chair, hands crossed over his chest. "Ask me anything you want to know."

"Anything?" *How would you feel about becoming a daddy in seven months?* Probably not wise to lead with that one.

"Sure," he said. "On one condition."

Damn. She'd known this supposed cease-fire was too good to be true. "I am not sleeping with you again just to find out your favorite color."

"I didn't ask you to," he pointed out. "My condition is simple. For every question you ask, I get to ask one as well. You can even choose who goes first."

Sounded fair, and as he'd mentioned, all those pageants sure had given her a wealth of practice in dodging sticky questions. "All right, why did you take this job when you were making more money at the sportswear corporation in Oklahoma?"

"Your grandmother is quite persuasive. I don't need the money. But I do need a challenge."

"Is that what I am to you? A challenge?"

He smiled, hazel eyes glinting. "That's another question when I haven't asked you anything."

"All right, your turn." She sighed warily, her tummy flipping with nerves and a hint more morning sickness. "Ask away."

"What's your favorite color?"

She blinked fast, waiting for the other shoe to drop. "Seriously? That's it?"

"Do you want a tougher question? Something more personal? Because I can think of more than one of that sort."

"Fuchsia," she blurted. "My favorite color is fuchsia. What's yours?"

"Don't care."

"Then why ask me my favorite?" She couldn't help but wonder.

"I've found I can tell a lot about a person by their choice. I catalogue those picks, like crayons in a box, and track the trends. It's like analyzing data in the workplace."

"Wait. Seriously?" She held up a hand as something else occurred to her. "You're working for a jewelry empire and you don't care about the nuances of beauty in jewel tones? Just an overall trend of some Crayola personality test?"

"I care about tracking sales data. I'm not a designer. I have people for that. A good boss knows who to promote based on job performance—not bloodlines." He hinted at that distrust of nepotism again. "What made you choose to stay in the family business rather than strike out on your own?"

She searched for the right words to explain something innate. "It's in my blood, all I can ever remember wanting to do. In fact, my earliest memories are of accompanying my grandfather to work."

"What did you do at the company as a toddler?"

"You'll have to wait. It's my turn to ask. Based on all that cataloguing of favorite color trends, what do you think would be your favorite color—if you ever decided to choose one?"

"What?" He looked at her as if he was dizzy from following her through a maze.

"What type of person are you? If I'm fuchsia, what are you?"

"Um, navy blue, maybe dark gray."

Why did she want to know? "You didn't think about that, did you? I believe you just made up an answer."

"Prove it," he said smugly, crossing his arms over his chest. Even through the black shirt, she could see the outline of muscles in his arm. His smile was genuine, if not a little playful, and his eyebrow cocked with such arrogance that she couldn't look away.

She scrunched her nose. "You're not playing fair with this question game."

He leaned forward again, closer this time. "I don't know the answer to your color question and I really want to get to my question. What did you do with your grandfather at work?"

She found herself drawn in by the timbre of his voice as much as the steel in his eyes. "He asked me to help him make a necklace for Gran's birthday. Picking out the stones. Choosing which of his designs I liked the best. It was…magical."

"Your grandparents are important to you." He was a perceptive man.

She needed to remember that.

"My grandmother is the primary reason I'm here. She and Gramps were more parents to me than my own—which is no great secret to anyone who's been around for any length of time. I hate that I'm missing even a day with her on this trip, but this is what she wants."

"If making your grandmother happy is that important, that brings me back to my first question. Why have you been avoiding me?"

There was no more hiding the truth from him or herself.

"I'm not sure how to be in the same room with you without thinking about the day we met."

Amie's admission still rattled around in Preston's brain even hours later after they'd checked into their Los Angeles hotel on California's renowned Gold Coast. He paced around the sitting area between their rooms, picture windows overlooking the water. Crystal, brass and high-end upholstery filled the place. He wasn't much on décor, but he knew "good" when he was around it. He hadn't grown up with this kind of luxury, but he'd grown accustomed to it over the years climbing the corporate ladder.

A knock sounded at the door. "Room service."

Preston went to admit the catering staff, allowing them to set up the wet bar with a tray of fruit and vegetables, plus a selection of finger sandwiches and teas. He'd asked what a light lunch would be for a woman and he had to admit the spread looked good. There would be food at the gala tonight, but he thought Amie might like something ahead of time.

Tipping the servers, he went to Amie's door and knocked.

"Amie?" The door nudged open. It must not have been latched in the first place.

A silver ball of fur streaked past his feet.

"Roscoe!" Amie streaked just as fast, wearing a T-shirt and cotton shorts that were…short. He probably shouldn't have noticed that when she was chasing her escapee cat.

But her hair was in a topknot on her head. No jewelry anywhere. And she had a down-to-earth appeal that kicked him square in the chest. It took him a minute to move past that and notice that she sidestepped a baby grand piano and one-of-a-kind furnishings like a shifty running back, finally pouncing on Roscoe before he slipped into Preston's room.

"Those were some moves," he drawled, trying hard to lift his eyes from the sight of her bare thighs.

"I might not have had to move so fast if I'd had a little help." She arched an eyebrow at him, no trace of makeup on features that didn't need it.

"I was…distracted." He couldn't help a slow grin at her glare. "I'll help now though. Do you need his carrier?"

He peered inside her bedroom and noticed a spread of papers on her bed. Sketches of jewelry designs that she'd inked in with bright, bold colors in snakeskin patterns.

"Wait." She hurried over, brushing past him even as he moved into her room. "I don't need the carrier."

He couldn't take his eyes off the sketches. "You did all these?"

It was a significant amount of work. They weren't rough sketches. They'd been drawn in meticulous detail, large enough to really see the interlocking-chain design.

"It's nothing." She started gathering the papers, stacking them hurriedly, but carefully, too. Even as she juggled a cat in her arms.

"Nothing?" How could she write off such obvious hard work as nothing? "I hope you're not taking them to a competitor."

He was only half joking. Why else would she be trying to whisk them out of sight?

"Don't be silly." Skimming aside all the papers, she secured the cat in her bathroom, closing the door. "I saw the lunch spread out there." She yanked a black silk robe off the top of her suitcase, colorful clothes exploding out of it in every direction. "It looks delicious."

A curious response. Preston tucked it away, not wanting to risk upsetting the accord they were trying to find.

"I hoped there would be something you would like." He followed her back out into the living area.

She slipped her robe on, covering up her luscious bare legs. But when she turned and smiled at him, he had to admit that was just as much of a treat.

"As it happens, I am famished."

Later that evening, he twisted open a bottled water, waiting for Amie to finish dressing for their evening out—although thinking about her a door away showering? Not wise. Not when they had to spend so much time together.

He'd already changed into a tuxedo for the gala at the Natural History Museum. It was almost like taking Amie on a date—well, for him, anyway, since work permeated every aspect of his adult life.

A date?

Was that what this week was about? Starting up a relationship with her in spite of the fact he was fifteen years her senior—and her boss? Damn it, he didn't want to be that cliché. But he couldn't get her out of his mind.

The door to Amie's room clicked and...damn.

He set his bottle down slowly. The sight of her knocked the wind out of him. He'd spent so much time keeping professional distance, sometimes the impact of her just caught him unaware. She carried off a boho style all her own. One of a kind in so many ways.

She stood in the doorway, wearing a rhinestone halter top attached to a filmy peach skirt to the floor. Buff-colored cowboy boots peeked out with diamond anklets around them. Her hair, normally loose, was gathered in a tight braid and fell over her right shoulder. Only Amie could carry off such an eclectic pairing.

God, she was magnificent, and his body fired to life in answer. Who was he kidding? He noticed her every minute of every day—whether she was in no makeup and a T-shirt, or dressed to impress.

He pulled a rose from the arrangement on the wet bar. "You look damn hot and I bet you know it."

"Your flattery overwhelms me." She rolled her eyes but took the flower anyway, bringing it to her nose and inhaling. "Mmm."

"Plenty of people flatter you. You want to be respected for more than your looks or being a McNair, and I see that. Now, let's go wow the business world." He extended his elbow.

She stared at him in confusion for three blinks of her long eyelashes before she tucked her hand around his arm. "Lead the way."

He guided her to the penthouse elevator and tapped the button, the touch of her hand searing through his jacket. "I meant it when I said your work speaks for itself, no last name needed."

"Thank you, Preston. I appreciate that, truly," she said as the door slid open and they stepped inside. Together. "You know all about my family—thanks to our infamous nepotism—"

"I didn't say your family doesn't deserve their jobs—well, other than your father." He shrugged, wondering why he felt the need to shoot himself in the foot. "Sorry if that offends you."

"I can't condemn you for speaking the obvious." She snapped the bud off the long stem and tucked the flower into her long braid that draped over her shoulder, anchoring it with ribbon at the end. "I'm curious, though… Back to our questions game, what about your family?"

He went still for an instant, weighing his words. "No chance of nepotism in my family. There was no family business to join into. My father worked for a waste disposal company, injured his back and went on disability. My mother worked for a cleaning service. Mostly cleaning condos for a real estate company."

"It sounds like they had a difficult time financially." She leaned back against a mirrored wall, the lights glinting off her sequined top.

They had, and he'd been so determined to do differently by his family, sometimes he'd forgotten the positive parts of his childhood. "My dad may have been laid up, but he studied with me every day. He wanted to make sure I had more choices than he did. Than my mother did."

"Where are they now?"

The floors counted down as they descended toward ground level where their car waited, elevator music tuned to the Mozart station.

"I bought them a condominium in Florida, complete with maid service." He may have failed his ex and his daughter, but he'd done right by his parents.

"You support them? That's really lovely."

"I have more than enough money. Why wouldn't I?" His gaze dipped to the small of her back, visible in the mirrored wall behind her.

"Not everyone would. Do you get to see them often?"

"Not as often as I would like." He pulled his eyes

back up to her face, lingering for a second on the rose tucked in her hair. "I think you owe me about a dozen questions."

"All right, then ask," she answered with an ease that said he was making progress breaking through the awkwardness between them.

There was a chance for...hell, who was he kidding? He wanted a chance to have her again. In a bed. The attraction wasn't going away. It increased every day and was wrecking their work environment. Tonight was just a reminder of how damn hard it was to be professional with her. He wanted to free her from the layers of fabric, feel her body against his again.

"I'm going to save my questions for later, after work." He swept his arm toward the lobby, already looking forward to the ride back up the elevator.

Amie had been a part of Diamonds in the Rough since graduating from college with a double major in art and business. But until recently, she hadn't given a lot of thought to the expanded business that went into marketing the product. She'd assumed the pieces would come together for her at the right time, especially after her cousin had stepped down to pursue his own dreams.

God, that was brave of him to do.

She felt like a coward right now, afraid to tell Preston about the baby. This week was supposed to be about finding that courage, and the more time she spent with him, the more questions she had.

She stepped out of the limo in front of the Natural History Museum, the red carpet filled with LA elite and top players in Hollywood. Diamonds in the Rough collections would be displayed throughout. The evening passed in a blur of schmoozing, seeing her rustic gem designs and others artfully showcased throughout the Southwest exhibit—beside everything, from a stuffed longhorn steer, to a locomotive light, to portraits of the diverse people who'd shaped Western history.

She was a part of this, the McNair legacy, and she couldn't deny Preston was in command. He owned the room, quietly and confidently, alongside some of the most famous men and women in the country. Hooking them. No doubt there would be Diamonds in the Rough pieces adorning actors and actresses at music and movie awards shows.

By the end of the night, she felt light, excited about the business in a way she couldn't recall since she'd been a child making a necklace with her grandfather. She just wished she knew what Preston thought of her designs when he'd seen those sketches earlier in the day. Why hadn't he said anything?

But he had been thoughtful so far on this trip. The questions game had helped her learn things about him. The lunch he'd ordered—so obviously full of chick food that he'd selected items with her in mind—had been a sweet gesture, and so welcome, considering that her appetite really kicked in later in the day.

The business part of the event was winding down and the attendees were free to explore the museum for the remaining hour the company had rented the venue. Amie hooked arms with Preston, wondering if maybe, just maybe, they were going to find level ground after all.

She stared upward in wonder at the butterfly exhibit. Monarchs and a zillion other kinds she'd never thought to learn the names of glided, landed, soared again. Her imagination took flight along with them. "This museum was a genius idea for the display."

"It's about art. You design art every bit as beautiful, Amie."

She stopped, turning to face him. "I think that's the nicest thing you've ever said to me."

A half smile ticked a dimple in his craggy, handsome face. "Considering how little we've talked, that's not saying much."

"You know, you haven't been exactly accessible, yourself." She wanted to touch him, to stroke those strands of gray at his temples and see if they had a different texture.

"What do you mean?" All hard edges, he made such a contrast to those delicate yellow butterflies drifting behind him.

"You're a broody and moody workaholic." Even with butterflies as a backdrop.

"I'm the boss. I have to maintain a certain professional distance, and I'm certainly not going to set a bad example by taking long lunches and checking out early," he said with more of that broody moody authority. His mouth formed a tight line that she wanted to tease open.

"It's more than that." She tilted her head to the side, wondering if it was her imagination that his eyes lingered on her outfit now. And had all night, even amidst the A-list guests with plunging necklines. The thought sent satisfaction and desire through her. "You're not the warm fuzzy, approachable type."

"No. I've staked my reputation on being a leader not a team player. Besides, I'm also fifteen years your senior. You realize that, right?"

Did that bother him? She hadn't thought about it beyond thinking how well he carried it. The gray streaks at his temples, the hard, defined angles in his face. And those keen, calculating eyes. The man exuded pure sex appeal and would no matter what age. But she couldn't just dismiss what he'd said.

"The years between our birth dates would be an issue if I was a teenager. Ew. And illegal. But I'm far beyond that stage of life. So I don't see it as an excuse for distant behavior—" she took the plunge for her baby "—outside the office."

His eyes narrowed. "So you're saying outside the office is okay?" He took a step closer, still not touching but near enough that one deep breath would brush her chest against his. "Because I was under the distinct impression you didn't want to pursue the relationship because I'm the boss. And quite frankly, I agree that's problematic on a lot of levels if not handled carefully."

"Of course," she murmured, having thought through all of them. "You're right."

He studied her for a long moment, eyes so perceptive she wondered if he could pluck her secret thoughts right out of her head. Instead, his voice lowered to a level that hummed along her skin.

"But you're open to discussion," he pressed. "What are we going to do about working at the same company when there's still this connection?"

A butterfly landed on his shoulder and in that moment he was so very approachable. So much so, she couldn't think about anything but how scared she'd been since that stick turned pink.

"I guess that's what this week is supposed to be about."

She sure hoped he had answers, because she couldn't seem to figure out any.

Only one answer ever sprang to her mind when she got this close to Preston. And it had a lot to do with what he called a "connection." On her end, it felt more like a riot of emotions combined with raw lust and—quite honestly—a little bit of magic.

What else could explain her attraction to the off-limits cowboy CEO with a butterfly on one shoulder?

She chewed her bottom lip and before she could second-guess herself, she arched up onto her toes for what could be the last kiss she would ever have with Preston.

Four

Preston had Amie back in his arms again and the feel of her was better than any memory he'd held on to of that night in the coatroom. And his memories had been pretty damn awesome.

Her lips parted under the press of his, yielding in a way that could only happen when they were kissing and she wasn't snapping at him, just purring. Right now, with her mouth under his, there were no arguments. No doubts. Even in her yielding, she was sure of herself. Of the kiss. The silken stroke of her tongue along his told him as much while he skimmed a touch down her bare arms and up again, her halter top giving him delicious access to her shoulders. The slender warmth of her neck.

He breathed her in, deepening the kiss.

The press of her curves against his body sent his pulse into overdrive. The exotic scent of her musk- and-clove perfume tempted him, begged him to touch her. Everywhere. He enjoyed the silkiness of her hair as he stroked his hands over her braid. But he needed to touch more of her. Needed to feel her skin against his. She leaned into his fingertips as he ran them down her spine. Her nimble fingers played along his neck and over his shoulders. Every touch sent snaps of electricity through him until he backed her into a wall, his body shielding them from view if anyone walked in.

He hadn't tasted her enough that first time. Hell, he could kiss her for days and not get enough of her taste. She was such a flash of bright color in his world that he could see her like a damn kaleidoscope even behind his eyelids as they kissed.

More than that, she intrigued him. This woman who was won over by butterflies more than flowers or extravagant gifts. So different than his other relationships. She was unique. Special. And he should be old enough to know better, but still, she drew him in. Age and their work connection and his own shortcomings in relationships be damned. He wanted her, ached to have her.

And from the way she moved, Preston could tell Amie wanted it too. Her touch spurred him to take the chance. He kissed along her neck, nipping her shoulder. "Let's go back to the hotel. That is completely not the workplace and a helluva lot roomier than a coat closet."

Her head fell back and she blinked fast, long black eyelashes fluttering to focus. "What?"

"I want to take my time with you." His hands glided down her bare arms slowly, resting finally on her hips. A smile snaked across his lips. "I want to live out every fantasy I wish we'd had time for two months ago."

"Ohmigosh." The fog from her eyes cleared and horror replaced passion. "What did we just do?"

"We kissed. Like two consenting adults who've been going damn crazy with frustration for the past two months trying to ignore the connection." He was losing ground fast and needed her to understand. "This is not about a repeat of the coatroom. This is about two adults attracted to each other. That's all."

She raised an eyebrow, face turning cold. Like marble. "Do you sleep with every person you're attracted to?"

He hadn't considered she might wonder about his motivations. It seemed odd that such a confident, sexy woman could have insecurities, too, but as he thought back to those sketches she'd tried to hide from him, he had to wonder. "I meant it when I said I'm not a one-night-stand person and I believed you were being honest, too."

"You're saying we should…what?" She angled her head to the side, butterflies swirling behind her in a display. Her blue eyes steeled against him. "That we go on dates? That we sleep together?"

"Honestly? I was thinking we would do both." There would be issues to deal with, datingwise, but he wasn't a man who tolerated sneaking around.

"What about all the things you said earlier?" She backed out of his embrace and crossed her arms over her chest defensively. "You're my boss and older than I am. That you're not a team player."

Good question. And that meant she was considering it. He was closer to winning. "We keep our relationship separate when we're at work with a little less ice and obvious static. We're both professionals."

She shook her head, the rose slipping loose from

her braid. It tumbled to the floor behind her, landing silently. "It isn't that simple."

It felt simple enough to him, especially seeing the way her fingers trembled lightly as she skimmed them across her lips where he'd just kissed her. His gaze followed the path of that sensual touch, hungry to show her how very, very simple—elemental—this could be.

"Why not?" he asked instead, thirsty for more of her. "What's the harm in trying a date? Or more. See what happens? Can't be more awkward than the past two months."

Indecision flickered through her eyes, just a flash before she held up a hand. "Don't try to win me over with your corporate pitch. I am not okay with the way you've cleared house and tampered with the family culture at McNair. You can save your closing-deal number. I know how you operate, and who knows, maybe my head's next on the chopping block."

"That's not in the cards," he said without hesitation.

Her throat moved in a slow swallow of relief. "Well, I'm not some account to win over."

"You most definitely are not." She was more. So much more.

Amie shook her head. "Save it."

A tight line smoothed her plump lips into an expression that he couldn't readily identify. Pain? Hesitation? He wasn't sure. And while he realized he would have to put his plans on hold for now, he was not giving up. Not on this woman.

Amie broke his gaze, turned around and made for the door. She stepped on the flower, smearing the red petals on the ground.

Preston stared at the ground, breathing in the scent of roses for a moment while he contemplated his next move.

The ride back to the hotel in the limousine was awkward, to say the least. Amie couldn't stop thinking about the kiss in the butterfly gallery. How much she wanted to take Preston up on his proposition. In fact, she very well might have if she hadn't been pregnant. But she was and she had to keep that in mind at all times for her baby's sake.

Preston sat across from her, giving her space. Although she could sense he was only biding his time. She'd watched him at work often enough to know his tactics. Telling him to back down wouldn't work. She needed to come up with a plan of her own.

Soon.

Her cell phone rang inside her pewter handbag. The bag, while stylish, was full of essentials. She batted around a mess of receipts and makeup, digging for the ringing phone. In the seat next to her, she dumped her lip gloss, mints and amethyst-and-pearl compact. Finally, the purse was empty enough to find her phone. She fumbled with the turquoise clasp. Her grandmother's name flashed across the screen. Her gut clenched in fear.

She grabbed the phone and answered fast. "Gran, it's late in Texas. What's the matter?"

Preston's forehead creased and he looked at her, a question in his eyes. She averted her gaze. Now wasn't the time to worry about Preston. Not when her grandmother was this sick.

"Nothing's wrong, dear." Her grandmother's voice

came across weaker but steady. "I'm just calling to see how the party at the museum went."

"The party? You're calling for an after-action report now?" she asked incredulously. "It's after midnight there, Gran. We can talk tomorrow. You should be asleep."

Her grandmother snorted on the other end of the line. "All I do is lie around in bed and rest. It wrecks my sense of day and night."

"Are you feeling all right?" Amie lowered her voice, wishing for a moment of privacy. Her grandmother's illness was hard for her to deal with. She hated to think of her grandmother awake in pain.

"You just saw me this weekend. I'm the same."

Dying. Moments ticking away while Amie was stuck going to parties. It wasn't fair. She wanted to be at her side. To soak up the precious, borrowed time with her grandmother.

"And I'm going to worry about you every single hour of every day because I love you and you're so very important to me."

"You're a sweet girl. My only granddaughter. I was so excited when you were born."

"Sweet? Me?" She laughed softly. "Not really, but then neither are you. I like to think I inherited my feistiness from you."

Her grandmother chuckled along with her, then laughed harder until she coughed. Clearing her throat, she continued, "I am proud of you and I believe you can make this work. Now, tell me. How is it going?"

"The LA party was a success. The museum setting was brilliant." The kiss with Preston was incredible, but that part would not appear in any reports. "The photographer took lots of photos. You should have them on your computer to look through in the morning. If you're still having trouble resting, some pictures may have already arrived."

"Photos of you with Preston? I want to see how the two of you work together."

Alarms sounded in her head. Had her grandmother picked up on some vibe between her and Preston? She couldn't possibly know about the baby. Amie settled on a simple answer. "We were a unified front for the company."

"So you're working through the differences that fast? I'm not buying it, dear."

"We're trying." She looked across the limo, her eyes meeting his. Had he been watching her so intently the whole time? Concern etched in his face. Genuine concern. It'd be so easy to let her guard fall, even now. "For you, Gran. Now, please, get some rest. We won't let you down."

The line disconnected and Amie realized more than her baby's well-being was at stake here. Her grandmother's peace of mind needed to stay in the forefront. They needed to smooth things over. And fast. She could make it through the week, smile for pictures with him. Amie couldn't afford to weaken again around Preston. She had to stay strong and make sure every step was taken on her terms. She needed to reclaim some control.

Preston angled back, his arms along the leather limo seat. "Everything okay?"

"Sure. No crisis." The last thing she wanted to tell him was that she suspected her grandmother could have ulterior motives beyond solidifying business relations. "She just wanted to check in."

"And that's all?" His hazel eyes narrowed in disbelief. The shadows in the limousine softened his features, making him seem more approachable. "I don't think so."

"What are you? Psychic?" She gripped the edges of the seat as the limo turned a corner. The driver took the corner hard, and she lurched toward Preston.

"I just know." He lifted his index finger to the side of his temple and tapped twice. "It's part of what makes me the boss," he said, his confidence filling the seat as tangibly as his broad shoulders.

"That—" she paused for effect, then grinned "—and your arrogance."

He laughed, apparently not daunted in the least. "Confidence is important. You're one to talk, by the way."

She opted to ignore that part. "Aren't you going to ask why she called so late?"

The smile faded from his handsome face. "Tell me."

"She's having trouble sleeping because she's in bed so much." And Amie wanted to be there with her to keep her company, but her grandmother wanted her here for whatever reason. For a test. "It tears me up inside to think of her confined like that. She's always been such a vibrant, dynamic woman. She's the one who taught me to ride. Alex, Stone and I would spend hours out on the trails with her and Gramps."

"I'm sorry. This is such an unfair way for her life to end."

"I'm grateful she can still talk, that she's still herself. The thought of…"

The limousine stopped short, and Amie fell forward, landing her onto Preston's lap. He reached out to catch her instinctively. Heat flooded her cheeks as his warm hands helped her back to an upright position. This was exactly the kind of situation she needed to guard herself against. Thank heaven they had arrived at the hotel. Amie was exhausted with worry for her grandmother, her child and her feelings.

She peered out the window only to realize they'd stopped a couple of blocks short of the hotel. Preston frowned, but she was closer to the window separating them from the chauffeur. She tapped on the pane, signaling the driver.

The window slid opened. "Yes, Mr. Armstrong? Miss McNair?"

"Is there a problem?"

The uniformed driver scratched under his hat. "There's a pileup that has traffic blocked ahead of us and there's no backing up. I'm afraid we're stuck until it clears. The minifridge is stocked."

Alone? In the limo with Preston for who knew how long?

Amie snatched up her pewter clutch bag. "We'll just walk. The hotel is only two blocks and this highway congestion is never going to let up."

The chauffeur looked to Preston, who shrugged. "Whatever the lady wants."

Amie stepped out into the warm night. Whatever she wanted? If only life could be that simple.

Preston shot out of the limo, stunned at how fast she'd bolted. No way in hell was he letting her walk around the streets of LA alone, regardless of how safe the area was supposed to be. It was still a city, far different from the open spaces of Texas. Besides that, she looked exactly like what she was—an extraordinarily beautiful and wealthy woman, both of which could attract the wrong sort of attention. Five sprints later, he'd caught her, her sequined top glinting in the night.

He shortened his strides to measure his pace to Amie's as he scanned the traffic-jammed street. The famous LA traffic was no joke. People honked their horns, and music with heavy bass from a parked car filled the night air. The hotel was located in a good section of LA, but his instincts still stayed on alert. There were plenty of places, even in the good areas of the city that could be a threat to two pedestrians. He placed a palm on the small of her back possessively as they walked. He glanced at her, narrowing his eyes and daring her to argue. "If you don't want my hand on you then we get back in the limo."

She sighed, tucking her handbag against her side. "We need to set some ground rules for the rest of this trip."

At least she was still talking to him. That was progress over the past two months of the great chill. "Such as?"

He continued to scan the area as they walked down the empty sidewalk. They had made it one block away from the limo. The street signs were caked brown from the smog. To a native Oklahoma kid, cities like LA felt dirty and overcrowded, even in the upscale areas. The sooner they were back at the hotel, the better. Maybe he could convince her to stay for a glass or two of wine in the hotel's restaurant.

"We have to work together for years to come," she said with her chin jutting, exposing her elegant neck.

He wanted to kiss her, starting at her neck. The taste of her two months ago and in the exhibit this evening wasn't nearly enough. Preston's attention wandered from her neck to the seductive swish of her filmy skirt.

Her boot heels clicked against the pavement, a steady drumming sound that matched the evenness of her voice. "We need to figure out how to make that happen without the attraction interfering."

"I still don't see what that has to do with denying the pull between us altogether."

"You mean have an affair."

"We *are* adults. Sex happens sometimes." The more he thought about it, the more it made sense. Even though they worked together, there was an equality to their stance since her family was the major stockholder. And she clearly didn't want a long-term relationship, thank God, since he'd already been there, wrecked that with his ex-wife. "Fighting the attraction isn't working. An affair makes sense."

"That brings me back to my original point. Affairs more often than not end…messy." She clutched her purse to her stomach. "We can't afford that."

"Then we agree that when the time comes to move on, we'll be cordial." He guided her past other pedestrians making their way down the sidewalk. Blue-and-red lights flashed in the distance as first responders pushed through the backed-up traffic to get to the three-car pileup.

"Preston, I hear what you're saying, but it's not that simple anymore." Her throat moved with a long swallow. "We can't afford to take that risk. The stakes are too high. Far too high."

There was such worry in her eyes, an unmistakable fear. Panic tore at her face.

He squeezed her elbow lightly. "I think that until

we face this head-on and give it a try, the tension will only get worse and interfere with the job all the more."

"Spoken like a man who doesn't take no for an answer."

"I didn't imagine what just happened or what happened two months ago."

She glanced up at him, her eyes full of more of that worry he didn't understand—but a yearning he understood all too well.

Chewing her bottom lip, she glanced at him. "Preston, can we go back to the original plan of getting to know each other better and take it from there?"

"Are you asking me to win you over?" The prospect filled him with a rush of excitement and hope.

"No," she said quickly, "I didn't mean that, exactly. Just…just… I'm asking you to be honest."

He measured his words, searching for the best way to win his way around her. "Okay, but on one condition."

"What would that be?" she asked warily.

"That we use this time together as dates. Real, honest-to-God, get-to-know-each-other dates. You'll see firsthand that we can balance work and romance."

Her jaw dropped. "Dating? You're serious."

"Absolutely, take our time."

She fidgeted with her purse gripped in her hands. "And when you say take our time, how long are you talking?"

"However long it takes. Trust me, I don't take this lightly. I'm not the type to let relationships into the workplace, never have been. You're just that damn amazing."

"Flattery already? I haven't agreed yet, so you can hold back on the wooing." For the first time since the kiss in the exhibit, Amie looked relaxed. Receptive.

The smile on her face reached her eyes, setting them aglow in the muted streetlight. She shoved him with her shoulder playfully. This was the Amie he wanted to get to know.

"I only speak the truth." God, she was mesmerizing. So much so, it was hard as hell to see anything but the stars shining in her deep blue eyes.

So hard he almost missed the shadowy figure lunging from behind a billboard. The man was broad, built and hardened by the streets. His frenetic eyes focused on Amie with a repugnant leer. On instinct, Preston stepped in front of her. Crooks like this never risked leaving people alive to identify them, especially when drugs were making their decisions for them.

The man loomed in front of them, a knife in hand, waving it menacingly. Erratically. "Give me your cash and jewelry now and nobody gets hurt."

Five

"Amie, get back." Preston pushed her behind him, the street lamp casting a halogen halo over the man with a knife, his face shadowed by the brim of a ball cap. "We don't want anyone to get hurt."

Fear chilled Amie so thoroughly her boots felt frozen to the pavement. She stared at the jagged-edge blade glistening in the night.

"Then pass over your money, dude, and quit screwing around here." The broad shouldered young guy stood close, looking from side to side, jittery. The rest of the world oblivious or uncaring. Or perhaps too busy rubbernecking over the three-car pileup to notice a simple purse snatcher by a trash can.

In a flash, Preston swept a foot behind the guy, knocking him to the ground, stunning Amie with the speed and power. Preston stomped a foot on the crook's wrist, pressing until the criminal screamed. His fist un-furled and he released the jagged knife.

The clatter of metal on concrete released Amie from her daze. She sprinted toward the flashing lights at the car accident. Surely there had to be a cop there who could assist.

"Help, please," she called out, waving one hand and hitching the hem of her layered skirt with the other. "Someone tried to rob us. My…boss has him restrained. The man had a knife. My…date…has him restrained."

A few heads turned, two rescue workers returning to their efforts to dislodge a woman from a smashed-up car. But one cop disengaged from the accident scene.

"Yes, ma'am?" The policeman with a shaved head and steely jaw jogged closer.

Thank God. She waved for him to follow her.

"Over here, by the closed toy store." Her heart in her throat, she raced back to Preston.

A small crowd had gathered around the fallen thief, suddenly interested, after all. The onlookers hungrily digested the scene, pointing and murmuring at Preston, who had the young man pinned to the ground with his knee planted on the guy's back, gripping the assail-ant's hands.

The officer and Amie pushed past the crowd, walk-ing with determined footsteps to Preston. Relief de-flated her fear, but even relief didn't keep her knees from trembling as she thought of how wrong this could have gone. And she had a baby to think about now. Preston's baby. If something had happened to either of them… She started toward him, needing to touch him and feel him vibrantly alive. But he shook his head, keeping her at bay until he passed over the crook.

"Officer," Preston said, "that's his knife there. You'll find his prints since he didn't bother to wear gloves. I didn't touch it."

The policeman knelt beside them and secured the man's hands with cuffs. "I've got this now, sir. I'll be right back to take your statements." He read the guy his rights and walked him to a police cruiser.

Standing, Preston straightened his jacket and cupped her shoulder to steer her away from the subdued criminal. "Are you hurt, Amie?"

"I should be asking you that." She pressed her hands to her chest, vaguely aware of camera flashes in the background. Photos of the wreck? Cell phones were everywhere these days. "You're the one who took on the man with the knife. Thanks to you, there's not a scratch on me. You acted so quickly. I thought we would have just handed over our money."

"He was high on something." Preston's jaw flexed with tension. "I couldn't trust him to walk away, not even in this crowd."

"I'm just glad you were here with me. I'm sorry I forced us to walk and put you in danger."

"It could have happened anywhere, anytime. All that matters is you're okay." He clasped her elbow and nodded to the policeman. "We should go inside to wait for the cops to take our statement. The last thing I want is for someone else to try a repeat."

"Of course. I know I've already apologized, but I am so sorry for leaving the limo." Guilt pinched tighter than her boots as she strode through the lobby doors of their hotel, passed a small group of guests peering out the windows onto the street outside. The posh interior felt like a different world. "Where did you learn to defend yourself like that?"

"I grew up in a neighborhood where you had to look out for yourself." He gestured to a green velvet sofa by the window overlooking the street.

"Still, that was such a risky move to make." She sank onto the couch and smoothed her skirt. "You could have been injured—or worse."

"Less risky than trusting a twitchy user to let us go unharmed. My only concern was keeping you safe." He sketched a finger down the braid trailing over her shoulder. "I could see in his eyes he was never going to let us walk away and risk having us ID him. He wanted you. I couldn't let that happen."

Unable to resist, she leaned her cheek against his hand. "Thank you for keeping us safe."

"Us?"

She bit her lip, realizing she'd almost let it slip about the baby at a totally awkward and public time. "Us— as in you and me." She stood quickly when the door to the hotel opened, relieved at the intrusion. "I think I see the officer coming this way to speak with us now."

Amie sat on her bed, cloaked in her favorite black silk robe, absently stroking her cat. The cat purred loudly, but refused to lie down on her lap. He was fidgety.

She felt just like Roscoe. He refused to sit down, to commit to a direction. Just like her. She couldn't stop thinking about this evening, either. About the whole varied experience. Her kiss with Preston. Her grandmother's desires. Her child. The man with the knife. All of it swirled around her head.

"Oh, Roscoe, what am I supposed to do?"

The cat nudged her hand in response. "Thanks, kitty. That's clearly very helpful. Great advice."

She stopped petting the cat, pushed herself off the bed and made her way to the minifridge. Water. She needed some water.

Things with Preston were more complicated than ever. She wanted to be with him. Wanted to let herself give in to him.

It wasn't that easy. Her own happiness wasn't the only consideration. She unscrewed the water bottle cap and took a swig of water.

Roscoe slinked off the bed and rubbed up against Amie's legs, threading around her feet with determination. He let out a low mew. He sounded more like a kitten than an old cat.

"All right, Roscoe, let's get you settled for the night. I've got your favorite treats."

Whenever they traveled, Amie made sure to pack the best assortment of toys for the cat. He was so loyal, her constant companion. She dug around Roscoe's traveling bag and pulled out a can of tuna, a bowl, a can opener and a blue mouse toy.

Absently, Amie drained the tuna water into the bowl and set it on the ground. The cat rushed the bowl, eager to lap up the treat. Roscoe didn't actually like the fish, just the water. Small indulgences.

Which, if she were being honest, is what she wanted with Preston. A small bit of fun.

It was more than that though. The way he looked at her tonight when her grandmother had called. He had such genuine concern in that handsome face of his. In those kind hazel eyes. And he had saved her. Stood up to that mugger without a moment's hesitation. So protective of her already.

And that was part of the problem. If she had let it slip that she was pregnant, Preston would stay close to her for the baby's sake. She would never be able to tell what he really felt for her. And selfish as it was, she wanted to know. Needed to know.

Glancing at the clock, Amie realized she was late in giving Roscoe his insulin injections. She readied the needle, scooped Roscoe up and pinched the extra skin around his neck. The cat was perfectly still.

"Good boy. You're such a good boy. I always know what to expect from you, Roscoe," she said softly as she slid the needle into his scruff.

"Brave kitty. That wasn't so bad, was it?" She capped the needle and rubbed under his chin. Roscoe circled once on her lap, sat down and purred.

She still had to figure out Preston. Tomorrow, in New York City, she would get to know him better. Which was what she had started to consider just before she'd realized she was pregnant. Baby announcements could wait a while longer. There was something about him that made her want to hold out. Just a little longer.

Preston hadn't found much sleep after the holdup. Instead, he had paced restlessly around the suite replaying events and how damn wrong the evening could have gone. How something could have happened to Amie. And how deeply that would have affected him.

She'd come to mean more to him than he'd realized. So much more.

He was still processing that after their flight across the country to New York City the next morning. Their event wasn't until tomorrow evening, which normally meant he would fill the free day with work. However, he found himself wanting to spend every moment with Amie. When he couldn't sleep the night before, he'd heard her moving about in her room for a long while, but just as he weakened and started to knock, all noise ceased. She settled for the night, leaving him to his thoughts and an aching need to be with her. The trauma of the attack must have worn her out, because she slept during most of the flight, too.

Now that he had New York City at his disposal, he didn't intend to waste an instant of his time alone here with her.

Figuring out what to do for one of the wealthiest women in the country hadn't been easy, but then he'd always enjoyed a challenge.

He'd arranged for a rickshaw to take them to Central Park to attend a Wild West film festival. The muggy day had eased with the setting sun, a pleasant breeze added to the wind from the ride. The *click, click, click* of the cyclist pedaling along the street was rhythmic, lulling. Amie sat beside him in killer shorts and heels with a flowy shirt that the wind molded to all her beautiful curves.

She leaned back, her high ponytail sleek and swinging with the pace of the horses. Her eyes took in the scenery. "I love New York, I always have."

"Always?" He propped a foot up on the other seat across from them, not remembering the last time he'd relaxed in the city. Hell, most people he knew probably wouldn't even recognize him in khaki shorts and a polo shirt. He'd spent all his time in planes, boardrooms and carefully chosen social functions for years.

"My grandparents used to bring Alex and me here as kids. We would see a show, do some shopping." Her blue eyes turned sentimental as they passed Rockefeller Center, a lighter blue as she offered him a small smile.

"I can see why that would give the town good memories."

She glanced at crowded streets as tourists jostled for pictures. "My grandmother always let me choose my own clothes, no worries about impressing a pageant judge."

"You didn't enjoy any part of the pageants?"

"To be honest, I did at first. I liked that my mom spent time with me. I enjoyed the attention. And I really enjoyed getting to have a Mountain Dew and Pixy Stix if the pageant ran past bedtime and I needed a pick-me-up." She shrugged sheepishly, her shoulder brushing his in the confines of the small rickshaw. "Later, though, I wanted to enter the competitions that included talent and grades and community service. But my mother told me that would be a waste of time. I stood a better chance at the ones based only on looks." She stopped short and held up an elegant hand, a silver bracelet wrapped from wrist to elbow. "I don't mean that to sound vain. Scratch everything I said. I shouldn't have—"

"I heard what you meant." And he couldn't imagine ever having said something like that to his daughter. That kind of behavior was inexcusable. "You're clearly a talented artist and intelligent individual."

She snorted inelegantly. "You have to say that because my grandmother owns the company."

"No, actually, I don't," he said with a raised eyebrow as they turned in to Central Park, the sound of street musicians drifting on the wind as the sunset hour turned the sky to golds and pinks. "If I didn't believe in your work I would have moved you to another department."

"Even if that made my grandmother angry?" she pressed.

Did she really think he was only pursuing her for her grandmother's approval? He could clear that much up at least. "My condition to signing on was I have complete authority over hiring."

"But my father still works for the company and we know he doesn't do anything." Her cheeks flushed with color.

And he understood that. She had one helluva work ethic he respected.

"Your father doesn't get a salary from the company coffers so it's not an issue for me. He has an office where he holds social meetings with possible connections. I can live with that."

"It's awkward," she said through clenched teeth, absently toying with her bracelet. "I don't want to be an embarrassment."

He slid his arm along the back of the leather seat and cupped her shoulders. "There's not a chance anyone can miss your work ethic and talent. The other designers are solid, and the occasional design from your cousin adds variety. But the sales numbers for your designs speak for themselves, putting you at the top of the heap."

She glanced at him, her mouth quivering, tempting him. "Thank you. I appreciate that."

"Just stating business." Which meant that wouldn't be a good time to kiss her. He searched for a distracting subject to keep him from kissing her in front of all of New York. Not that anyone would care. "What about vacations with your parents?"

"We went to my pageants and my brother's rodeos together."

"But what about vacations?"

"They took those on their own to have together time as a couple, which is great, of course. And if Alex or I won, then all the better."

So her parents only had time for her and her brother if they were competing like show horses? He didn't like the sound of that at all. No wonder she was so concerned with rising to the top of the company. It wasn't about success but the only way she would know to feel valued.

She rested a hand lightly on his knee. "What about you? What kind of vacations did you go on as a kid?"

His body leaped in response to her touch and it took him a second to focus on her question. "My folks didn't have much money, but we went camping and trail riding. You may remember me telling you my mom worked for a cleaning service. She worked overtime cleaning offices for a stable, so we got discount rates and we could ride. It was actually therapeutic for my dad's injury."

"Your mom sounds awesome." She smiled with that million-watt grin that had stolen his breath from across a room. "So you're the real-deal cowboy. Is that what brought you to Diamonds in the Rough?"

"It was part of the allure of the job offer." He liked riding to unwind after a long day at the office. It gave him peace of mind.

"So, where are we going?"

"Wild West film festival in Central Park. Our first date."

"Date?" Her delicately arched eyebrows shot upward.

"What we talked about last night. Dating. Spending

time together. How did you put it?" He scratched his temple, then pointed. "I'm 'wooing' you."

The bicyclist braked to a stop close to the Sheep Meadow portion of the park, an open field teeming with people, with plenty of visible security. After last night's scare with the purse snatcher, he'd wondered if he should just lock them both up in their suite. But he also knew too well he couldn't control everything. So he would keep her close. Which was how he wanted her.

Snagging a folded blanket and tucking it under his arm, he jumped to the ground and extended a hand for her. She stepped down gracefully, her slim fingers resting in his, her unique silver-and-turquoise ring a walking advertisement for her talents. They walked side by side through the crowd to find a seat. Some were in chairs but others sprawled on blankets. His preference for tonight. He saw her eyes landing on a food vendor and he waved for an order of pizza and bottled waters before they sat down for tonight's first feature under the stars.

He spread the red plaid blanket while she arranged the food. Families and couples dotted the field. A few strollers and kids running in the last light of day. Some people had brought extravagant picnics, complete with linen, silver and candelabra. But most of the attendees had just showed up in jeans with a blanket. Amie seemed content with their spot. She extended her legs and bit off the end of a slice of pepperoni pizza, chasing the oozing cheese with her mouth. Groaning. Pleasure obvious.

"Oh my God, this is the best piece of pizza I have ever eaten in my life."

"So you're a sucker for a pizza pie," he said, lifting up a piece for himself. "I did not expect that."

"And I didn't expect this for a date, but it's perfect. Just what I needed after all the stuffiness of the airplane travel and galas."

"I thought you would enjoy the fresh-air venue after so much time indoors."

She nodded, swiping her lips with a napkin. "The downside to office work is missing being outside. My brother managed to blend both, running the ranch."

"I agree one hundred percent. That's part of what drew me to Texas and this job." In fact, he'd had it written into the contract that he would have access to the ranch. "Someday I want to build a big spread of my own to live the kind of life I dreamed of as a kid. My folks could come visit. At any rate, tonight I figured the outdoor ride would work better, too, in the event of another traffic jam."

"Better than being stuck in the limo." She tipped back a swig of water.

"Spoken like a person who's grown up wealthy." He couldn't resist commenting, even though that had been his life for a long time, too.

He'd never forgotten his roots. Or how lucky he was today.

She crinkled her nose and set aside her water. "I guess that came out snobby."

"Not snobby. Just…a sign that you grew up privileged."

She tipped her head. "Is that a problem for you?"

"It's just a challenge figuring out ways to romance you." He threaded his fingers through her ponytail.

"And we've established you like a challenge." Her eyes held his.

"Don't start with the negative." He tapped her lips. "Just be in the moment."

"You really are charming under all that gruff business exterior." Her mouth moved against his fingertips. "How did you stay single so long?"

His hand fell away and he looked forward at the blank movie screen, due to glow to life at any minute. "I was married, but we got divorced ten years ago."

She went still beside him, her long legs straight beside his, almost touching. "I'm sorry."

"Me, too." And he was. He hated how much they'd hurt and disappointed each other. Most of all, he hated what had happened to their child. His throat threatened to close. "But we married too young. We gave it a good shot, and it just didn't work out."

"Do you have children?"

His blood turned to ice in his veins. "I have no children."

He could practically hear her thinking through that. His heart slammed harder.

"Do you not like kids?" she asked, her voice tentative.

"I like kids fine." He paused, stared up at the sky then back at her, needing to be honest if this stood a chance of…what? Anything. So he told her as much as he could force past his lips. "I had a daughter. She died."

"Oh, Preston, that's so sad." She rested her hand on top of his on the blanket. "Do you mind if I ask what happened?"

His publicity people had done a damn good job keeping those details hidden from the public, even better than he'd known if the McNairs hadn't discovered those details in the background search they'd undoubtedly conducted before hiring him.

"It was an accident." He cleared his throat. He couldn't talk about this, not the rest. He scrambled for something, anything— "Look, the first movie is starting."

A black-and-white film crackled to life on the screen, the projected version maintaining the authenticity of the original as the Western-style font blazed across the screen with a lasso frame decorating the title. It wouldn't be the first time Preston had lost himself in a place where Gary Cooper and Roy Rogers could still make sense of the world.

She looked as if she might press for more, so he slid his arm along her back and pulled her to his side, wanting just to be with her. Enjoy this.

"Amie. Movie. Okay?"

She relented, leaning against his chest with a sigh. "Right. Sure. I didn't mean to push you to talk about something painful."

"It's all right. Another time, maybe."

For now, he had her in his arms and that helped ease the pain inside him in a way he hadn't felt in a long time. A way he looked forward to exploring more fully when they returned to their hotel.

Six

Nerves pattered in Amie's stomach as the elevator doors slid closed on their way up to their penthouse suite in Midtown Manhattan. The evening in the park had been amazing, romantic, fun. Everything a first real date should be. And surprisingly, he hadn't made a move on her other than sliding his arm around her, being a gentleman but undeniably interested in her. She hadn't felt so mellow and happy in…she couldn't remember when.

Was this the real Preston? Was this what they could have had if she'd dated him rather than impulsively leaping into a coat closet with him? God, that night was so surreal now. But they'd actually been together, no denying their impulsive coupling.

She leaned back against the mirrored wall, just looking at him, soaking in the sight of him. Casual. Approachable. His hazel eyes softened as he held her gaze. Heat flushed through her. Everything felt right. Natural. Could she just indulge for a little while longer and see where it went?

The high-speed elevator brought them to their floor in record time, the doors opening on the west half of the tower, thanks to the private code they'd keyed in for their room. The east-side doors went to a different suite.

She took a deep breath and reached to take Preston's arm as she stepped off the elevator on their private quarters. Only to have Roscoe bolt into the elevator—something that shouldn't have happened because she'd secured the kitty in her bathroom before she'd left.

Alarms sounded in her head as she squeezed Preston's hand. She went rigid, cold. "Someone's been in our suite. I locked up Roscoe…maybe a maid let him out?"

Preston's arm shot out to block her path. "After what happened in LA, I'm not taking any chances. Get back in the elevator. Call Security while I go in. What the hell is it with all the security around these places?"

He charged forward and her stomach knotted with fear for him. The events of last night replayed in her head. She had the baby to consider, but she couldn't just leave him here. She held the elevator door open while reaching for her cell phone.

Across the room, someone sat up on the sofa. A familiar someone in jeans, cowboy boots and a plain black T-shirt.

Her twin.

"Hey there, sister." Alex stood, sweeping a hand through his dark brown hair. "I happened to be in the neighborhood and figured I would say hello."

* * *

Suspicion seared through Preston as he strode toward Amie's twin brother. Here. In Manhattan. In their suite. Did the guy have some kind of brotherly radar that Preston was making progress with Amie? Their night at the park had been everything he'd hoped it could be.

He'd had plans to take things further tonight, but clearly that had been blocked by a towering, suspicious cowboy sibling.

Preston sauntered toward Alex McNair, aware of Amie rushing up behind him. "What are you doing here in New York?"

Alex extended an arm and hooked his sister in for a quick hug before backing up and keeping his arm draped protectively over her shoulders. "I brought Nina and Cody to see a matinee on Broadway, like Gran and Gramps used to do with us. Cody okayed the plan once he heard the show has animals in it. And my fiancée could use some pampering with a shopping trip in New York, some spa time along with that show. Amie, you're welcome to join in."

Amie narrowed her eyes, sticking her brother with an accusatory stare. "And you just happened to choose the day I would be here as well? The hotel staff must have fond memories of you from past trips that they gave you access to my suite."

Her brother shrugged. "I think our family has made a favorable—and lucrative—impression on the management in the past. I spent almost a whole summer here once when I was determined to leave the rodeo life behind." He huffed out a long breath. "Anyhow, there's the Diamonds in the Rough show tomorrow. I figured why not bring Nina and show our support for the family business."

"Where is Nina?"

"Settling into the other penthouse suite next door, getting Cody unpacked and oriented before he goes to sleep." Nina's son had autism and changes in routine could be difficult.

"I'll see if she needs help." She slipped from under his arm, but pinned him with a laser gaze of matching blue eyes. "But we're still going to talk later."

As Alex gave her the code to access the other suite, Preston couldn't help but watch the sway of her hips when she left, wishing like hell this evening could have ended differently.

Alex cleared his throat. "That's my sister you're ogling. Eyes up."

Preston pivoted on his heels and walked to the bar, pulling out two beers. The last thing he needed was this oversize cowboy brother breathing down his neck personally—or professionally. "Did your grandmother send you to check on the event tomorrow?"

And did this have something to do with the McNair matriarch calling her granddaughter yesterday? Preston passed his uninvited guest a longneck.

Alex took the Belgian brew. "My grandmother has nothing to do with this. It's all me. I'm checking in on my sister. You and her together?" He shook his head. "That worries me."

"Amie is an adult. Perhaps you should listen to what she has to say on the subject." He tipped back the yeasty brew.

"I realize that. Doesn't make me any less of a protective brother." He took a long drag from the bottle.

"You're known for being a distant dude. I don't want my sister to get hurt. She puts on a tough act, but she's been pushed around by the family for too long."

"I think you underestimate your sister if you think anyone can push her around." Preston tilted his head to the side.

Alex's eyebrows shot up in surprise. "You have a point there. But that's the Amie you know now and you haven't known her that long." The child's voice echoed from the other suite and Alex looked away quickly. "Let's go next door to check on them. I want to make sure Cody's still okay with all the change." Preston wanted to push for more now, but Alex had already started for the door leading to the second penthouse through the shared elevator. He punched in the code. The doors swept open to reveal the two women sitting on the living room floor with a young, blond-haired boy—Cody. An intricate puzzle lay on the coffee table.

The suite was much the same as its mate, other than the use of silver and blues rather than reds and golds for the lavish accommodations. Preston hadn't grown up in this sort of world, but he'd earned his way into the life of the rich and famous. He hoped he'd kept his feet and priorities planted, much like the young mom over there with her child. There hadn't been much time for him to get to know Alex's recent fiancée and her son, but he'd been impressed by her down-to-earth ways and her devotion to her child.

Amie glanced up, her eyes lighting as she looked at Preston before she shifted her attention back to the puzzle self-consciously. Nina reached up to clasp hands with Alex briefly, connecting without taking her attention off her four-year-old son. Alex kissed the top of her head full of red curls before dropping to sit on the window seat overlooking the buildings lighting up the night skyline.

Preston joined him, curious what this gathering held in store—and what he could learn about Amie.

She helped Cody match pieces in the puzzle, a Monet image far more advanced than a four-year-old could normally put together. But Mariah had told him Cody was a savant at art, and Amie had a gift for helping tap into that connection with the child. She was good with kids and that touched something in him he hadn't thought about in a long while.

Alex set down his bottle on the window ledge. "You asked about my sister," he said softly. "Do you want to know as a boss or for more personal reasons?"

Might as well be honest. He wasn't having any luck hiding his attraction to her. And maybe Alex would respect the straight talk. "This has nothing to do with business. I would like to get to know her better."

"Okay then." Alex nodded slowly, his eyes settling on his sister, fiancée and future stepson. "Did Amie ever tell you about the time Stone and I put Kool-Aid in Amie's showerhead right before the Miss Stampede Queen pageant? I didn't think she would ever forgive either of us for turning her hair pink. Not to mention her skin."

Where was he going with this story? "Seriously?"

"Mom never could figure out which one of us to blame. I did it, but she was convinced Stone egged me on." A smile twitched.

"And the truth?"

His grin faded. "I wanted to help her, and Stone was more of a rebel, the idea man behind the prank. He left a gag book open to a particular page right on my desk."

Preston envisioned Amie stepping out of that shower covered in pink dye—um, better not to think overmuch on that image. "I bet Amie was furious."

"Not really. She wasn't as into the pageant gig as Mom likes to think. It was pretty much the only way she could get attention from our mother."

"That sucks."

"It was worse when she was little. As she got older, she started to rebel." He rolled the beer bottle between his palms. "When we were seventeen, she didn't want to win the Miss Honey Bee Pageant—and given how many pageants she'd won in the past, it wasn't arrogant of her to assume she would run away with that crown. But back to that time. She didn't want to go because the Honey Bee Queen had to attend the county fair and she wouldn't be able to attend homecoming."

"What did you do that time?" He was getting an image of these three growing up together, protecting each other from dysfunctional parents but bonded by the love of their grandparents.

"Nothing too terrible. We went boating the day before the competition, and we stayed out so long we got sunburned. I told Mom the engine stalled. Amie looked like a lobster." His reminiscent grin went tight. "Mom made her compete anyway. Just slathered her in more makeup. Amie got second runner-up."

"Seriously?"

"Scout's honor." He held up his fingers. "I offered to cut her hair but she nixed that, so we opted for the sunburn instead. I was never sure if she opted out of the haircut idea out of vanity or because Mom would have just bought a wig."

Preston studied the beautiful, eclectic woman sitting on the floor patiently piecing together a puzzle with Cody. She was focused on the child's wishes, on the child himself. She was an amazing woman in so many ways.

But he also could see how her upbringing would have left her with some hefty trust issues. Was her brother right to be worried? Because Preston was beginning to wonder if he had enough left inside him to give this woman who deserved—and would demand—one hundred percent.

Amie had felt jittery all evening watching Preston and her brother huddled together talking. What was Alex telling him? What did Preston want to know? She would find out soon enough now that Cody had calmed down enough to go to sleep. The puzzle had helped soothe him in the new locale. Nina was tucking him in now.

Preston had stepped onto the balcony to take an overseas business call. A breeze swept in through the open balcony door, carrying in his low and rumbly voice.

Amie rushed over to her brother as he straightened the puzzle on the coffee table, Monet's *Water Lily Pond*, a puzzle she'd gifted Cody with to connect through their love of art.

She knelt beside her brother. "Alex, be honest. Did Gran send you here to spy on me?"

He rocked back on his boot heels. "No, but that answers a big question. So Gran sent you on this trip for your inheritance test."

"I didn't say that," she hedged, crossing her arms.

"You don't have to."

She sank back onto her bottom, hugging her knees. "You tricked me."

"You fell for it…" He sat beside her and tugged her ponytail. "I just want to make sure you're okay. Preston is a shark. It's clear you two have something going on and I don't want you to get hurt."

Her heart hammered as she hugged her knees tighter. So it was that obvious. Their attraction was visible. But…that also meant Preston looked equally interested, enough to be noticed. And though Alex was playing the protective brother, the confirmation of Preston's interest gave her hope.

"If you think Preston's such a bad guy, why haven't you said something to Gran? You have influence with her."

"He's one helluva businessman and he will make the company successful, which is good for all of us. That doesn't mean I want him having anything to do with my sister."

She appreciated that he cared, but at the same time it bothered her that no one in this family seemed to think she could look after herself. Her pageant days might be long behind her, but people in her family were still so intent on making decisions for her. She didn't even want to consider her brother's reaction if he found out she was pregnant.

Deep breath. That wasn't important now. Not yet. One crisis, one task at a time.

Preston stepped back into the suite, closing the balcony door. He might be a shark, but damn, he took her breath away and set her senses on fire.

And time was running out fast to figure out how to deal with that.

* * *

Preston palmed Amie's back and led her into their suite, all too aware that her brother was so damn close. This whole dating ritual felt alien at forty-six years old. He wasn't a high schooler to sit on the sofa and be grilled by dad.

But Amie was tight with her family and there was no dodging all those concerned relatives. Truth be told, Alex's insights helped, even if he'd meant them as a warning.

Amie stepped into their suite and spun on her heels fast. "I can't wait another second to know. What were you and Alex talking about while I played with Cody?"

"Business." Images of Amie with pink tinged hair and a sunburn filled his mind, making her all the more approachable. Vulnerable.

Beautiful.

"That's all?" She perched her hands on her hips. "Somehow I'm having trouble believing you just talked about Diamonds in the Rough. My brother's known to be protective. It can't be coincidence that he showed up here now."

"Of course it's not a coincidence. He cares about you." Preston guided her deeper into the room, over to the balcony and their view of the Hudson River. He missed the outdoors. Needed the clarity. "But I can handle a worried relative."

"I hope so." She gripped the balcony railing, the NYC skyline lighting up the night, glittering like manufactured touchable stars. This was as romantic a setting as the park. Maybe the evening wasn't lost. Not yet. "I don't need any more conflict in my life right now."

A rogue thought struck him. "Did you tell him what happened between us?"

"No, of course not." Her eyes went wide with unmistakable horror. She shook her head. "I do *not* share that kind of information with him. That would be…creepy. But we're twins. There's an instinct between us. I'm certain he's here to check up on me. So I'll ask again. What did you two talk about?"

"Business—and yes, we talked about you." He skimmed his fingers over her high cheekbones and along her silky ponytail. "He shared stories about your pageant days and pranks you pulled to get out of attending some."

She angled closer, her feet tucked between his. "Why in the world would he do that?"

"I suspect he was lobbying to make sure I know you're more than a pretty face." He cupped the back of her neck. "But I already knew that."

"How so?" Her hand flattened against his chest, no hesitation.

There was a physical ease growing between them. It felt familiar. Comfortable. Natural.

"I work with you. You're damn smart." He tapped her temple. "Underestimating you would be a big mistake on anyone's part."

"Still—" she swayed even closer, bringing her lips inches away from his mouth "—it wasn't my brain that landed us in that coat closet together, since we hadn't even met."

Unable to resist her, all of her—body and brain—he sketched his mouth over hers. "Don't I know it."

Seven

His kiss sent Amie's already simmering passion into a full flame. She was so tired of fighting the attraction and had precious little time left to explore it before she told him about the baby. Tonight had been magical in a million ways, from their date in the park, to seeing him hang out with her brother and future nephew. In his own way, Preston fit. Or rather, she wanted him to fit.

But thinking that far ahead threatened to send her into a panic, so she focused on the present. On the warm stroke of his tongue with the taste of beer and pizza. The bold stroke of his hands along her spine, over her bottom to cup her hips and bring her closer. The press of his arousal sent a rush of power through her. This was real, happening again, not just another dream at night that left her feeling frustrated and aching.

He angled back to meet her eyes. "Are we headed for the bedroom?"

"Is that where you want to be?"

"You don't even have to ask that question."

"Neither do you. My only suggestion—" she looped her arms around his neck and she walked backward, sidestepping her cat "—let's begin in the shower."

His eyes flamed. "I like the way you think."

Their clothes fell away, leaving a trail of clothes as they walked into the Florentine-marble bathroom with an oversize steam rain shower and multiple body jets. He pulled a condom from his leather shaving kit, setting it inside the shower stall as he turned on the sprays, but stayed outside while the water heated.

"You're even more beautiful than I remember." He held her at arm's length, his eyes sweeping her curves and bringing tingles of awareness along her skin as surely as if he'd stroked her. "It's been driving me crazy the past two months thinking about that dark coat closet, wishing we had chosen a place with light and time. Hating like hell that it seemed we wouldn't get another chance."

She savored the breadth of his shoulders, the hard cut of muscles along his chest covered in dark hair. His narrow hips drew her eyes, her attention held by the thick arousal against his stomach.

She trailed her fingers down his chest, lower, his stomach muscles tensing visibly. "That night seems so surreal now."

With one finger, she traced the rigid length of him. His hard-on twitched against her touch and he groaned low in his throat.

His hazel eyes went steely with desire. "It happened."

"Believe me, I know." Her fingers wrapped around

the length of him. "I remember every detail, every moment."

He stepped closer, his hands cradling and caressing both her breasts. "This is going to be even better. I'm going to take my time."

She arched into his touch. "Promises?"

"I'm a man of my word." Dipping his head to kiss her again, he backed her into the shower.

No more reservations. She would have this and worry about the consequences tomorrow.

Preston backed Amie against the tile wall, taking the shower spray against his back. Her breasts filled his hands, the hardened peaks pressing into his palms as he stroked and caressed, then plucked with his thumbs... and mouth.

The spray pelted over their naked bodies, the beads of water mingling with sweat and need. Steam filled the shower stall, creating an even greater sense of privacy, a barrier between them and the outside world. For so long he'd ached for her, dreamed of having her totally. To learn every curve of her that he hadn't had time to explore before. She'd shut him out for so long. He wasn't a hundred percent sure why she'd changed her mind now, but he sure as hell wasn't turning his back on the chance to win her over.

He took a bar of soap in his hands, savoring the task in front of him. He applied all his focus to taking his time. Discovering all her secrets. All the places she liked to be touched best.

Steam surrounded them, a misty warm cloud along her wet skin while he worked up a lavender lather. She shifted from one foot to the other, drawing his eye toward long, slender legs slick with shower spray. Setting down the bar of soap, he reached for her shoulders and massaged the suds all over her.

Preston grinned hungrily, watching as her eyes drifted closed for a long moment, her muscles easing beneath his touch. He brushed kisses across her spiky, wet lashes while he slid his hands lower, kneading her high, full breasts until her knees seemed to give out from underneath her, making her sway. He pressed her to the tile wall with his hips, holding her upright.

Her breath caught as she reached for the soap, too, her fingers fumbling with it somewhere behind his back while he thumbed one dusky pink nipple to taut attention. She sighed in his ear, a throaty rush of breathless pleasure that only deepened when he took her in his mouth.

The soap fell from her hands and landed somewhere around his feet, but he couldn't stir himself to retrieve it. Not when her back arched the way it did right now, her whole body attuned to his slightest movement. Just like that first night when they'd danced. When they'd made love.

The chemistry at work was undeniable.

Still, she'd wanted a shower and he planned to deliver. So he forced himself back to hunt for shampoo.

Water saturated her hair, deepening the dark brown to ebony, and he squeezed the fruity-scented concoction into the locks, working it through, massaging her scalp while she hummed her pleasure. His hands slicked along the soaked strands, down her back to cup her bottom and bring her closer again. Skin to skin.

She sipped a kiss from him. "No more waiting. Now."

"And again in bed."

"Yes," she whispered, passing him the condom from the ledge.

He pressed inside her, moving, claiming.

The clamp of her around him was better than memories. The warmth of her body, the writhing of her hips was perfection. Bathroom lights and moonbeams streamed through the panes over her curves. No darkness. No shadows.

Just steam carrying the scent of soap and sex.

Her gasping breaths ramped, faster, her breasts pressing against him as her desire grew. He could feel it. Sense it. Her hand slapped against the glass wall as she braced herself, sliding down the condensation. Her head falling back, neck vulnerable.

As she unraveled with her orgasm, it was difficult to tell what was hotter—her or the steaming water. Finally, finally, he let himself go and thrust faster, deeper, wringing fresh sighs of pleasure from her as he found his own mind-shattering release.

And he knew he'd made the right decision. They would date, sleep together, work together, keeping it all civil and incredible.

They had all the time in the world.

Time was moving so fast. Knowing she was stuck in a twilight dream and unable to pull herself out, she rolled from side to side in the sheets, the Egyptian cotton sliding against her skin like Preston's touch. Her mind filled with an out-of-control reel, the past and present tangled, the night in the closet meshing with their encounter in the shower. Their clothes on from that night, but wet and plastered to their bodies. The peach-colored satin dress clung to her skin and shower spray slid from the brim of his Stetson.

She breathed in his scent, clean but spicy, too. Masculine. Heady. His touch warmed her where he touched her waist. Her hand.

The energy between them crackled like static through a rainstorm, crackling, dangerous along her skin. The music from that evening mingled with the percussion of the showerheads hitting the wall, their bodies, the floor. She breathed in and he breathed out. The writhing of their movements—dancing, making love, synced up effortlessly, her body responding to the slightest movement of his, shadowing his steps as she fell deeper into the spell of his hazel eyes.

The dim lighting of the coatroom and shower cast his face in shadows as she arched up into his kiss, his arms strong around her but loose enough she could leave if she wanted. But the last thing she wanted was to stop even though her mind shouted that she couldn't see his face, she didn't know who she was with. She needed to wipe away the water, let in the sunshine and see him. Know him.

Except pleasure pulsed through her at the angling of his mouth over hers, the touch of his tongue to hers. The kiss went deeper, faster, spiraling out of control. She pressed herself to the hard planes of his body. She lost herself in the kiss again, in the dream. In the feel and fantasy of this torrid dream that had her pressing her legs together in a delicious aching need for release.

Her breasts tingled and tightened into hard beads and her hands moved restlessly under the covers searching for him...but they were in the shower and the closet. And the hard length of his erection pressed against her stomach, a heavy pressure that burned right through the silky dress she'd worn.

She couldn't deny how much she wanted this. Him. Now.

He started to ease back and she stopped him, gripping his lapels. Slipping her hand into his tuxedo jacket, she let her fingers stroke across the muscled heat of his chest, water sloshing over them in her tangled mind. This was a man, the very best kind, powerful in body and mind.

His hands were back on her just as fast, roving, keeping the flame burning and—

Her breath was knocked from her.

She blinked awake, gasping for air as her cat stared back at her, perched on her chest. "Roscoe?"

The rascal must have jumped on her chest, worried over her restless dreams. She reached beside her and Preston still snoozed away, his breath heavy with sleep. She ran soft fingers on his forearm, unable to quiet her mind.

Eyes bleary, she stared at the digital clock on the nightstand: 1:30 a.m. A sigh escaped her lips. She needed to move. To think. To find clarity rather than thrash around in dreams she didn't understand.

Lifting Roscoe off and setting him on the floor, she carefully slipped out of the bed. He didn't stir. Neither did Preston. After the shower, they'd moved to the bed, slept, woken to make love again, taking their time, learning the nuances of each other. Then drifted off again. But still, she was restless.

From the floor, Amie grabbed Preston's T-shirt and put it on. It fell midthigh, like a short dress from her pageant days. But it smelled like Preston's musky cologne. It reassured her. Steadied her.

On tiptoe, she moved to the white chaise lounge across the room. The hand-stamped Venetian velvet made a gorgeous addition to the suite, and the kind of textural art that she loved best. She ran an appreciative hand along the pattern as she plopped down, clutching an oversize silk pillow to her stomach. Roscoe pattered over to her, tail straight up, shaking with excitement and affection. He jumped up, pawed at her until she lowered the pillow. He sat in her lap, purring, squinting his blue eyes at her. Roscoe always knew when she needed someone. When she needed comfort.

And damn. She needed that now more than ever.

Light from the city poured in through the window, allowing Amie to see Preston's figure in bed. He was a wonderful man. Caring. Confident. And more important, he seemed to believe in her. In her designs—at least the ones that she'd openly shared with him—and in her ability to make decisions.

Reaching for her stomach, Amie sighed deeply. There were too many unknowns.

For a moment, she allowed herself to think about what it might have been like if they had dated over the past couple of months. What they would be like. Would he be helping her pick out a nursery theme? Would he be offering names?

"Roscoe kitty, why is this so complicated?" she whispered. Roscoe simply looked up at her, purring still, and stretched his front paws to her belly. "We used a condom. I never sneak off into coat closets. And it's so hard to regret anything."

She scratched his head, wondering about what her

baby would look like. What life with her baby would look like. No, life with *their* baby. With his hazel eyes and her thick dark hair, chubby cheeks. Her heart went tight at the image of Preston smiling, rocking that child in his arms. If only life could be that simple, that easy. Had she blown her chance at it already?

Roscoe jumped from her lap and sprinted back to the bed, curling around Preston's head. Amie stayed for a moment on the chaise lounge before crawling back into bed, wanting to have Preston's warmth against her skin.

He stirred as she found her way back into his arms. He squeezed her tightly, and kissed the nape of her neck.

His breath was warm against her neck. If only things were different, less complicated. Somehow she would have to find a way to fix things between them. Wishing wasn't enough. She needed to act and soon.

Amie watched the clock for another few minutes before drifting to sleep.

After a catnap, Amie curled up against his side, the Egyptian cotton sheets tangled around their legs.

They were so good together it almost scared her, making her want to hesitate pushing for action and savor this just a while longer. It was just one night.

Preston stroked her bare shoulder while moving his toe under the sheet to entertain Roscoe. The cat pawed and pounced at the movement. "I'm disappointed your brother thinks I'm the bad guy."

"Well, you have cut a wide swath through the staff, firing off longtime employees we've grown to know and care about for years," she pointed out, tugging lightly at his chest hair.

He closed a hand around hers as Roscoe waddled slowly up the bed. "You mean, I saved the corporation."

"*Saved* is a strong word." She flattened her palm to his chest, his heartbeat steady and strong. "I would say you bolstered things."

"Semantics."

And likely why her grandmother had put him in charge instead of her.

Still, she frowned. "We lost a lot of talented people. Talented loyal people. I feel they deserved better from the company."

"It wouldn't help those talented and loyal people if the company started losing money. And that's what we were looking at. The employees don't thrive if the organization isn't thriving." He spoke with surprising passion, opening their blinds a bit with the remote control beside the bed, exposing an incredible view of the city lights in the middle of the night. "You know how many companies reorganize and then leave their people sweating it out for months afterward, worrying about their jobs? I happen to think it's kinder to circumvent the drama and the questions, making cuts as quickly and painlessly as possible."

"None of it was painless." Although she understood his point. She'd had friends who had been caught in corporate takeovers, worrying about their jobs for months while they navigated shifting seas at work.

"That's what severance packages are for." He shrugged. "I take personnel issues very, very seriously. I honestly believe the people are the backbone of any good company. That's not lip service. That's a fact. I happen to think it's one of the things your grandmother liked best about my philosophy when we first met."

"I believe you." She could see what had won over her grandmother. Preston might seem bottom line oriented. And he was. But he did care. "You just…look at things differently than me."

She wondered what he saw out that window overlooking the city right now. While she saw the lights and play of the moon over the river, he no doubt focused on other things.

"Different is not bad. Most artists are empathetic by nature. It's what makes them thrive in their work."

"Oh, really?" She grinned for a moment, realizing she'd never separate the man from the arrogance for long. But he was a smart man. And he'd obviously spent some time thinking about this kind of thing.

"Really."

They were quiet for a moment as she tried to process this new side of Preston. A side, she had to admit, appealed to her.

"I'm trying to see your take on things. My whole family has been more on edge recently because of Gran's cancer, so maybe not all the McNairs have given you a fair chance." That worry inside her—the fear that dogged her about the woman she loved most in the world—had been a large part of what had driven her into Preston's arms in the first place. "You're an outsider, so it will take us a while to trust you."

He lifted a strand of her hair. "Do *you* trust me?"

What a loaded question. She tugged the sheet up farther over her breasts, avoiding his eyes. "I trust you can lead Diamonds in the Rough."

"But you still wish it was in family hands."

Except then she wouldn't have met him and she wouldn't have this baby she loved more and more every day. Life was complicated. She opted for an honest answer—about the company. "I understand where my area of expertise falls at the company, but I still resent that I was not even considered for the CEO's position. I wasn't consulted about the choice. It stings."

"I'm sorry to hear that." He sat up, studying her face with those perceptive CEO eyes of his. "Your cousin didn't want the job. Did you?"

"I wanted to be considered." She sat up as well, hugging her knees to her chest.

"What makes you think you weren't?"

She rolled her eyes. "My family has never taken me seriously." Roscoe curled under her hand to be rubbed. "I'm the eccentric one, the airheaded beauty queen."

"You've proven you're at the top of your field at Diamonds in the Rough. Your more rustic designs are catching on like wildfire across the country and in England. You deserve to be proud of that. We all have a role to play."

She thought about the designs that weren't rustic. The ones he hadn't asked her much about. They might be all wrong for Diamonds in the Rough.

"I guess I just feel all the more need to prove there's no nepotism. My grandmother gives my father an office with a title and his name on the door."

"Your father's position is as a figurehead," he said matter-of-factly. "We know that. You contribute work, founding entire design lines. Sounds to me like you don't take yourself seriously."

She snapped back at the observation. One that was perhaps a little too astute for her peace of mind.

"Maybe you're right. And maybe you're not." She slid

off the bed, taking the sheet with her. "But I do know one thing for sure. I'm starving."

Seemed she was hungry all the time lately once the morning sickness passed. Her time was definitely running out to tell him about the baby. She'd rambled on about trust and yet she was lying to him in one of the worst ways possible.

They'd taken a big step here tonight. She just hoped the connection they'd made was enough to carry them through the news she had to tell him.

Preston leaned against the wet bar, facing the bay of windows looking out over one of the best views in Manhattan, but his eyes zeroed in on Amie. She perched on a leather bar stool wrapped in a sheet and eating a sliced pear, cheese and crackers from the cut-crystal dish as though she were a starved athlete. He'd learned to read people over the years, a survival skill in his job world. And he could see something huge weighed on her mind.

Nudging aside her empty plate and sliding it across the smooth granite countertop, she dabbed a napkin along the corners of her mouth with overplayed care. She folded the crisp linen napkin, set it down and pressed the crease nervously. "We need to talk."

Damn. He'd known something was off with her from the second she'd rolled out of bed. "Forget the speech about how we shouldn't have done this and it will never happen again. There's an attraction between us we've tried to deny and that hasn't worked. I say it's time to quit fighting it."

"Things aren't quite that simple." She pressed the napkin crease again and again.

"They can be. You can't deny what's between us any

longer, especially not after tonight." He picked up her hand and linked fingers, even the simple touch crackling the air with attraction.

"I hear you." She squeezed his hand, a sadness creeping across her face and catching in her eyes. "And in a different world things could have played out over the months."

"Different world?" He struggled to follow her words and for an astute CEO, he just wasn't getting it. But he wasn't letting go. "Is this because I head the company? It's not like I'm your boss any more than you're mine, since your family owns the business. That puts us on even footing."

She shook her head, tousled hair sliding over her cheek. "It's more complicated." She jerked her hand free and pushed her hair back with agitated fingers. "I've been looking for the right time—the right way—to tell you."

Tell him what? To go to hell? That she was seeing someone else? "Just say it."

She sat up straighter, her hands falling away from her head and settling to rest over her stomach. "I'm pregnant. And the baby is yours."

Eight

"You're pregnant?"

Preston's flat tone and stunned expression didn't give Amie much hope for an enthusiastic reception. She tucked the sheet more securely around her, wishing she'd chosen her timing better to make the announcement, when she felt less vulnerable from making love with him.

When she had on some clothes and he was wearing more than sweatpants low slung on his sexy narrow hips.

Arming herself with a bracing breath at least, she met his shocked gaze head-on. "Apparently the condom didn't work—welcome to the world of the two percent fail rate. And before you ask, I haven't been with anyone else in over six months, so I am absolutely certain the baby is yours."

He gave a rough nod. Swallowed visibly.

"I wasn't questioning. I trust your honesty." He thrust his hands through his tousled dark hair, the dusting of silver strands on the side a hint more pronounced in his stress. "I'm just...stunned."

She tipped her chin, trying to squelch the ache of disappointment in her heart that he hadn't...what? Just turned a cartwheel? Or hugged her and asked how she was feeling? Make her feel connected to him since they'd created this new life together? She knew better than to hope for those things. But that didn't stop the sting of hurt just the same.

"I don't expect anything from you. I'm able to support myself. I would hope for the baby's sake you would want to be a part of his or her life, but if you decide otherwise, I am not going to force you to pretend to care."

"Whoa, hold on. I didn't say I'm out of the picture." He started pacing restlessly around the luxury suite, the same way he did whenever he went into thinking mode in the boardroom. "I've had less than a minute to process this. I'm forty-six years old. This isn't the news I was expecting. I'm past that stage of my life."

She remembered his child who'd died and her heart softened. No doubt her baby would stir all the more difficult emotions for him. Yes, she understood that. Wished he would have confided more in her when she'd asked him about it. But he hadn't wanted that kind of intimacy between them.

His decision. And damn it, this wasn't easy for her, either. This baby was coming no matter what.

"Fine then." She clasped the sheet between her breasts and slid off the bar stool. "My baby. I'll take care of him or her and you can move on with the next stage of your life."

He clasped her elbow gently and stopped pacing. "Lower your defenses, Amie. This is my baby, too. And I may not be as young as most new parents, but I'm not Methuselah." He massaged her arm, his touch tender but his face still guarded. "I'm all in. Whatever you and the child need, I'm here for you both. I will be an active part of his or her life."

"Thanks for doing your duty," she said dryly, easing her arm away.

He sighed heavily. "Apparently I'm not expressing myself well."

"No, I'm hearing you just fine. And more than that, I can see in your face this news doesn't please you in the least." A knot started in her throat. Damn hormonal emotions.

"Are *you* happy?"

His question caught her off guard. She hadn't spent a lot of time thinking about her own emotions. She'd focused more on Preston's and her grandmother's reactions. "I'm nervous. But yes, there are days I have these images of what he or she will be like, and I'm happy."

"Pardon me for being human. You've had a while to process this surprise." He clasped her hand, holding firm. "Give me time to get over the shock of your being pregnant and I'll get to the happy part."

She eased a step closer, not quite ready to relent. "Well, forgive me if I'm skeptical."

Holding her gaze, he sat on the sofa, tugging her hand carefully until finally she sat on his lap and he held her close. They didn't speak and she let herself soak up the feeling of his arms around her. Maybe, just maybe, they could work things out in a way no one would be hurt or feel disappointed.

He rubbed his hands up and down her back. "Holy crap," he said slowly, realization lighting his eyes. "This is why you've been avoiding me lately."

"Ya think?" She pressed her cheek against his steady heartbeat.

"What about before you found out you were pregnant? Why did you give me the deep freeze then?"

Now, *that* surprised her. How could he be so clueless? "You honestly don't know?"

He shook his head. "Afraid not. Enlighten me."

"You were firing Diamonds in the Rough employees at the speed of light." She slid off his lap to sit beside him, the warm fuzzy moment over as indignation crept up her spine. "The poor staff was literally put on the island watching people voted off every day."

"You don't agree with the business decisions I made." He arched a dark eyebrow.

"Not all of them. No," she admitted.

"But you can't deny the company is thriving now. Those who are still working for us have jobs that are more secure than ever. With luck, we'll be able to hire more back."

Could that be true? Could she trust him? "When will that happen?"

"When the numbers speak."

She stifled disappointment at his typical double-talk answer. "Numbers don't talk. People do."

He spread his hands. "That's why you're the artist and I'm the CEO."

"And we're both now parents of this baby." She shot to her feet, feeling more hopeless than before that they could find a middle ground together. "I need to shower and rest. I just can't talk about this anymore."

Before she did something weak and vulnerable like curl up and cry against his chest. She dashed back to her bedroom and closed herself inside, alone with her cat and an even bigger tangle of emotions.

Maybe a better man would have gone after her.

Preston could not be that man. Not right now. Not when this news had ripped him raw.

Charging into his bedroom, he found his workout clothes and pulled on a clean T-shirt and running shorts. Socks. Shoes. He focused on the routine to keep himself from putting a hole through the nearest wall.

Amie pregnant. His daughter had died giving birth... The two events spun together. Clouded his mind. He needed to move.

He sprinted out of the suite and down fifty-two flights of stairs from the penthouse suite. He headed west on East Fifty-seventh Street and picked up his pace. Midtown was far quieter in the small hours of the morning. While it may be the city that never sleeps, 4:30 a.m. didn't attract the same kind of crowds. Cabs raced to the stoplights in the freedom of no traffic. Bars and clubs in unlikely places spilled music and colored lights out onto the sidewalk, making him dart around the occasional red velvet ropes set up on the street.

And Amie was pregnant.

Lungs burning, he hit Central Park before he realized where he'd been headed. Maybe not the wisest place to run after dark, but he pitied anyone who tried to mess with him. He'd love an excuse to throw a punch. Or ten. Anything to make this ache in his chest go away. The fire behind his eyes.

He'd lost his baby girl to a pregnancy. And now *Amie was pregnant*.

Tripping on a tree root as he darted off the sidewalk into the grass, he almost fell onto a homeless guy sleeping on a green painted bench, his face covered with newspaper.

"You okay, man?" the guy asked, a hand shoving aside last week's sports section as he stared up at Preston.

He nodded. Started running again.

Slower.

He spotted the pond up ahead and followed the path around it. Now and then a cab pulled onto one of the roads through the park, headlights flashing over him. A few street lamps lit his way. Nocturnal birds called out from the trees all around the pond, the conservancy efforts having made this portion of the park feel like being out in the country. Exactly what he needed.

Space. Air. Stillness.

Slowing his steps even more, he paced alongside the water's edge until he'd circled almost the whole way around. He hoped he'd sweat out the worst of the crushing fear for Amie. For his unborn child. He'd loved his daughter so much. Even during the years where he hadn't gotten to see Leslie much, he took joy and pride in knowing she was in the world. A small piece of him, but better than him. The very best of him.

Losing Leslie had cut so deep he'd barely stood it. There was the pain of losing her. Compounded by the fact that she'd died without getting to hold the infant she'd given up everything to have. And made even worse by the pain of knowing how much she hadn't wanted her own father in her life.

When Leslie had died, he'd taken time off from work—something he'd never done. Listless weeks he could hardly remember. But a company crisis had saved him. Forced him to dedicate everything he had to bending the corporate world to his will. There had been a grim satisfaction in that. And it had saved his sanity.

Now, he was going to face all that again. With Amie.

"You sure you're okay, man?" a gruff man's voice shouted to him from several yards away.

For a second, Preston figured voices in his head was just about right for the hell of the past hour. But then he saw a flash of newspaper waving at him from another bench surrounded by bushes and flowers. Lights illuminated the plantings—and the homeless man he'd almost tripped on before. The guy's grizzled beard and shaggy hair were so long they flowed over his T-shirt, but he held up both hands as if to show him he meant no harm.

"I'm good. Thanks. Just out for a jog."

But was it too much to ask to be alone with his thoughts?

"Sorry, dude," the scratchy voice rasped in the quiet of predawn when the sounds of night bugs were still more prominent than the rattle of diesel engines and squealing brakes in the distance. "Had a friend that came here to…er…end it all." The guy scratched his beard. "Got that same feeling when you sprinted past me."

"No problems here—" he started. But seeing the older guy's patches on a tattered jacket—military badges, Preston stopped with the bs answer. "Running off some old ghosts. But I'm…okay."

Scared spitless of having another child. Worried he might fail this baby the same way he'd let down Leslie… but he was going to find a way to get himself together.

Man up.

"Hard to keep 'em off your heels some days. I've had that kind, too." The man nodded thoughtfully, staring out at the pond.

Laughter nearby interrupted as a young couple stumbled past, sounding intoxicated as they held on to one another, doubled over with hilarity while the street lamps glinted off their matching face piercings.

Preston needed to get out of here. Get his butt back to the hotel and be there for Amie. For his child.

And the only way to do that? Wall off those emotions—the ghosts on his heels—and just focus on her. Getting through this. He was a man of honor and he would stand by her. His family.

His eyes burned even as he thought it.

Striding over to the older man, Preston took a deep breath.

"Thank you for your service." He held out his hand, knowing in his gut the man was a veteran fallen on hard times.

Sure enough, the guy grinned. A few teeth were missing. But his eyes held plenty of wisdom.

"You're welcome, son." His weathered grip was strong. "You might try surprising those ghosts sometime, by the way. Stop and turn instead of running. One of these days, you'll give them hell."

"I'll remember that." With a nod, Preston launched into a run, turning his feet back toward the luxury hotel that seemed a million miles away from this place.

He wasn't ready to battle any ghosts today. But for now he would count it a victory if he could talk to Amie about this child without breaking out in a cold sweat.

First, though? He needed to run faster, arrange with the concierge to find help for his veteran angel.

Then Preston would be ready to ask Amie to marry him.

The next day passed in a blur for Amie. She couldn't get a read on Preston. He'd been the perfect gentleman, but it was all so...perfect. Too perfect. He'd closed himself off from her in a way she couldn't explain but couldn't miss.

Technically, he'd done nothing wrong. They'd shared breakfast in the hotel dining room with Alex, Nina and Cody, then attended a Broadway matinee together. In fact, they'd spent the entire day together, leaving not one free moment alone to talk about the baby.

In another half hour, they would be leaving for the Diamonds in the Rough gala being held at the Waldorf Astoria. For now, Preston sprawled on the floor with Cody, playing with action figures from the children's performance they'd seen today. They were watching her future nephew while Alex and Nina got dressed. The sitter would be arriving soon—one of the camp counselors Cody had met and grown fond of. She was from home being flown in so Cody would have a familiar face to care for him.

Meanwhile, Preston looked too damn enticing playing in tuxedo pants and his shirt. No jacket or tie yet, just his suspenders and cummerbund. His broad hands moved the little lions, marching them over a mountain they'd built from throw pillows.

He was clearly at ease with children. But then, he'd told her he'd been a father and that his daughter had died. This new baby had to be bringing up old memories—good and painful ones. She should have thought of that before now.

The elevator door opened and Amie glanced over to see Nina walking through, wearing a floor-length black dress, simple other than the plunging neckline with a long yellow diamond pendant. Her red curly hair was upswept in a riot of spirals.

Amie rose from her chair and greeted Nina, grasping her hands. "You look amazing. I'm sorry if Alex caused you any trouble dragging you here to check up on me."

"A woman's never too old to play dress up. This is a fun break." She grinned, twirling, her silky dress swirling around her feet, a flash of gorgeous Jimmy Choo heels beneath. "And you, oh my, you do have a way of making a statement."

"This old rag?" Amie winked, but she couldn't deny she'd dressed to the nines, too. It was a kind of armor, a way to stabilize herself. The Grecian-style red dress was gathered on one shoulder, leaving the other bare, exposed. The gown was cinched on one hip with a brass medallion, a long slit up one leg. She hooked arms with her future sister-in-law and walked to the window seat where they could talk without Cody overhearing. And where she could gain a little distance from the appeal of Preston.

Amie sat in the window seat, cars below moving at the typical New York snail's pace. "How's Cody adjusting to your decision to stay at the ranch?"

"It's a love-hate thing." She smoothed her dress over her knees, her eyes lingering affectionately on her blond son. "He likes that we're going to live there now that Alex and I are engaged. He adores being around horses all the time. He gets along so well with Alex. Your brother is wonderful at getting through to him—and willing to learn more every day. He wants to go with me to interview new doctors and therapists for Cody. But it's all happened so fast, which makes it tough, because new routines upset Cody tremendously."

Amie chewed her lip before asking, "I hope you don't take this the wrong way, but why choose to come to New York now?"

"Alex is worried about you, and Cody was upset over him leaving, so we came along. Your brother says you haven't been yourself lately. I don't know you well enough to compare, but you do seem very...stressed."

Having someone to confide in felt good, but she didn't know how much she could tell her brother's fiancée, a woman none of them had known for very long at all, given the whirlwind romance. She needed to share the news with her grandmother first. And before she did that, she wanted to have things in order with Preston, to have a plan in place. Amie settled for a general—and still truthful—answer. "Gran's cancer progressing has us all worried."

"I can understand that. I mentioned the same to Alex, but he says it's different. He can sense it because of the twin connection."

Amie glanced down at her hands, anxiously twisting the four gold and topaz rings she'd chosen to go with her dress. "Things have been difficult at work."

Nina glanced at Preston, then back at her. "It's clear there's a chemistry, but I can see how that would be complicated. I'm here if you ever need someone to talk to."

She clasped Nina's hands, noticing they both wore one of the newest Diamonds in the Rough pieces, a sun and moon facing each other in silver and gold. "Thank you. I appreciate it and am sure I'll be taking you up on that soon."

"Just not today?"

Amie shook her head, smiling warmly. "Soon."

The elevator slid open again and her twin strode into the suite. Cody shot to his feet, carrying one of the lions to show him, chattering about the imaginary game he'd been playing with Preston.

Amie rose quickly. Too quickly. Her head started swimming and the room spun. Oh God. She reached for the wall, but her line of sight was narrowing to a pinpoint. Damn it, damn it, she was going to pass out.

Dimly, she realized Preston was rushing toward her. "Amie? Are you okay?" He caught her under the arms as her legs gave way. "Is it the baby?"

"Baby?" Alex barked.

"Baby?" Nina whispered.

"Baby, baby, baby," Cody chanted.

Preston swept her up as she fought back the dizziness. He settled her onto the sofa. "Amie?"

"I'm fine," she said, the room already stabilizing. "I just stood up too fast, and I could use some supper."

"Baby," Alex said again in a menacing tone, walking closer. "What the hell is going on here?"

Preston shot him a dagger glare. "Do not upset Amie."

Still, Alex walked closer. "My *sister* is pregnant?"

Nina gripped his arm. "Alex, I don't think this is the time or the place. When Amie's ready to talk, we can have a civil discussion. Maybe we should give them some space?"

Alex kept walking toward Preston as if Nina hadn't

spoken. "I'm asking you now. Is my sister pregnant and is the baby yours?"

Preston stood, his shoulders broad and braced, staring down her angry twin. "Yes, the baby is mine."

Oh God. Her twin was the quiet one in the family, but fiercely protective. So it was no surprise when he drew back his fist.

And punched Preston in the jaw.

Nine

Amie launched forward, shouting at her brother, tugging on his arm as he pulled back for another hit. "Alex, what the hell are you doing?"

Preston stumbled a step but stayed on his feet. His eyes went steely as he stared down Alex but pointed to her. "Amie, step out of the way." He zeroed in on Alex, that same alertness in Preston's body that she'd witnessed right before he took down a criminal on an LA street corner. "McNair, get yourself under control. Think about how this is upsetting your fiancée and Cody."

The young boy with autism was sitting on the floor with wide eyes, hugging his knees while rocking back and forth. Alex cursed softly, then kneeled beside his future stepson, all his focus shifting. "It's okay, Cody. I just lost my temper. Grown-ups do that sometimes. I'm sorry, buddy. Would you like to go back to our room with your mom?"

Cody nodded, standing, moving over to his mom. Nina cast a cautious look over her shoulder before shuttling her son out of the suite.

Alex took a deep breath, but his tense face said he wasn't backing down as he stared at Preston. "You knocked up my sister."

Amie gasped, stepping between them, hands raised. "Excuse me, but I am an adult. I make my own choices, and while I am expecting a baby, I take offense at the phrase 'knocked up.' I would also appreciate it if you didn't shout the pregnancy to the world. This is my business. I don't know why you're going all Cro-Magnon."

"Seriously? It doesn't take a math whiz to realize that since you haven't been around very long, the kid was conceived before you even had a chance to really get to know my—"

Preston growled, "Watch where you're headed with what you're saying. I let you have that first punch free and clear. But push me or say anything to Amie and I'm taking you down."

Alex's jaw jutted. "You can try."

Amie pressed a hand on each man's chest. "Stop. Both of you. You're both stressing me out and that's not good for the baby."

Alex's eyes narrowed, but she felt him ease a fraction. "Sister, you're manipulating me. I don't like that."

She patted her twin and looked into his familiar eyes, finally seeing more love than anger. "But I'm right. Thank you for your concern, but I'm okay. Go see Nina and Cody before you say something you'll regret. Your family needs you."

With a tight nod, Alex hugged her quickly. "Love you, Amie." He leveled a look toward Preston before backing away. "Be good to her or there will be hell to pay."

He stalked away and the elevator doors slid closed, leaving her alone with Preston. She reached to touch his jaw carefully along the red mark turning light purple. "Are you hurt?"

Her gaze ran all over him, taking in the powerful shoulders and chest. But his hands were impossibly gentle as they landed on her arms.

"It's nothing. I've taken worse. I just need to know you're all right."

Was she? Not really. Her heart pounded double time and she just wanted life to settle down. But there was nothing she could do about that. "I'm fine, and we have the party to attend."

His hand brushed her cheek, smoothing away a tendril that had slid out of place.

"We'll talk later," he promised.

A good thing or bad? She honestly didn't know. His expression was impossible to read. Cool despite his warm touch, and that worried her. Life had been so much simpler when they were in a coat closet and shower.

Five hours later, Amie put together an ice pack from the limo minifridge. The gala had been a success from a business standpoint, with the displays echoed by edible-desert versions the guests feasted on with relish. But the event hadn't been nearly as pleasant from a personal perspective. Nina and Alex had opted to stay at the hotel with Cody. And Preston had been distant and remote but utterly in control. He'd done his job impeccably. He'd been a consummate gentleman and efficient CEO as he chose a few key people to speak with, applying just the right amount of charisma on a night that called for a personal touch. He'd even laughed off questions about his bruised face, saying he'd run into a street light while jogging.

But even so, there was still no sign of the tender lover, the man she'd started to think she could have a relationship with. He'd shut down on her ever since the baby news. She needed to get past that polite wall again, for her child's sake—and yes, for her own peace of mind.

Preston sat in the plush leather limo seat, collar unbuttoned, looking handsomely disheveled. Clutching the ice pack, Amie inched next to him, closing the space between them.

She pressed the bag of ice against his jaw and the light purple bruise. "I'm so sorry my brother hit you."

"He loves you. He didn't break anything. It's okay." He seemed to have turned the explosive moment into a simple math equation, reducing it to a balance sheet with a measurable figure. Always a businessman. Calculating.

"It's not okay. It was awful." She shivered thinking of the moment her brother had taken a swing at Preston. She dabbed the ice pack along his jaw while the limo slowed for a red light. "Can we at least talk honestly here instead of this cool and distant approach? If you've decided you're not okay with the baby, after all, just tell me. I can't take living in limbo." Her heart slammed as she waited for his response. In what way had he decided to coolly solve this complicated equation?

"I've already told you I'm going to be a part of the

baby's life." He smiled, then winced, his jaw clearly sore. "I want to be in your life, too."

"I hear the words, but your eyes are not the same." He was still closed off. She could see it in the way he refused to really look at her. "Something's wrong and you're not telling me. I know this has happened fast, but we don't have the luxury of unlimited time. Not with a baby on the way."

He tugged the ice pack from her hand and tossed it aside in irritation. "I'm giving you everything I have."

"*Giving* me?"

"Everything I have. Yes," he said, his voice clipped. "This is all there is."

"What does that mean?" she pressed, not even sure what she was searching for from him, but certainly not this. "You either want to be with me or you don't."

His jaw flexed, his stormy eyes darting back and forth for an instant before he finally exhaled, his head falling back against the leather seat. "I told you I had a daughter and that she died. This new baby has brought up a lot of memories. Tough memories to deal with."

Her heart softened. She'd suspected this, but to hear him say it—it took the fight right out of her. She smoothed a hand down his arm, the fine fabric of his tuxedo warm from his body. "Tell me, Preston, please. Let me know what's going on inside you. Your daughter is my baby's sister. I want to know—I need to know."

The car started forward, the tinted windows muting the headlights and street lamps on Park Avenue, past an older residential section of the city. She saw the lights reflect on Preston's face while he seemed to debate what to tell her.

Finally, his throat moved in a long hard swallow. "Leslie was just eighteen when she died."

So young, so tragic. And at the same time, Amie realized he'd lived a whole other life before walking into hers just two months ago. He'd told her more than once he considered himself too old for her. She didn't agree but could see right now why he felt that way.

Hoping he wouldn't close her out again, she kept rubbing his arm. "You said she had an accident. I can only imagine how that must still hurt." Her voice was soft, gentle. She brimmed with the ache to be someone he could trust. The car slowed to a stop again, and this time, the flood of red brake lights nearby created a crimson glow inside the limo.

He shook his head. "I don't think anyone gets over losing a child. And the fact that Leslie's death was preventable eats me alive every day."

Preventable? He'd said it was an accident, but clearly he'd said so to brush people—her—off. But not tonight. They'd moved past that. They were tied together for life through this baby. "What happened?"

"It's a long story without a simple answer." He turned his head toward her, his eyes full of pain.

"I'm listening." A sympathetic, encouraging smile brushed her lips as she squeezed his hand.

"Her mother and I split when Leslie was just finishing elementary school. They both hated me for leaving." He winced over that part, the pain flashing again. "And Leslie hated her mother for staying. There was no reasoning with her. She became an out-of-control teenager. Some say she would have been that way regardless, but I worked too much and missed so many of my scheduled visitations. Time I can never get back." He rested his elbow on his knee, dropping his head into his hands.

"I'm sure you did the best you could." She rubbed circles along his broad back, their car stuck in gridlock just a few minutes from their hotel.

She suspected they wouldn't be moving anywhere for a while. And this time, she had no intention of leaving the limo.

"How can you be so certain?" he asked softly.

"You're a perfectionist. You hold yourself to a standard so high most would be crushed."

His laugh was bitter as he sat up again. "That's my business persona. My parenting skills were sorely lacking. I thought by giving her nice things I didn't have as a kid, I was being a good dad. Trust me, I see how screwed up that is now."

"How did she die?" she pressed again.

"She ran away from home at seventeen with her loser boyfriend," he said, the bitterness in his voice unmistakable. "She got pregnant, didn't get proper prenatal care. She died and the baby didn't make it. Something called placenta previa. She went into premature labor and by the time she got to the ER…it was too late."

Amie stifled a gasp, the story so much worse than she'd expected, so painful. So terribly tragic. "No wonder you're worried about becoming a parent again."

Losing his daughter through a pregnancy added a whole other layer to his emotions where Amie's baby was concerned. It made sense now that he'd looked so rattled when she'd told him. The lines of worry that etched in his jaw all evening made more sense. Seemed more reasonable.

"It's tough not to worry about your health and the

baby. It's all I can think about sometimes, all the things that could go wrong." His eyes sheened over. He stared out in front of them.

An ambulance honked nearby, lights flashing while it went up on the sidewalk to get through the jam.

"I'm taking care of myself and am absolutely getting the best care available." Clasping his hands in both of hers, she pressed his to her stomach.

He froze again, his palm broad and warm through her silky dress. Preston stared at her stomach before meeting her gaze. His face was contorted with a sadness she could not quite comprehend. "That's not what's scaring me most."

"What then?"

"I'm scared as hell of loving another child and screwing up—" his voice came out ragged, tortured "—of having my soul ripped out if something happens to him or her. I can't go through that again. My heart died that day, Amie. I don't think I have anything left to give the two of you and that's so damn unfair."

He squeezed his eyes closed, no tears escaping, and she knew that just meant he kept them bottled up inside with all that pain and misplaced guilt.

"Preston? Preston," she said again until he looked at her. "You seem to care a lot more than you like to let on. I can see it in your eyes."

"You're seeing what you want to see."

"Trust me—" she cupped his face and couldn't help but notice he left his hands on her stomach where their baby grew "—I may be an artist, but I'm the most starkly realistic one in the family."

She was far more practical than people gave her credit for, a side effect of having her every move scrutinized by a stage mother—a mother she did not intend to emulate.

Her thoughts were cut short by the soft chime of a bell that preceded an announcement from the driver.

"Excuse me, Mr. Armstrong. My apologies for choosing this route, sir. There's an overturned bus ahead. Looks like we may be stuck here for a while."

Preston hit the speaker button. "Not a problem. Thank you for the update."

Releasing the light on the communications panel, he stared at her in the dim light of the luxury car, his eyes bright with inscrutable emotions slowly shifting to…hunger.

It was her only warning before he leaned closer and pressed his mouth to hers, kissing her. Not a quick kiss. But the kind that promised more.

So much more.

The old hurt and anger roiled inside him. But this time, instead of running it out, he had Amie's hands on him. Amie's soft voice in his ear and slender body shifting beside him on the limo seat. It was tough to resist her on a good day. And this day? The last twenty-four hours had shredded him.

All the emotions surged and shifted into one inescapable need.

He kissed her hard. Deep. But he made sure to be gentle with his hands and his body. He skimmed a touch along her bare shoulders, feeling her shiver and tremble. She was exquisitely sensitive. He'd been an ass not to see the signs of her pregnancy earlier. But now? It seemed written all over her body.

In the way she quivered against him when he did

something small, like nip her ear the way he did now. Or when he licked his way down her neck and her skin broke out in goose bumps.

The limo windows were the blackout kind. No one could see in. The partition window was secured, he'd double-checked it on the communications panel. Doors locked. Traffic jam keeping them right here for a long time.

So he didn't quit kissing her. He laid her back on the seat and stretched out alongside her, never breaking his kiss down her chest to the swell of her breast. More delicious evidence of her pregnancy. He'd just thought her curves were even more lush than he'd remembered from that first wild night together. But now, he cupped the weight of them in both hands, savoring the way she felt almost as much as he liked hearing her breath catch.

Dipping his head to the valley between her breasts, he nudged aside the pin on her red Grecian gown, essentially undoing all her clothes with just one touch. A red lace bra molded to her curves, but a flick of the front hinge had that falling away, too.

Impatient as hell, needing to lose himself in her—in this—he circled one tight crest with his tongue even as he slid his hand up her thigh. She arched and sighed beneath his touch, totally on board with this plan. He nudged aside the lace panties she wore, feeling her warmth right through the thin fabric.

"Amie." He said her name so she would open her eyes.

Put all that brilliant blue focus on him as he touched her. She was a beautiful woman, but damn…so much more than that. He watched her lips part as he slid a

touch inside her. Her eyes fell closed again. Her thighs
clamping tight to his hand to hold the touch there.

As if he was going anywhere.

He covered her mouth with his again, working her
with his hand until he felt the rhythm of her sighs and
throaty little hums of pleasure. Finding the pace she
liked best, he took her higher. Teased her. Tempted her.

He wanted to draw it out. To make it last, but she
had her own ideas. She captured his wrist in her hand.
Held him right where she wanted him most.

"You like that?" He repeated the circling motion,
bending to draw on one breast. Then the other. "I like
it, too."

"More," she demanded, voice rasping, her blue gaze
landing on his.

Complying, he drove her right where she needed to
be, her cries of completion sweet music in his ear as
she found her release.

Another day, he might have given her a little time to
recover herself. Or taken her to that peak a second time
while she was so delectably willing in his arms. But
just then, that dark, hungry need returned, his emotions
churning to the surface. Reminding him how damn
much he needed her.

"Preston?" She smoothed her fingers along his shoulder, making him realize he hadn't even removed his
jacket.

He ditched it now, sitting up on the seat.

"I'm going to bring you up here, sweetheart," he
crooned as he peeled away her panties and then lifted
her. Gently. Carefully. He moved her onto his lap so
she straddled him.

Her thighs splayed over his, remnants of her red silk

gown still clung to her thighs and waist. She unfastened his belt and tuxedo pants, freeing him from his boxers. He watched her, her dark hair mostly falling around her shoulders, the updo sacrificed to their frenzy.

She stroked him, fingers cool and nimble as she guided him closer to where she wanted him.

Grasping her hips, he lifted her high and then eased her down. Down. Deeper.

Perfect.

Everything else fell away. Her slick heat surrounded him, holding him tight. Her hands fell to his chest where she steadied herself. She brushed a kiss along his cheek, urging him on. Telling him what she needed in a way that only fueled him up. His hands molded to her waist. Smoothed up to her breasts.

He had a lot of other ideas for his hands, too. But she gripped his wrists again. Pinned them to the limo seat on either side of his head as if she had him captive. She arched an eyebrow at him. Teasing.

But then things got crazy. She swayed her hips in a dance that about turned him inside out. Lifting up on her knees, she found a rhythm she liked and took them both higher. Faster. And he let her. Not thinking right now—great idea. He took everything she was giving him.

When her grip slipped on his wrists, though, he sensed she was close. He held her waist, taking over, pushing them the rest of the way. Her release squeezed him hard, spurring his own. With no condom between them, the pleasure seemed to last all the longer, the pregnancy issue moot at this point, and hell if that didn't feel…so good.

Wrung dry, he shuddered a deep sigh and folded her

against him. Holding her. Kissing her bare shoulder as a silk strand of her dark hair teased his nose. He spanned a hand along her back, rubbing slow circles while he tried to find his breath again.

He couldn't bear to think about the past anymore. And thinking about the future raked him raw with fears as well. Walling off the past didn't mean he had to wall himself off from the future. He just wanted to lose himself in the present, with Amie.

"I'm sorry for being distant earlier today. I just needed some time to myself to think."

"I know." She shifted against him, resituating herself so she sat beside him, her head tucked against his chest. Her hand covering his heart. "I've had more time to process this than you, and even for me I feel like I can't wrap my head around it. Everything is changing so fast. Both with my grandmother and the baby."

"Let me help you. Your whole family works together and depends on each other. We're tied now through this child, so let me into that circle." He hoped it was the right time for this—the most important pitch of his life.

But it needed to happen and he couldn't fail. She meant too much to him.

"What do you have in mind?" She lifted her head, eyeing him as the limousine finally inched forward.

Preston took her hands in his and hoped his eyes didn't betray his fears. The time had come to tear down some walls and start letting her in if they would stand a chance at building a future together.

"Let's get married."

Ten

"Married?" Shock chilled Amie to the core, the leather crackling under her as she inched back to look into Preston's eyes. She'd expected him to pursue her because of the baby. But she hadn't expected this. It felt too forced, too sudden. Too rehearsed. "You have got to be kidding."

"I'm completely serious." His voice was steady, eyes trained on her face.

Amie shook her head in disbelief. "We've only known each other a couple of months. That's a huge leap to take just because I'm pregnant."

She knew he was only proposing because of the baby, and maybe even to secure things at the company, too. Old insecurities flamed to life inside her and she couldn't shut them down no matter how much she wanted to believe their connection was special. That given more time, they could have gotten to this place on their own. And maybe they would have. But now there was no way to separate fact from fiction.

Preston reached for her hand. He ran his thumb over her knuckles. His face etched calmness. Stability. Reminding her of his boardroom demeanor, where he focused on the goal and calmly maneuvered his way there. Her gut wrenched.

"Sure, it hasn't been long, but you can't deny we have something good going here. We have an attraction beyond anything I've experienced. We get along now that you're not icing me out at the office. We work well together. I know we can build a future together for ourselves and this baby."

A part of her heart leaped at the idea of being married to Preston. He was a good man. Protective. Confident. Sexy as hell. But she wouldn't settle for being his end goal just because he felt as if he should marry her. Ever since her pageant days, people had taken it upon themselves to judge what was best for her. To tell her what she needed, what she desired. For so long, she hadn't cared about the outcome of the pageants, so she let herself be told what to wear, what act to perform and how to answer interview questions.

Was Preston just like that, deciding this was the most logical outcome to their problem? Deciding what was best for her? She couldn't allow herself to take the path of least resistance just because it was simple. And the man in question was irresistibly appealing. She owed her baby better.

She wanted to trust what he said, but she needed more from him. Was it so wrong to want him to want her, child and company aside? "We don't have to decide now. We have a few months to think this through."

"I take it that's a no." He still held her hand, but his grip loosened.

"I just want us to make the right choices—for ourselves and the baby. We still have time with the Atlanta event before we have to face the family at home…"

"Family." He slumped back in the seat, dropping her hand. Running his fingers through his hair, he let out a pent-up sigh. "I hadn't thought about all of them."

"And your parents. Do you have other family?"

He shook his head. "Not since Leslie died."

"Do you still communicate with your ex-wife?" Amie knew so little about his life before the company. Before her. They were tied together through this child. And if he was going to make hasty decisions, she would make sure she balanced that with all the important angles he was overlooking.

He blinked in surprise but answered quickly. "Not often or regularly. Last I heard, she and her new husband moved to Georgia. They adopted two children, siblings that had been orphaned."

"And you're okay with her remarrying and having kids?" Her breath caught in her throat, heart pounding as she asked the question.

"Of course I'm all right with that. I want her to move on and have a future."

Yet he hadn't moved on for himself. Or was that what he was trying to do now? So tough to tell when she didn't know much about him or his past. "What was your daughter like when she was little?"

"Feisty, independent." He laughed out the words. Preston's gaze seemed to turn inward. Thoughtful.

Amie knew in that moment how much he had loved his daughter.

"Sounds like her father." Amie grinned at him, placing her hand on his knee, leaning closer. This was a hard subject for him. She wanted to make sure he didn't close up on her. And that he knew she was here to listen.

"Except for the pigtails."

"Now, that's an image." Her smile widened. "What color was her hair?"

"Dark, like mine. She was an active child. She walked early, loved her trike. I bought her a pony, a fat little bay mare from Chincoteague, Virginia. She loved the books about the ponies from that island. It seemed suited that she had a formerly wild pony as her own." He hung his head. "My ex said I used gifts to make up for lack of time."

"That could be true, but it also sounds like you knew her and her wishes. Time together doesn't always translate to a quality relationship anyway. My parents spent plenty of time with me and never had a clue what I wanted to do or what gifts I may have preferred."

"I appreciate you trying to let me off the hook. But I made mistakes. I have to live with that. I'm going to do my best not to make the same mistakes with this child." Genuine promises shone in his eyes.

Amie desperately wanted to believe that's what she was seeing. "My baby's lucky to have you as a father."

"Our baby," he softly corrected her.

"Right, I'm still adjusting, too." She was fidgety. Her fingertips smoothed back her hair, but nothing was out of place—unlike her insides that were a mess.

"I want to be more than the dad. I want to be there. With you and the baby."

"I told you, I need more time to think about the proposal." Her voice edged with more steel than she intended. While she was starting to have a clearer picture of Preston the father, the image of Preston the husband was still elusive. And she would not settle. She needed someone that genuinely wanted her.

Preston considered her words. Amie could see him recalculating. "Well then, how about we move in together and if we decide to get married one day, we can head to the courthouse. Let me at least be there to help you through the pregnancy day by day."

"I have a houseful of servants." She was thinking practically, suspecting he was doing the same.

"Good. Because I suck at doing laundry." He offered her a causal grin. "So is that a yes to moving in together?"

She studied his face, trying to get a read on him. If only she had spent the past two months getting to know him. She might have been able to tell something from the light in his hazel eyes. "Let's enjoy the next couple of days and decide after the Atlanta show so we have a plan in place when we talk to our families."

He studied her at length as if he intended to press, then nodded. "I can live with that." He slid his hand behind her neck, fingers massaging her scalp. "In the meantime, I intend to make the most of every second to fully and completely seduce you."

She looped her arms around his neck. "Maybe I intend to seduce you first."

Preston lint rolled cat fur from his tuxedo, making sure not a stray hair was in sight. Tonight was important. And not just for the gala. It meant more than sell-ing jewelry and making this line succeed.

He needed to sell Amie on the idea of them. She hadn't outright rejected the idea of them together, but she wouldn't commit to the proposal. He could see hesi-tation and questions in her eyes.

If she would just say yes, he could do away with so many of those fears. He had meant what he said about wanting to be there for their baby. For her. He wanted to do this right.

There had to be a way to convince her that he was serious about her. That he wanted to pamper and take care of her and their unborn child.

She was an amazing woman. Independent. And she was smarter than she gave herself credit for. Her artistic instincts were brilliant and he hated that she couldn't see how much she was worth to the company. To him in particular.

Amie riled him, made him want to try harder. There was something in the way she carried herself, in her sarcasm and eclectic flair that drew him in. No one but Amie would ever consider taking an elderly and sickly cat on a business trip just to ensure proper care was administered. Her heart was so big. He wanted a place in it.

He'd been racking his brain on how to show her he cared. How to prove to her practical nature that he cared. Or maybe…

He stopped the mindless brushing of his tuxedo jacket and put the lint roller down on the floor for Ros-coe to play with—the cat was a primo escape artist, sneaking out of Amie's room. Maybe he didn't need to show her he cared so much as show her that he believed in her.

Hadn't she said that no one in her family took her seriously? That she wasn't even asked about heading the company? A plan came together in his mind as he thought of ways he could show her just how much he valued her. She might think his efforts to prove his faith in her were just corporate maneuvering. And— he had to admit—the plan he had in mind was straight out of his boardroom toolbox. But for a woman who felt as if she hadn't been taken seriously in the business world, it might help her to understand that he saw her differently.

That he recognized more than her legendary beauty or her obvious wealth. He respected the hell out of her.

Picking up his cell phone, he tapped the lint roller into motion for Roscoe again while trotting out some instructions to his personal assistant to get the ball rolling on his idea.

A few moments later, his work was interrupted when the door to his suite clicked open and Amie stepped through the threshold. She was radiant.

Yes, beautiful, but so much more.

He would convince her to marry him, one way or another. He had to.

Amie was used to working close to home, which meant she wore casual business attire some days and ranch clothes on others. All these galas so close together gave her flashbacks to her pageant days. Except at least she got to choose her own clothes now. No more traditional stage garb like the kind her mother insisted on as her "manager."

Now she could let her creative impulses run free.
And yes, she had to confess, she enjoyed watching the
heat flame in Preston's eyes every time she made an
entrance.

Since she'd pushed the edgy boundaries before, she
went for a simpler look tonight, a fitted gold lace dress
that flared around her feet. Her hair was slicked back
into a tight bun. Simple, classic cat eyeliner and nude
lips. Dangling hammered-flat gold earrings and multiple wide bracelets were engraved with her favorite
quotes from her favorite poets. All the words of encouragement and perseverance were strung around her
wrists. There to remind her to breathe.

She walked down the grand winding staircase at the
Saint Regis Hotel where they were staying and holding
the event. No getting trapped in a limo together tonight.

Her body heated at the memory of making love in
the backseat. And continuing through the night when
they'd returned to their hotel. The trip on the private
jet had been too quick and full of business for any deep
conversation, but that marriage proposal still hung in
the air between them.

Could she really just move in with him and see what
happened over the next few months? She wished she
knew the answer or saw some kind of sign. She felt
adrift with nowhere to turn. Her mother wouldn't be a
help at all. Her brother had made his adversarial position
clear. And she didn't want to burden her grandmother.

Her fingers clenched around Preston's elbow as they
reached the bottom of the staircase, noise from the jewelry show already drifting down the hall along with
music from a string quartet.

Preston glanced at her. "Are you feeling all right? Tired? Or dizzy?"

"I'm feeling fine," she said quickly. Of course, he'd meant the baby, not the proposal or her feelings. "I'm taking my prenatal vitamins religiously. I promise."

"Just making sure you aren't overdoing it. It's been a hectic week." He patted her arm. "Let's get to the party and find some food."

Okay, more pregnancy concerns, but it was thoughtful and she was starving. She spotted a waiter heading into the ballroom with a silver platter of persimmon pear caprese toast. Another with what looked like goat cheese and beets. Her mouth watered.

"Definitely food. Sooner rather than later."

He smiled down at her with such light in his eyes she felt hope flutter to life inside her. Maybe, just maybe, they could be happy, sharing great sex and working hard to build a future together. They were both driven people. If they set their minds to this…

He dropped a quick kiss on her lips before escorting her into the ballroom teeming with jewelry displays on models strategically seated and standing on small themed stages throughout the room. As songs changed, they changed jewels from the display cases beside them. More than just a runway event, they'd created an interactive jewelry fashion show to play throughout the evening. She was quite proud of the execution of this idea, the thematic podiums echoing the various Diamonds in the Rough lines.

She snagged an appetizer from a passing waiter. Cheese truffle with chives. She could have eaten a dozen. Her mouth full, she looked around the domed space, searching for the contacts she needed to make.

Taking her time to work the room, she sampled her way along the perimeter.

Preston went still beside her, stopping her short of her goal of a mini lobster soufflé.

"What's wrong?" She followed his gaze and realized his attention was focused on a lovely blonde in a pale blue dress walking toward them on the arm of a distinguished-looking man in a conservative tux. "Preston?"

"Amie…" He paused, his forehead furrowing. "I'm not sure how to tell you this or why she's here, but—"

The woman stopped directly in front of them. "Hello, Preston, it's been too long, but you're looking good." She extended her hand to Amie. "I'm Dara West. I used to be married to Preston."

After an awkward introduction to Amie, Preston cornered his ex-wife by the triple chocolate fondue fountains surrounded by fruit and small delicacies. She always had adored her sweets. That had gotten him out of trouble more times than he could count. He'd known they were through the day she'd thrown a box of her favorite Godiva's exclusive G Collection chocolates at his head after he missed Leslie's fourth-grade dance recital because he'd worked late. No good excuse.

"Dara, what the hell are you doing here?"

"I do keep up with your life thanks to the internet and an occasional Google search. I saw photos of you and Amie in the social pages. I know you, and I could see there's a connection between the two of you. I was curious." She picked up a glass of champagne from a passing waiter.

"And your husband doesn't mind?" Preston raised his eyebrows in disbelief.

"Bradley and I are secure. Solid. Besides, coming here gave us an excuse for a weekend away together. Mom and Dad are thrilled to watch the kids."

"The kids are—" he swallowed hard, thinking back to the photograph she'd sent—a family, a complete family "—beautiful. Thank you for the Christmas card."

"I'm happy..." Dara's voice trailed, became leaden. She shook her head. "Well, there was a time I didn't think that happy was possible. But I love Bradley, unconditionally, and I've worked hard to find happiness again after what you and I went through. I keep hoping you'll find a way to be happy, too."

Leslie's death had shredded Dara as deeply as it had hurt him. He knew that.

"So here you are, checking up on my happy meter." Preston's arms crossed over his chest.

"Checking up to make sure Amie McNair is worthy of you." She gestured with her champagne flute to Amie, who was standing chatting with a potential client. She took Preston's breath away with her understated charm and love for the company, for people.

He threw back his head and laughed. "You are something else, Dara. But thank you. I can take care of myself. Truth be told, Amie's too good for me."

"Spoken like the gentleman you've always been."

"Not always." Preston's eyes darkened, muscles tensing. He had spent years ignoring and burying his past. His ex. His dead child and premature grandchild. These past few days had brought every painful memory lurching back to the surface. "I'm sorry I let you and Leslie down. Sorrier than you'll ever know."

"Casting blame takes away from thoughts of remembering her. I want to remember her and smile." She looked thoughtfully at him. And she seemed to be at peace.

"How did you do it?"

"Do what?" Dara's green eyes looked back inquisitively.

Preston let out a long-held breath. He shrugged his shoulders. "Get up the guts to have another child in your life?"

She nodded her head in understanding. "I have a mother's love to give and nowhere to pour it. There are children who need that love."

"You're a good woman. I was an idiot to let you get away."

"You aren't about to hit on me, are you?"

"Our time passed before Leslie died. I know that." The weight of the past threatened to drag him under. He needed to lighten the mood. Fast. "Besides, your husband would kick my ass."

"He would try. But we both know you could take him." She winked at him, tossing her blond hair over her shoulder with a dramatic flick of the hand.

"Flattery? You surprise me." He laughed. The conversation was easier than he could have ever imagined, than he felt he deserved.

"I've realized our breakup wasn't entirely your fault. I had my part in how things went south between us."

"That's kind of you to say, but I know—"

"Stop. You don't have to protect me from myself. I take responsibility for my own actions. That's a part of how I was able to move forward and enjoy my future." Dara smiled at him.

If she could move on, could he? Could he stop running from those old ghosts?

He sighed, the words falling out before he could weigh the wisdom or why of speaking them. "Amie is pregnant. The baby's mine."

Her eyes flashed with only an instant's surprise, then total joy. "Congratulations. That's wonderful news."

"It is." Pain crept into his words.

"Then why aren't you smiling?"

"Amie won't marry me. I'm having to work my ass off just to get her to agree to let us move in together."

"She doesn't love you in return?"

He scratched the back of his neck. "We, uh, didn't talk about love."

Dara rolled her eyes. "She won't marry a man who doesn't love her, who only proposed to her because she's pregnant. Hmm…" She tapped her chin in mock thought. "I wonder why she said no. That would have been enough to sell me."

Sarcasm dripped. And yet, the theatrical delivery helped him get the message. Sometimes he needed things spelled out for him.

Damn. How could he be so successful in the business world and such a screwup in the relationship department? Of course Amie wanted more from him. How had he overlooked that? "Okay, I hear you. And by the way, you're funnier than I remember."

"And I'm hoping you still remember how to be romantic. There was a time you were quite good at that. You do love her, don't you?"

"This is not the way I saw this conversation going," Preston admitted.

She raised an inquisitive brow at him. "But you're not denying it."

"Because I can't." Realization bubbled in his stomach.

She rolled her eyes, tilting her glass back to Amie. "Well, don't tell me. Tell her."

Eleven

Amie kept her cat in her lap on the flight back to Fort Worth, needing the comfort of stroking Roscoe. The rhythm of Roscoe's purring was the only thing anchoring her. The last week had left her raw. Vulnerable. She had spanned a year's worth of emotions over the course of a few days. How could it have only been a week since her grandmother gave her orders to travel with Preston, to make peace with him for the future of the company?

She felt anything but peaceful after seeing the way Preston greeted his ex-wife. It was obvious he had feelings for her. It didn't matter that Dara had moved on with a new family. Amie hadn't been able to take her eyes off Preston with his former wife at the party in Atlanta, mesmerized by the emotions she saw broadcast through his hazel eyes.

Emotions she'd never seen for her.

She'd hardly slept afterward, her stomach churning all night, knowing that Preston didn't care for her that way. Knowing she didn't have a fraction of his heart. His offer to stay, to marry her, was not out of desire or longing for her.

Roscoe nudged closer, standing to make his feline presence felt. She brushed her fingers behind his ear, doing her best to keep herself from shedding tears on the flight home. Instead, Amie concentrated hard on Roscoe's purring. She could only imagine the turmoil that would erupt over her news, especially with the memory of Alex's reaction weighing on her heart.

She needed to do what she could to control the family response. Which meant talking to Preston. And she wasn't ready to face more questions about marriage or moving in. She needed time and space to think.

Stroking the senior Siamese, fur soft under her fingers, she hoped it was a good time to broach the topic. On her terms. "Now that Alex and Nina know, it's only a matter of time before word gets out."

Preston stretched out his long legs, crossing his boots at the ankles, wearing faded jeans with his suit jacket now that the galas were done. "Do you think they would talk, even if you asked them to keep their silence? I assume you asked them to wait for you to make your own announcement."

"I did ask before they left. Nina won't say a word and no one will guess from her behavior. But Alex? Even if he keeps his silence, I'm not so sure he can hold back his emotions. He's mad—which I think is ridiculous because I'm a consenting adult. I am damn tired of this family treating me like a flighty nitwit who doesn't know her own mind. So it's going to be time to tell them soon."

"They're your family," he said, his hand resting on his Stetson beside him as if he took comfort from it the way she did her cat. "You have my support in however you decide to handle the announcement. I do want to be there with you."

"Okay, I'm all right with that. I think we need to tell them about the baby after the final event in Fort Worth. We can say we're still working out the details between us, but that we're committed to doing the best by our child."

"You can say that and I'll support you. That doesn't mean I agree with you." He leaned forward, elbows on his knees, eyes skimming her turquoise and gold–trimmed maxidress, taking in every inch of her as he always did. "I want to marry you. I would like them to know that."

"No, absolutely not." She shook her head adamantly, remembering the way he'd looked at his ex. The shine in his eyes and warm quality of his face as they slipped into easy conversation. That, more than anything, had assured her she was making the right decision. She would not rush into this and wind up with only a shell of a man doing his duty. "They'll all pressure me to say yes and I can't take all of them coming at me that way."

He frowned.

"What?" Did he know she was withholding her deeper concerns?

"If they say so much as a cross word to you, I'm going to have trouble with that. I don't relish the notion of all of them coming swinging at me, but I'll handle it."

The thought of another fight breaking out made her shiver. A follow-up thought popped to mind. "Is that why you proposed? Because you care what they think?"

"Hell, no, and frankly I'm offended you think that of me." He held her eyes with unwavering intensity. "I proposed because I want us to be a family. I want us to bring up the baby together, no split-time parenting."

Something she wanted, too. But was that enough to build a marriage on?

"And if it doesn't work out between us and things turn acrimonious?"

"It will work out. I care about you, Amie." He said it so earnestly she wanted to believe he meant more than that. "I won't fail again."

He wouldn't fail? Like they were a work project? The thought sent her spiraling. His honor and protectiveness weren't in question. But she wanted more from him than just "caring" about her. She wanted… Her heart lurched as if the plane had lost altitude, realization making her unsteady.

She loved him. She loved Preston Armstrong. And she wanted him to propose because he loved her, too.

Preston was losing control fast. Something had shifted with Amie during their discussion on the flight. She'd shut down and clammed up. He'd seen this volatile woman go through many emotions, but closed off? That was never one of them. Even when she was icy, it was that cold ice that burned. This shutdown came from buried emotions. She'd left the plane as quickly as possible, abandoning her luggage except for her cat. She'd even taken the waiting limo and said she needed to leave immediately, mumbling an excuse about needing to get a vial for the cat.

He didn't know what he'd done to flip things so fast other than asking to marry her, for heaven's sake. He'd even told her he cared about her, as Dara had reminded him to say. And it hadn't made things better. In fact, they were worse off than before, and he wasn't sure what move to make next.

He'd caught a ride from one of the flight-line crew back to the ranch to find her. She wasn't answering her phone. He got out to the ranch, a buzz of activity with vacationers taking riding lessons and the kids' camp off to the side. The resort side of the main lodge was busy, as well, but the private living quarters looked quiet.

He saw the limo backing up beside the barn, attempting to turn around to leave. He jogged over and knocked on the chauffeur's window.

The electric window slid down. "Yes, Mr. Armstrong? I was just coming back to pick you up. Miss McNair said you were conferring with the pilot."

"I found my way back. Thanks. Which way did Miss McNair go?"

"She handed the cat to one of the staffers and headed to the barn. She said she needed to ride Crystal to clear the cobwebs."

Riding? Pregnant? Was that wise? Panic rolled in his gut.

"Thank you for the information," Preston said, already jogging toward the main barn. He readied his personal sorrel quarter horse, Chance, waving aside the stable hand that offered to help. Leather creaking, he swung up into the saddle. He looked down at the stable hand. "Which way did Amie ride off?"

The employee pointed toward the forest to the east, away from the kids' camp. Off to privacy and away from the more beaten trails. Preston urged Chance forward. The horse leaped instinctively, digging hooves into earth with as much desperation as Preston felt. He set off after her, unsure what he would say when he found her but knowing he couldn't leave things this way.

The wind whistled in his ear as his horse galloped. He gave Chance his head, pressing his legs into the horse's sides. He needed to find her. Quickly. While the speed was safe for him, it made him afraid to think of Amie racing over trees and creeks—afraid for their child and for her.

Finally—thank God—finally, he saw her in the distance, her dark brown hair streaming behind her as she took the trail with her white Arabian.

She sat deep in her seat, a saddle of black and silver with a bridle to match. She looked like something out of some Western fairy tale. Her long dress flowed and rippled, hints of bare leg flashing above her turquoise cowboy boots. She was intriguing. Gorgeous. Wild and untamable. Infuriating.

Irresistible.

He galloped alongside, shouting, "Amie, slow down. Let's talk."

"Let's ride," she shouted back, hair whipping across her face.

Crystal's pace opened up and the space between them doubled. Tripled. Her grace, even here, was perfect. The way her arm fell casually to her side. She moved in perfect time to the mare's beat.

God, how he wanted to take her up on that offer and just let loose on their horses, riding the expanse of the land. But he had to be careful, for her sake.

He pushed Chance onward, making sure he was close enough to be heard. "Are you sure this is safe for you and the baby?"

Her face creased and she didn't stop, but she slowed to a trot. She sat perfectly balanced, reins gathered in one hand as she swiveled to face him. "You know, pregnant women ride horses, drive cars and even go swimming. It's quite the revolution."

"I'm not laughing." He eased his quarter horse to a trot in step with hers and reached to take her reins.

Her eyes flashed with fury at his taking the lead. "Duly noted and not surprising."

"Please, get off the horse," he said through clenched teeth.

"I wouldn't risk my child," she snapped.

"*Our* child," he snapped back, slowing Chance to a halt.

"Walking up the stairs is more dangerous than riding this horse." Still, she slid off Crystal's back, her boot thudding the ground beside his.

"Then I guess you'll be taking the elevator."

"Are you one of those smothering kinds?" Her chin jutted, challenge in her eyes as she took her horse's reins back. She stroked the Arabian's arched neck and clucked softly to her. Crystal sprung to attention as Amie guided her around Preston.

"I'm one of those careful kinds. It's how I've become such a successful businessman. Why would I take more care with work than with my personal life? I'm learning about balancing that."

"Good point. If it makes you more comfortable, I won't ride again once I return my horse to the stable." She withdrew from him again.

Shutting down.

"What's wrong?" he probed, dropping his horse's reins, effectively ground tying the well-trained mount.

"Nothing." She tightened her grip on the polished leather of her horse's reins, not slowing down. Continuing away from him, to the forest line.

"Damn it, Amie, you're upset about something."

"We don't know each other well enough for you to read my emotions." She stopped. Turned.

"Are we going back to that again? Fine, I won't press for marriage. We'll go back to dating."

"I'm not some fragile flower." She dropped the reins at her feet, leaving Crystal as she stomped toward him. "I'm not an airheaded person who's too stupid to live. Treat me like an equal, damn it."

He didn't have a clue what she meant. Why she was so angry. Or what the hell had gotten under her skin. But he knew a spark when he saw it, and she was sparking all over him.

"Treat you like an equal?" He fought for calm. Control. Couldn't seem to find any as he dragged in a harsh breath. "Remember—you asked me to."

Her brows furrowed for all of an instant before she seemed to guess his sensual intent. He angled toward her.

But she beat him to it, lunging closer to fling her arms around his neck and damn near kiss his socks off.

His brain raised a protest for about a fraction of a second—shouldn't they be talking?—before his body got fully on board with this plan.

He wanted this. Needed this.

Lifting her off her feet, he backed her up against the trunk of a massive bald cypress tree, hiding her from view, even though they were far from the ranch and not close to any trails. Her hands already worked the buttons of his shirt, her lips dipping to follow where her fingers had been. He reached to skim a hand under her hem, letting the dress bunch around her thighs while he cupped a palm between her legs.

Her head fell back, eyes closed, lips parted. She was so responsive. So hot and ready for him. Despite everything that didn't work for them, this did. The electric connection that torched away anything else.

With one hand he palmed her thigh, lifting her leg to wrap around his waist and giving himself better access. With his other hand, he slipped beneath her panties to stroke her until she went breathless, her fingernails catching on his back as she held herself still for his touch.

She amped him up so much. Unfastening the fly of his denim, he shoved aside her underwear just enough to take her. The thin strip of lace gave way anyhow, leaving her naked as he sank deeper inside her.

His groan mingled with her soft whimper, the pleasure undeniable. He cupped her cheek with one hand and slid a palm behind her back, making sure not to press her into the tree bark. She didn't seem to notice, though, her hands stroking through his hair and down his back. She kissed his chest and breathed along his skin, warming his flesh, driving him out of his mind with her sweet, sexy ways.

A breeze rose, scattering a few old leaves around his feet and plastering his shirt to his back. Amie's hair lifted, blowing around him, too. She tipped her head back as if she enjoyed the feel of it. The wildness of it. He edged a shoulder sideways a little so he didn't block her from the brunt of it, letting her feel the force of it on her face.

Her eyes popped open then, blue gaze meeting his

for one fierce, unguarded moment, and she smiled at him in a way that dazzled the hell out of him. Made him want her more. Forever.

Fueled by frenzy and too much emotion, he thrust into her again. And again.

"Preston!" She called his name in a hoarse rush right before she found her release, her body convulsing around him in the soft clench of feminine muscles.

He followed her a moment later, his own fulfillment slamming through him. His heart pounded hard against his chest, their bodies sealed together while they twitched through aftershocks of a passion bigger than the Texas sky.

When she went still against him, he could almost feel the taut strain creeping into her shoulders and back. Just like that first time they'd been together, the aftermath went tense as she relegated him to a place outside her life. He settled her on her own feet.

His head rested in the crook of her neck, his breath coming in pants as he struggled to get his galloping heartbeat under control. "Amie, you're tearing me apart here."

He remembered that moment of connection when the wind had kicked up. He hadn't imagined that.

Yet now, her hands smoothed along his hair, over his shoulders, but her eyes were distant. "I'm sorry, Preston, I'm so sorry." A sigh shuddered through her. "I just think this is all too much too fast. We should keep our distance until we figure out a plan. It's the only way to stay objective."

A cold lump settled in his gut as he angled back. "Are you dumping me?"

She smoothed her dress into place, not meeting his gaze. "I'm protecting us and our child from heartbreak."

Too damn stunned to know what to say. It wasn't often he'd been struck speechless, but right now was one of those times. He could only stare at her as she moved away from him, talking softly to Crystal as she approached her horse and then stroked the animal's muzzle.

She swung up on her horse again. She didn't race off, giving him time to make the trip with her. She kept the pace at a slow trot, but she didn't look at him or speak again all the way to the stable. Once they returned, she slid off her horse, handed the reins to a stable hand and walked away.

Her silence and stiff spine spoke louder than words. Preston waved off the stable hand, insisting on untacking Chance on his own. He needed time to think. Spending time in the barn was more productive then locking himself up indoors.

Inhaling the smell of sweat and hay, Preston attached his horse to the crossties. He loosened the girth, gave Chance a pat on the shoulder and heaved the saddle off. The sorrel shuddered from withers to tailbone as his saddle was removed.

Preston dutifully brushed and hosed the horse down. Once again, he found himself escaping in a rhythm of routine. Avoiding ghosts.

His window of time to win her over had closed unless he came up with a Hail Mary fast. A way to break through her insecurities and let her know how much she meant to him. How much he cared.

Cared?

With a sinking sensation in his chest, he knew that

was far too tame to describe the way he felt right now. Her rejection gutted him after lovemaking that had been one of the most incredible experiences of his life. After a week of witnessing her talent, her generosity and her warmhearted ways up close.

"Cared" was the cop-out of a man too scared to face his own ghosts. But he was ready to do battle now. Because he knew that he felt a whole lot more than that for Amie.

He loved that woman. Heart, body and soul.

Twelve

Amie had never felt less in the mood for a party.

But this final wrap-up of the Diamonds in the Rough promotional tour was crucial to finishing off her deal with her grandmother. And beyond any "deal," she wanted Gran to be happy. This would likely be her last celebration, a fact that tore at Amie's already raw emotions.

Preston's overprotectiveness, his anger, then his tender lovemaking had been every bit as much of a roller coaster of feelings as her own. What were they doing to each other? How could love be so damn complicated?

She stepped into the largest barn, an open space used for entertaining, the same location her cousin had used for his wedding just a week ago. Rustic elegance. The signature of Diamonds in the Rough.

Bales of hay and leather saddles made eclectic showcases for high-end jewelry with pricey stones and intricate carvings. And not just women's jewelry but men's as well, along with belt buckles and boots. Light from the chandeliers refracted off the jewels, sending sparkles glistening throughout the room and over the guests. The room was bathed in splintered, glittering light. All the indications of a lovely evening. One she couldn't enjoy.

Amie had reached into the back of her closet for a gown, barely registering what she wore. Somehow, she'd ended up in one of her old pageant gowns. A black strapless number, fitted at the top with a floor-length, poofy tulle skirt studded with tiny diamonds and silver flecks. She'd always felt like the bad Disney princess in this gown. And it was too darn tight across the chest now, thanks to her pregnancy breasts. Her cleavage was getting more attention from some men than the jewels.

She just had to get through the evening without crying over the mess she'd made of things with Preston. And then she saw him across the room, looking as sexy and brooding as ever in a black tux with a bolo tie and Stetson, cowboy boots polished. He looked so...

How could she love him so much and still have so many doubts?

Her stomach rumbled and she realized she'd been so upset she'd forgotten to eat. She turned toward the buffet, only to stop short. Her parents were standing there. On a good day, dealing with them was taxing. But tonight? Tonight they threatened to send her nerves out of control. Undo what little stability she had.

She and her brother had always thought her mother's collagen-puffy lips and cheek implants had changed her appearance until she looked like a distant-relative version of herself. Not her mother, yet eerily familiar. Her father always worked to look like an efficient businessman. Ironic as hell, since Garnet McNair carried an in-name-only title with the company, some kind of director of overseas relations. Which just meant he could pretend he worked as he traveled the world. Mariah only requested that he wine and dine possible contacts and charm them. On the company credit card, of course. Her parents were masters at wringing money out of Gran. But they would have to learn to live within their trust-fund means soon enough.

Her eyes burned with tears at the thought and she turned away fast, searching for Gran. She found her grandmother in the back of the room, away from the noise, sitting in her wheelchair, holding court with different loyal business contacts.

Amie angled through the crowd, smiling and nodding, her full-skirted gown brushing tables, chairs and people on her way past. As she neared, Gran ended her conversation with two jewel suppliers and turned her attention to Amie.

Gran patted the chair next to her. "Your business trip seems to have been a success."

"We completed the events." She smoothed the back of her dress and sat in a cloud of black tulle. Her hair was swept back on one side with a large pewter-and-diamond comb, leaving half the silky mass to fall over her shoulder.

"So you believe you and Preston can work together? You can accept him as the CEO of Diamonds in the Rough?"

It would be so easy to just say yes. Instead, she found

herself asking, "Gran, why didn't you ever ask me if I wanted to be considered for the job?"

"Did you want the job?"

"God, no," she answered quickly, surprising even herself. "I believe I could do it, but I'm like Gramps. I'm the artist. I just wanted to be considered. To be asked."

Her grandmother took her hand and squeezed, her grip still firm in spite of her thin frailty. "I know you could have handled the job, but I also knew you wouldn't want it. I assumed you understood that. You are my amazing girl, everything I could have hoped for as the next matriarch to lead the family. *The family.* You know that's much more important than the company. You are the McNair glue that's going to keep our empire cohesive—Diamonds in the Rough, Hidden Gem Ranch and HorsePower Cowkid Camp."

Her grandmother's words surprised—and touched—her. "You really think so?" Amie's own words came out in a half whisper.

"I do." She nodded with confidence. "And if you feel the artist well is drying up and you need a change of pace, I can also see you on the board of directors, even leading the table someday. You're a force to be reckoned with, my girl."

Tears welled in her eyes that had nothing to do with hormones and everything to do with a lifetime bond she felt to this woman who'd been the true mother figure in her life.

She leaned in to hug her grandmother. "I love you, Gran."

Her grandmother wrapped her in a hug, the familiar scent of gardenias enveloping her with memories. "I love you, too, Amie dear."

Amie held on tighter, her voice choking. "I'm going to miss you so very much."

"I know, sweetie." Gran pulled back, brushing the two fat teardrops from Amie's cheeks. "And I'm sorry we didn't have more time together. But I am at peace about all of you and the legacy your grandfather and I built. I miss him. We're going to have a beautiful reunion in heaven, he and I."

Amie smiled, wobbly but heartfelt. "Say hello to him for me."

"I will." She touched Amie's stomach lightly. "If it's a girl, will you name her for me?"

Amie blinked in surprise. "You know?"

"I suspected, yes, and I am assuming Preston is the father." She narrowed her gaze. "I didn't miss the quick exit you two made for a certain coat closet that first night."

Oh, but those eyes had always seen so much, hadn't they?

Amie could only nod slowly, her eyes darting to Preston then back to her grandmother. "Is that why you sent me on the trip?"

"I didn't know then, actually, just knew there was something between you and Preston. I guessed about the baby when you got back."

"How?" She had to know what gave them away.

"He treats you like spun glass."

Amie winced. Now, wasn't that a sore subject? "I don't want him to be with me because of the baby or the business."

"Good Lord, Amie, have you looked in that man's eyes when he's watching you? He's been in love with you since day one."

Amie shook her head, wanting to believe but still too scared to hope. "You're just seeing what you want to see."

Her grandmother took her face in her cool hands. "You're afraid to see what's really there. But take a look. Take a risk. The payoff is beyond anything you can imagine. Watch with your heart rather than your eyes." Her voice softened and she cut off any chance of response as the chandeliers dimmed. A spotlight illuminated the dais where the band finished their song and Preston stepped up to the microphone.

Amie's throat burned as she looked at him. And wished.

"Thank you, everyone, for joining us here this evening." His voice still made her nerve endings twitch to life, just like that first night when they'd met. "For those of you who may not know my face, I'm Preston Armstrong, the CEO of Diamonds in the Rough. I'm also known as the interloper brought into a tight-knit family business."

He paused as laughter rippled through the room. Once the silence settled again, he continued, "I'm a man of numbers, a businessman, but in my soul I appreciate the beauty of art my skill set could never create. However, it is my honor to use my experience in the business world to bring that beauty into the lives of others."

That's what she wanted, too. She found herself nodding, embracing his company philosophy in a way she hadn't allowed herself to before. She'd been so busy avoiding him, she truly hadn't let herself hear the good things he was doing for the business.

"And on that note," he continued, gesturing toward a

screen that immediately illuminated. "The art speaks so much better than I ever could. So I'll turn over the stage now for our presentation of Diamonds in the Rough's most popular brands—as well as unveiling an exclusive first look at a new line in development by our top designer, Amie McNair. It is our hope that this new direction will add a division to the company that will bring new jobs into our community." His gaze found hers in the audience. Warmth radiated from his eyes. "And now, if you'll all turn your eyes to the screen, I give you… the heart and lifeblood of Diamonds in the Rough."

Fingers sliding into her grandmother's hand, Amie's heart leaped into her throat at his words.

The film presentation held so many of her designs, even Amie hadn't realized until then just how large her stylistic imprint had been on the company. Guests oohed and aahed as audibly as they had over the fireworks at Stone and Johanna's wedding, the jewelry brought to life with cinematic flair.

And then the screen scrolled an announcement for the future, images from her sketchbook fading in and out, the snake-themed coils she'd designed, the patterns of their markings inspiring interlocking pieces for multicolored chains in precious metal. They were more urban and sophisticated than the rustic-luxury items that were the company cornerstone, potential crossover items for a younger, more international market, while staying true to her roots.

This was the new program he'd spoken of. The new division that could create jobs and bring some of their former employees back. Realizing how well this man knew her—how well he had listened—made her heart swell. Truly listened to her wishes, her choices, even her style. He let her be—herself. Something she didn't take for granted after the way she'd grown up. He didn't stuff her into a category.

He accepted her. Flaws and all. And she owed him the same acceptance. She needed to take her grandmother's advice and be brave, take the future waiting for her.

Shining right before her eyes.

Preston sat on a bale of hay on the stage, the barn quiet in the aftermath of the final stop on their gala tour. A success in attendance, and the feedback on his presentation had been unanimously positive from the board of directors.

But there was still one person left to hear from, the opinion that mattered most.

Amie's.

As if conjured from his thoughts, she walked into the empty barn, weaving around the tables and chairs that would be cleared away in the morning. She was a vision, wearing her version of a "little black dress." So very Amie. She was one of a kind and he wouldn't have her any other way. He needed to tell her that, in no uncertain terms, to let her know he loved her. No more running. No more cop-outs. No more ghosts. She was worth every risk. Had always been worth the risks.

Her dress swished as she walked. "Thank you."

"For what?"

She stopped in front of him, her gown brushing his knees, blue eyes shining. "For the presentation. For your faith in my work. For loving me."

Her pronouncement stunned him. How did she...? Hell, he wasn't sure what to think. He slid off the stage and stood in front of her. "You know that? I was about to tell you and you've preempted my speech. But you trust that I do love you, right? I have since the first time I saw you. I can't explain it, but I do." He gathered her into his arms and held her close, something he'd feared he might never get to do again.

She tucked closer against his chest. "It would have helped if you'd told me sooner."

"My ex-wife said something a lot like that," he muttered under his breath.

She angled back to look up at him. "You talked to your ex about me?" She waved and shook her head. "Never mind. That doesn't matter. Why didn't you listen to her?"

"I guess I'm thickheaded."

"But not unteachable. The McNairs are strong-willed people, too. We can be difficult, but we are so worth the effort." Her smile was brighter than diamonds.

He cupped her waist and lifted her to sit on one of the saddles that had been used to display studded reins.

"Amie, I want you to marry me. This is about you. Nothing and no one else. You've turned my life upside down from the moment we met. I haven't been able to stop thinking about you, and yes, wanting you. But for so many more reasons than the fact that you're hot as hell. You're smart and strong. You're loyal and loving. I need that—I need you—in my life. Please make me the happiest man alive and say we can spend the rest of our lives together."

She tugged him close until they were face-to-face, close enough to kiss. "I want nothing more than to marry you. I've fallen crazy, impulsively, in love with you. No matter how hard I've tried to fight it, I can't help myself."

He listened to her, hardly daring to believe how fortunate he'd been to find her. To win her.

"I can't help myself, either." He traced the line of her jaw. The soft fullness of her lips. "I've built a reputation on being the most controlled person in the room, the CEO with the cool head, and yet you took one look at me and undid all that without saying a word."

Angling his lips over hers, he brushed a kiss along her mouth. A tender, forever kind of kiss.

He gathered her in his arms, trailing hands across her silky bare shoulders. Through the soft fall of dark hair that blanketed one arm. He breathed her in, her scent imprinted on his brain the way the feel of her had imprinted itself on his body.

Deepening the kiss, he stroked along her lower lip, demanding entrance she was only too willing to give, her whole body sighing into his as the tension left muscles at last. He kissed and kissed her, not caring about anything else but this moment with her. They might have forever, but he wanted to savor every moment with her, not taking any of this for granted.

He pulled her hips to his, knowing his whole world was in his arms. In her. He was a lucky, lucky man.

Ending the kiss with a final nip on her bottom lip. "Mind telling me why you fought something this amazing?"

"You know why," she said, her blue eyes swimming with emotion. "The fear of losing love is scary."

Of course. The answer was so simple and so complex at the same time. He'd fought against those same fears. "I can't promise a perfect, trouble-free future.

But I can promise you'll never have to doubt me or my love for you."

"You're a man of your word."

"That I am. And I look forward to proving that every day."

Epilogue

Nine months later

Amie smiled with pride as her husband thanked the family for attending the outdoor baptism held at their private new spread on the Hidden Gem Ranch property. Their home—having built a house of their own on five acres, away from the resort activity.

Preston stood with her in the landscaped gardens full of multicolored flowers, their own private jewel box of petals. He spoke to their guests as they stood together under a bower of roses holding their twins. "Amie and I can't thank you enough for joining us in celebrating the joy of our two precious—vocal—bundles of joy, Mariah Armstrong and McNair Armstrong."

He paused for the laughter before continuing the speech he'd spent more time preparing for than any boardroom presentation. He was excited—and so proud. She'd never known she could be so exhausted and happy all at once. She took her squawking son from Preston, while her husband held their daughter and kept speaking to their families—hers and his. His parents were regulars now, flying up for visits.

Amie inhaled the sweet scent of baby shampoo, McNair's unbelievably soft cheek pressed to hers. Perfection.

She should have considered she might be pregnant with twins, given she was a twin herself, but she'd still been stunned when the doctor picked up two heartbeats and then the ultrasound showed two babies. Her pregnancy had been blessedly uneventful. She'd even made it to thirty-eight weeks pregnant, giving birth to a seven-pound daughter and six-pound son.

Alex had joked she'd always been an over-the-top kind of person. Preston had just smiled, declaring her and the babies perfect.

As much as she'd missed her grandmother that day, she could feel her spirit smiling down in happiness. She felt that feeling even now, all around them, celebrating the family. With the sun shining on their happy haven, their family and closest friends beside them to help them celebrate, Amie had never felt more blessed. Family truly was everything.

She smiled up at Preston as he talked about the joys of second chances, expressing his gratitude for being a part of their family. She snuggled McNair closer, her heart overflowing with love for her babies. Their babies.

Johanna and Stone had adopted a toddler daughter six months ago and since seeing the babies, their little girl was already asking for a sibling. Alex and Nina had married last month, and Cody was already calling her Aunt Amie. He was a McNair in all the ways that counted. He had taken his job of watching over Roscoe the cat very seriously today, and Amie was pretty sure Roscoe the cat took his job watching over Cody darn seriously, too.

The cat twined around the boy's feet where they played together in the rock garden between the lilies of the valley and the gardenias.

And what a treat to have their house complete in time for the baptism. The three-story stucco home had airy porches and large rooms with plenty of space for the children to play while she and Preston watched in awe. She couldn't imagine the awe would ever go away.

She worked on designs from home three days a week, and Preston had installed an office for himself in their house to spend more time with his family. They were making it work, being with their children and keeping the McNair legacy alive. She wasn't sure she was ready to call herself a matriarch any time too soon, the way Gran had mentioned, but then again, it felt right to host all of her and his family here, under her roof. She had large shoes to fill, but she would enjoy trying.

Her parents might not have given her the upbringing she'd hoped for, but they seemed to be embracing the grandparent role with Alex's stepson and now with little Mariah and McNair. They'd come today and so far had been pleasant—maybe they'd all learned the importance of family and acceptance after losing Gran.

Preston wrapped up his speech and waved for everyone to help themselves to the brunch buffet by the pool. The beautiful chaos commenced. Preston kissed her cheek before stepping away to speak with his parents.

Alex stepped beside her, sliding a brotherly arm around her shoulder. "Gran would love all these kids playing on the lawn."

Amie could swear she smelled her grandmother's gardenia cologne on the breeze. "A familiar sight, that's for sure."

Their cousin Stone joined them, the three as close as siblings, having grown up under Mariah's care. "Our parents all seem to be better at grandparenting than taking care of their own children. I can live with that."

"True," Amie agreed. "Gran would be happy about that, too."

Stone nodded to her husband. "Preston's working out well on a lot of levels." High praise from the former CEO of Diamonds in the Rough. "You look happy. And the company's in capable hands."

Alex shook his head wryly. "Funny how that all worked out. Hell, I even like the guy."

Amie grinned up at her brother and cousin. "Love you guys."

They both tugged her ponytail at the same time.

Alex said, "Love you, diva."

Stone said, "Love you, brat."

And the teasing didn't bother her in the least. She heard the affection. They both rejoined their wives as Preston brought Mariah over, one tiny foot peeking out of a pink lightweight blanket.

"Everything okay?" he asked.

"Absolutely perfect." She leaned back against his shoulder and kissed her daughter's foot before tucking it back under the blanket. She felt the studious weight of his gaze and looked up to find his eyes serious. "What?"

"You've made me happier than I ever thought I could be. I hope you know that."

"I do," she promised. And meant it. "That's a very reciprocal feeling. Do we still have a date later tonight after the babies are asleep and the nanny can watch over them?"

"Yes, ma'am, we do." He skimmed a kiss over her lips. "I have a surprise cooked up for you, something to do with a nighttime picnic in the backyard, complete with a private showing of a Wild West film on an outdoor screen. I might have even arranged for someone's favorite pizza in all the world to be specially flown in for the occasion."

Amie laughed, remembering their perfect date in Central Park. "You wouldn't be so extravagant."

"Possibly just this once." He brushed a kiss along her lips. "I'm still in the honeymoon phase of this marriage, Amie. You're going to have to excuse my indulgent side."

Her heart warmed that he took so much time to think about what she liked.

The rest of the party fell away—even with family and babies and a senior cat at their feet.

"I think I can make special accommodations for you," she whispered, gazing up into the hazel eyes that captivated her. Fascinated her. Loved her. "I wonder how long this honeymoon phase lasts."

"I have it on good authority it can last a lifetime if we're careful." He brushed a kiss on her cheek. Her nose.

"Is that so?" Happiness curled her toes as she looked out over their party. Their family. "I wonder who told you such a thing."

"Those words of wisdom came from Mariah Mc-Nair herself. She was one of the two smartest women I've ever met."

Amie's heart squeezed tight. Happy tears threatened. So she laid another kiss on McNair's head and then kissed Preston, too.

Sometimes, no words were needed.

* * * * *

If you loved Amie's romance,
pick up the other books in the
DIAMONDS IN THE ROUGH *series*
from USA TODAY *bestselling author*
Catherine Mann

ONE GOOD COWBOY
PURSUED BY THE RICH RANCHER

With a smile, Kelly picked up the sleepy bundle, holding him close, loving the sensation of her tiny son against her heart.

Henry had Jace's dark lashes, even his dimples. Kelly shook her head, still in disbelief that Jace had moved here. She should have known he would come back to stir up the painful memories it had taken her months to overcome.

Forcing the negative thoughts from her mind, she kissed Henry's little head and went to the kitchen to get some aspirin.

As she reached for the medicine, she heard her brother talking to someone in the next room. Curious, she rounded the corner just in time to see Jace Compton step inside the small living room.

Immediate and total panic set into every fiber of her being.

"You left your purse in the truck." He held the small bag out to her.

She glared. Stepping forward she snatched the purse from his hand then turned toward the bedroom, hoping he'd go out the same way he came in.

"Kelly?"

She stopped. This was so not happening. Jace walked over to where she stood. His gaze was fixed on the baby in her arms.

"Who do we have here?"

LONE STAR
BABY BOMBSHELL

BY
LAUREN CANAN

MILLS
BOON

Published in Great Britain 2015
by Mills & Boon, an imprint of Harlequin (UK) Limited,
Eton House, 18-24 Paradise Road, Richmond, Surrey, TW9 1SR

© 2015 Sarah Cannon

ISBN: 978-0-263-25269-9

51-0715

Lauren Canan, born and raised amid the cattle ranches of Texas, climbed a fence and jumped onto the back of her first horse at age three. She still maintains the punishment was worth the experience. She grew up listening to her dad tell stories of make-believe and was always encouraged to let her imagination soar. The multi-award-winning author and recipient of the 2014 Golden Heart® Award happily spends her days penning her favorite kind of stories: those of two people who, against all odds, meet, fall in love and live happily ever after—which is the way it should be. In her spare time she enjoys playing guitar, piano and dulcimer in acoustic club jams and getting lots of kisses and wags from her four-legged fuzzy babies. Visit Lauren's website at www.laurencanan.com. She would love to hear from you!

Special thanks to two brilliant authors who kindly
gave their time and expertise. Kathleen Gregory,
I could not have done this without you.
Angi Morgan, you are my forever hero!
Thank you for all you do.

To Jill Marsal of the Marsal-Lyon Literary Agency.
You made all the difference.
Thank you for believing in me.

To my editor, Charles Griemsman,
for your endless patience and encouragement.
You are the best.

To Laurel Hamrick for being there
when I needed to whine!

And to Terry, my real-life hero, who taught me the
true meaning of love and happily-ever-afters.

One

Kelly Michaels slowed the car as she neared the twelve-foot-high black wrought-iron gates banked by native stone walls on either side. A bronze plaque on the left welcomed her to the C Bar Ranch. She stretched to reach the keypad and entered the code Don Honeycutt, the Realtor, had provided.

With a resounding *click*, the gates swung open, separating the giant *C* set in the center. She followed the long winding drive flanked by centuries-old oak trees towering over lush green pastures. She pulled around to the staff entrance. The home was enormous. It was more mansion than typical ranch house. But new construction was generally a breeze to clean. Gathering the implements out of the trunk, she went inside.

Her instructions were to clean two bedrooms and adjoining baths upstairs plus the den, office, foyer and kitchen downstairs. She should be able to wrap this up in time to get ready for the annual music festival and dance that evening. The generous pay she earned occasionally cleaning new homes for the local Realtor was more than worth the effort. It had once been her only income, but even after she landed a job consistent with her field of study, she'd held on to this one and the financial bonus it offered.

She started on the second-floor master suite, working her way downstairs. Some furniture had been delivered. New bedding and pillows lay on the mattresses. Kelly quickly and efficiently put everything in order. An interior designer would probably complete the rooms in accordance with the new owner's preferences.

She loved the smell and freshness of a new home. Holidays in this house would be amazing. A turkey roasting in the oven while pumpkin and coconut pies cooled on the dark granite counters. The aroma of spices and home-baked bread filling the air. She could imagine laughter and teasing banter filling the great space while children played hide-and-seek around a huge tree. She envied the family who would live here. At least, she hoped it was a family. The gossip around town said the old ranch had been purchased by an out-of-state corporation for employee retreats. It would be a shame if no one actually lived in this beautiful home.

A couple hours later, while rinsing the last of the soap from the kitchen sink, she heard the door in the utility room open and close. Must be Don checking on her progress. She smiled, knowing she'd completed the house, just as requested.

"Kelly?"

The breath caught in her throat and all outward motion stopped. The voice did not belong to Don Honeycutt. Her heart slammed against the walls of her chest as denial overwhelmed her mind. *It couldn't be.* Bracing herself against the counter, she turned and stared incredulously at the man standing less than four feet away.

"Jace." His name came out a whisper, a testament to the pure shock pummeling her from every direction. She blinked her eyes, willing her mind to convey it was only an illusion.

But the illusion was very real.

In the year since she'd seen him, he'd changed very little. His rugged good looks hadn't diminished. If anything, he appeared even more handsome than before, something she wouldn't have thought possible. The deep line of his jaw was smooth now, missing the bearded shadow he'd had before. His dark hair was cut several inches shorter. The tiny scar was still visible, the only imperfection of full lips that could widen into a devilish grin showing perfect white teeth, a smile irresistible to most everyone, male or female, young or old.

Kelly swallowed hard. She knew the touch of those lips. A man in his prime, he took extraordinary care to stay in top physical condition. It was, after all, part of his job. Part of who he was. She hadn't known it before, but she certainly knew it now.

"What are you doing here?" His deep, graveled voice mirrored her surprise, sending goose bumps over her skin.

With a wet sponge in one hand and a can of powdered cleanser in the other, she thought the answer should be obvious.

"I might ask you the same question." But she feared she already knew the answer. The giant *C* on the front gate apparently stood for Compton. Suddenly the huge mansion took on the dimensions of a shoe box as the walls came crashing in. "You bought this ranch?" She needed to hear him confirm her worst fears.

"Yeah. I did."

Her heart dropped to her knees. "I...I've just finished. I'll get out of your way."

She grabbed the mop, broom and bucket of cleaning paraphernalia and without another glance in his direction, headed for the door, her mind spinning.

"Kelly, wait. You don't have to—"

She ignored him and all but ran through the side door. Why would Jace Compton, a man with the world at his fingertips, move to this tiny Texas town?

The outside lamp over the side porch provided dim light against the growing darkness. She tossed the cleaning supplies inside the car, not caring where they landed. Her hands shook so severely it took three tries to insert the key into the ignition of the twenty-year-old Buick. It responded in kind, quivering equally as badly as her hands while the engine struggled to engage. After she'd made several attempts and repeated silent pleas to *start*, it became clear the old car wasn't going anywhere.

This couldn't be happening.

Her cell phone lay on the seat next to her, but even if it found a signal there was no one to call. By now her friends were at the music festival along with most of the county. It was the single largest event of the year in their small community, and she would not spoil their evening even though it was a long walk home. If only Mrs. Jenkins, her babysitter, could still drive. She had a nagging fear in the pit of her stomach that this downward spiral had not yet reached rock bottom.

Resting her forehead against the steering wheel, she closed her eyes, giving in to the memories flooding her mind, to the sharp pain once again slicing her heart into tiny pieces. The best and the worst wrapped up in one package. And the name on the label was Jace Compton.

When she'd first tried to reach him at the cell number he'd provided, she got at a voice mail message that Jace Compton—not Jack Campbell, the name he'd given her when they met—was out of the country. And the mailbox was full. Who was Jace Compton? A call out to the ranch where he'd claimed he worked provided the answer. The man to whom she'd given her heart, body and soul, the man who'd said she was so special he never wanted to let her go, was not Jack Campbell, the ranch hand. He was Jace Compton, an award-winning actor and multi-millionaire living in California, having some fun at her expense. The ranch foreman had given her another number to try, but it was disconnected.

As the memories of that day surfaced once again, shame rolled over her in a mind-numbing wave just as it had for months after she'd learned the truth. She'd been so stupid. Her initial awareness that he looked familiar had been easily dismissed with a "Yeah. I get that a lot." No doubt he

would have had a pat answer even if she'd asked more point-
edly. He'd set out to seduce her and she'd fallen hard. She'd
wanted to believe him, to trust him, so any suspicions that
he might not be who he claimed were ignored.

Weeks after he'd left, when she finally learned his true
identity, it seemed as if his picture was everywhere. Photos
and headlines depicting the wild beach parties, shocking affairs with married women and his playboy lifestyle in general headlined the rag sheets at the grocery store checkout
lines and the celebrity programs on television.

She'd finally managed to track down his manager, who
had been clear and threatening. She meant nothing to Mr.
Compton. They'd had a fling. So what? Jace had lots of
flings. Unless she was prepared for a court battle over cus-
todial rights, which Jace would assuredly win, she should
take the manager's advice and handle the situation herself.
Numbly, Kelly had hung up the phone. She hadn't slept that
night. Or the next. She'd just sat in the little wooden chair in
her bedroom and stared at nothing while her mind bounced
between disbelief and utter devastation.

Nine months later, as she lay in the hospital bed praying for her baby to survive the complications of the birth,
one of the hospital volunteers brought Kelly a magazine to
read. On the front cover, the charismatic, drop-dead gorgeous Jace Compton had again been named Bachelor of the
Year. The handsome face seemed to mock her as the tears
spilled over and ran down her face.

Why had he come back?

After a year she thought she'd finally put it all behind
her. The tears and sleepless nights, the regrets and countless
waves of humiliation as time after time her mind relived
how easily she'd fallen for his deception. Yet at the same
time, despite the lies, the yearning for his touch refused to
go away. The memories of his incredible smile fading to
a look of serious intent; the knowing glint in his eyes seconds before his lips covered hers, taking her fully, deeply,

until she never wanted him to let her go. His powerful arms holding her, his hard body locked to hers, his hot breath and deep voice teasing, whispering sinful things in her ear, tempting her in ways she'd never imagined, always leaving her gloriously satisfied yet wanting more.

Apparently, he hadn't had the same sentiments. If those thoughts ever entered his head, he'd quickly pushed them away. From the minute he'd boarded the plane back to California, she'd become a distant memory. To him it had just been a vacation in the north Texas ranching community with her supplying a few fringe benefits on the side.

Two raps on the car window brought her back to the here and now. Determined to keep her anger at bay, she pushed open the door and Jace took a step back. Standing at a height of well over six feet, he was wearing well-worn jeans that hugged long, muscular legs. His left arm rested on the door frame while his right settled on the roof, effectively trapping her within the boundary of his heavy arms. Getting out of the car brought her within mere inches of the hard wall of his chest. Muscles rippled under the ash-gray T-shirt, the sleeves stretching to accommodate thick biceps.

Kelly didn't want to be this close to him. She didn't want to look into his eyes, but his large stature blocked everything else as if he was purposely giving her no choice. Finally, she looked up, their gazes locked, and for an instant, time stopped. It was still there. In the deep green depths a flicker of the raw passion that once bound them together with such intensity, a passion that slam-dunked any rational thought into nonexistence.

The scent of expensive cologne surrounded her. In spite of the months of heartache, some small part of her still yearned for his touch, which was nothing short of insanity. What she needed was for him to disappear. Again.

"Please step back and let me pass." Her voice, raw with unreleased emotion, held fierce determination. He did as she asked and dropped his arms to his side. "I'll have the car off your property as soon as possible."

Without a backward glance, Kelly took off down the driveway on foot.

"Don't you have a phone? Someone you can call?"

She ignored him and increased her pace.

"You want to use mine?" She heard him mutter a curse.

Her complete focus was to get off this property and away from him as fast as possible. Her mind was still reeling from the fact that he was here. He'd bought land and built a large house, usually an indication of permanency. The thought did nothing to brighten her spirits. Somehow she should have prepared for this even though logic was screaming *how could you have known*? But he had friends in the area. He'd been staying with them when they first met. He'd commented many times that he loved the general region. Why had she never considered the possibility that he would come back? She was an idiot. And now she was going to pay for it.

She didn't hear the truck on the concrete driveway until Jace pulled up next to her.

"Kelly, you can't walk all the way to town. It has to be close to six or seven miles and it's almost dark."

Hearing him so close once again still had the same effect. Her body came to life as irrational hunger for him ran rampant. She clenched her teeth and pulled the evening air deep into her lungs as tears of resentment burned her eyes. She refused to let them fall. He was right about it getting dark. And he'd guessed right about the distance. But she kept walking. She'd be every kind of fool to climb inside that truck.

In spite of her refusal to stop, he continued to roll along next to her.

"Kelly, get in the truck and let me take you home."

"No. Thank you."

The tall gates opened as she reached the end of his property. She went through them and cut to the left onto the white-rock county road. The gravel made it harder to walk, but she refused to slow her pace. The Bar H Ranch was just a couple of miles away. Shea, her husband, Alec, or one of their ranch hands would give her a ride home. In hindsight, she should have called, but her only thought was to get away from Jace. Surely everyone hadn't gone to the festival. But if they had, she would sit on the porch and wait.

Why did Jace have to come back to Calico Springs? It was a small community where everybody knew one another. Eventually someone would tell him about Kelly Michaels and the baby who almost died when he was born four months ago. And Jace would know. He would do the math and figure out the baby was his. Another wave of panic slammed into her. What was she going to do? What *could* she do?

The iron gates clanged shut and she realized he was no longer following her. Apparently, he'd only driven to the end of his driveway and turned back. Good enough. The farther away he stayed the better. Taking a deep breath, she willed her heart to slow its pace.

The consequences of Jace finding out about Henry were beyond comprehension. She had to steel herself against the urge to break into a dead run to more quickly get home to her baby. Regardless of how much money he had and how well he could lie, Jace was not getting custody, no matter what she had to do or where she had to go.

The sun had set, darkening the sky to deep purple. Shadows of the trees and tall grass along the road faded into the overall darkness of the landscape. She wished for a flashlight. Even though the road was still easy to distinguish from the surroundings, the creatures that might slither out to soak up the last of the afternoon warmth were not.

The thought brought her to a heightened sense of awareness. A wrong step might land her in a world of trouble and there was no one in shouting distance if she needed help. If anything happened to her, who would care for Henry?

Right now, her baby should be enjoying his bath before going to sleep thanks to the wonderful woman who kept him while Kelly worked. Because of the festival, no one expected her home early. She swallowed back the touch of alarm. *Think positive.* Once she reached the Bar H Ranch she'd be home free.

As if to dispute that optimistic thought, lightning flashed across the sky followed by deep, rolling thunder. Kelly groaned, not daring to think this night could get any worse.

Jace Compton took in a deep breath of frustration, his jaw muscles working overtime. He couldn't believe Kelly had been in his house. Cleaning it, no less. How bizarre was that? He'd hoped he could find her if he moved to Calico Springs. But he never considered she'd be in the house, and he wasn't prepared for the immediate anger and the glaring gaze shooting beams of blue-green fire in his direction.

Apparently, she'd found out he'd lied about his identity when he was here before. He hoped she would give him a chance to explain. He'd had twenty-five precious days on a neighboring ranch to kick back, relax and be himself, just a guy who'd grown up on the south side of Chicago. The last thing he wanted was someone to discover his identity. Over the years he'd become proficient at staying well under the radar. He'd had no idea when they first met that their relationship would develop into something so much more.

Kelly had accepted that he was a cowhand from a nearby ranch, and there had never been a right time to tell her differently. In hindsight he hadn't wanted to take a chance on putting a wedge between them and that special something they'd found in each other. It was a timeless journey where they were the only two people in the world. It was perfect. When she returned his kisses, he'd known she was kissing *him*, the regular guy, not the wealthy celebrity. It was a damn good feeling. When the time came to leave, he wrestled with his conscience, wanting to tell Kelly the truth. Finally he decided to wait until he returned to Calico Springs. He hadn't expected the four-month interim period he'd planned to expand to over a year.

On the outside, the Kelly he remembered had changed, and those changes immediately had his libido sitting up and taking notice. The curves of her body were decidedly more feminine, more mature, more alluring than those of the model-thin young woman he remembered. She exuded health and considerably more sex appeal than he recalled, making him wonder how he'd ever torn himself away. The long blond locks that used to flow free and silky around the delicate features of her face were pulled to the back of her head in a ponytail, giving her face a different, intensely alluring quality, accenting the almond shape of her eyes. Jace had never seen eyes that color. They were the same brilliance and shade as the turquoise waters of the Mediterranean. Only tonight, instead of containing a welcoming sparkle, they'd reflected more than a small trace of annoyance when she stared at him as if the devil himself had come to life.

While he'd anticipated she would be a bit perturbed if she learned he'd lied about his identity, he didn't expect the high level of animosity she'd shown today. Was she angry because he'd lied or was it because she'd missed an opportunity to gain some of the wealth? Thinking of Kelly in that light didn't sit well. At all.

Some people thought they'd found the proverbial pot of gold when they caught his attention, a fact that galled Jace to his core. People always wanted something, whether it was money or five minutes worth of fame. Making action films was his job. Not who he was. He hated the phony facade he had to maintain, and the ridiculously implausible stories he had to validate all for the sake of keeping his name in the media, all to keep the publicity going. Finding someone who liked him for himself was a rarity. He hoped Kelly would understand. He really hoped she would.

When he'd returned to California, he'd talked nonstop about the young woman he met in Texas. He'd even mentioned buying a place to be close to her until she finished her degree. Two days later, his manager, Bret, handed him a PI report indicating Kelly was a con artist with a rap sheet a mile long, citing numerous jailed offenses. Jace hadn't wanted to believe it then and still had a hard time believing it now.

By the time six months had passed, with the filming of his latest movie hitting one roadblock after another, it no longer mattered if she had a record or not. He probably would never see her again. He'd felt more than a small twinge of loss at the thought. He'd managed to push their time together to the back of his mind until Garret Walker, the friend who had invited him to Texas, called asking if he was still interested in buying some land in the area. Suddenly in his mind's eye, all he saw was Kelly. The memories of holding her in his arms and the pure enjoyment he'd found being with her far outweighed any past crimes she may have committed. He kept Bret's warning in mind. He'd be a fool not to. But Kelly Michaels just didn't fit the mold of a crook. Perhaps she'd had a rough life? They'd never spoken in detail about her past, so all he could do was speculate. But after the way she'd almost run from his house today, it probably didn't matter one way or the other. Apparently she'd made her decision that their relationship would not continue. While he couldn't justify it in his mind, he once again felt a deep loss.

He rubbed the back of his neck. Kelly was out there in the dark, determined to walk all the way to town. He'd returned to the house to give her a chance to calm down and allow him time to get a grip. The instant he'd recognized her, his body had surged to readiness while a vapor of heat surrounded him. It was the same reaction he'd felt the very first time he'd ever seen her in the local feed store when he'd gone with Garret to place an order. The immediate attraction had overwhelmed him then, and today was no different. It was like a giant magnet pulling them together regardless of the circumstances. And when she'd stepped out of her car and her incredible scent of spring rain and nutmeg reached him, he hadn't wanted to move away, his body immediately swelling with need.

But with Kelly, it went beyond physical beauty and sex appeal, although she had plenty of that to turn any man's head. It was the look in her eyes that made him believe he could accomplish anything. Hell, when he'd held her in his arms he could fly. Her soft Southern drawl and impish nature had him bouncing off the walls and loving every second. Had it all been an act? He still didn't know the answer and probably—sadly—never would.

Raindrops began to splatter against the windowpane. He turned toward the door, intent on giving her a ride into town. His glance fell on the thin strap of a pale pink purse hanging over the back of a kitchen chair. As he lifted it from the chair back, the sound of thunder rolled over the house, followed by flashes of lightning.

With purse in hand, he headed back to the truck, ignoring the first heavy raindrops. Whether she was angry with him or not, he wasn't about to leave her outside in the dark and the quickly approaching storm. He'd make sure she got home safely, this time accepting no excuses.

Whether she liked it or not.

Two

Isn't this gonna be a basket full of fun?

Kelly eyed the sky as the thunder rumbled overhead. She didn't dare tempt fate by asking what else might go wrong. Picking up the pace, she topped the next hill just as a bolt of lightning struck a tree straight ahead. Seconds later, the sky opened up and a downpour provided the answer to her unspoken question.

Crossing her arms over her chest, she gritted her teeth and kept walking. The warm temperatures of the afternoon took a nosedive as the chilling rain continued to hammer away, stinging her face, making it hard to see. The strong wind gusts made each step forward a challenge to her determination.

Suddenly the glare of headlights from behind illuminated the road and the white blanket of rain ahead of her. She moved to the right, hoping it wasn't a bunch of liquored-up high school kids out for an evening of fun and harassment. She got her wish, but not in a way she'd wanted.

"Kelly," Jace's voice barked through the darkness as he pulled up beside her. "Get in the truck."

She continued walking.

"You're being a complete idiot," he insisted.

"You're entitled to your opinion." She had to yell to be heard over the downpour.

"You have ten seconds to get your ass inside this truck."

"Or what?"

"Or I'm going to pick you up and put you in here myself."

She turned to face him, her eyes narrowing in a glare.

"Get. In. Now." The darkness concealed his expression, but his angry tone came across loud and clear. She had little doubt he'd do exactly what he threatened.

Just do it and get home to Henry.

She looked from Jace to the dark, seemingly endless road ahead. A blustery gust of rain-filled wind assisted the return of her sanity. Biting her tongue, she walked to the truck and opened the passenger door.

"I'm wet," she unnecessarily disclosed, taking in the truck's beautiful interior.

He muttered a curse. "Everything is wet. I don't care. Get in the damn truck." His demand was accented by a loud crack of lightning directly overhead. She grabbed the hold-bar above the opening and pulled herself up and inside, closing the door behind her. Jace immediately raised the passenger window.

In the warmth of the cab, her teeth began to chatter as uncontrolled shivers assailed her body. Jace quickly adjusted the heat. The new-car smell and the earthy scent of his cologne swirled in the warm air around her. She leaned back against the rich leather and buckled her seat belt. Without another word, Jace hit the gas, sending the truck speeding toward town.

Town. Home. Kelly didn't want him to know where she lived. It took away the small sense of protection, even if it was only an illusion. In Calico Springs, population six thousand, it wasn't hard to find anybody.

"Just take me to the ranch up ahead. The entrance is on the left. I know the owners. They'll drive me the rest of the way home."

No response.

As the big truck ate up the miles, she anxiously searched to the left of the headlights for the big gate to the Bar H Ranch. Finally, the reflection of the stone pillars shone just ahead.

"There," she pointed. "Just pull in…"

The truck didn't slow as it approached, then passed, the driveway.

"You missed it." She looked behind them. "Turn around."

Jace glanced at her, then returned his focus to the road. "No reason to force anyone else out in this weather."

"*Force* anyone else? Like I forced you to be out here?" she challenged, still resenting the fact that he'd coerced her inside the truck to begin with. Never mind that she was grateful to be out of the storm.

"That's not the way I meant it. Of course you didn't." He glanced over as she sat back in the seat, her arms crossed over her chest. "And you didn't leave your handbag in my kitchen on purpose." He held up the small rectangular purse. "And you didn't know it was my house you were cleaning or that I would be arriving around six. Kelly, if you want to see me again…just say so."

Kelly's head snapped around, her jaw dropping. "Stop this truck."

Instead of slowing, he asked, "Shall I take that as a no?" as a grin spread over his handsome features.

"Yes."

"Yes?"

"Yes, I mean no."

Jace pursed his lips as though holding back another grin. "Your sense of humor isn't quite as good as I remember."

"No? Try saying something remotely funny."

He made no further comment. Kelly glared at him for another few seconds before she sat back in the seat, expelled an angry breath and accepted her fate. It was surreal. To not see him for so long, then to suddenly be in the close confines of a pickup cab as they barreled into the darkness. She glanced at him from the corner of her eye. His big hands on the wheel, his sharp jawline and those full lips caused an unwelcome need to stir deep in her belly, a need she hadn't felt for over a year.

She remembered everything: every touch, every erotic whisper, the teasing humor and the arguments over nothing that always ended with his lips on hers. Swallowing hard, Kelly inhaled deeply and turned away, fighting to clear her mind, hoping he couldn't detect her body's traitorous response.

"So," she said, clearing her throat, looking straight ahead, "I can't imagine this tiny spot on the map holding any interest for you. Big celebrity. Small town. Why are you here?"

For a few minutes, she thought he wasn't going to answer her question.

"I needed some downtime," he finally said. "I have a friend who lives in the area, as you know, and this seemed to be as good a place as any."

"You buy an entire ranch to take a break?"

He shrugged.

"And you call me an idiot."

Obviously, he didn't care to share his true intentions with her, which suited her just fine. She should be used to his lies and secrets by now.

"What about you?" he asked.

"What about me?"

"Still in school?"

"No."

So much had happened over the past year his question seemed strange. Her life had changed so radically it felt as though she was answering for someone else. The massive heart attack that had taken her grandfather had been sudden and devastating. Then the bank foreclosed on his farm, leaving Kelly and her younger brother to scramble for another place to live. And just when she thought things couldn't possibly get any worse, she'd discovered she was pregnant by a man who'd hidden his identity, then all but disappeared.

That sobering thought assisted in her return to reality.

"Why did you lie?" It came out a whisper. The question seemed to break free of her mouth, not waiting on her brain to give its permission. "Why did you think it necessary?" He'd wanted someone to share his bed while here visiting friends. She got that. But why lie about who he was? And why promise to call or come back if he'd known all along he wouldn't?

"What does it matter now?"

"The truth always matters."

"I gave you a name. That should have been enough. If you'd known my true identity it would have made a difference in our relationship."

She stared at him in amazement. "Is it tough carrying around all that arrogance?" She shook her head.

"It's not arrogance," he shot back. "If you'd realized who I was you would have—" He inhaled deeply and blew it out.

"What? I would have what? Not thought of you as Jekyll and Hyde? Not known you would rather climb a tree and tell a lie than stand on the ground and tell the truth? Not felt like I was being played? All of the above?"

"You would have treated me differently." Almost under his breath, he muttered, "They all do. And you were not being played. Ever."

"*They all do?* Who is *they*?"

She saw his hand grip the steering wheel in a tight fist. "What I do for a living had nothing to do with us." He glanced at her through the dim glow on the dash lights. "People hear my name and suddenly they can't see *me*. I should have told you the truth, but I wanted you to know *me*, Kelly. I'm just a man. And I enjoy being seen as one instead of all the damned hype. I intended to explain when I got back here. I intended to tell you the truth."

"Really. Why? If, as you say, a name doesn't matter, why bother?"

She heard him expel a deep sigh. "You're purposely twisting this around."

"I am?"

She heard his huff of frustration.

"We were two people who met and enjoyed being together. At least I enjoyed being with you. Why did it need to be more complicated than that? Or am I missing something?"

Her eyes shot toward him. Had he really said that with a straight face? She couldn't hold back a snort. "You do realize you're trying to justify your deception?" The man wouldn't recognize truth if it smacked him in the face. "Unbelievable." She'd gotten her answer. She should have saved herself the trouble of asking. "At least I provided you and your friends with a good laugh."

Heat rolled up her neck at the thought of his wealthy friends laughing about his affair with a stupid country bumpkin. How easily she'd bought into his deception.

"I never laughed." His tone indicated surprise she would think that. He glanced at her, the hard masculine mouth pulled to a taut line, his eyebrows drown into a frown. "Our relationship wasn't a joke. At least not to me. And I had every intention of coming back and talking to you. I'd hoped you would understand."

"I'm sure you did." The anger rolled off her tongue. "But things happen, right?"

"Yeah. I guess they do. For instance, you never told me which correctional center you were in. Apparently I'm not the only one who can be accused of keeping secrets."

Her head snapped around toward him. *What did he just say?* For several seconds she couldn't speak. Had she heard him correctly? "*What?*"

"I said I—"

She raised her hand, palm side toward him. "Does someone write this stuff for you or do you make it up all by yourself?" He expected her to buy the excuse he hadn't come back because he thought she was in *jail*? She shook her head in amazement. "You really need to seek help."

The man she remembered had clearly changed. She

couldn't help but ask herself which one was the real Jace Compton. "Turn left at the light."

"Left?"

"We live in town now." Jace was remembering her grandfather's small farm.

"Kelly, are you saying you don't have a criminal record?"

"Duhhh. Are you saying you honestly thought I *did*?"

"But—"

"You know what, Jack… Jace—whatever your name is today—just don't say anything else." She'd heard more than enough. "Obviously, you're incapable of being honest. I don't care anymore, all right? I don't care why you lied. I don't care why you never came back. I don't give a rat's behind who you are and I don't want to sit here and listen to your wild excuses. I'm sorry I even brought it up."

Jace didn't speak again, but Kelly felt the anger crackling in the air between them.

The route took them south, toward the low-rent side of town where the small forty-year-old houses marred the landscape and even a fresh coat of paint did little to hide the weathered conditions along the rutted streets. Inside the houses lived people like herself, who worked too hard for too little. But she refused to be embarrassed. The house was old and small, but it was clean. It had a new roof and the amount she paid for rent couldn't be beat. "Third street to the right and down a block. On the right. It's the white house with green shutters."

With her hand on the door handle, Kelly made ready her escape. But by the time they pulled up to the curb and she remembered to unfasten the seat belt, Jace held the door for her, seemingly oblivious to the rain.

Her younger brother stood on the front porch leaning on one of the support posts. The glow of the outside light fanned out over the small front yard.

Jace nodded toward the teen. "How ya doing?"

Kelly watched Matt's body language shift as he recognized Jace. It was clear he was having a hard time believing it. He stared at the big man standing next to the truck.

"You're… Are you? You're Jace Compton!" Matt's eyes were as big as dessert plates as his mouth dropped open in sheer astonishment.

"Matt, go inside," Kelly ordered.

"You want to come in?" Her younger brother totally ignored her request. Anger tinged with fear coursed through her, quickening her steps to the house. This was so not happening. What if Matt had picked up Henry from the sitter?

"No," she stated firmly, and turned back to Jace. "I don't think that's a good idea. Thanks for the ride. It was very… enlightening."

Jace made no reply, just stared at her through the soft glow from the porch light. Kelly hurried to the house. "Matt, get inside." When he didn't move, she snapped, "Now."

"But Kelly—" he looked as though she'd just told him to rob a bank "—do you know who that is?"

The question was almost laughable. Almost.

"Have a good night," Jace called from the curb.

Kelly grabbed Matt by the arm and pulled him inside. At fifteen, her brother already stood a couple of inches taller than her own five foot seven and pulling him anywhere was a challenge. This time, with the adrenaline flowing, she managed. She closed the front door and prepared for the onslaught. She didn't have to wait long.

"I can't believe you." Matt glared in her direction. "*The* Jace Compton at our house and you wouldn't let him come inside. What is your deal? Are you like…crazy?"

"Matt…" There was no way to explain.

"Forget all the movies. He still holds the record for completed passes in the entire NFL. The *record*, Kelly. The guy is a football legend."

Matt lived and breathed football, so she understood what he was saying. But her brother didn't know Jace Compton. Unfortunately, she did.

"Come to think of it—" Matt frowned "—what were you doing in his truck? How did you—?"

"He bought the old Miller spread and had a new house built so Don asked me to clean it. When I finished, the car wouldn't start."

"Jace Compton is living here? In Calico Springs? Like *permanently*?" With each question, Matt's voice rose in excitement. His eyes were wide with elation. He hadn't even taken note of the fact that they had no transportation.

"I really don't know." Kelly didn't want to discuss it. Jace had chosen to keep his reasons for being here to himself, so there was really nothing to tell Matt. She just wanted the man to stay as far away from her small family as possible. "I'm gonna walk down to Mrs. Jenkins's and pick up Henry."

"He's here." Matt was clearly still annoyed, his tone full of frustration. "Mrs. J fed him and got him ready for bed. Football practice was canceled because of the rain so I brought him home."

"Thanks, Matt." She smiled and walked toward the small bedroom she shared with her son. Bless the elderly woman down the street who kept Henry while Kelly worked and who refused to accept one penny for her efforts.

The baby slept in his favorite position, on his tummy, his little butt in the air. Kelly pulled off her wet T-shirt and jeans and grabbed her old robe from the closet. Then, unable to resist, she approached the crib and softly caressed the little head. Sensing his mother's touch, Henry stirred. With a smile, Kelly picked up the sleepy bundle, holding him close, loving the sensation of her tiny son against her heart.

Henry had Jace's dark lashes, even his dimples. Kelly shook her head, still in disbelief that he'd moved here. She should have known Jace would come back to stir up the painful memories it had taken months to overcome. He was no different from her father. Love 'em and leave 'em and not give a damn who he hurt in the process. Move on to the next conquest and never look back. Only this time, the man in question had looked back.

Because of her father's lies and cheating, her mom had taken her own life. That was when dear ole dad had disappeared for good. Kelly had made a pledge then and there that she'd never let a man get close to her. And she'd kept up her resolve. Until Jace. She shook her head at the irony. The one man she'd made the mistake of trusting made her father look like a guppy compared to a twenty-foot shark. And look where it had gotten her.

Forcing the negative thoughts from her mind, she kissed Henry's little head and walked toward the kitchen and the aspirin bottle. Her own head was pounding. After the last hour, she might take two. The very idea that Jace actually believed she'd been in jail was…laughable.

But she wasn't laughing. The man apparently believed his own hype. He really did live in a world of make-believe.

She reached for the aspirin bottle and heard Matt talking to someone in the next room. Curious, she rounded the corner just in time to see Jace Compton step inside the small living room.

Immediate and total panic set into every fiber of her being.

"You, ah, left your purse in the truck." He held the small bag out to her, his eyes glinting wickedly. "Practice makes perfect?"

She glared. She stepped forward and snatched the purse from his hand, and then turned toward the bedroom, hoping he'd go out the same way he came in.

"Kelly?"

She stopped. This was so not happening. Jace walked over to where she stood. His gaze focused on the baby in her arms before those green eyes pinned her to the spot.

"Who do we have here?"

Three

It was here. The moment she'd dreaded since the day Henry was born. She looked down at the baby in her arms, hoping Jace wouldn't see the panic that engulfed her.

"This is Henry," she said and swallowed hard.

"Yours?"

She blinked more than once at his question. Apparently his manager hadn't lied when he'd said he wouldn't tell Jace about the pregnancy. He'd never even told Jace she called.

"Yes," she finally answered. "He's all mine."

Jace looked at her, and then glanced back at the baby. Henry kicked his feet, blowing some of his best baby bubbles for the strange man.

"He's cute," Jace murmured. "How old is he?"

No surprise he would ask. She had to give him an answer. To avoid a reply might only increase his curiosity. "Four months."

She saw the wheels turning in Jace's head as he did the math and knew what conclusion he reached: Henry could be his son. He looked at Kelly again, as though searching for a different answer. His full lips were pulled into a straight line of contemplation.

"I'm Kelly's brother, Matt." Her brother grinned from ear to ear, obviously dying to talk to his hero. Kelly welcomed the interruption.

"Nice to meet you, Matt." That killer grin spread across Jace's face. He held out his hand and Matt shook it. Matt was so excited, it was as if he rose two feet above the ground.

"So Kelly says you're living in Calico Springs now?"

Jace nodded, his eyes shifting toward Kelly for an instant and then back to Matt.

"Yeah. I bought an old ranch north of town. Have a friend who has been in horse racing for thirty years. I always wanted to have land and horses. He talked me into trying my hand at raising some thoroughbreds. There's enough room to bring in some cattle later if I decide to expand."

"Oh man, that's cool." Matt's entire body vibrated in excitement. Matt pointed to a chair. "Can you stay a couple of minutes?"

"Sure."

As they sat down, Matt asked, "Do you still throw a ball?"

"Oh, yeah. Any chance I get." Jace's heart-stopping grin reappeared. "I'd still be a wide receiver if the knee hadn't gotten bent the wrong way. Do you play?"

"Yeah. Well, it's where we all started. What position?"

"Hey, it's where we all started. What position?"

As the football banter between the two continued, Kelly eased out of the room. She put Henry down in the crib, and then collapsed onto the small wooden chair by the door. When would this day finally end? Jace Compton, the lying, two-faced multimillionaire, was sitting in her living room talking with her brother, probably speculating if he'd just been two feet away from his own son. And from the sound of their animated conversation, the two guys shared a common interest. This was going to get worse before it got better.

She wouldn't think it odd of the Jace she'd met last year. A regular guy. One who fit into the world she knew: a guy who loved cheeseburgers, hot rods and practical jokes. He'd been a decent, down-to-earth guy who'd talked of everyday things. No arrogance. No haughtiness. But it seemed unbelievable the suave wealthy superstar who traveled the globe would sit in an old house and enjoy conversing with a fifteen-year-old kid. It was as though Jace was two different people. In spite of everything, deep inside she still wanted to paint him as a good guy. But she knew he was anything but.

Breathe deep. She'd told no one the identity of Henry's father, not even Matt. Infants didn't resemble either parent enough for someone to see a resemblance. Did they? Most babies had dimples. Maybe she'd get through this.

To her brother, Jace was a true hero, a superstar both in his action films and on the football field. The chance to talk to *the great Jace Compton* one-on-one was beyond exciting. She got that. But she would exercise caution. Usually a fair judge of character, apparently she'd misjudged Jace once. She wouldn't make the same mistake again.

The two voices filled the small space as Kelly grabbed dry clothes and headed for a hot shower. When she emerged some twenty minutes later, all was quiet. She saw the glow under her brother's door and heard the faint sound of music coming from inside. She pulled the air deep into her lungs and blew it out as relief loosened the muscles of her neck and shoulders. Like a major storm that dropped down from the sky without warning, Jace had again breezed in and out, this time leaving no damage behind. But more storms would come. Jace wouldn't let this go. She knew in her gut he hadn't been convinced. He would think about it. Remember their time together. And he would be back.

As Jace drove through the small town square headed north toward the ranch, he couldn't get Kelly and her baby out of his mind. His heart had dropped to his knees when he first saw the infant in her arms. The last thing he'd expected was for Kelly to have a child. Then the idea had hit him hard. *Was he the father?* He'd always been so careful. He didn't want to have any kids. He knew all too well what the title of dad meant in his family.

To this day, he could still vividly remember the smell of

burned grease and scorched onions that had filled every corner of the shoddy apartment above the fast-food joint where he and his parents lived when he was around ten or eleven. It was during that time that something had happened. Something had changed. He never knew what. His mother had refused to discuss any of it. But his father had begun drinking and the arguments between them had grown worse. Louder. More intense. Then the abuse had started, his dad taking his fist to the first one he saw when he walked through the door. To try to protect his mom, Jace had endured a lot of it. His mother had been the strong one, taking her son away from the horrific situation. A couple of times after the divorce, his father had found them and it got bad before the cops arrived. Even after all these years, Jace still hadn't completely let go of his hatred of the man. And he would always admire his mom's strength of will.

Finally, in the predawn hours of a Sunday morning, two police officers had stood outside their door. They'd explained that her ex, George Compton, had been killed in an alley behind a bar. Jace's only thought had been that some stranger got to the bastard before he could.

Jace could still feel the sinking sensation he'd experienced when reality hit that night. In that moment, with those two cops standing at the door, he'd had an epiphany. He was George Compton's son.

He'd never put it into perspective before. His primary focus had always been survival. He and his father shared the same face and deep jaw. They had the same green eyes. Same color hair. If they were so much alike on the outside, it had to be true for the inside. When Jace had realized that, the earth seemed to tilt and spin.

Before he turned sixteen, he'd been in and out of juvie a half dozen times for altercations with guys in the neighborhood and at school who had somehow found out about his dad and wanted to see if the son was as worthless. He'd had so many suspensions he never did figure out how they'd let him stay in school. His junior year, he'd tried out for football on a dare. He put himself up against classmates who had been active in the sport since fifth grade and wanted to see Jace Compton go down. They were merciless on the new kid, which suited Jace just fine. He'd poured out all his aggression on the field. It was his saving grace. And, as it turned out, football was something he was good at. After three games, he'd earned the respect of a lot of his teammates. His grades came up, and just before graduation he was offered a college scholarship. His love of the sport carried him almost four years. Then amazingly he'd been picked up by the pros. No one knew that every tackle he made, he was taking down George Compton. Every catch and subsequent dash for the goalpost was a *screw you* to his old man.

After a freak injury ended his football career, Jace began to work with young athletes. He enjoyed teaching them about his favorite sport anytime he got the chance. But any hope that he'd someday have kids and a family of his own had been stomped into the ground a long time ago, beaten out of him by his father's fists.

Still, the idea of Kelly bearing his son was immediately, unbelievably gratifying. His body surged to readiness. Protective instincts rallied to the surface, taking him to a place he'd never been before.

He took a deep breath, pulling the humid night air into his lungs. If the child was his, why hadn't Kelly called? He knew instinctively she wouldn't have kept something so important from him. It wasn't her way. And surely she would want help with the baby, child support...*something*. Most women would beat a path to their attorney as soon as a pregnancy was confirmed. There had been two women who had actually schemed to make Jace think they were pregnant just to get rings on their fingers or obtain a few million dollars in their bank accounts.

But Kelly wasn't like other women. He would be wise to

keep that in mind. It wasn't only her beauty that drew him to her. She was feisty and independent to a fault. She was intelligent and decisively stubborn. Her convictions and beliefs ran deep, and her sense of right and wrong went to the core.

What phone number had he given her before he left? He couldn't remember. The security he had to maintain made it damn near impossible to reach him by phone unless one knew the phrase or identifying password. It changed every few weeks. Had he provided his private cell number? His gut tightened. If she'd tried to call when she realized she was expecting and couldn't get through his security, she would be…furious. Suddenly all the little pieces fell into place with the force and impact of a nuclear implosion.

Dammit to hell.

He slammed on the brakes, bringing the truck to a screeching stop. Jerking it into reverse, he backed into a side street, turned around and headed back to Kelly's house. No wonder she'd wanted to get away from him and been so angry. Not only had he lied to her, but he'd gotten her pregnant and left the country. Then the first time he saw her in over a year he'd called her a crook.

Jace wanted to punch something other than a punching bag. Bret better be glad he was a thousand miles away. Jace had zero doubt his manager had lied to keep Jace from coming back to her. That he'd ever bought into that crap about Kelly having a criminal record caused a giant ball of rage to churn in his gut. His instincts had told him not to believe Bret at the time. Why the hell hadn't he listened to them? Bret probably saw her as a threat to his future income. If Jace quit the films, his manager's gravy-train run would be over.

But while it was easy enough to blame his manager, ultimately, in this, there was no one to blame but himself.

His mind returned to Kelly. A thousand questions hit him with pinpoint accuracy and he couldn't answer even one of them. Did he have a child? A son? Despite using precautionary measures, it was more than possible. When he'd held Kelly in his arms, the passion was intense beyond anything he'd ever experienced. He'd never wanted to let her go. His desire for her was insatiable. Their nights together had turned into days, and then back into nights. It began as hot sexual need. But by the time he had to leave, that white-hot passion had expanded into the blending of two souls. Even now, just thinking about her, those blue-green eyes crazy with need for him, the scent of her shampoo, the feel of her silky skin and the soft cries as her desire crested at the pinnacle of their lovemaking, had parts of him hard and throbbing. Kelly had a way of making him crazy. Apparently some things didn't change.

Kelly sighed with relief knowing she'd skirted one confrontation, but was equally aware there would be more to come. Jace wouldn't give up and just go away. She knew him that well. He went at everything he did with dogged determination. Whether it was training a filly at the ranch where he'd stayed a year ago or hiding his identity from the world. From her. While it had been a shock to learn his real name and profession, it didn't come as a surprise how easily he'd duped her. Jace Compton was proficient at anything he set out to do. It was small wonder he was highly acclaimed as an actor. And according to Matt, Jace had received the same admiration when he played pro football. It was all or nothing. *Defeat* wasn't a word in his vocabulary.

But she qualified the thought: it was possible he hadn't as yet come up against a mother protecting her child. Whatever rules governed his life would fly out the window. There were no offsides or penalties. No interceptions. No retakes. Kelly might not be a match for him on a football field or a movie set, but Jace would encounter significant resistance if he tried to push into her life with intentions of taking her child. Figuratively, he'd be lucky if he came out with only minor scratches and a limp.

She'd just turned off the kitchen light and was headed to her bedroom when a hard knock on the front door stopped her in her tracks. *Surely not.* Surely Jace wouldn't come back here tonight. But intuition told her he was standing on the porch. Squaring her shoulders, she returned to the front room and opened the door.

"We need to talk."

It was neither a demand nor a question, but somewhere in between. She wasn't about to act as though she didn't know what he wanted to discuss. With a glance back at Matt's closed door, she stepped outside, closing the front door behind her. She absently noticed the rain had stopped. A cooling breeze touched her skin. Somewhere in the distance crickets chirped. But her focus was on the big man who stood in front of her, almost a silhouette in the night.

"Is the baby mine?"

Kelly wanted to be anywhere but here. She had often envisioned this moment, but at the same time kidded herself into believing it would never happen. She drew in a deep breath. She couldn't lie to a man about his own child. Regardless of what he'd done to her, he had the right to know the truth. It was what he might try to do with that truth that had her on the brink of panic.

"Yes."

"Kelly, why didn't you tell me? The cell number I gave you should have worked."

He didn't question whether she was telling the truth, a fact that surprised her. But his voice held frustration mixed with anger. She knew only too well what those feelings felt like.

As many times and in as many ways as she'd tried and failed to reach him, his question sounded ridiculous. Part of her wanted to go back inside the house and close the door behind her, refusing to give him a second more of her time. The other part of her wanted to share the wonder of their beautiful son. The little things that made him laugh.

The way he mouthed what would someday be words. The overall amazement of him.

Did Jace deserve to know such things? Did he even care? She'd wasted months of her life alternately wishing he would come back and hoping he never would. In her mind she'd practiced what she would say if she ever saw him again, all sorts of scenarios with a wide variety of outcomes. Now that the moment was here, she didn't have a clue how to proceed or what to say. She crossed her arms over her chest and faced him.

"I did try to reach you. It was a bit of a challenge since I didn't even know your name."

"Kelly—" He raked his hand through his hair.

"The cell number you gave me kicked over to a voice mail box that was full. You really should learn to delete your old messages. Some new ones might be important."

She'd swear he cringed.

"I was able to contact your friend, Garret. The son of the rancher you stayed with last year? He gave me another number and a password, but apparently he had it wrong or it had been disconnected.

"I did speak with your manager. Bret... Gold-something. Goldberg? Goldman? Is that right? It took me about a week to track him down. Another five weeks to get him on the phone. He didn't think it was such a good idea that I talk with you."

She ignored the obscenities that fell from Jace's mouth.

"I tried a couple more times to reach you through your cell, but after a few months, I gave up. So. Now you know. You have a son. Belated congratulations."

Kelly could hear the sarcasm in her own voice but made no effort to conceal it.

"Kelly... I screwed up, okay?"

She shook her head. "No, you didn't. Screwing up is when you do something accidentally. Not when it's done on purpose. And so, no. In this case, it isn't okay. You lied.

You lied to me from the moment we met. Then you disappeared and never looked back."

How many nights had she lain in bed, consumed with the need to hold him, to touch him, to hear his voice again? At times the want had been almost unbearable, her mind elevating it to the level of death. Had he ever thought of her? Did he even remember any part of their time together?

She could sense his aura now, feel the warmth from his body through the darkness, and that same need ran through her like liquid fire. What was it about this man that made her want to forget the past year? Just forget everything and step into his arms and feel his touch once again? The thought made her angry, and she held on to that emotion. She couldn't be weak. She had to think of Henry and be strong.

"I understand why you're mad. You have every right to be."

"Yes. I do. And before you accuse me of getting pregnant on purpose, I didn't. I had a career plan and had envisioned a vastly different future. I have no way to prove it and I don't intend to try. Now, did you want anything else? Or are we finished?"

"I…I don't know. I've only known I had a son for two minutes."

"Give it about nine months. Maybe it will soak in." She hesitated, looking absently at the worn paint on the porch where they stood. "He…he almost died, you know?" Her voice broke; tears burned her eyes. "When he was born? They thought I would lose him. For six days, it was hour to hour, minute to minute. But he's a tough little guy. He may not have been expected or wanted but… Yeah. He's strong. And he's smart." She quickly swiped the tears from her cheeks. "If he gets his strength from his father, I'm grateful to you for that."

"I want to take care of you. Both of you."

Logic demanded she consider if it was fair to Henry to

deny the financial assistance Jace was more than capable of providing. But they were doing okay. Henry wanted for nothing and she didn't want to open Pandora's Box. She shook her head. "We don't need to be *taken care of.* I want nothing from you. And he doesn't need anything from you. There are no shackles here. Contrary to popular belief, I've never tried to con anyone. Or entrap them. I'm not about to start now. So just…you know, carry on with your life. Throw your wild parties. Make your films. It's a little late for regrets, so don't give us a second thought. We'll be fine."

It took a long time before he could swallow the huge wedge of emotion caught in his throat. Jace couldn't let it end this way. In light of this new overwhelming discovery that he had a son, he instantly thought of his own upbringing and the monster it had made of him. For now it lay dormant inside, but eventually it would awaken. He should distance himself from Kelly and the baby. But his heart throbbed with the idea they had a son. They'd created a child. *He was a father.* That, in itself, was enough to mess up any man's mind. And regardless of how hard he fought to hold on, his common sense went down the tubes.

"I want to be in his life." The words fell from his lips as though he was determined to be heard regardless of the consequences.

"Then what?" She shrugged. "Get your attorneys involved? Let them decide on a visitation schedule that meets with your own agenda? See him when you have time or when you happen to be in the country? Introduce him to all your lady friends vying to be his new mommy? Let him grow up seeing his dad's face on TV or the big screen? I'm sure the other kids will someday envy him for that. Wow." Her sarcasm was obvious. "Maybe have your secretary send an expensive gift on his birthday? That's always a nice touch."

"Dammit, Kelly. I don't know how to answer you. I

haven't had a chance to work anything out." He held her gaze as though it was a lifeline while experiencing a rush of emotions he didn't want to feel and had no clue how to deal with.

"Then let me answer the questions for you. No. No to you seeing him once or twice a year. No to long-distance phone calls and the inevitable excuses when you miss his birthday. Or his first spelling bee. Or his first softball game. No to him being a media spectacle. He deserves more, and I won't step aside and let you do that to him. Somehow I'll stop you if you try."

He ran a hand over his face. *Dammit.* He couldn't deny that a lot of what she said was true. She'd pretty much nailed what would happen if his life continued as it had for the past twelve years. He was more than ready for some normal in his crazy life. He wanted a home, a family. But he didn't know how to change, and if he was honest with himself, he didn't know if he wanted to. The work, the travel, the physical aspects of it, the concentration needed…it was the only thing keeping the monster inside at bay.

It was a damned if you do, damned if you don't situation. He should take the out she was offering, make sure Kelly had plenty of money in her bank account and leave them both alone before he caused them to be thrown into the media spotlight, which she would no doubt view as under the bus. Before he became abusive like his old man. It made Jace every kind of selfish for wanting to keep them in his life. But he did. And how convoluted was that?

Despite her show of bravado, he wanted to pull her into his arms, hold her close and promise he would make everything okay. But he couldn't. He didn't know how to make her believe things would work out when he had doubts about it himself. He knew he had to do *something.* But the answer of how to make this right seemed worlds away.

After all she'd been through Kelly had more internal fortitude than anyone he'd ever known, with the single exception of his mom. But while Kelly's resilience and internal strength were admirable, he couldn't leave things as they were regardless of what she said she wanted or, in fact, didn't want.

"He is my son."

"Yes." She nodded. "He is."

"And you want me to just walk away?"

She looked down, as though giving her answer serious thought. "I'm telling you that you have a choice. His life will not revolve around yours. I won't stand by while you break his heart, then try and pick up the pieces after you again disappear."

"Kelly—"

She raised her hand to silence him.

"That said…" She hesitated as if making up her mind about a difficult decision. "I have plans for tomorrow, but if you want to see him while you're here, come by Monday afternoon. I get home around five thirty. He's still too young to form any attachment or be upset when you leave." She again brushed at a spot just below her eye. He heard a soft sniff. "I'm not doing this to be mean, Jace. You have every right to see your son. He's beautiful. You will be so proud. I…I wish you could be in his life always. Every day. But we both know that isn't realistic. And I have to protect Henry, even if it's from his own father."

"We can work this out, Kelly. I know we can."

Her eyes found his through the darkness. "Maybe," she whispered.

Maybe was better than *no*. Jace would take it for the time being. He understood what she was saying. Between the travel his career required and the fear that he might someday become as abusive as his father, he couldn't argue—even though he wanted to.

"I have to be up early in the morning. It's late."

"Okay. Monday. Five thirty. I'll see you then."

Kelly nodded, stepped inside and closed the door.

* * *

Jace blindly turned and walked to his truck. His emotions were all over the place. Even though he didn't like it at all, he had to give merit to Kelly's need to protect the baby. He wanted to be angry with her, his mind playing out the possibilities of what would have happened if he hadn't come back. Would she have waited until the child was grown to introduce them? Or simply raised the boy to believe he had no father? Either way was unacceptable. Yet on the heels of that thought was the fact that she had tried to reach him. He had no doubt she'd tried. It was a vicious circle and it all came back to him. He'd screwed up. Royally.

He climbed inside the truck, slamming the door quite a bit harder than was needed. All the regrets, all the shouldas and couldas, were tripping through his mind. But the big question was: what was he going to do now? It was so overwhelming he wished he had reason to doubt his paternity. But he knew, without any doubt, the baby was his. Kelly just wasn't a person who would make up something like this. Some would. But not Kelly.

Inasmuch as she intended her life to continue as it had so far, Jace knew it wouldn't happen. Her world was about to change and, from her perspective, not necessarily for the better. Sooner or later the media would find out about the ranch. It was only a matter of time. And eventually there was a very good possibility they would discover Kelly and their son. Especially if she'd listed Jace's name on the birth certificate. It would turn her life into a media circus, one she was not equipped to handle. He'd dealt with overzealous fans many times and knew what they were capable of. It wouldn't be safe for Kelly or the baby, and he could not stand back and let that happen.

He pulled away from the curb and headed for the ranch. *He had a son.* Even knowing all the obstacles in front of them, the idea of having a child was enthralling. The more the fact soaked in, the more incredible it became.

How could he go forward and not include Kelly and the baby in his life? Her vulnerability, her innocence about the world and the people in it who would use her for a stepping-stone to further their career, concerned him. The overwhelming desire to take care of her and the baby fought the knowledge that it could never happen because someday he could hurt them. A surge of intense feelings for her made him ache inside. The war that raged was the most intense pain he'd ever experienced. Broken bones had nothing on the anguish tearing his insides to shreds.

If he cared about Kelly, about his son, he needed to walk away. But where would he find the strength to do so?

Four

"Thanks so much for the ride, Gerri," Kelly told her friend as together they walked through the outside glass doors and down the steps of Great West Insurance. "I really do appreciate it."

"Not a problem, ever. You know that."

Kelly still hadn't found anyone to check out her car. With fall roundup in full swing, all the guys she knew had either signed on as ranch hands for the extra wages or had something else going on. The local garage had offered to send someone out, but wanted one hundred and fifty dollars just to make the trip to Jace's ranch. She'd told the mechanic she'd have to get back with him, biting her tongue to keep from calling him a crook.

The car had been on her mind constantly since she'd left Jace's home two days ago. Knowing it still sat on his property was unsettling; it was a tie to him she didn't want.

But as they turned onto her street, Kelly had to blink twice. Her old car sat in the driveway, and parked next to the curb was Jace's dark metallic-blue pickup.

"Hey, Kelly," Gerri said. "Looks like someone decided to help you out after all."

When Gerri pulled up behind the truck, Kelly saw Matt and Jace tossing a football across the expanse of three front yards.

"Yeah. Maybe. I'll see you tomorrow. Thanks again."

Kelly walked toward Mrs. Jenkins's house, hoping Gerri would drive away. Thankfully, she did, sticking her hand out the open window to wave goodbye as the Toyota continued down the street.

Mrs. Jenkins's home was only two houses down and around the corner. She was lucky to have such a kind and loving woman to keep the baby while she worked. Mrs. Jenkins's family had moved to another state the previous year and she longed for her own children and grandchildren. She'd assured Kelly that keeping Henry was a joy. It filled a void in her life. It was a great solution for all concerned.

Returning to her house with Henry, Kelly had just set the baby bag on the sofa and still had Henry in her arms when she saw Jace walking toward the door. Her heart immediately began doing flip-flops. Even the warmth of the baby snuggled against her couldn't make her relax. What she wouldn't give for Jace to be a regular person with a normal job. Maybe then things would have turned out differently. But why waste her time wishing for something that wasn't even in the realm of possibility? She didn't want to keep Jace from his son. But at the same time, his father's world was not a place the baby should be.

As soon as Jace spotted her standing behind the screen door with the baby in her arms, that infamous smile spread across his face. Kelly pushed open the door and bade him to enter. Gingerly, Jace reached out and touched Henry's hand. The baby laughed and grabbed the offered finger, kicking his feet in excitement.

"Hi, buddy." The acceptance was immediate. Apparently on both sides. "He's amazing."

"Would you like to hold him?"

Jace nodded, his eyes switching from Kelly to the baby, then back to Kelly. A twinge of heat surged through her body. Jace was so masculine, so totally male, every hormone she had was screaming to get closer. It was unsettling. His earthy aroma swirled around her, and she swallowed hard.

"Take a seat," she offered, clearing her throat, then placed the little bundle in his father's arms. Henry looked so tiny, and Jace looked so awkward, so out of place, but she couldn't miss the look of pride in his handsome features. As she silently watched father and son interact for the first time, she couldn't help but ask herself how Jace could look even sexier when he held the baby. His tanned arms and dark features were such a contrast to Henry's pale skin and hair. The sheer sexuality rolled off him in waves. So male. So powerful. So compelling. She ran the fingers of one hand through her hair in an effort to regain control of her wayward thoughts.

"He's just starting to respond to voices and smiles. He can almost roll over from his tummy onto his back. One day soon I'll go in the bedroom and find him trying to pull up and stand. His pediatrician said he is exceptional in both his mental and physical development."

Jace nodded, still staring at the baby as if he were in a trance. Kelly knew the feeling. The first time she'd been allowed to hold her son, she'd been captivated. A miniature of his father, complete with dimples, Henry was going to be a heartbreaker someday.

Just like his dad.

While Jace held his son, speaking softly to him and chuckling at his antics, Kelly eased into the kitchen and took her cell phone from her purse. Bringing up the camera, she returned to the living room and clicked away. This was a memorable moment for all three of them.

"If you'll give me your email address, I'll send them to you."

"Thanks, Kelly," Jace said in a tone that indicated he really did appreciate the gesture.

She returned to the chair and sat down.

"Tell me more about him."

She shrugged. Where to begin? "He's a happy baby. He loves the water and bath time. He has a small yellow plastic duck he will try and grab. His efforts send water splashing in every direction and it makes him laugh, so he splashes some more. My coworkers bought him a little swing. You wind it up and it will stay in motion about half an hour. Henry loves that, too."

"How did you choose his name?"

"Henry was my grandfather's name."

Jace nodded.

"His…his middle name is Jason."

Jace's head shot up and that green gaze held hers. "You named him after me?"

Kelly shrugged. "It seemed like the right thing to do." The warmth of a blush touched her cheeks as the glint of surprise and obvious happiness showed in his eyes. "I've started reading to him. Of course he doesn't understand what I'm saying, but he seems to like it."

"He responds to the sound of your voice." Jace looked at her. "Like father, like son."

For an instant their eyes met and held. Kelly swallowed hard, fighting against a sudden overwhelming sense of loss. It felt as though somebody had reached in and ripped out everything inside. Which was crazy. How long would this man have such a compelling effect on her? His voice had always sent shivers across her skin, and now was no different. She remembered lying on the blanket under the shade of a giant oak tree, her head resting on his muscled chest, held close and protected in his heavy arms. She remembered how good just being in his presence had made her feel.

Pushing away those memories, Kelly continued to share small things about Henry's life. She kept her gaze locked on the baby. She didn't need any more remembrances of Jace distracting her. The recollections she'd managed to bury could stay buried. Feeling his arms around her again would never happen. The past was best left in the past.

Eventually their quiet conversation lulled the baby to sleep. Kelly took him from Jace and put him in his crib, covering him with his blue puppy blanket. When she returned Jace was standing at the front door.

"Do I have you to thank for getting my car home?"

He shrugged those broad shoulders. "No big deal."

"I called everyone I knew and no one had time to look at it." She felt the need to assure him she'd tried to get the car out of his way. "How much do I owe you?"

He shook his head and shrugged. "I just turned the key. You must have given it too much gas and flooded the engine. Desperation for a quick getaway sometimes causes that to happen."

She ignored the gibe. "Well, thank you."

"No problem." He hesitated. "I'd like to invite Matt out to the ranch to throw some footballs. Maybe I can give him some pointers."

"He would love that. He is so into football, and as you will soon discover if you haven't already, you're his hero. But Jace, don't do it because you feel in any way obligated. Eventually, Matt would figure it out and—"

"Gotcha. No worries there. He seems like a good kid. My mom will be staying at the ranch but won't be here for a few days, so tossing the ball with Matt will be great. Brings back the good old days." He grinned and pushed open the door as Matt came jogging up to the porch. "It gets dark around nine. I'll have him home about then."

The afternoon visits and the ball practice with Matt at the ranch became everyday events. Over the next two weeks, Kelly's anger and resentment slowly began to wane to a controllable level. It was so odd having Jace back in her life. Every day she expected him to not show up. But he hadn't missed a day yet. Initially she'd had some sleepless nights, her mind trying to answer the big question: What now? Where was this going? What was he eventually going to do? Did his plans include an attempt to take Henry?

Jace was a brief moment in her past. He had no part in her future other than being her son's father. Never again would she be back in his arms. Ever.

Pushing open the heavy glass door of the insurance company where she worked as assistant customer service rep, Kelly headed toward the side of the building and the employee parking lot. It had been a long day. But it helped keep her mind focused, leaving no time to think about Jace.

Most of the time.

Rounding the outside corner of the building, heading toward the parking lot, she immediately spotted the very subject of her thoughts leaning against her car, his arms crossed over his broad chest. Her heart skipped a beat. Her determination to keep their past where it belonged was an ongoing battle, and every time she saw him, it grew more difficult.

Inside she was jumble of nerves, wanting him to stay away yet missing him, then hating herself for it. Every time a dark blue truck passed, she had to look to see if it was him. When told she had an incoming call at work, she anxiously picked up the receiver, prepared to hear his deep voice on the other end. Errands around town had her searching the faces in the crowd for him.

Now the pulse surged through her veins as she took in the sight of him, and her mind rushed to figure out why he was here.

"Do you have a minute?" he asked when she reached the car.

Kelly shrugged.

Jace hesitated, as though looking for the right words. "I received a phone call about an hour ago. A friend in the media owes me a couple of favors. He called to let me know someone found out I'm the primary stockholder in a company that recently bought a ranch in Calico Springs, Texas. The news media will probably be staking out the ranch by this evening or soon after. Reporters can be ruthless. They can dig up facts you thought were long buried."

Why was he telling her this? This didn't concern her. And if the media discovered Henry was Jace's son, she couldn't stop it.

"So, why tell me? It's not any of my business."

"I'm afraid it might be only a matter of time until they find out about Henry."

"Are you asking me to deny Henry is your son if anyone should inquire? Sorry if he's an embarrassment for you." She adjusted the strap of her purse on her shoulder. "Excuse me. You're blocking the door. I need to get home."

Jace didn't move.

"That's not what I'm saying at all. Kelly, other than his middle name, did you put my name on his birth certificate? As the father?"

She nodded.

"If anyone finds out about Henry, this will blow up into a very big deal. You won't be safe, or at the least, you will be surrounded by the press. Night and day. Everywhere you go. They will follow you to work. They will find out who keeps the baby during the day and do what they have to in order to get a picture. They could even go to Matt's school."

Jace had to see the skepticism on her face. "So...I'll just tell them to leave my property," she countered. "And once the school year begins they should be able to keep any stranger, reporter or not, away from Matt. I mean, they can't just—"

"They can and they will."

"No." She gritted her teeth to keep her anger in check. "No. This will not happen. Dammit, Jace. Keep your media mania on your side of the street and leave my side alone. This was exactly what I told you I didn't want to happen to Henry."

"I know. And I'm sorry. I'd change it if I could."

"So what's the answer? Why are you telling me all of this if there is no way to stop it?"

"You and Henry and Matt need to move out to the ranch as soon as possible."

Her eyebrows shot straight up as she looked at him with

open disbelief. "Yeah. Right. That is so not going to happen."

"Kelly, you're not equipped to deal with this on your own. I have a full security staff in place 24/7." Jace glanced toward a black sedan parked across the street and nodded. The man behind the wheel nodded back.

"You've got to be kidding." He had to be. "Jace, you're blowing this way out of proportion. This is Calico Springs, population six thousand and two. It isn't Los Angeles. It's a quiet little ranching community. Things like you're describing just don't happen here. Now if you'll please step aside, I really need to go and pick up Henry."

With a muttered curse, Jace moved toward the front of the car and opened the door for her. Kelly didn't hesitate to throw her purse onto the passenger seat and slip behind the wheel.

"Take this." He handed her a cell phone. "Just punch Call. There are only three people who will answer it—a couple of my security team and me. If you get into trouble, change your mind or need to reach me, use it."

This was taking on the ambiance of a James Bond thriller. "Are you kidding me?"

Jace looked down at her and shook his head. He wasn't smiling. A small trickle of fear ran down her spine. She took the phone and slipped it into the side pouch of her purse. It seemed easier than arguing about it.

"I won't be coming back in the afternoons. There's too much of a risk someone will see me. Kelly, I really do wish you would—"

"We'll be fine." She turned on the ignition and put the car into reverse. "I'll let Matt know you won't be stopping by for a while."

Jace didn't nod. He said nothing more. He stood in the same spot as she backed out of the parking space and turned toward home.

It must be tough to live your life always looking over

your shoulder. In a way she found it sad. To become so
successful in your chosen career that you actually become
a target of the very people you sought to entertain. But it
was a life he'd chosen. Consequently, he had to deal with
the repercussions. It didn't mean she had to.

Five

An unfamiliar sound woke Kelly from her sleep. Frowning, she rubbed her eyes and listened more intently. It sounded like people talking outside her house. She threw the covers back and rolled out of bed. It was early morning, still not completely light. She checked on Henry and adjusted his blanket. He'd slept through the night, so he would be ready for his breakfast soon.

Without bothering to turn on a light, she headed toward the living room, literally bumping into Matt in the hallway.

"Do you hear that?" It took a major shakedown every morning to get Matt to even open his eyes. For him to be awake at this hour...

"Yeah. I heard it."

"What is it?"

"I'm not sure." Separating the blinds just enough to see, they both looked out the front windows. In the predawn light, Kelly saw people. About a dozen of them. And cars and vans lining both sides of the street.

"What's going on, Kelly?" Before she could speak, Matt added, "I'm going out and see what's happening."

"No! Matt. Don't go outside."

In the ever-increasing light Kelly now saw the cameras and the white vans with satellite antennas on top. People were talking among themselves, calling out instructions to their crews. Large black power cords lay over the ground. She swallowed hard. Jace had told her the truth. Anger flared that he had brought this madness to their family, but it was temporarily pushed aside by concern for Henry and Matt.

"Matt, go get dressed and ready for school. You can't be late the second day. Find something to eat for breakfast. There are waffles in the freezer. Fresh fruit in the bowl on the table."

"This is wild." His eyes were as wide as saucers. "Those are reporters, right? Is all this because Jace comes here to visit?"

"No. Not exactly." She didn't know how her brother would take the news, but it was time he was told. Before he heard it on television. "This is because Henry is Jace's son."

Matt's jaw hung open; his eyes went ever wider. "*What? Oh, man. Are you kidding me? You had a thing with Jace and you never told me? When? How? Where? Are you serious?"

Kelly nodded. "Yes. But it's…complicated. And we don't have time to discuss it now."

"Does Jace know?"

Kelly rubbed her temples. "Yes."

"Henry is Jace Compton's *son*?"

Clearly Matt was struggling with this truth.

"So that's why he invited me out to his place to throw the ball."

Wow. Left field. His disappointment was obvious. "No. Absolutely not. You guys share a love of football and the two of you seemed to…click. He thinks the world of you, Matt. I would never lie about that. He's told me so on more than one occasion." The very last thing she wanted to add to this insanity was hurt feelings. She'd told Matt the truth. She just hoped he would believe it.

Matt was silent for a few worrying seconds. "Okay," he nodded. "Okay. Good. That's cool." The side of his mouth drew up in a half grin and he looked squarely at his sister. "I guess I'm not the only one in this family he *clicked* with."

She felt the heated blush cover her neck and face. Her

eyes narrowed into a glare. "Right now, Matthew Douglas Michaels, I would advise you not to go there. Go get dressed."

Matt headed for his bedroom, a wide grin across his face. His body language was decidedly springy with a bit of teenage swagger thrown in. He was on the *ins* with a superstar. And no doubt he thought he had something on her, as well. From the number of people standing outside their house, he would have to get in line.

With Henry changed and dressed, she went into the kitchen to ready his food. Her purse was on the kitchen table and the cell phone Jace had given her began to ring. When she pulled it out of her bag, she saw there had been numerous calls. She'd never heard it.

"Hello?"

"Why in the hell haven't you answered your phone?" Jace bellowed out, his frustration obvious. "I've been trying to reach you for thirty minutes. Are you all right? Is Henry—?"

"Henry is fine. We're all fine. There are some people outside. They have cameras. I guess you were right. It appears the media found us."

She heard him take a deep breath and blow it out. Kelly couldn't remember Jace ever getting angry or upset about anything. Clearly he was experiencing some anxiety now. Did he actually think something was going to happen to them in Calico Springs?

"Stay in the house. Keep the doors locked. Tom Stanton, my head of security, just arrived and is standing by outside your house. Let us know when you're ready and he'll bring you guys to the ranch and we—"

"Jace, no. I'm not coming to your ranch. I thought I made that clear. I've got to go to work and Matt has to be in school—" she switched Henry to her other arm and checked her watch "—in twenty minutes. I need to take the baby to the sitter's, then be on my way."

"Kelly, I don't think that would be—"

"Please don't waste either of our time telling me you don't think it's a good idea. If you want to help us, we need to get Henry safely to the babysitter and Matt to school."

A prolonged silence met her statement. "Kelly, you can't go on expecting your life to stay the way it was. I'm sorry, honey."

She heard the sincerity in his tone. His endearment made her heart beat a bit faster, her breathing become shallow. His rich baritone voice calling her honey caused a memory to flash in her mind. Jace's arms around her, his hand covering hers as she gripped the end of a fishing pole. They'd been on the edge of a clear blue pond located in an area of the ranch where he'd stayed last year. It had felt as if they were the only two people on earth. Jace had removed his shirt and shoes, leaving only the well-worn, slightly ripped jeans. She'd had a two-pound bass on the line, the first fish she'd ever caught. When it broke the surface of the water, bending and flouncing in an effort to get free of the hook, she hadn't been able to contain the screams of excitement. And she couldn't forget Jace's laughter at her animated enthusiasm. Then the fish had fallen back into the water and seconds later the line went slack. She'd lost it. Jace had hugged her close and murmured, "I'm sorry, honey. Let's see if we can catch him again." But as she'd turned into his arms the fish was forgotten. The soft rays of the summer sun had been joined by the hot sparkle of desire in his eyes and the burning of his hungry lips.

Would she ever be immune to him? To his voice? His touch? How much longer until she could stop having to fight her own body in order to maintain some small amount of control? Kelly brushed the hair back from her face, striving for practicality. She didn't need to turn into one of Jace Compton's groupies, and the past had shown her that was the most she could ever be.

"Kelly? Are you there?"

"Uh...yeah. Yeah. Jace, I can't walk away from my life. Apparently, you can't walk away from yours, either. Matt has to go to school and I need to get dressed and go to work." Why couldn't he understand? Had he been living the high life so long he could no longer relate to ordinary people living ordinary lives?

He finally agreed, but she could tell by his tone he didn't like it. "I'll have Tom send two men to the front door. Tell them where you want to go."

Three days later the craziness had not subsided and her cell phone wouldn't stop ringing. There was no sign the media were giving up. Not only had they increased their ranks, they had been joined by some of the town's residents, their own curiosity compelling them to be part of the excitement. There were what appeared to be tailgate parties going on just past her driveway as far down the street as she could see in both directions, with dozens of lawn chairs lining the yards on both sides. Her home had become a freak show. For the first time in her life, Kelly felt claustrophobia stir her anger.

The switchboard at work had been bombarded with calls since that first day, overwhelming the phone lines. Just after lunch today she'd had a rather unpleasant one-on-one with her boss, who'd recommended she take off early, adding she had a week of vacation and suggested she use it until she got her life in some semblance of order. And now, apparently, her cell number had been discovered and passed out, free for the taking.

Every day, Jace's security team picked Matt up and escorted him home. He was having a great time with all the excitement, enjoying the sudden popularity and inspiring the envy of his classmates, which only added to her growing frustration.

Pacing around the small house, her mind was filled with murderous thoughts, and all of them revolved around Jace.

How could he do this? And why wouldn't he stop it? *I want to be in your life*, he'd said. Ha! What a joke. This media mania was exactly what she'd wanted to avoid. How dare he dump this on her front doorstep?

The cell phone Jace had provided began to ring.

"Hello?"

"Ms. Michaels, this is Tom Stanton of Jace's security detail. Would you like your mail?"

"My *mail*?" Why not? What else did she have to do? "Yeah. Sure."

"One of our men will deliver it to your back door in two minutes."

"Thanks." It seemed as if they were going to a lot of trouble. She mostly received advertisements addressed to "resident," which immediately went into the trash.

At the man's knock, Kelly opened the door. With a respectful nod, he brought in her mail. Three large bags of it.

"What...? What is all this?"

"They're all addressed to you. Probably fan letters."

"Fan letters?" Was he kidding?

By the time Matt got home, Kelly was just about to open the second bag. Sitting on the living room floor with Henry playing on a thick blanket next to her, she'd spent the past three hours reading pure crazy.

"You know," Matt said as he walked to where she sat, "we should sell popcorn to those people outside. Make some money off this. What are you doing?" Frowning, he dumped his books onto the sofa. "What is all this?"

"Fan letters." She didn't look up, but she could feel Matt's surprise mixed with excitement from four feet away. "Have a seat. I wouldn't want you to miss one second of this *wonderful* experience."

Ignoring her sarcasm, Matt quickly found a place on the floor and pulled a handful of letters out of the newly opened bag.

"Ha!" Matt laughed. "This girl wants to have Jace's baby

but is happy for you in spite of you beating her to it." He picked up another and began reading.

"Kelly?"

She noticed his face narrow into a serious frown. "You'd better take a look at this." He handed the page to her.

The letter was filled with alarming descriptions of what they intended to do to Kelly and the baby. Off-the-wall acts of violence directed at her and Henry. She felt the blood leave her face as she realized the implications. Suddenly a crashing sound from the bedroom made her jump. It sounded as if a vase had shattered. "Matt, stay with Henry."

Kelly scrambled to her feet and hurried in that direction.

"Sorry about your vase." A woman about her age was standing inside the bedroom, looking around.

"Who are you? How did you get inside my house?" Kelly's voice was about three octaves higher than normal.

The woman shrugged and looked toward the bed. "Through the window. Is that where Jace Compton sleeps?" She spoke as though she was in a daze, as if she'd just stumbled into Neverland. The woman walked over to the bed, smoothed her hands over the covers, and then proceeded to crawl on top of the mattress.

"What are you doing? Get off my bed!"

"It's so soft," the woman said, completely ignoring Kelly's angry demand. "Wow."

Kelly ran for kitchen table and the phone Jace had provided. Her call was immediately answered.

"There is someone in my bedroom." She could hear the anger in her own voice. "She said she climbed in through the window. She's *in* my bed and refuses to leave."

The line went dead and within seconds men were coming in every door to her small house, guns drawn, with Tom Stanton leading the charge. The woman was seized and handcuffed. Notification of the break-in was called into the police, all handled in a practiced and flawless manner by the men in Jace's security detail.

Kelly went back to the front room and picked up Henry. Matt stood next to her, not saying a word.

"The police will need a statement, Ms. Michaels. They should be here any minute."

Kelly nodded and sat down on the sofa, holding Henry close.

"I think you need to see this." Matt shoved a letter into Tom's hand.

"Where did you get this, son?" Tom frowned.

"In the mail. We were reading all this mail." He gestured to letters spread over the floor and one of the bags, still partially full, next to the sofa. "Most of them are stupid. But this one…"

Tom took out his phone and punched a number before turning and walking out of the room. Kelly could hear his voice. She couldn't understand what he said or who he was talking to.

But she had a pretty good idea.

Six

It took Jace most of the drive from the ranch to Kelly's house to bring his temper under a small bit of control. Tom's phone call had his heart racing, his fear for their safety mounting. *Someone had gotten into their house.* The lives of both Kelly and his son had been threatened. He blew out an angry sigh. Kelly was going to listen to reason. This time he was not going to accept any damned excuses. If he had to play the role of bad guy, so be it. If pleas didn't work, maybe a bluff would. One way or the other, she was leaving that house.

He knew in time the press's feeding frenzy would die down. News of him having a child was enough of a story to bring the cameras to Texas. But no one wanted to read old news. Eventually, some new story would replace the old. The question was, how long until this was considered old? A call to Bret was necessary to ensure he didn't do anything to prolong this mess. The last thing any of them needed was for the manager to jump into the mayhem and milk it for all it was worth.

Putting his sunglasses in place, Jace got out of the truck with two members of his security team, one behind and one next to him. He ignored the shouts from the reporters and what had to be a quarter of the town's population standing behind the yellow tape. Three police cars, lights flashing, were blocking off the street, the officers trying unsuccessfully to disband the gawkers. With more calm than he felt, Jace opened the front door of the house and stepped inside.

Kelly was sitting on the couch, holding Henry. Matt sat on the floor next to her, reading letters. Tom, two of his men and two police officers stood in the small kitchen, quietly talking among themselves.

When Jace approached Kelly, she glared at him with a force that could hurt if it had any substance. But his concern effectively deflected any anger she might have and replaced it with some of his own. He crouched down next to the sofa, his face only inches from hers.

"Are you guys okay?"

"Physically. Obviously I don't appreciate that woman sneaking into my house and crawling up on my bed. You were supposed to do something. She broke my grandmother's vase."

"I'm about to do something. Kelly, this is finished. Do you understand?" His gaze caught hers and he didn't let go. "You're going to pack some clothes and you and Matt and Henry are moving to the ranch until this blows over."

"I don't want to live in your house."

"That's too damn bad." Jace could feel the tight control he had on his temper slipping. "You'd rather stay here and have someone break into your house again? Next time, it might be someone worse than that mentally disturbed woman. It might be the crazed idiot who wrote that letter. Don't be stupid, Kelly." He could hear the growl in his own voice.

Her quick intake of breath and the flash of surprise in her blue-green eyes told him he'd crossed the line. *Damn.* For the first time in his life, with Kelly of all people, the mother of his child, he was in danger of letting his anger override his common sense, doing exactly what he'd been afraid of for so many years. He clenched his jaw in an effort to maintain control. He had to keep it together. For Kelly. He felt a wave of guilt wash over him for what he'd said.

He reached out and gently took her face in his hands, determined to make her understand. "What if someone took

Henry?" Her eyes widened. Apparently the thought had not occurred to her. "A ransom demand is not that far-fetched."

"Then stop it," she snapped at him, a whispered plea. "You caused all of this. We were fine until you came back. Make them leave us alone."

"I'm trying, but it isn't that simple and you're smart enough to know that. I intend to do everything in my power to give the reporters what they want and see if I can make them leave. But the ranch is the only place I can protect you until that happens."

Jace let his hands drop and she looked down at Henry, who was sleeping peacefully in her arms. Jace could see the resentment in her face, the need for all of this to go away. She was frustrated and angry and probably a little scared all at the same time. He knew Kelly well enough to know she was going to try to bluff him out of their moving to the ranch. And no way was that going to happen.

"We can go to my friend Gerri's apartment and—"

"Do you really think that will make any difference?"

As she thought about his question, she moistened her lower lip with her tongue. He remembered all too well his mouth doing the same thing—tasting those lips, sucking the nectar from them before going deeper, enjoying the sweet taste he'd found in the hidden recesses of her mouth.

"I don't know. But I'm not moving to your house."

Jace ran a hand through his hair and huffed out some of the frustration. "Kelly, I can't legally make any demands of you, but Henry is my son and one way or the other, he is leaving this house. Now. It isn't safe. If I have to, I'll get a court order giving me temporary custody. And don't imagine any judge is going to stand by and let a five-month-old baby live in a threatening environment."

He hated playing the badass, but clearly they were in danger. If something happened to any of them he would never forgive himself. At this point it wasn't beneath him to toss her over his shoulder and carry her out kicking and screaming. If that's what it took, so be it. He *would* to keep them safe.

Pale and distraught, she looked up at him. Apparently just the mention of taking her child was enough to terrify her. Jace knew a surge of guilt for what he'd said, but he had to get her to relocate somewhere safe.

"Kelly? It doesn't have to be forever." He ignored the extra beat of his heart and the odd sinking feeling in his gut when he spoke those words.

She nodded. "You don't have to threaten."

"I apologize. You're making the right decision."

"Don't patronize me, either. You're giving me no choice. Of course I'm concerned for Henry's safety. You have to realize how…uncomfortable this will be for me. And in the meantime I expect you to make all this insanity go away."

She would try the patience of a saint. His eyes held hers for countless seconds, and he became aware that he was almost close enough to kiss her. He wanted to. Even now. Even in the middle of this crazy situation. He remembered holding her, making love to her. His body was hard with expectation and he knew she wouldn't be the only one uncomfortable while she lived under his roof. Only a few steps down the hall from his bedroom.

Kelly watched as Jace stood and walked over to Tom. There was a lot of nodding during their low, quiet discussion. Minutes later, they disappeared out the front door. Kelly listened to the muffled conversations as Jace apparently talked to the press. Ten minutes later, they came back inside.

"Here's what we're going to do," Jace said, returning to where Kelly sat. "It's almost dark. That will work to our advantage. Tom will have a car in front of the house in a few minutes, allowing time for some of the media to disperse. It's the same dark green SUV that's been taking you to work. Go to the car. Don't stop for anything. You know the drill."

Kelly stood and handed Henry to his father. Jace accepted the baby as if it were something he did every day. Which, come to think of it, he did. Or at least, he had for two weeks.

"I need to get some things together, unless you have his formula and plenty of diapers?" Knowing the answer, Kelly turned toward the bedroom. With her heart racing, she grabbed the baby bag and shoved it full of bottles, formula, baby food, clothes, diapers and a couple of stuffed toys. She pulled a small suitcase from the closet and packed jeans, assorted T-shirts, toiletries and a few more baby items.

Thirty minutes later it was time to go.

Matt stood waiting by the door. He wore a backpack, no doubt full of clothes, and held a tote bag with his books.

Jace stepped up behind them, still holding Henry. Kelly watched through the front windows as a green vehicle pulled up in front.

"It's here."

The short walk to the SUV was made without incident, although Kelly could feel the bevy of cameras recording every step. The throng of people standing behind the yellow tape surged forward when Jace emerged with his new baby. That provided a few seconds of apprehension but again, his security team took control. The ride to the grocery store parking lot where a helicopter awaited was made with no problems. Soon they were leaving the ground, quickly ascending into the darkened sky. Kelly watched the baby, afraid the sound would frighten him. But Henry took it in stride and continued to chew on Jace's shirt. Teething. Jace would have a major wet spot by the time they landed. Welcome to fatherhood.

"Cool," Matt muttered in fascination as he looked out the window.

In minutes they descended into the clearing of a pasture behind the stately home, setting down on a large round landing pad. The pilot immediately killed the engine, and they were escorted to waiting vehicles. The ride to the house was made in silence other than Henry's babble. Part of her wanted to be grateful to Jace for stepping in to keep Henry safe. The other part resented the fact that were it not for him, the protection wouldn't be needed in the first place.

The mansion was ablaze with lights. Jace escorted them down a path, his hand on her lower back.

"This is Carmen." Jace introduced a robust Hispanic woman who came forward with a welcoming smile as soon as they entered the house. "I need to speak with Tom. Carmen will take you all upstairs and show you where you'll be staying."

Not for long, Kelly thought, her mind slowly coming back on track. She took the baby from Jace and they followed the housekeeper up the stairs. Kelly remembered the day she'd cleaned the house and thought what a great place it was for a family. Never in a million years would she have guessed it would be her own family, let alone that she'd be living here with Jace. She swallowed hard.

The bedroom she was shown was only slightly smaller than the two rooms she'd cleaned a few weeks ago. The color scheme was green and blue pastel. It presented a relaxing and welcoming feel.

"You are next door, Mr. Matt," Carmen said in a strong accent. "This way. Make yourselves at home." She smiled at the baby in Kelly's arms. "I have four daughters, two sons and five grandbabies. Anything you need for your baby, you let me know, Mrs. Compton. I know what to do."

"Thank you. But I'm not…" Carmen and Matt disappeared around the corner before Kelly could explain she was *not* Mrs. Compton. She never would be. But why bother to correct her? They wouldn't be here long enough for it to make any difference.

Henry had finally wound down and was fast asleep in her arms. She put him in the center of the large bed, his little arms falling out to the side as he slept.

Living under Jace's roof was a bad idea. Every time Jace came close to her, memories jumped to the front of her mind. When he spoke, her eyes automatically focused on his mouth, on those lips that could do amazing things. When those all-knowing green eyes gleamed with passion, a chill went across her skin.

She had to keep this situation in perspective. There was no doubt any number of women who had felt exactly the same way about Jace Compton. She had to be one in a very long list who experienced the same pleasures in his arms. She was not a hormone-driven, nitwitted adolescent. She'd survived Jace once. She could do it again. She was here now only because of Henry. Even though the attraction was still strong, she would do well to remember the months after Jace had left and the fact that he'd never given her a second thought.

After unpacking, Kelly paced, not knowing what to do. She switched on the flat-screen TV and ran through the channel options, but found nothing that would hold her attention and turned it off. Her gaze fell on the door to the large bathroom. Venturing inside she passed through the powder room with its antique mirrors and vases of freshly cut flowers on dark marble countertops. Next was a shower large enough for four or five people and a whirlpool tub of equal size. She hurried back to the bedroom and placed pillows all around the edge of the bed to safeguard Henry while he slept. After covering the baby with his blue blanket and assuring herself he was sleeping peacefully, she headed back into the bathroom.

Pouring her favorite lavender bath salts into the quickly filling tub, she turned on the jets and climbed in. Lying back, she closed her eyes and gave in to the sheer luxury that enveloped her. The streams of the water coursing around her, against her back, her sides and neck, through her legs, soon began to reduce the stress of the past few days.

The memory of another time came unbidden to her mind.

There had been no tub at the ranch where Jace had stayed, but they'd made do with the shower.

For the first time in her life, Kelly saw a perfect example of the human male body. Broad shoulders blocked the water from reaching her as the moisture cascaded down over his corded neck and arms. Jace soaped his large hands and began to rub them slowly over every inch of her body, over her breasts, down her stomach, between her legs.

He was heavy with arousal and the air left her lungs as she stared, unable to tear her eyes away. She realized she'd never seen a man in this way before. There was no hiding under the blanket of modesty. He wanted to see every inch of her and offered her the same.

"See anything you like?"

Her gaze shot upward and met his. She could feel the blush spread over her face and neck. Obviously, Jace had no problem with modesty. He seemed totally unconcerned that she was seeing him naked. And aroused. Or that his size had her eyes bugging out of her head.

Jace had noted the blush. "Have you never seen a man before?" He tilted his head.

She swallowed. "Not...not like this."

He continued to watch her for several seconds. "How old were you? Late teens?"

"Yes."

"Quickie in the backseat?"

She nodded.

She saw a look of understanding cross his face. Instinct said her onetime experiment with teenage sex was not even close to what she was about to experience with the fully mature man who stood before her.

"Makes me curious what else you haven't experienced." His head dipped toward hers and he muttered against her lips, "Let's find out."

Without waiting for an answer, Jace took her lips in a deep, penetrating kiss that rocked her senses. He caught her

*hands and held them, palms up, as he poured the scented
soap into them. Kelly stared at her hands for countless seconds, knowing what he was asking of her. Her heart beat
in an accelerated rhythm as she contemplated what she
was about to do.*

*Almost of their own accord, her hands moved to his large
body. Slowly she began to rub the slick soap over his smooth
skin, covering the hard wall of his chest and arms, loving
the feel of the muscles that rippled beneath her hands.*

*She let them glide up to his massive shoulders and neck,
then once again over his chest. She couldn't keep from looking into his eyes. He watched her with the look of a cat
playing with a mouse. So intense was his focus, her hands
stilled in their journey of discovery.*

*He took them and slowly pushed them down his body.
"Touch me," he whispered, placing her fingers around his
sex.*

*She tore her eyes from his face to look at the hard pound
of flesh in her hands. Her gaze returned to his face, blue
eyes meeting green, as she stood there, frozen, unable to
release him yet unable to move. Her breathing becoming
almost nonexistent.*

*"Let me help you, honey," he whispered. He began to
move her hand against the silken flesh covering the under-
lying steel of his erection. It was an amazing sensation, and
she caught on fast.*

*Jace lowered his head, and his lips again found hers. She
opened her mouth and welcomed him in. His arms came
around her as the warm water cascaded over their embrace.*

*His hand squeezed her hip then moved on to rub the sen-
sitive area between her legs, encouraging her to open to
him. She moved against his hand in an effort to quench the
fire burning deep. Two fingers eased inside, and a shudder
ran rampant through her entire body. With a muffled moan,
she fell back against the shower wall as the mind-blowing
sensations overtook her.*

"Kelly," Jace groaned, his voice rough with need. Suddenly, his control seemed to snap. He lifted her, positioned her and pushed deep inside.

She felt a sudden draft of cold air mingle with the warm moisture of the bathroom seconds before his warm lips touched the sensitive curve where her neck and shoulder joined. A soft moan escaped her lips and, eyes closed, she turned into his mouth. Hungry lips covered hers, his tongue searching and finding what he sought. Her wet hands rose to hold his face, the need for him strong, essential. She gripped the back of his hair in a fist.

"Mmmm." He groaned, his deep, husky voice breaking the silence.

The memory ended with a shocking recoil, as if she'd had ice water thrown in her face. Her eyes shot open to find Jace leaning over the tub, his handsome face mere inches from hers. Kelly gasped in shock. She could feel herself flush with embarrassment over the memory she'd been reliving. Apparently, at some point they had merged with the present. She prayed his talents didn't include mind reading.

Jace's intense expression increased the simmering heat the daydream had generated. She held her arms over her breasts as she glared at Jace. He stood to full height, hands on his hips, his eyes moving over her naked body with an undeniable gleam.

"What are you doing in here?" Kelly spat the words, but Jace only pursed his lips as though hiding a grin and made no move to leave.

"I'm about to make love to you."

Seven

"You have no right to walk in here just because you own the house."

"You didn't appear to mind."

"I…I was just…"

He tilted his head, eyebrows raised, waiting for her to squirm out of this one. When she didn't reply, the gleam in those forest-green eyes intensified. "I know exactly what you were doing, Kelly. Instead of relying on memories, why don't you let me give you the real thing?"

Kelly frantically looked for a towel. "I need you to leave."

"Actually, I was headed to my room and heard Henry crying. After repeated knocks, I grew concerned. Would you rather I ignore his cries in the future?"

"He wasn't crying."

"As a matter of fact, he was. I gave him his pacifier and sat with him a few minutes and he went back to sleep."

"Well, you didn't have to come in *here*."

"I thought you might want to know about Henry." He pursed his lips, his green eyes glinting with humor. "There's nothing I haven't seen before, Kelly." His low voice caused shivers to run up her arms.

"That's not the point."

"No?"

"No."

He grabbed an oversize fluffy white towel and held it up for her. Kelly clambered out of the bath and down the few steps, and Jace wrapped the towel around her; his arms remained, holding her close.

"I've missed you." His low voice caused shivers to run over her skin.

"No, you haven't."

"Kelly, I want to work through this. I made mistakes. But they were not done intentionally."

She stepped back and his hands fell to his side.

"You miss the point. I don't care."

"I think you're letting your pride talk for you."

"And I think your libido is dictating to you."

"And that's a bad thing?"

She folded a corner of the towel between her breasts and moved away from him into the dressing area. She refused to argue. Especially when she might not win. Grabbing her comb, she began to work through the tangles, praying he would leave.

He stood in the entrance to the bathroom, leaning casually against the wall, watching her. The mirrored reflection did nothing to diminish his pure male presence, making her want to do all sorts of things she shouldn't. Unbidden, her mind kept reliving moments from before, and Jace was apparently more than willing to repeat every single one of them. She wouldn't go there again. She couldn't. The first time, his leaving, his lying, had almost destroyed her. For her own sake, and Henry's, she would not jump back in that rabbit hole again.

Having finished her task, she returned to the bedroom in search of fresh clothes. A peek toward the bed confirmed Henry was fast asleep, his blue pacifier moving slightly as he sucked on it. Jace stood next to her gazing down at the baby, and then shifted his focus to her. What she saw in his eyes was pride for his son, but more: she saw concern. He honestly cared about his son. He'd heard Henry crying and stopped to check on him. The blue pacifier was proof Jace had been telling the truth. That meant he'd sat next to the baby and given comfort until Henry went back to sleep. For perhaps the first time since they'd met, she saw more than a sexy body and killer smile. She saw a glimpse into the heart of the person Jace was inside. And that was a little bit daunting. She didn't want to like Jace Compton.

"I need to check on Matt." She walked to the bureau, removing a clean shirt and jeans.

Jace nodded, this time taking the hint, and walked out the door.

Matt was happily absorbed in a car racing game on his Xbox. To him, this was a grand adventure. He'd better enjoy it while it lasted.

She returned to her room and pulled on her old cotton gown and slipped into bed next to Henry. She had to leave here. She couldn't stay in this house with Jace. He might want to pick up where they'd left off, and she knew her defenses were sadly lacking. Loving him might not be something she could control. Making love to him was not going to happen.

Regardless of how much she might want it to.

"But I don't understand." Kelly blinked back the tears. "I had a week of vacation and it's only been...five days." *Crap.* She'd just quashed her own defense.

"Are you saying you'll be back on Monday?" Her boss was usually a fair man, but this was a low blow. "I should warn you, the press are still camped out at all the exits here. Frankly, this is becoming a problem."

The voice on the other end of the line was apologetic but firm. The work was piling up and they had to get someone in to deal with it.

The call ended and Kelly sank down onto one of the kitchen chairs, totally devastated. Reluctantly, she'd agreed to give up her job. Her boss had called her work top-notch and said that if there was an opening when she was ready to come back, she would certainly be considered for reemployment. He'd again offered his apologies, and then it was over. The call as well as her hope for the immediate future.

This was a nightmare that kept on giving.

"Hey, Kelly." Matt hurried into the den. "Turn on the TV." Matt found the remote and switched on the set himself. A news conference was in full swing. "Now we know where Jace has been for two days."

"I didn't know we cared."

"Yes, I've always liked Texas." Jace's handsome face filled the screen as he spoke.

"Rumors are rampant that you and a woman, Kelly Michaels, have a child? Can you comment on that?" a reporter asked off camera.

Without hesitation, Jace nodded, that award-winning grin flashing perfect white teeth. "Yes. We have a son. We're both very happy. Very excited."

A bevy of questions followed his statement. Kelly didn't see how he could understand any of them, but he soon responded, "I'll provide some pictures when he's older. I'm sure you can appreciate the safety concerns."

Another round of questions, and then, "I can't say where we will live at this juncture. Currently we are enjoying some solitude in Texas. There's always a chance we'll come back to LA. We haven't made a decision."

"Are you planning to get married?" someone asked.

Kelly's heart stopped in her throat, anticipating what Jace would say to that.

"Right now we haven't made any plans. We just want to enjoy our son and some quiet time together. I hope you can respect our privacy, give us a little room."

The subject changed to his next film role. Did Jace think he would get the lead in the rumored blockbuster due to start filming in three months? Again that smile. "You guys will probably know that before I do." He got the laughing response he no doubt intended. After a few more softballs like that, he called an end to the press conference. "Okay. That's all I have for today. Thanks."

He turned and disappeared into the hotel lobby, security stepping in to prevent the throngs of reporters from following him inside. At least he was keeping his promise to do what he could to make the media leave them alone. She just hoped it worked.

"Awesome." Matt turned off the television. "Tell me you're not excited to be here."

"I'm not excited to be here." Kelly met her brother's eyes with a deadpan expression.

"Kelly—"

"I just lost my job, Matt. Soon we'll have no home to go back to. And before you say it, no. We can't continue to live here." She wasn't about to go into the reasons with her kid brother. How could she even begin to explain the complicated emotional mess between Jace and herself? And where would she find another job? In the small community, jobs weren't plentiful.

"I need a personal assistant."

Kelly swung around to find a petite woman with beautiful auburn hair standing in the open doorway. The intricate lines around her eyes seemed to make them sparkle. Her welcoming smile looked very familiar.

"I'm Mona," she introduced herself. "Jason's mother. And you must be Kelly."

"Yes."

"I'm sorry I wasn't here to greet you when you arrived," she said as she walked toward them. "It took longer than anticipated to take care of some lose ends before leaving California. This must be Matt? Very nice to meet you. Jason has talked nonstop about you both."

She stopped in front of where Kelly sat balancing Henry on her knees. "And who is this handsome little man?" The look that softened her face spoke volumes.

"This is Henry." Kelly looked up and smiled.

A wet sheen glistened in the older woman's eyes. For the longest time, Mona stared, unmoving, at the baby in Kelly's arms, her gaze taking in every inch of her grandson, from his head to his feet. Kelly held him with his back against her chest. He kicked his feet while he tried his best to fit his little fist into his mouth. Jace's mother tried valiantly to hold back the tears of joy. It was all there in her face: overwhelming delight, pride and immediate acceptance.

"Would you care to hold him?" Henry loved people. He'd never been intimidated or shown any fear of strangers, and this was someone he might want to know better. Mona pulled out a chair and sat down. She took a moment to compose herself, wiping away the tears now falling from her face. Then she smiled at Kelly.

"I would love to."

Matt headed for his room and another round on Xbox. Mona took Henry in her arms and for a time seemed to be mesmerized. Kelly sat down, content to watch the first meeting between Henry and his grandmother unfold.

As it turned out, she was serious about the job offer. Mona headed an organization that raised money for several charities. One in particular that helped abused women and children was apparently very special to her. For that one she always held an annual ball and banquet in early October. And she needed assistance.

Kelly wasn't entirely sure how Mona did it, but Kelly soon found herself agreeing to help and worse, agreeing to continue to help until the charity ball, which was over a month away. She was losing it. That's all there was to it. But she would not live under Jace's roof forever. Absolutely not. She might be crazy but she wasn't stupid.

She'd give the big news event another week to blow over. Then no matter what, she was taking Matt and Henry and going home. Remaining in Jace's house was a seriously foolish idea. She liked to think she was strong as far as determination and resolve. But she knew if she had a weak spot,

Jace was it. If she caved, she'd be setting herself up for more heartache. That was something she didn't want or need.

As the helicopter began its descent, Jace again thought about who would be waiting for him at the door when he arrived. Kelly. His son. Matt and his mom. A small family. The kind of family he'd wished for most of his life. Granted, he wasn't exactly returning to a loving family unit who would welcome him with open arms, but he wasn't coming back to an empty house. It was a family. Sort of. And it was his.

Matt already had become a great friend. And Henry…a living miracle. Something Jace had never let himself envision. His son. A little face that would someday resemble his own. A young life with everything ahead of him. And Jace wanted to give him the world.

Kelly was the core. She brought it all together. She was the reason he was here, the driving force that had prompted him to purchase this ranch in Texas. The time spent with her last year had been nothing short of bliss. This community of kind strangers, along with the gently sloping hills and valleys, had brought serenity to his soul. It was the dream of a future he'd never before let himself imagine, but for a brief moment in time, he could pretend. Had it all been his imagination? He intended to find out.

He sighed and pulled a hand over his face. The only thing worse than wanting a real home and family was having one and knowing it couldn't last.

"Where is Kelly?" Jace asked his mother as he entered the large kitchen. His mom sat at the table munching on a slice of Carmen's homemade butternut bread. She didn't answer his question, merely took another sip of her coffee, not meeting his eyes. Jace frowned, his senses going on full alert.

"Mom?"

"I believe she had some things she needed to do."

"Did she leave the ranch?"

"Don't worry, dear. She'll be back as soon as she can."

Dammit to hell. He took the cell from his pocket and punched Tom's number. His head of security answered on the first ring.

"She said she had to get some things and she wanted her car," Tom said, answering Jace's unasked question. "Murphy drove her to town, and when they reached her house she told him to leave. Jace, you know we're limited in what we can do. If she tells us to get lost…"

"Yeah, I know. Was there anyone at her house?"

"Just a few dozen determined gawkers. She'll be fine if she stays under the radar. I don't foresee any problems."

Obviously Tom didn't know Kelly.

"What time did she leave?"

"Ten o'clock."

"Thanks."

Kelly was independent as hell. He just hadn't thought she would push her luck to this extent. She knew what could happen. Apparently, whatever she was up to, in her mind it was worth taking the risk.

Jace glanced at his watch and frowned. Two o'clock. It didn't take half a day to make the drive from town. Jace headed outside and jumped into the truck. Three miles down the road, he spotted her, trudging toward his place, baby in her arms, her ponytail swinging side to side.

"Do I need to guess?" he asked as he pulled up next to her.

She didn't look amused.

He threw the truck into Park and walked around to open the passenger door, helping her and the baby inside, and then tossed the bags, purse and brown paper sack she was carrying onto the backseat. He hoped to hell that wasn't her lunch, but he suspected it was. Miss Independence. He had to wonder how far she'd walked.

He turned the pickup around and headed back to the ranch. "I'm getting you a phone."

"I have a phone. I can't get a signal out here."

"Then I'm getting you a better one."

"No, you're not. The one I have works fine in town."

"What about while you're living out here? It's not smart to have a baby and no way to call for help if you need it."

"You're right. I'll buy a new one eventually."

"And what are you going to do between now and then if something happens?"

"With no transportation, I doubt it will be a problem," she answered dully. "First, I need to get the car fixed."

"That piece of junk isn't worth repairing," Jace muttered under his breath. He glanced her way. She was smiling down at the baby, who cooed and held on to his mother's finger. "Pick out a new car and have it delivered tomorrow."

"No."

Jace gritted his teeth and rubbed his neck. "You have got to be the most stubborn, hardheaded woman I've ever come across in my life."

"*Me?* Look in the mirror. Why do you keep pushing? Why do you keep insisting I take things from you? Frankly, it's getting old."

Goddammit.

"I don't need your help. We've already had this discussion. Maybe you should write it down and tape it to your forehead?"

Kelly was the only woman who came close to bringing him to his knees out of pure frustration. And she didn't have to touch him to do it.

"Why did you go into town?"

"I wanted my car."

He snorted.

She glared.

"You mother kindly offered me a job. Temporarily. I have to have transportation to get to the ranch."

"You're staying at the ranch."

"We can't keep living in your house."

"Why not?"

She presented him with a deadpan stare. The silence was deafening.

Okay, so he knew why not. The attraction between them, the pheromones, so powerful that they pulled him to her like a winch and a steel cable. He would have to be dead not to feel it. But he didn't want her to leave the ranch, and it wasn't only because of the safety issue. And it wasn't solely because he wanted to take her to his bed.

He wanted Kelly to like him again.

"Maybe there's another option."

"Like what?" She frowned.

Jace applied the brakes. Coming to a halt, he threw the truck into Reverse. Backing up some fifty feet he turned into a small, one-lane gravel road that disappeared into the trees. In less than a quarter of a mile the road ended at a small white house. Jace pulled up to the side and killed the motor.

"When I bought the ranch, there were four small houses on the property, originally built for ranch hands. I had them updated along with the main house. The ranch foreman lives in one, my head trainer in the second. The third was redesigned for my security team. This is the fourth. It's empty. It has its own entrance separate from the ranch, three bedrooms, a bath and a small kitchen."

"Are you saying…? I can't move here."

"Why not? The house is just sitting here. I have no plans to use it."

She had to admit it was better than living in his house. Barely. Kelly had been concerned about his close proximity if she worked for his mother. Living in his house was her single biggest worry when she'd agreed to help Mona. But this might be a temporary solution.

Or not.

"I don't know…"

"Kelly, don't be so stubborn about everything. This is a great idea."

She snorted at the absurdity. "No, it's not."

She didn't like it. A sense of unease churned inside. If she moved here, she would be totally reliant on Jace for everything. And it didn't come with an expiration date. There was no until-the-end-of-the-month move-out date. And that wasn't a good feeling.

"At least think about it. It makes sense."

"I like living in town."

"You haven't seen the inside of the cabin."

"I don't care. Why would I move out here just for a few months? Seems like an awful lot of trouble. I'm already indebted to your mother for a job. I'm not going to ask you for a place to live as well."

"I don't recall you asking."

Kelly turned to face him. His vivid emerald eyes made her want to waver, but she held firm. "Jace, I have two people who rely on me. I can't take the chance you won't suddenly decide to sell this place. Then where would we be? No job. No home. And you'd be gone without so much as a backward glance, just like before."

A glint of resentment darkened his eyes to the color of singed leaves; the barely perceptible narrowing of his eyes said he was ready to defend himself against her challenge. His jaw muscles tightened, his mouth straightening to a hard line. Then in an instant it was gone, replaced with a look more closely resembling determination.

"You will *never* have to worry about a job or a place to live or money in your bank account. *Deal with it.*"

Her eyes narrowed. "You might be okay with your ex-lover living on your ranch like some kind of leech. I'm not. I'm sure I've already been branded a gold digger. I *hate* that. Moving here... Word would get out and only make it worse."

"I really don't give a damn what anyone else thinks," Jace responded, slight traces of annoyance in his tone. He looked at her, his olive eyes intense and thoughtful. Then he dropped a bombshell. "But if you're that concerned about public opinion, marry me, Kelly. Problem solved."

Eight

Kelly had to steady herself. "That isn't funny."

"I didn't intend it to be."

"Then you're out of your mind."

"Why?"

She turned away from him, looking out the side window without really seeing. She shook her head, swallowing down the bile that rose in her throat. "Do you honestly expect me to respond to a joke? Having a child together does not a marriage make."

"I can come up with more reasons."

"Being good together in bed is not a valid reason, either." It didn't take the mental aptitude of Einstein to guess where his mind was going.

"At least you admit it." He raised his eyebrows as if daring her to deny it.

Kelly fought to keep him from seeing the hurt churning inside. She'd never expected him to say those words even in jest. A little part of her died at the realization that Jace viewed marriage as a joke. A prank. To him life was a game. That fact above all made his words seem almost cruel.

This was a pie-in-the-face wake-up call about how Jace viewed life. She'd always suspected, but never really let herself believe it.

She'd had a front-row seat during her parents' marital atrocity. She'd seen her father's feelings of obligation turn to disinterest, then disgust and finally hatred. He'd maliciously mocked her mother's love, seemingly taking glee in her anguish.

Her mother may have settled for a man who didn't love her, but Kelly was not interested in starring in the sequel. She wanted someone who loved her and wanted to be with her, not a man who felt trapped by circumstance. Despite the deterioration of her parents' marriage, Kelly still believed in the rightness of marriage. It was an ideal she held close to her heart, harboring a childhood dream that maybe someday she could have a chance to do it better. But it wouldn't be with Jace Compton, Mr. Love-'em-and-Leave-'em.

There was a time she would have jumped at the chance to marry the man she'd met and fallen in love with fifteen months ago. But even then, it had to be because he loved her. Not because he felt obligated.

The only reason Jace was spending time with her now was because of his son and the mess he'd created in their lives. Once his baby revelation died down, he'd be out of here so fast his exit would suck the leaves off the trees. Marry today. Divorce tomorrow. Fodder for the gossips and a publicity boon. No harm done. Life goes on.

How had his life morphed into such a bizarre existence?

She blinked the moisture from her eyes and gritted her teeth to overcome her momentary weakness. Inside, a mature, sensible woman battled an immature fool who was willing to believe anything, go anywhere, do anything, just to be with him. Reach for the stars and the delusion of happily-ever-after.

The single common thread between the two conflicting forces was love. She loved Jace. Behind all the barriers protecting her heart, she'd never stopped. But he must never know. She couldn't bear the shame and the mockery that would undoubtedly follow if Jace and the world ever found out.

"Come on. At least look at the cabin."

"No." Her voice was almost a whisper. She released her death grip on the seat, folding her hands in her lap.

"I would prefer you stay in the main house but I understand your need for some privacy. At least wait until you've seen the house before you decide?"

"Jace…"

Walking around the front of the F250, he opened the passenger-side door.

"Come on. Get out."

"Please. Just let it go."

The humor left his face. It was as though he'd suddenly realized something had changed. He looked at her questioningly.

"I respect your need for independence, Kelly. But you're letting your hatred of me overshadow your common sense. I have no intention of selling this place. Mom needs it as much as I do." His eyes were steady as his gaze held hers. "And we both need you."

His deep voice and those last words shook her to the core. Kelly wanted to reach out and touch the strong, handsome face only inches from her own. She wanted to feel his arms around her again despite how badly he'd hurt her. But she'd already used up her share of idiocy for a lifetime.

"I don't hate you, Jace."

For long seconds, neither moved. Then Jace leaned toward her. Ignoring the warning bells going off inside her head, Kelly didn't back away. His lips touched hers, warm, tentative, as though asking for permission. The subtle fragrance of his natural male scent surrounded her. She felt the slight rasp of his day-old five-o'clock shadow as his tongue entered her mouth, bringing with it the rich taste of coffee and the tantalizing taste of pure male. Her right hand lifted to rest on his powerful shoulder. God help her. It was as if fifteen long months had shriveled down to yesterday, his touch both familiar and new.

With a sudden squeal and a string of happy jabber from

Henry, who chose that moment to awaken from the nap in Kelly's arms, Jace drew back, watching her closely. Frowning, he lifted her face to his, his thumbs gently wiping away her tears.

"Why the tears, Kelly?"

She gave her best impression of a laugh. "Don't know what you're talking about."

He continued to watch her, his look intense. "Kelly—?"

"Just don't say anything else, okay? I'm…I'm just grateful. For the offer of the house. That's all."

She knew that look on his face. He didn't buy the gratitude excuse for a second. Unlike him, she was no actress. He would let it go for now, but he wouldn't drop it completely.

He reached to take Henry from her arms, and then held out his hand to her. Kelly reluctantly accepted his help getting out of the truck. His hand was big and warm, his grip strong and sure around hers. The baby laughed, then began sucking on his forefinger, his feet in a simulated run. They walked to the front of the cabin where Jace unlocked the door.

It was nice. The small kitchen was the same size as the one in her rental. A breakfast bar separated it from the living area, and a high-beamed ceiling gave a spacious feel.

"The bedrooms and bathroom are through there." Jace nodded in a direction behind her. The entire house was fresh and clean. The bathroom fixtures and kitchen appliances appeared new. It was already furnished with a sofa, stools for the breakfast bar and beds.

Jace dangled a key in front of her.

"It isn't bait. This is not a trap. It's yours if you want it. No expectations. No hidden agenda. As you saw, it has its own entrance, its own driveway. You'll have the only key." He tilted his head and waited for her decision.

Chewing her bottom lip, she looked back over the spacious room and then returned her gaze to Jace. "Why are you doing this?"

"Does there have to be a reason other than practicality?" He readjusted his stance as though ready for another battle. "That doesn't answer my question, does it?"

Her mind said she was about to make another huge mistake. She hated weakness, especially in herself. Being weak caused regrets and all kinds of pain. Why did everything have to be so hard? Why did her world suddenly seem to revolve around this man? It was like being strapped to a merry-go-round as it spun faster and faster out of control until the very breath was sucked from your lungs. By the time you realized you had to get off, you knew doing so was really going to hurt.

"You have to live somewhere, and staying at your house in town right now is not a good option. You don't want to live in the main house with me. This is a sensible, workable alternative. The rent on your house in town has already been paid through the end of the year—so don't feel you're trapped here. And I intend to replace your car—which I refuse to argue about."

Despite what had just happened between them, Kelly reached out and took the key from his hand. Her heartbeat increased as she turned it over and over in her fingers. She nodded her head in reluctant acceptance. It was only a couple of hundred yards farther away from him than she was now. But she'd take what she could get.

Jace stepped outside, still holding Henry. "This path leads to the back door of the house. Follow it in the opposite direction and you'll be at the main barn."

Together they returned to his truck. He helped her inside, handed her the baby and got behind the wheel.

"You had no right to pay my rent."

Jace didn't comment as he started the motor but just pursed his lips, obviously biting back a grin, and shook his head as though he'd expected her to say exactly that. She didn't like charity and she damn sure didn't like being a foregone conclusion.

They headed back to the main road, made the short ride around to Jace's front gate and on to his house in silence. Kelly had to wonder where all this would end. She was increasingly becoming part of his life and it frightened her. Putting up a brave front was hard to do. And getting more difficult every day. A wave of reality washed over her and she swallowed hard. Change was always a scary thing. In her life it had never been for the better.

It's only temporary, she reminded herself. *It isn't forever.*

On Friday afternoon, three of Jace's ranch hands moved the boxes she'd packed from her house in town to the cabin on the ranch. Jace stood next to her while they unloaded the truck. He appeared content to hold Henry, even responded to his gibberish. It surprised Kelly how Jace and the baby seemed to have already formed a bond. While it worried her, she had to resign herself to the fact that it was done. If Henry became upset when it was time for them to leave here, she'd have to handle it then as best she could. Mr. Playboy of the Year was definitely becoming a hands-on father. Who would have thought?

"That's the last of it," the ranch foreman told Kelly as two lanky cowboys walked out of the cabin. "We put the baby bed together for you. Looks like all that's left is for you to unpack and settle in."

"Thanks so much, Sam. Thanks, guys."

"I appreciate it, Sam," Jace added, ambling up to where they stood.

"You bet. Jace, you take care of that baby." Sam grinned and seated himself behind the wheel of the old truck. The cowboys tipped their hats, already walking toward the barn. "Good to have you here at the ranch, Mrs. Compton." Sam gunned the motor and with a wave out the window, took off down the driveway.

"I'm not… Ahhh." Kelly stomped her foot in frustration. "*Why* does everyone keep calling me that?"

Jace's free hand shot up, palm toward her. "I'm not saying a word."

With a glare in his direction, Kelly took Henry and went into the house. Standing in the center of the living room, she glanced at the boxes stacked around her. It seemed so... permanent. The anxiety she'd been pushing aside all week came back front and center. She couldn't let go of the feeling that this was a bad decision.

She put Henry in his swing and began unpacking and arranging their things. Several hours later everything was done, the beds were made, the empty boxes flattened and placed outside next to the small front porch.

That evening after she fed and bathed Henry and put him to bed for the night, she ventured outside. Two old metal chairs, one yellow, one green, sat on the extended concrete slab that served as a front porch. The weather was unusually cool for this time of year. Slipping into the nearest chair, she leaned back, closed her eyes and savored the beautiful evening.

"Looks like someone is enjoying this fine weather."

Kelly jumped at the sound of the male voice.

"Sorry." The man held his hands up. "Didn't mean to scare you."

"That's okay." Her eyes focused on the tall, lean man standing a few feet in front of her. His shaggy blond hair and welcoming smile immediately put her at ease. "It seemed like a good time to put my feet up and relax."

"I know the feeling." He took off his hat. "I'm Sylvester Decker, one of the trainers here at the ranch. People just call me Decker."

"Oh. Of course. It's nice to meet you. Occasionally I see you guys leading a horse from one area to another. There's a chestnut, almost the color of a new penny, with flaxen mane and tail and three white socks. Beautiful."

"That would be Classy Lady." He put one foot on the concrete slab and leaned toward her, resting his arms on his knee and holding his hat in his hands. "And you're right. She's a nice filly. Great bloodlines, but in the racing game, that's not an absolute guarantee. You should come to the main barn area sometime and see them up close. Do you ride?"

"I used to. One of my best friends lives at the neighboring ranch, the Bar H. When we were in school, she used to invite me out for weekends and we would go riding. It was great."

Decker suddenly straightened and took a step back. "Hey, Jace."

"Decker," Jace responded as he stepped out of the shadows into the muted light from the barn. Jace had obviously followed the path from the house, but neither Kelly nor Decker had heard him approach until he was standing in front of her small cabin.

"I just stopped by to welcome our new neighbor to the ranch."

Jace didn't reply. He watched the man like a predator protecting his territory. His eyes almost glowed in the darkness, giving the impression of a panther returning to its lair to find another male stalking the entrance. The air suddenly became thick with the sizzle of animosity. Kelly couldn't help but wonder if Decker sensed it or if it was just her imagination.

"Well, I'll leave you two to talk. It was nice to meet you, Kelly."

"You, too, Decker."

"Don't forget to come see the fillies."

"Thanks. I'd like that."

The cowboy slipped his hat back in place, his long strides carrying him down the path toward the barn until he disappeared into the night.

Jace motioned to the chair next to Kelly. "Mind if I sit down?" He didn't wait for an answer. He lowered his bulk into the old metal rocker, leaned back and brought one booted foot to rest on his knee. "So how goes it with you and Mom? Everything okay?"

"She's great. I love the work. I was afraid it was... That she offered me the job because..."

"You thought it was charity."

"Yeah." Kelly nodded. "But it's not. There's really a lot to do."

"Mom had two full-time assistants when she lived in Los Angeles." Jace cut her a glance, a smile tugging at the corners of his lips. "Be careful what you asked for."

Kelly had to smile. "We're finishing the invitations and considering a theme for the charity ball in October."

"Ah, yes. Mom usually hosts several events a year for different causes, but this one is her favorite. Over the years, it has taken on a life of its own. Be forewarned."

The soft glow of the lights from the barn in the distance provided the only light. Somewhere deep in the trees, a lone cricket chirped and two owls called to each other. Suddenly the tiny porch seemed very intimate. With only a soft breeze passing through the trees, Jace's heady male scent seemed to surround her. She could feel his heat. Her body automatically gravitated toward him. She couldn't help but wonder if he knew the effect he had on her. But no doubt he had the same effect on most women. It was as natural to him as breathing, and he'd probably stopped paying any attention years ago.

He adjusted his position and his knee touched her leg. The small point of contact became a focal point in her mind. She swallowed convulsively. This close, he was entirely too disturbing. Kelly hadn't realized the chairs were so close. Now she fought the temptation to move hers. But her mind and body were giving mixed signals on which way to move it. Jace didn't seem to notice the contact. He sat back, appearing completely relaxed.

"It's too bad there are so many trees out here," Jace said. "They block the view of the sky."

Her gaze automatically veered upward. All she could see were the leaves on the lower branches, which caught the glow of light from the barn.

"I remember watching Texas sunsets until they faded into night. Suddenly, the sky became full of stars." She felt his eyes on her. "Everywhere."

"Yes," she whispered before she could catch herself. She knew he was referring to the nights they'd spent together, him holding her close while they watched the stars through the window twinkle in the midnight sky. Then Jace would put his lips on hers and make similar stars burst in an explosive grand finale before the free fall back to earth.

"Do you still look at the stars, Kelly?"

That brought her out of the past and slammed her face-first into the present.

"No." She shook her head. "Not anymore." She cleared her throat. "Decker said you have some good bloodlines."

"I like what I see so far."

Kelly chanced a glance in his direction. He was looking directly at her; a wicked light glittered in his eyes. She quickly looked away. "I grew up with the cattle ranches, but never saw anything like you're putting together."

He nodded. "It's a challenge. A lot more involved than I originally thought, and we're just getting started. Every day is a new challenge. It's not easy, but definitely well worth the effort. I'm hoping patience and determination will pay off in the long run."

Kelly swallowed hard. She could swear every word out of his mouth referred to her. To them.

"Kelly..." he said, his voice husky.

She couldn't stop herself from turning toward him. Their gazes met and held. In that instant, she wanted to again feel his lips on hers. She wanted to turn the page and let them start fresh. Allow her the chance to make this superstar believe in love. The forever kind. The kind that wasn't a joke. Unbidden, her gaze lowered to his mouth, so tempting. So close.

Electricity sizzled in the air. Her heartbeat increased as the heat of unwanted arousal bloomed in her lower regions, causing her body temperature to rise. He leaned toward her.

He gripped the back of her neck and gently drew her to him. His tongue moistened her lips, tempting her to open to him. She drew air deep into her lungs, but rather than clearing her head and pulling her out of the spell she seemed to be under, inhaling his essence tempted her to come closer. With a fevered sigh, she tilted her head the slightest bit and opened her lips, and Jace took full advantage, entering her mouth, deepening the embrace.

A filament of sanity threaded its way into her mind, and she clung to that small thread. With all the internal strength she could muster, she turned her head, separating her lips from the smoldering heat of his.

"I should go and check on Henry," she whispered, still fighting to retain some clarity of thought, her voice breathy from his kiss. Jace's gaze held hers for a long moment before he released her. Taking a deep breath, Kelly pushed against the metal arms of the chair and rose to her feet. More than anything, she wanted to kiss him forever. She wanted to relive the passion that detonated the stars. And she was edging ever closer to doing something really stupid. "If you'll excuse me, I'll say good-night."

The gleam in his dark eyes clearly told her he understood more than she wanted him to. "Good night, Kelly."

She hurried inside and closed the door. When she was sure Jace was gone, she stepped back outside and crossed the lawn until she came to a spot where the trees parted and offered an unobstructed view of the sky.

She'd lied to Jace. She'd never stopped looking at the stars. At *their* star. One winked at her and she smiled, peace settling in her heart for the first time in a long while.

Kelly had wondered if he remembered the dinners across

a candlelit table, the days spent together under the warm rays of the sun, the nights in his arms as they watched the night sky. She'd doubted it. Compared to the beautiful women he dated, she was nothing. A piece of wheat toast compared to a fine French pastry.

But she'd been wrong. Jace remembered.

But all things considered, did it really make any difference?

Nine

There was something going on with Kelly. It was barely perceptible, and if it were not for his years of training as an actor, he wouldn't have picked up on it. But there was something infinitesimally different in her voice, in her eyes. She had distanced herself from him, even more so than when he'd first come back to Calico Springs. She'd erected a wall that hadn't been there before. He just couldn't get a handle on what had happened. What had changed?

As he walked back to the house, his mind whirled in quiet speculation. He'd noticed the difference around the time she agreed to move into the cabin. Had moving from the main house upset her? Did she want to stay with him instead? Surely she knew the choice was hers. He replayed their conversation in his mind. He recalled that her only objection had involved wanting to return to her home.

She seemed to like her job. His mother had told him Kelly was a delight to work with. Her attention to detail, her intuitiveness as to the direction his mom wanted to go with the charity event, her suggestions… Everything was great. His mother had a baby bed, a swing and a truckload of toys brought in and they were both enjoying Henry.

But something was off. He had no doubt it was something he'd said or done, but he had no clue what it could be.

Whatever the reason, Kelly was right. He should keep his distance. He needed to stop pursuing her. He couldn't give her the forever she undoubtedly wanted and deserved. And Henry. He knew he needed to stay clear of the baby.

But he was drawn to him just like he was to Kelly. It was crazy. Something inside compelled him to be as close to them as possible while it lasted. Henry had already grown so much during their short stay on the ranch. By the time Jace returned from another film project, his son would be walking. And talking. And if Jace distanced himself the way he needed to, the coming years would pass without him ever knowing his son. Without Henry knowing his father.

All things considered, maybe that wasn't such a bad thing.

Kelly straightened the desk and gathered Henry's things in preparation to leave for the day. Before she could pick up Henry, Jace stepped inside the room.

"Can I borrow your assistant?" He looked first at his mom before switching his gaze to Kelly. "Thought you might like to see the horses. I remember you mentioning it to Decker."

Kelly glanced at Mona and received a nod of encouragement. "Henry will be just fine. And I don't mind a bit. You go ahead."

Jace's hand was warm against her lower back as he guided her down the path to the large structure. It was wrong to enjoy his closeness, his touch. But she did. And she was not about to ask him to stop. When they reached the wide-open double doors of the barn they were greeted with knickers from the stalls on both sides of the aisle. The earthy scent of rich, sweet alfalfa, leather and the horses filled the air. The beautiful chestnut filly she'd seen being led back to the barn one day immediately caught her eye through the bars on the top half of the stalls. As Kelly approached, the filly's ears pricked forward in curiosity as she continued chewing her evening grain.

"She's so beautiful," Kelly murmured. The young mare's coat gleamed like polished copper. "I saw her being led from the round exercise pen once. She's even more magnificent up close."

Jace smiled, reached forward and opened the top half of the stall door, giving Kelly unrestricted access. The filly stepped over and put her head through the opening. Kelly couldn't resist stroking the silky neck.

"Hey, sweetheart." She couldn't contain the full grin from spreading across her face. "Oh Jace, she's amazing."

"Most thoroughbreds are pretty high-strung. This one seems a lot calmer. Don't know how that will play out on the track. But she seems to genuinely like people."

"Does she like carrots? Or apples?"

"I really couldn't tell you." He appeared surprised at the question.

"I'll bet she does. And she'll be fast, won't you, pretty lady? I never knew you liked horses, Jace."

He stepped around to the other side of the filly, giving her a pat. "As a kid, I dreamed about someday having a ranch." He shrugged. "There used to be a small carnival that came to our area once or twice a year and it had pony rides for the kids. That's the first place I headed. Never wanted to get down. Then a few years ago, I had to learn to ride pretty proficiently for a part in a film. Once I was trained, every spare second I wasn't needed on the set, I would spend riding. We were filming in New Mexico on a large ranch near Santa Fe. You could ride for miles."

"I can relate. Your neighbor just down the road at the Bar H is one of my oldest friends. Growing up we spent most of our summers on the back of a horse. We'd pack food and water in the saddlebags and off we'd go. Her dad used to get so mad when we were late getting back. A few times it was well past dark and he was *livid*." Kelly grinned at the memories. "Their land backed up to the national forest and grasslands. We found an old gate and that was it. We headed for that entrance every time."

Kelly glanced from the filly to Jace. He was grinning, the

small laugh lines showing at the corners of his eyes while attractive grooves appeared on either side of his mouth. "What?"

He shook his head. "I just never pictured you for a cowgirl."

"I don't know if that's a compliment or an insult." She smiled up at him. "But I love horses. I think your place might border the grasslands, as well. You might want to have someone check it out. You can ride for days. Shea and I would get so turned around. Oh my gosh. I still don't know how we always managed to make it home. I think the horses were our saving grace."

She saw an amused glitter in his dark eyes. She swallowed nervously, not believing she'd just talked so freely with him. But then, she always had. Between them, conversation had flowed easily as they discovered more and more about each other, their likes and dislikes. They had so many common interests. Food. Music. Gazing at the stars on cloudless nights.

"I did the same thing," he said, closing the stall door. "I would ride out so far from base camp in New Mexico, at times I had no idea which way was up. But the horse always knew where its evening meal would be."

In this environment with the scents and sounds of nature surrounding them, and the easy banter between them, Jace was again the guy she met almost a year and a half ago. Silent alarms began clanging in her head. Needing to put some distance between them, she walked down to the next stall. Inside was a horse with a slightly darker coat than the filly.

"This is Chesapeake Dream," Jace offered as he opened the top of the door.

Like the first filly, she came forward and curiously sniffed the two humans who stood in front of her. "She's the one we think will bring it home. She's not yet three, so Lee is taking her training slow, but she's been on the track a couple of times and has really shown some speed."

Kelly reached out to run her hand down the velvety neck. After a few minutes, Jace closed the stall door and Kelly moved down the aisle. She passed an empty stall and proceeded to the next one. Through the metal bars, she saw a magnificent thoroughbred with a coat as black as polished ebony. This one was a lot bigger than the others.

She opened the top of the stall door as Jace had previously done, but this time the greeting was not sweet. It happened so fast. One second she was peeking over the opening, the next the horse had wheeled around, ears flat against its head, teeth bared, ready to take a chunk out of any part of her he could reach. It lunged for her and only Jace's quick action saved her from a vicious bite. A loud, angry scream from the horse followed the near miss.

For several moments, Kelly stood in Jace's arms, trying to slow her racing heart. She'd never had a close call with something that big and that vicious; she'd never been attacked by any animal. She turned her face into the soft, muscle-hugging T-shirt and deeply inhaled Jace's familiar scent as she fought to overcome the fright.

"Kelly, honey, are you all right?"

All she could do was nod. For a few minutes, Kelly stood in his embrace, feeling his strength and power, not wanting to step away.

"That was my fault." His chin rested on the top of her head while his large hand rubbed her back. "This is a stallion here for breeding. The crew is working on the stud barn, but it isn't ready yet. I should have warned you not to open this door. His...job...keeps him a little testy."

Kelly closed her eyes, letting the deep reverberation of Jace's voice calm her. Then, taking a deep breath, she stepped out of his arms and felt a chill that hadn't been there before.

"I should have realized it wasn't a filly by the sheer size of him." She looked at the gleaming black stallion, still aggressively pawing the ground, nostrils flaring, and couldn't help but shiver. That had been a close call. "He's beautiful, though."

She shifted her gaze to Jace's face. Hot fire blazed in his eyes. Despite knowing better, she wanted to walk into that flame until it singed every part of her. In that moment, she wanted Jace to put his arms back around her and hold her forever, consequences be damned.

His gaze held hers as his hands cupped her face. "Kelly," he whispered, his voice graveled and deep.

Every cell in her body screamed for his touch; her lips ached to say *yes*. But Kelly knew there was no future with Jace. He would go back to making his films. Back to the worldwide party scene that was his life. It was inevitable. The ranch was not his home. He'd even told her he'd bought it for some downtime. How could she walk into a situation knowing firsthand how it would end? She hadn't had that foresight before, but this time there was no excuse. And she was frightened. Of herself. Because she loved him. And her resolve to keep Jace at arm's length was weakening more every day.

She stepped back, out of his arms, and he let her go. She knew he could see the desire in her eyes, but she wouldn't say the words he wanted to hear. The words she longed to say.

One of the ranch hands came around the corner, his gaze taking in the two of them standing next to the stall. "Hey, Jace. Glad I caught you. Evening, ma'am."

Kelly gave a forced smile and nodded.

"Lee got the papers for that last colt you bought and said they didn't look right. He told me if I saw you to ask if you could stop by his place in the morning or give him a call."

While the two men talked, Kelly ambled on toward the back of the massive structure. Off to the right she heard something, a small sound coming out of one of the stalls. Curious, she walked in that direction, and the sound gradually got louder. It was a cat. Kelly opened the empty stall door and peeked inside. In the far corner, encased in shadows, a small gray-striped tabby lay on the straw.

"Hi, little one." It meowed in response and sat up. When it did, Kelly spotted more gray underneath where it had been lying. The cat was a female. And she had babies. Three tiny kittens, two gray, one gold, lay sleeping, cuddled together in the bed of straw. The mother showed no fear as she walked to Kelly and rubbed against her legs. Bending over, she ran her hand over the soft fur. Then felt the ribs. The cat was half starved.

Kelly lit out of the stall at a dead run, no second guessing, no consideration needed when an animal, especially a mother, needed help. She didn't slow when she passed Jace and the cowhand, still talking in the center of the isle.

"Kelly?"

"I'll be right back."

She ran out of the barn and down the path to the main house. Entering the kitchen, she grabbed milk from the fridge, and from the pantry, a tin of potted meat, a can of tuna and a breakfast bowl. Racing to the bathroom, she snatched two towels, deep pile and velvety soft. Dumping the food and bowl into one of the towels, she grabbed the carton of milk and ran back to the barn, again passing Jace and the cowboy. She couldn't help but notice a look of curiosity on their faces.

Kelly carefully lifted the kittens and placed them in the center of one of the towels. She folded the second one in half and spread it over the little indention in the hay before gently placing the babies back in the little nest. Mama cat was watching but voiced no concern, as if she understood the human was trying to help. Soon the little cat was enjoying her meat, milk and then some fresh water, eating as if she hadn't had food in a week. Which she probably hadn't.

Kelly felt exhilarated. To be able to help out such tiny, helpless little things in a place that, to them, must be so big and scary was a good feeling. It was with that glow of happiness she turned and saw Jace standing behind her.

He didn't speak for a long moment. "I take it we have guests?"

Kelly quickly shook her head. "Aren't they precious? The mother was so hungry, you can feel her ribs." The smile on her face wavered. "You don't mind, do you, Jace?"

He entered the stall and knelt down next to her, shaking his head. Reaching out, he stroked the cat's back, and then returned his gaze to Kelly. "So what's her name?"

Kelly was radiant. Her face glowed with the innocence of a child on Christmas morning. It was the first time since he'd been back he'd seen that smile and the sparkle in her eyes.

She chewed her bottom lip and damned if he didn't feel a surge of hot need in his groin.

"How about Jacemina? Or…"

"How about Cat?"

"No," she scolded in that you-should-be-ashamed mother's tone. "It has to be a real name. She deserves a real name."

"I had an aunt named Martha," Jace offered. Where that came from he would never know. "Mom's older sister."

"Martha." She said it out loud. He could see the name rolling around in her head. She looked up at him, grinning ear to ear. "It's perfect." And before he had time to let the idea soak in that he now had a cat named Martha who was, apparently, the proud mother of three, Kelly hurled herself toward him. His arms automatically went around her. "Thank you, Jace!"

Jace swallowed hard. Kelly was exactly where he wanted her to be. And she was happy and bubbling. Not because she was in his arms, but because she'd found a cat. His male pride took a hit, but hell, he'd take what he could get.

She finished her spontaneous hug and sat back on her heels. Her eyes moved over his face and a more intense look came into them.

"You're really a very sweet and kind person." She frowned, tilting her head. "I don't know if I ever realized that about you. It's not the same thing as being nice." Of her own volition, she leaned toward him. "Or sexy," she added, placing her lips against his.

His erection jumped to full attention. One arm pulled her closer while his other hand threaded through the silken strands of her long hair. He deepened the kiss, immediate need surging through his body.

"You taste so good," she murmured and he almost lost it. Right there in front of Martha Cat and her babies. Gently, Jace turned her into his arms, her head resting on his upper arm as he held her, his mouth never leaving hers. The moist heat of the kiss sent a shock wave rolling through him. His heart raced, showing no sign of slowing down anytime soon. Her hands cupped the sides of his face and for long moments he enjoyed the pure delight of her touch, the warmth of her body against his, every breath she took. Finally, reluctantly, he pulled back, knowing where they were headed and realizing it would embarrass her if one of the crew walked by.

As she lay in his arms, with her long hair falling over his sleeve and against his shirt, those blue-green eyes holding him spellbound, she reached up and played at his lower lip with her finger, exploring, bringing him to the edge of madness. With a slight movement, he took her finger inside his mouth, sucking, nipping lightly with his teeth. She was killing him. He wanted her beyond anything he'd ever wanted in his life.

"Who'd have thunk it?" She grinned, popped her finger out of his mouth and tapped him on the nose. "Tough guy Jace Compton is a mush melon inside. A sweet, kind man who rescues little kitties."

"Yeah," Jace muttered, reluctantly rising to his feet, pulling Kelly with him. "Who'd have thunk it?"

Ten

Together they headed back to the main house to get Henry. His mother did a double take when they walked into the den, laughing and clearly happy, Jace's arm around Kelly's shoulder. Henry was in the playpen next to where she sat on the sofa paging through fashion magazines.

"Has someone been playing in the hay?" Her smile of welcome turned into a grin of speculation. Her eyes twinkled.

Jace ran a hand through his hair, dislodging several twigs of straw. He then reached over and pulled some from Kelly's long strands.

"Sorry we're late," Kelly said as she walked over to give Mona a hug. "The horses are incredible. There's one that's the color of a copper penny. Mona, you must come out and see her. And the best part—we found *kittens*." She turned and looked at Jace, excitement lighting up her face. "Tell her, Jace."

"We found kittens."

"A mother and three tiny babies. She is almost starved. But I think she'll be okay. She is so sweet. I owe you and Jace for a can of tuna and milk."

"Not a problem, sweetheart. I love cats."

"So do I." Kelly reached for Henry. "Jace named her Martha."

"Did he?" There was a wicked light in her eyes. "Martha Compton. Who would have ever thought?"

"Aunt Martha hated my father," Jace dutifully explained,

seeing the confusion on Kelly's face. "The names Martha and Compton are not synonymous with any feelings remotely seen as warm and fuzzy. That should be a very strong cat." His mother chuckled and Jace leaned over and gave her a kiss on the cheek. "I'm going to walk Kelly back to the cabin."

"I won't wait up." She stood from the sofa. "You both have a good evening. Kelly, perhaps tomorrow you will take me to see the kittens?"

"Absolutely."

With Jace carrying Henry, they walked through the evening shadows to the small house in the trees. Jace followed her inside.

"Do you have time to hold him while I warm his bottle?"

"Sure." As Kelly headed to the kitchen, Jace wondered at the feel of his tiny son in his arms, the weight of his compact little body. It did strange things to Jace's heart. *His son.* He rubbed his face against the downy hair, loving the smell of baby powder, captivated by the little baby sounds. Henry's fist was again planted in his mouth, the sound of his lips smacking interspersed with words only Henry could understand. His head bobbled as he perched on his father's arm. Too soon he began to squirm and whimper.

"What's a matter, Henry?" No amount of coaxing would calm him down. "Kelly, is something wrong?" Jace asked in a concerned tone. "Is he sick?"

"Just hungry." Kelly came forward with the bottle. "Our little man has a very good appetite. Want to feed him?"

His eyes shot to her. It was an offer he hadn't expected. "Yeah. I'd like that."

"Find a seat."

Kelly found it hard to suppress a grin at Jace's intense expression. He sat down, still holding a fussing baby against his chest.

"You need to lay him back in your arms. Pretend he's a football," she suggested.

Nodding, Jace positioned Henry on his left arm, cuddled against his chest.

"Good." Kelly handed him the bottle.

Seeing Henry in his little blue rompers held so lovingly by his big tough dad caused her throat to constrict with emotion. She'd never let herself envision the picture in front of her. A small twinge of sadness touched her heart at the way fate had set their course adrift in different directions. Over the few weeks Jace had been back in her life and now seeing him like this, she knew he would be a great father. *If onlys* flooded her mind. But there was no going back. And there was no going forward. Not together. Destiny wasn't that kind.

Jace seemed to have fallen into a trance as he stared down at the baby in his arms. Henry took his bottle with gusto, his tiny hand gripping Jace's little finger.

"He's amazing," Jace murmured, and then gazed up at Kelly. "He looks just like you."

"No." She shook her head, quick to disagree. "He looks like *you*. Even has your dimples. I hope he doesn't become as bullheaded."

Jace made a huffing sound. She leaned against the wall, content to watch as Jace fed his son.

"I never intended to have kids," Jace said unexpectedly, his eyes glued on his son. "I never pictured a child in my life. Like you said, I'm gone more than I'm home. And even then, there's always something I have to do, something going on. It never stops. Meetings, overnight trips, PR campaigns... This is the longest I've ever managed to stay put."

She shrugged. He hadn't said anything she hadn't already suspected. "It's your job. It's what you do." *It's your choice.*

"Yeah." His tone was not happy. He glanced over at Kelly. "Do you think about his future? Who he will be? What he'll want to do with his life?"

"Every day."

Jace's gaze returned to the baby in his arms. The look on

Jace's face was intense. It was as though his mind had taken him to another place. And not necessarily a good place.

"He's so amazing. From his fingers to his toes…he's perfect. And so innocent." He watched Henry slurp on his evening feeding. After a few long moments, Jace's gaze returned to Kelly. "I don't understand people who would ever hurt a child," he blurted out.

Kelly's eyes widened in surprise. Where did that come from? Had Jace witnessed abuse at some point in his past? Might that be a reason Jace didn't want a family?

"There are all kinds of people, Jace," she said gently, wanting to take away the misery in his expression. "You above all know that, with the oddball fans you have to deal with. You just have to make sure to keep your child safe and well away from any potential harm. That's just part of the job of being a father."

She saw his jaw muscles clench. He nodded and swallowed hard.

"Yeah." Then he seemed to realize the path his mind was on and changed the subject. "When did your grandfather pass away?"

"Um…about a week after you left."

"Was he sick very long?"

"No. Some developers were after his farm and I think he was really stressed over that. They claimed his title was invalid. I came home from school the week after New Year's and found him. He'd had a massive stroke. By the time the paramedics got there it was too late. A letter of eviction was on the floor next to him."

She couldn't stop the sudden rush of moisture that burned her eyes. She lowered her head, hoping Jace wouldn't notice.

"What happened to your parents, if you don't mind my asking?"

It was Kelly's turn to take a few minutes to formulate her answer. She hadn't expected the question, didn't quite know what to say and wasn't at all sure she wanted to go there. It had been a really great evening, and talking about her parents was jumping off a very high cliff with no possibility of a good outcome at the bottom. Finally, she decided to leave off the sugarcoating and tell him the truth. Let him read into it what he would.

"My father, apparently, wasn't happy at home. Like you, he traveled a lot. But even when he was home, there were other women. Lots of other women. A couple of them were the mothers of my classmates. *That* was fun."

Jace frowned. "How do you mean?"

"My classmates blamed me for breaking up their homes..." It wasn't something she wanted to remember. "Gossip was rampant. The stories grew bigger and bigger. It...it was a tough time for us." Her dad was the playboy of the year if the rumor mill was to be believed. But Kelly didn't say it out loud. What good could come of it? "Mom refused to leave him. She just numbed her pain with liquor and pills. She finally got the right combination when I was sixteen." Tears sprang to Kelly's eyes. She put her hand over her mouth, taking a few seconds to get her emotions under control. She rubbed the tears away and blinked hard. "Sorry. Anyway, Dad came to the funeral, but we never saw him again after that."

"*Damn.* I'm sorry, Kelly."

She shrugged. "He didn't care. He wasn't meant to be married. All he wanted was a good time. Gramps was a kind man and we loved him. I hate to think what might have happened had he not stepped forward and taken us in. I finished high school, got a student loan, started at the university and for a while, life went on. Until he died. Then it was Matt and me against the world." She had to smile. "I think we did pretty good. You couldn't ask for a better brother, but don't you dare tell Matt I said that." *Keep it light. Grit your teeth and get through this.*

She'd lost her parents because her father was a two-faced cheating bastard who was too spineless to end the mar-

riage. Her mother had been too weak to leave him. She'd
lost Gramps after a wealthy man and his high-priced attorneys found or fabricated a loophole in the deed and took
his farm. And here she sat, smack in the middle of a lion's
den, Jace being both a philanderer and as wealthy as they
come. She'd given birth to his baby and already experienced the temptation to return to his bed. She was as big a
fool as her mother.

The silence that filled the room was deafening. Gone
was the lighthearted camaraderie from earlier. It would be
so easy to let the rest of the tears fall. But she refused. The
very last thing she wanted was Jace's pity. She had to wonder if he saw the similarities between him and her father. At
least Jace hadn't gotten married before he'd begun *chasing
the skirts*, as Gramps used to call it. He'd never had anything good to say about Kelly's father. She couldn't help
but speculate what her grandpa would have thought of Jace.

The loud sound of Henry sucking on an empty bottle
suddenly filled the room.

"I think he's finished." She stepped forward and took
the bottle, glad for the interruption.

"What's next?"

Kelly placed a cloth over Jace's shoulder. "Hold him upright next to your chest. Be careful to support his head. Put
one hand under his butt and gently pat his back with the
other. Just pretend your favorite starlet needs consoling."

Jace shot her a warning glance, and then wrestled Henry
around until he was against his shoulder. It was a sight to
behold. Jace's hand was as big as Henry's entire back. But
his touch was gentle, as though Henry were so fragile he
might break. In fact, Jace was only patting the folds of
Henry's shirt.

"You're gonna need to pat him a little harder if you want
to get that bubble out." The look Jace gave her was something close to panic. Some tabloid would pay big bucks for
a picture of this. "It's okay, Jace. He won't break."

Jace nodded and tried again. After considerable time had passed, Henry turned his head toward his father and appeared to nuzzle his neck. Seconds later, Kelly heard the burp. It was followed by a small stream of milk. Completely missing the cloth, it trickled down Jace's thick neck and into his shirt.

He looked up at Kelly, and the expression on his face was priceless. She hurried to take the baby.

"He's been a little fussy today. Teething. Sorry about that."

Jace cleared his throat and stood up. "No problem."

"He's ready for his bath and then bed."

"I think I know the feeling." He stood and reached for his shirt, pulling the wet material away from his neck.

Kelly bit her lip to keep from laughing. "Bath time can be fun."

"I couldn't agree more with you there," he said, his eyes glinting wickedly. "Baths and showers can be an amazingly good time."

Heat rushed up her neck. He was not talking about bathing a baby. She knew only too well what Jace could do with a bar of soap and a little warm water.

"But this time I think I'll pass." Jace stopped before he stepped outside, still holding his collar away from his skin. "Thanks for…this, Kelly."

"Sure." She covered her mouth with her hand in an effort to hold back a giggle. From smiles to tears and back to laughter. Such was a day spent in the presence of Jace Compton.

Jace followed the path back to the main house, his mind spinning, his gut churning. He and Kelly had been together only weeks before her grandfather died. At a time when she needed him the most, he was twelve hundred miles away listening to Bret tell him lies about her, insisting Jace not call her as he'd promised. By the day of the funeral, he'd been on his way to South America for a film shoot.

He rubbed the back of his neck, a sinking feeling in his gut. A man couldn't get a whole lot lower. He hadn't known her circumstances, but he should have called her before he ever boarded that plane. It explained so much: why she'd left school, why she worked two jobs, why she had to support Matt and her baby. Why, when he'd come to his senses and tried to call, the phone had been disconnected. No wonder she resented him. Hell. She had every right. It was a miracle she didn't hate him.

Did she think he was just like her father?

The thought sent a sickening surge through his body. His actions toward her so far, combined with the bullshit facade he had to perpetuate for the public... Yeah. He could see how she would. And there was not one damn thing he could do to change it.

He respected Kelly for her strength and tenacity. But he knew firsthand how fast that strength could fly out the window when facing down a cruel, vicious adversary twice your size: an intoxicated man determined to hurt you and your child. That his mother had survived and managed to hide them and keep them safe when his father got out of prison was nothing short of a miracle.

Not for the first time, Jace cursed his fate. Having Kelly and Henry here, seeing them, interacting with them, was everything he'd ever longed for. A perfect family. One he could never have. He'd been serious the day he'd told Kelly if she was concerned about public speculation to marry him. But she'd been right when she called him on it. A marriage between them could never last. But not for the reasons she thought. It had nothing to do with Henry. It was because there was a monster inside him, a monster that could hurt Kelly and the baby. Marriage would work fine on paper. Put the gossips to rest. But a real marriage and family, for him, could never happen.

Kelly was a temptation to which he'd become addicted.

He wanted her until it hurt; it was almost unbearable torment every time she came near.

He had to get a handle on it.

Kelly deserved a man who could give her forever. A guy who would pamper her and protect her, not turn on her someday. Not only had his old man convinced Jace he was worthless and then died before Jace could prove him wrong, he'd ensured, even after he was dead and buried, that his son's life was on a direct downhill course to hell.

Eleven

"I'll be damned," Jace muttered under his breath as he leaned out over the railing. They were grilling something. One of the cowboys had rolled in an outdoor grill from God knows where and they were actually grilling food—maybe hot dogs?—just outside of Kelly's cabin. Jace squinted to get a better look. There were binoculars in the study downstairs, but he refused to stoop to that level. Yet.

From the balcony outside his bedroom, he had a fairly clear view of the front of her little house. He'd first noticed the Friday night gathering three weeks ago. He'd heard laughter coming from that direction and stepped outside, wondering who it was and what could be so damned funny.

At first he'd seen old Sam, the ranch foreman, Decker and another trainer sitting out on the tiny porch with Kelly. The next weekend, he'd given into curiosity and looked again. This time they'd been joined by at least a half dozen cowboys, sitting on crates, laughing the night away. Even Matt later joined the party. The little group had grown until now almost every unmarried hand working on the ranch sat circled around that porch. And in the middle of all those lonesome, lusting, hungry men sat the princess bee herself. Kelly drew them like a budding flower, and every drone in the county wanted to get close in spite of the fact that some nights she bounced the baby on her lap. *His* baby. She'd invited him to stop by but he had no wish to join the crowd while they sat and ogled Kelly. It was none of his concern, but at the same time he fought the overwhelming urge to go down there and beat the living crap out of any one of the bastards who tried to put the moves on her.

Adding to his frustration was the knowledge that he'd been the one who had convinced her to move to the little house. He'd wanted her to be close. He'd never considered he wouldn't be the only one she would be close to.

And now they were cooking for her. *Dammit to hell.*

"Jace?" his mother called from inside his room. He turned and headed in that direction. If she caught a glimpse of the goings-on at the little cottage and him leaning over the balcony railing, she might get the wrong idea.

"What are you doing?"

Why did he suddenly feel like a ten-year-old who'd gotten caught with his hand in the cookie jar? He stepped inside and closed the door behind him. "Just getting some fresh air. What's up? Are you okay?"

"Oh, I'm fine. I was just curious if you'd gone to the party."

He couldn't miss the mischievous light dancing in her eyes. "Party?"

"The one at Kelly's cabin."

Damn. "I didn't know about any party."

"Uh-huh. Well, I'm sure you'd be welcome. Why don't you go down and join them?"

The last thing he wanted to do was be yet another bee blazing a trail to Kelly's sweet nectar. "I'm really kinda busy. Need to read the new script. I don't have time to go to a party."

"Right." Turning, she walked toward the door. "Whatever you say. Just wanted to let you know I'm going out this evening."

"Out? Where? With who?"

"Thomas—Dr. Sullivan—invited me to have dinner. He should be here anytime."

"Oh." Jace felt a twinge of uneasiness mixed with surprise. Granted, Sullivan was the town doctor who commanded a certain amount of respect, but what did they really know about him? Jace couldn't prevent visions of his father's fist slamming into her delicate jaw time after time from flashing through his mind. His instinct to protect her was strong. He supposed he should try to remember his mother was, after all, an adult. And the doctor wasn't his father. Still, Jace gritted his teeth. "I don't suppose you'd consider letting one of the security team—"

"Absolutely not."

He nodded. "Well, then have a good time."

"I intend to." She winked and turned toward the door to his suite. "Oh," she said over her shoulder, "the binoculars are in the desk in your office downstairs if they would help with your...work. Bye-bye."

Jace pulled both hands through his hair. Dammit to hell. He had to get a grip on this Kelly thing. He'd become like a daytime barn owl, practically living in the office in the main stable in an attempt to stay away from the house as much as possible. When he did give it up and return to the house, it was straight to the gym or his office to check emails. The new script had arrived, but it sat unread on his desk; Jace had found neither the concentration nor the motivation to even open the mailing envelope. Something had to change or he could plan on spending the rest of his nights pacing the balcony like some seriously messed-up loser.

It was impossible to treat Kelly as just a friend. He refused to be just another of the drooling, lusting men clustering around her. His body knew she was his and responded accordingly regardless of the time and place.

Kelly was the only one who ever came close to being *the* woman in his life. He'd been with beautiful women. He'd known women with kindness in their hearts. But Kelly had that unique something, that special quality that brought it all together. She was in a league of her own. A treasure that remained out of reach.

Jace suspected part of what had kept him from coming

back sooner was a deep-seated fear he was getting too involved with her. He'd begun picturing them together. Forever. He hadn't been prepared for that. And in light of the monster he might someday become, it had frightened him.

But now, over a year later, things had changed. He had a son. And he was still as infatuated with Kelly as he'd ever been. What would happen if he risked it? Kept her in his life? The idea was making him crazy.

Sleeping with another woman was not appealing. But if he persisted and seduced Kelly, he might hurt her someday. It was a hell of a dilemma.

A wave of laughter from outside drifted into the room. *Dammit to hell.*

"C Bar Ranch," Kelly said into the phone.

On Monday Jace asked her to take on the additional duty of answering his private line. Lee arrived with new horses and everyone was running in high gear. At least that was the excuse. Whether Kelly believed it was still open to speculation. Initially the calls went to his voice mail, but by Monday afternoon, that was full. Now, three days later, the calls were coming in fast and furious and Jace had yet to clear them from his phone. No surprise there.

"Just see if you can help them," he'd instructed. "Take their names and numbers. I'll call them back later. If it sounds urgent, try to page me."

They all sounded urgent. Kelly didn't like it. She didn't want to know who called him, hated talking to the smug-sounding women, but she hadn't come up with an acceptable reason to refuse. Yet.

"I have Joanna Reed calling for Jace Compton." The woman's voice was pleasant and professional. A nice change from most of the other callers.

"I'm sorry. Mr. Compton is not currently available. Perhaps I can help you?"

"No. Thank you. Miss Reed must speak directly with Mr. Compton. It's urgent she reach him as soon as possible."

Of course it was. "One moment, please. I'll try and page him." *Urgent* was the magic word. Kelly placed the call on hold and punched the intercom for the barn office. "Jace, you have a call on line one," she said, using their code for his private phone.

There was no answer. *Surprise. Surprise.*

"Jace, if you're there, please pick up."

"Kelly, this is Lee. Jace headed back to the house an hour ago. Don't know what to tell you past that."

"Okay. Thanks."

She punched the button for the house intercom. "Jace, a Miss Joanna Reed is holding on your private line." After waiting several seconds, Kelly returned to the caller. "I'm sorry. Mr. Compton isn't answering the page. Would you care to leave a message?"

She heard voices in the background, and then another voice came on the line.

"This is Joanna Reed. What is the problem?"

"As I've explained to your secretary, Mr. Compton is not near a phone. I'll be happy to take a—"

Her end of the conversation had caught Mona's attention. The older woman stood and walked toward Kelly's desk. Kelly put the call on speaker. Might as well share the wealth.

"Then find him. This is outrageous."

"I'm sorry, Ms. Reed. I seem to have lost the ability to make someone appear by snapping my fingers or twitching my nose. I'll be sure to get that checked. Again, I'll be glad to take your number."

"Do you honestly think he doesn't have it?"

"I really wouldn't know."

Kelly looked at Mona. This was ridiculous. Mona put her slender hand over her mouth to stifle a laugh as her shoulders began to shake.

"Will there be anything else?"

"Just one thing. I will reach Jace eventually and you might as well start packing up your things. You are gone."

"I appreciate the early notification."

"You can also tell Jace the next time he…needs me… I'll be busy. And the fault will be yours."

"Have a nice day."

Kelly terminated the call. Mona and Jace paid her well, but not nearly enough to take that crap.

"I'm not doing this," she said to Mona with as much calm as she could muster. It was the hundredth such call in the past three days, each one progressively worse than the last. Crazy women. Acting as if they owned Jace Compton.

"You might try the gym," Mona said, an impish twinkle in her eyes.

"Thanks." Kelly stomped out of the room and headed for the first-floor gym.

When she rounded the corner, sure enough, Jace was lying on a bench, his hands gripping a barbell with several weights on either end, straining to push it up and down. Beads of sweat ran down his face and neck, his biceps ballooning to an enormous size. She didn't want to startle him and cause an accident, so she stood next to the wall and waited. The man who usually flew in and trained with him every few days was not here. Should Jace be doing this alone?

Finally, he set the heavy bar on the rack and sat up. Grabbing a towel hanging nearby, he wiped his face and neck.

She cleared her throat. Jace saw her for the first time and tilted his head with a surprised look.

"Kelly?"

"I refuse to answer your phone. I *refuse*," she repeated, leaning forward, her hands perched at her waist.

His eyebrows rose. "Okay. Mind telling me why?"

"Like you don't know." She couldn't hold back a sarcastic laugh. "Do you have any idea how many lunatics call you in a day? Never mind. Of course you do. That's why you stuck me with the job. Then you refuse to answer my page and I'm the one who gets attacked."

"Attacked?" He stood up from the bench. His ragged cutoffs rode low on his waist and molded to the muscular hips and thighs. That's all he was wearing. The tanned flesh of his muscled chest and flat stomach glistened with perspiration.

Good Lord. Couldn't the man put on some clothes?

"They think I'm lying to them. Cherry Newton has called four times. Today. Do people make up these names? That sounds like a sandwich cookie you'd pull off a tree. She's threatening to have me arrested, insinuating I must have done something to you to keep you from talking to her. Cora Spager—Stagler —has called ten times. *Ten*. The last call, I had to sit and listen to her alternately rage and cry for almost an hour. I just got off the phone with the Wicked Witch of the West, who said I should tell you the next time you *needed* her—" Kelly made a snorting sound "—she wouldn't be available and it was entirely my fault. How exactly is it *my* fault? Oh, she also said that I should be forewarned—this is my last day of employment. Finally, some good news."

Kelly noted the grin he was trying to hide, and her irritation doubled. "This is not funny, Jace. Your idiotic calls are taking my time away from Mona and making me crazy."

"I'm sorry." The wicked glitter in his eyes told her he was not sorry at all. His spicy male scent was strong from his workout, and her body responded to the sight of his sculpted chest, sweaty and gleaming. She tried to swallow but her mouth had gone dry.

"Then hire an agency. Use a call center," she said in a ragged voice, then tried to clear her throat, fighting the response of her traitorous body. "But don't expect me to bite my lip while those ladies, and I use the term loosely, call me every name in the book."

As soon as she said the word *lip*, his eyes focused on that part of her face.

"Say no more." He moved closer. "Because no one is going to bite those lips but me."

"Jace." She began to back out of the room, shaking her head. "I'm serious."

"So am I."

"Don't do this."

"You feel it, too."

The husky timbre of his voice told her he sensed the change in her. She'd made a huge mistake coming to the gym. She fought to maintain her poise, taking calm, steady breaths. *Just get out of here.*

A smile played at the corners of his full lips. "I think you want me…to kiss you again."

Yes. "No." She again cleared her throat. "No, I don't." It was almost a whisper. Another step away from him and she felt the wall against her back. A heady sexual tension mixed with a touch of panic enveloped her.

"I damn sure want to kiss you. Hell, I want to do a lot more than that."

"Jace…"

He looped the small towel around his neck and placed his hands against the wall on either side of her head, his huge biceps bulging. She felt the coolness against her back, a vivid contrast to the smoldering heat radiating from him.

"It's making me crazy having you here, seeing you every day and never touching you."

Bending down, he placed his warm mouth against the very place under her ear he knew caused sweet shivers to run through her. She couldn't repress a little cry as her eyes closed and her skin sizzled. Her hands came up against his granite chest and she felt the strong steady beat of his heart.

"Kelly." His intonation was so deep, so mesmerizing, he held her captive using nothing more than his voice.

"You don't play fair," she murmured against his lips,

which were so tantalizingly close. She sounded breathy to her own ears. "We shouldn't do this."

"Who are you trying to convince? Me or yourself? Admit it, Kelly. Say you want me and let's stop this damned cat-and-mouse game."

"I don't think—"

"Good. I don't want you to think. Just go with your feelings."

With a small whimper, Kelly leaned forward, moving her lips even closer to his, seeking the pleasure she knew was there. Jace didn't wait a full heartbeat before his mouth took hers, fiercely, deeply, his tongue filling every crevice. "Say it, Kelly," he groaned, before kissing her again, intensely, with such passion she couldn't have spoken had she wanted to. She heard him growl, and his mouth opened wider, hungrily, as though he couldn't get enough.

Kelly was lost. She couldn't fight this. No one could. It was as though the power of the mythical god Zeus surged through him, proving that all the stories of his erotic escapades were true. Mere mortal women didn't stand a chance. Jace's arms came around her, pulling her closer to his hard frame. His arousal pressed against her belly, and like a branding iron, it singed her skin through her clothes, making sure she knew she was his. She couldn't stop the small moan forming deep in her throat, but it was swallowed by his hungry mouth.

His big hands slid under her hips, lifting her, pulling her tightly against him, making her feel his body's reaction to her, his heavy thickness leaving no doubt what he wanted. She wanted the same. She needed to feel him against her core with shameless intensity.

"Jace?"

A distant voice broke into the moment.

"Hey man, you in the gym?" The head trainer called out from the den, no doubt heading in their direction.

Jace lifted his head and stared into her eyes. "Someday

very soon, your luck is going to run out." He stepped back and dropped his arms. "Yeah," he called out to Lee, still holding her with his gaze.

"I'll make a deal with you, Kelly. Stop the damn Friday night smorgasbord and I'll take care of the phone calls."

Her mouth dropped open. "*That's* what answering your phone is about?" Jace saw her visiting with some of the ranch hands…and he was *jealous*? Jace Compton? The man wasn't jealous of anyone or anything on the planet. He could have any woman he wanted. But the aroused hunk standing two feet in front of her appeared deadly serious. "They are just a few nice cowboys who—"

"Who would take you to their bed in a heartbeat. You're the mother of *my* child," he snarled as if she didn't know that.

"And your point is?"

Jace's eyes narrowed, his nostrils flaring with emotion. "If you need sex, you come to me."

He did not just say that. "I'll tell you what, Compton. You hold your breath until that happens. See how that works for you."

With a last glare, Kelly turned and stomped to the door, colliding smack into the trainer as she rounded the corner. Only Lee's quick reflexes kept her from falling on her butt.

Her mind was blown. The very idea that Jace could ever be envious of the men on the ranch was just not believable. She was an employee in his house, which made her a convenience. That's all it was. He needed to get out of the house for a few days. He needed to be reminded there was an entire world waiting for him outside the boundaries of this ranch and that world was filled with beautiful, desirable women who would do anything to be with him. To say he was a very potent package was an understatement. And the idea that he could be in any way jealous… It was too much to take in.

It took a good part of the afternoon to push Jace's antics

in the gym out of her mind. With Henry napping and Mona there to watch him, Kelly finally went downstairs, gathered a can of cat food and a couple of apples, and headed for the barn. The need to make love with Jace again, to feel his hands and body work their magic, was eating her up inside. She might as well admit defeat. It didn't matter what she felt for him, be it mere physical attraction or something more: he was dangerous. In every single way that mattered. And that enticing element, in itself, would be her undoing.

Wednesday evening Kelly had just settled Henry for the night when there was a knock on the door. One of the ranch hands stood on the porch, his hat in his hands. Kelly remembered meeting him the day she'd moved in.

"Decker?"

"Evening, Kelly. Are you busy?"

"No." She shook her head. "I just put the baby to bed."

"They're having a barn dance at the Bar H spread to celebrate the birth of their daughter. I was curious if you were going and if you might need a ride."

"No, I mean, I didn't know anything about it. Shea and I haven't talked in months."

"Well, I realize it's late notice. I just found out about it myself. It's only intended for the employees and family, but I remember you saying you and Shea were close. I doubt they will mind if you crash the party."

"Oh, I'd love to go," she said, the idea of seeing her friend again immediately taking root. "But I don't have anyone to keep my son. Unless…" *Would Mona watch him for a couple of hours?* "I can ask Mona if she'll sit with the baby. How long did you plan to stay?"

"That's entirely up to you."

Stepping inside, she grabbed the cell off the kitchen counter and dialed Mona's private line. She answered in two rings. After Kelly explained what she needed, Mona enthusiastically agreed.

"I'll bring Henry to the house in just a few minutes. Thank you, Mona."

Decker grinned when she told him she had a babysitter.

"How about if I pick you up in front of the main house in about ten minutes?"

"Perfect."

It would be so great to see Shea again. They hadn't had a chance to visit in far too long. Between Kelly working two jobs and having a new baby to care for and Shea and Alec spending the summer in Europe, the opportunity just hadn't been there. She grabbed the baby bag, gathered a sleeping Henry in her arms and hurried to the main house, excitement at seeing her old friend quickening her steps.

She didn't see Jace as she climbed the stairs to Mona's suite. In fact, she hadn't seen him that day at all. She didn't know if he had as yet met Shea and her husband but maybe he would like to go. Mona was waiting at the top of the stairs, her arms reaching out to take the baby into her arms.

"Do you know where Jace is?"

"He's in Dallas talking with some people about a new film."

"Oh." So much for that idea. "Okay then. I'll see you later. Thanks so much for doing this, Mona."

Decker was waiting when she came back downstairs and they were on their way to the Bar H.

"Wow," Decker said as he turned his truck into the long, rambling driveway of Shea's ranch. "That's some house."

"Shea's husband, Alec, is an architect and builder. Shea was devastated when her old ranch house burned down. Alec went over and above when he built their new home." The sprawling three-story Victorian-style house with its turret towers and four chimneys peeking over the high roof was the talk of three counties.

"I guess. Man."

They pulled into the designated parking area. Kelly heard the music and laughter as soon as she opened her door. The aroma of mesquite logs burning in the large grill tempted all to come and bring their plate.

"I think I see Shea over there." Decker pointed to a huge oak tree. "Go ahead and say hello and I'll catch up with you later."

"Thanks, Decker." Kelly raced to where Shea sat in a lawn chair.

"Shea?"

"Oh my gosh. Kelly!" Shea rose to her feet and the two friends embraced. "It's so great to see you."

"Same here. You look so good."

"Let's get you a chair. I want to know everything that's been happening. How are Matt and Henry?"

"They're good." Kelly grinned as she pulled a vacant chair next to Shea's. "I'm so happy for you. Congratulations on your new baby."

"Thanks. I want you to see her before you leave."

"I would love to. How is Alec handling being the dad to a little girl?"

Shea rolled her eyes. "She has him rolled around her little finger. You'd think she was the only baby girl ever born." It was wonderful talking with Shea and the time passed much too quickly. Too soon it was time to go. But Shea wouldn't let her leave without seeing her new baby.

"Come meet Alexandra Christine." Shea led the way across the yard and into the house. After a short tour of the magnificent home, they went up the staircase to the nursery where a sitter sat reading. Shea lifted the infant from the crib.

"Oh, Shea. She's beautiful. She looks just like you!"

"That's what Alec says. I've never seen a man go totally off the deep end over a baby. He hired a nurse for the first six weeks, then questioned everything she said or did. After a few days he decided he knew what his daughter needed better than she did. I think her leaving was by mutual agreement."

Kelly smiled but was suddenly struck with the hopelessness of her own situation. To have Jace always around every day to watch his son grow and develop into a fine man was a dream Kelly kept locked away deep inside. She'd long ago accepted it would never happen. But in moments like this, she couldn't stop the hope from breaking free, only to have it wither and die in the chill of reality.

"It's so great we're neighbors now," Shea was saying. "You've gotta come over when you have time. Bring Henry."

Kelly nodded, not trusting her voice. If Shea noticed that she'd suddenly became quiet she said nothing. She just leaned over and gave Kelly a hug.

Outside, Kelly easily spotted Decker. When she approached him, his grin faded and he frowned in concern. She tried to smile but Decker apparently sensed something was wrong and asked if she was ready to leave. Was she that transparent? Not good.

"Thank you so much, Decker," she said as they made their back to his truck.

"No problem. I'm glad you got to see your friend." Decker was a nice guy, and with his blond hair and good looks, he certainly wasn't hard on the eyes. But he wasn't Jace.

She slipped from his truck and entered the house. Walking through the kitchen, she headed for the stairs, not bothering to turn on any lights. There was enough radiant light spilling into the house for her to see where she was going.

Before she reached the room Mona had deemed as a temporary nursery, a dark shadow on the left moved toward her. Kelly barely held in a shriek.

"Did you have a good night?"

"Jace. You scared me." What was he doing standing in a darkened hallway? "Yes. I did, thank you."

She moved forward but Jace stepped in front of her, blocking her way. Through the dim glow of the night-light Mona insisted on having at the top of the stairs, she could see he was dressed in only a pair of old jeans. And he wasn't smiling.

"I wasn't aware you were dating anyone."

Did he really have any right to know if she was or wasn't? How rude would it be to just keep walking?

She shrugged. "I'm not." She gave him that much and tried to step around him, wanting to get Henry and go to her cabin. Jace again blocked her way.

"That's not what it looked like to me."

Oh, here we go. Mr. Macho was back.

"You don't consider going out with Decker a date?" Jace continued.

"He gave me a ride to the Bar H," she explained, forcing her voice to remain calm. "Shea just had her baby a couple of weeks ago. Their ranch crew honored her and her husband with a party. They had a barbecue. It wasn't a date. And you weren't here. I asked Mona, thinking you might like to go. Do you know Shea and her husband, Alec?" No answer. "Do you know their ranch hands?" No answer. She'd take bets he was clenching his teeth.

Again she attempted to step to the side and continue on her way. And again, Jace blocked her path.

"Decker has a reputation, Kelly."

"So do you." She was starting to get angry.

"Did he kiss you?"

She glared at him, refusing to answer.

He rubbed the back of his neck, before meeting her gaze across the short space that separated them. "Do you think about us, Kelly? About those three weeks when we first met?" he asked in a low, husky tone.

Her heart increased in tempo. If only he knew.

Twelve

"Do you ever think about the time we spent together?"

"I... Jace, don't do this." She shook her head. Her emotions were already raw, splintered. After seeing Shea's baby and again facing the reality of her own situation, she felt as if she'd been pulled inside out, every nerve in her body scraped raw. Before her stood the man who had given her the world. Then taken it away.

"I think about it," he said as though needing her to know.

Something inside her snapped. "Then why didn't you call?" The unfairness suddenly overwhelmed her and she almost screamed the words as she blinked back angry tears. "Why didn't you come back? I will not be a convenience, Jace. I'll never again be simply a diversion to relieve some rich man's boredom. Now please let me by."

"You were never just a diversion. Dammit, Kelly."

He pulled her hard against him, his hot mouth coming down over hers. For a few seconds, she fought to be free of his arms, pushing against his wide shoulders, crying on the inside as she fought the overwhelming need to embrace him.

This was Jace. This was the man she loved. His lips, his scent, his voice, the feel of his powerful arms holding her firmly but gently, was what she'd longed for all those many months. This was the never-ending dream that came to her on those nights when she was too weak to push it away.

With a small desperate whimper of defeat, she gave in to her weakness, clutched the front of his shirt and opened her lips, letting him in. She kissed him back with an urgency propelled by the torturous need that had ripped at her soul for so many months. No longer held in check, the bittersweet memories pummeled the last remaining bits of her resolve. She gloried in his kiss once again, warmed by the heat of his body, his hard erection pressing against her stomach. His hungry mouth devoured hers as he pulled her closer. She felt his heart beating as fast as her own as his tongue explored the recesses of her mouth, enticing hers to do the same. His hands moved to cup her face, holding her to his, and she heard him moan.

He swept her into his arms and carried her into his bedroom and kicked the door closed behind them. Not breaking the kiss, Jace set her down next to the bed and made quick work removing her blouse. She absently felt him remove her bra, felt the cool air on her skin as his hands cupped her, squeezing gently, his thumbs playing across the sensitive nubs, making them harden under his touch. Bending down, he took one firm nipple into his mouth, sucking gently. Kelly moaned at the exquisite pleasure. Her back arched, her breasts swelled under his touch. He moved to the other breast, giving it the same attention. She heard the faint sound of a zipper being opened and her jeans were pushed down and over her hips. Then his mouth returned to hers and Kelly became lost in the sensation, in the gut-wrenching need overtaking her. Fisting her hands in his hair, she held on as the room began to spin. She felt a floating sensation, and then absently realized she was in his bed, covers thrown back, her jeans tugged from her legs.

He used his knee to ease her legs apart, and then settled on top of her. His hard erection pushed almost painfully, urgently against her core. His breath was hot against her skin as he kissed her neck, slowly moving to her ear, nipping and kissing her jaw before returning to her mouth.

A white-hot flow of heat coursed through her body, building into an unrelenting fire at the apex of her thighs. Her need reached a frantic level as she twisted, trying to adjust her position and take him inside. He was breathing hard as his lips and tongue continued to feed, the sheer heat of his mouth making her want to embrace him, to give in to what they both wanted.

Kelly was out of her mind. Her hips arched against him, conveying her need. She wanted to feel more of Jace. Inside her. Filling her.

Jace unzipped his jeans and let them fall. He felt a long-forgotten tingle at the base of his spine and knew he had to get inside her, fast. She was so damned hot he was going to lose it. Grabbing some protection from the drawer in his nightstand, he quickly put it in place. With Kelly, it had always been like this: a raw, gripping, almost unquenchable need that made them frantic in their actions to unite as one. With one hand, he tested her, two fingers pressed inside, eliciting a soft moan.

"Are you ready for me, Kelly?" he murmured against her ear.

Her body arched against his hand, silently conveying her need. With the pulse hammering in his veins he covered her, positioned his shaft at her core and experienced that tingle again, this time radiating up his spine, splintering his mind. Any illusions that he could take it slow went up in flames as he pushed his heavy length inside, filling her...

Sweat broke out on Jace's forehead and he knew taking this easy was not going to happen. With a rough growl, he pushed still deeper, unable to completely absorb the almost painful pleasure of the throbbing heat that encased him.

"Are you okay?"

She gave a partial nod and pulled his mouth back to hers.

As he began to move, she moaned, biting his lower lip, her hands gripping his back, attempting to hold him to her, expressing the same intense need that ran through him. His lips covered hers, his tongue filling her, simulating what was happening below.

Faster. Deeper. More intense. Until Jace lost hold on reality. He gripped her hips, raising her to him, and pushed even deeper. He rolled his hips and her head fell back against the pillow, her open mouth sending a clear message needing no words. As he took them to the next plane, he returned to the temptations of her lips and she drew his tongue inside, sucking hard. Jace's control snapped. He began to pummel against her, thrusting deeper and deeper with every stroke. He was going to lose it. Suddenly, Kelly stilled and cried out, all the air leaving her body as she arched up against him, shattering in raw pleasure. Her body clenching around him pushed Jace over the top. He couldn't hold back his own ragged moan as the intensity of his release overtook him, pulsating deep within her, spasm after spasm as if there were no end.

It seemed to take a millennium before the stars began to drift back down and settle in his totally shattered brain. His body lost its grip on whatever strength remained. Overwhelmed with heady weakness, he dropped to his side.

His hands found her face and he kissed her softly, loving the scent, the taste that was only Kelly. He felt her tremble as she kissed him back.

She was his.

"Did I hurt you?" he asked against her lips.

Her answer was a smile against his lips and a soft moan in the key of *no*.

The next morning, Kelly worked on the correspondence, logging the RSVPs for the charity gala and responding to both those who would be coming and, as a courtesy, those who would not.

She felt as though Mona could somehow tell what had happened between her son and Kelly just by looking at her face. Therefore, Kelly made every attempt not to look at Mona, turning a different direction if the older woman came into the doorway of her small office. If Mona noticed anything amiss, she chose to say nothing. But it wasn't Kelly's imagination that Jace's mom was smiling more than normal. But Kelly was, too; hopefully Mona didn't catch on.

The work was steady throughout the day. The detailed to-do list for the charity ball required Kelly's concentration, which kept her from reexperiencing the sensations brought by Jace's hands the night before. At least a little.

"Penny for your thoughts…" said a deep voice in her ear.

Kelly jumped and looked up to find the very subject of her thoughts directly in front of her. Bracing his hands on the edge of the small desk, Jace leaned toward her and raised his eyebrows, a small sexy smile on his full lips. She could feel the blush spread over her face.

Before she could respond, she heard Matt's voice call out, followed by footsteps running up the stairs. He entered the room in a full run.

"Kelly. Oh. Hi, Jace. Mrs. Compton." He was grinning from ear to ear. "Guess what happened today? You're never gonna believe it!" He was barely able to contain his enthusiasm. "Frank Gentry broke his leg during football practice!"

Kelly stared at him as though he'd lost his mind. She glanced at Mona, who had a curious look on her face. Jace straightened and placed his hands on his hips, as if waiting for more.

"This is *not* good news, Matt."

"Wait—his dad told Coach Hager he'll probably be out for the rest of the season. The coach talked to me privately and asked me to take his place. Oh, man. It's the *varsity* team, Kelly. I'll be the only sophomore on it."

"Oh my gosh. That's great, Matt." She jumped up from her chair and gave her brother a hug.

"Absolutely. Congratulations, Matt," Mona said.

"That's great, dude." Jace grinned.

"It's all because of you. All the pointers you gave me and how much you made me practice. Oh, man. Thanks, Jace."

"I didn't really do anything, but you are entirely welcome for whatever you think I did. I'm proud of you, Matt."

"I wish you could come to the game. It's this Friday—" he shrugged his shoulders "—but I know you probably can't." Matt turned to Kelly. "Cory is picking me up in a few minutes. He's the quarterback. We're gonna grab a burger and talk about some plays. I'll be home before ten," he added before bounding from the room.

"Do you have any plans for Friday evening?"

Her gaze shot to Jace in surprise. She shrugged. "Not that I know of."

"Want to go to a football game?" He was grinning from ear to ear.

"Matt's?"

"Yeah."

"I would love to go."

Matt's first varsity game. It would be doubly special to share it with Jace. The thought of being seen in public with him made her a bit nervous, but Matt had mentioned that most everyone in town knew Jace Compton was living among them. After the media reports that had lasted for weeks, the world probably knew. And apparently, Matt hadn't hidden the fact that he and his sister lived on the ranch. And really, why would he? So it was pointless for them to attend the game separately.

"I'll meet you in the kitchen. About six thirty?"

"Jace, what about you going out in public?"

He shrugged those broad shoulders. "I have no intention of living my life in hiding. Tom says it has been quiet for a couple of weeks. The folks of this community seem like good people. I really want to see Matt's game."

Kelly assured herself the inner excitement she felt was the anticipation over seeing Matt play, but she knew part of it was about going with Jace. As his date. It would be the first time they'd gone out together since he'd moved to this ranch.

As she counted down the days Kelly had to wonder what the news media might do if they saw her and Jace out and about together. All she could do was put her trust in Jace and hope that he knew what he was doing.

By six thirty on Friday, Kelly had joined Jace in the kitchen and soon they were on their way to the stadium, followed by two bodyguards in a separate vehicle.

The snare drums of the local band beat out a cadence, adding to the spirit and excitement in the air as the small entourage reached the front of the old wooden bleachers. They climbed the steps, heading to a spot that would give them a better view of the field and hopefully allow Jace some degree of anonymity. He didn't seem worried about it. His small two-person detachment would ensure his safety, handling any situation should it get out of hand. The two men were dressed in jeans and T-shirts with light jackets helping to camouflage the weapons they no doubt carried underneath; one of them led the way while the other brought up the rear.

"Fall is on its way," Kelly said as she sat down next to Jace.

"Are you cold?"

She shook her head. "No. It's a perfect temperature. I'm just glad we're past the worst of the Texas summer heat. You'll learn to appreciate November weather."

He laughed. "Be glad Matt isn't playing football in the northeast. I've been on the field when you couldn't see the yard lines for the snow. Played during a blizzard one year."

"How is that possible? How can anyone play in a blizzard?"

"The best way you can." He grinned.

"You loved it, didn't you?" She could see it in his eyes. Regardless of anything else Jace had accomplished in his life, his true love was football.

He nodded, his gaze on the field. "Yeah. I loved every

second," he said, and then turned to Kelly. The dark glitter of his eyes took her breath away. "It was the second best time of my life."

She smiled, immediately understanding his implication. The urge to lean toward him and taste those wickedly handsome lips was overwhelming.

The band began a rousing school fight song and everyone sprang to their feet, clapping and cheering as the home team broke through the colorful paper barrier and jogged onto the field. The black-and-gold uniforms of the Calico Springs Cougars stood out against the bright green turf. It was high school sports at its best. Jace, Kelly and the security team stood and cheered along with the other three hundred people in attendance.

It was surreal, being at a game in the town where she'd grown up, watching her kid brother among the varsity players, while standing next to Jace. The stadium lights made the colors more vivid; the air was thick with excitement. As they tossed the coin and the kickoff ensued, Kelly watched with pride as Matt took his place in the starting lineup.

As the game progressed, becoming more intense, Jace whistled and shouted his encouragement. When the Cougars made the first touchdown of the night, he pulled Kelly into his strong arms and hugged her in a tight embrace.

During halftime, Kelly noticed people walking below them as they made their way back and forth between the refreshment booth and their seats. They would look up at Jace and wave. If he saw them, Jace waved back, displaying that sparkling smile. Only a few approached, welcoming him to their community, wanting only to shake his hand. Their courtesy made Kelly feel a pride for her hometown she'd never really felt before.

"Would you like anything? Soft drink, coffee, hot dog?"

"No, thanks, I'm fine."

Her gaze wandered over his handsomely cut features, lingering for an instant on the strong line of his mouth. She couldn't stop herself from remembering how his kisses had so easily destroyed her preconceived notions of just how erotic a kiss could be. She'd way underestimated the power of a kiss. At least where Jace was concerned.

More than a little unnerved by the intensity of his glance, she forced her gaze back to the field with a shuddering breath.

By the third quarter, the score was tied. The Vikings had the ball. Their quarterback threw a pass and all eyes were on the ball as it soared through the air. At the last instant, it was intercepted. By Matt. Jace was on his feet, with Kelly close behind him. The crowd roared as Matt darted and circled in and around his opponents, jumping free of hands that would take him down. The spectators were on their feet as Matt ran down the length of the field toward the goal post, making it to the thirty yard line before he was finally tackled. Kelly was ecstatic. She swallowed past a lump in her throat as she clenched her hands together, overwhelmed with pride.

Jace caught her gaze and grinned at her reaction. He clearly shared in the pride she felt for her brother. With his run downfield, Matt had set his team up for an easy touchdown. He was the hero of the night.

When there were only three minutes remaining on the clock, Jace's security encouraged them to leave. With the home team ahead by two touchdowns, Jace hesitantly agreed.

"Do you mind?"

"Not at all. I think it's a good idea. Matt will understand. He's been talking all week about a postgame party at the pizza place. They'll no doubt rehash every second of the game. He's going to be floating on cloud nine for a month."

"He has every right to." Jace offered her his hand as he stood up, and she took it. "He did great. He still has this year plus two more to expand his knowledge and hone his skills before college. And he's a natural. He's got a chance at the pros, barring any injury, if that's what he wants."

"I wish Gramps could be here. But I'm grateful Matt has you. Thank you for all you've done for him, Jace."

He shrugged his shoulders. "It was my pleasure, whatever you think I did. Giving Matt some tips wasn't the reason for his accomplishments tonight. He did that all on his own."

As they walked out to the parking lot, she reflected on how she'd seen another facet of Jace Compton tonight. And she had to admit, she liked what she saw.

The drive back to the ranch was quiet, but it was an easy silence. Jace pulled into the main entrance and walked with Kelly through the trees to her cabin.

"I enjoyed it, Jace. Very much," she said as they went inside.

"So did I."

"I guess I'll see you tomorrow."

"Yeah. Tomorrow." For a few seconds their gazes locked across the darkened room.

Reaching out to her, Jace cupped her face, drawing her closer. Lowering his head, he gently kissed her, loving the softness of her lips, the taste of her. Her purely feminine essence called out to him and his body tensed in readiness.

He was about to pull away when she opened her lips to him. His heartbeat quickened and he deepened the kiss. His arms came around her, pulling her tightly to him; he loved the way her smaller body molded perfectly to his. He cupped the back of her head, his fingers lost in the silky texture of her hair. Raw need surged through his body, demanding he hold her close, ensuring she wouldn't turn away.

She was beyond tempting. The need to feel her underneath him once again, taking the pleasure he gave and giving it back ten times over, was eating him up inside. Kelly was everything he'd ever wanted in a woman. He never wanted to let her go.

But he knew it was wrong. She didn't need an affair. She needed a husband and a permanent home. He couldn't offer her either one.

Kelly moaned softly and Jace struggled to keep his passion under control. As the fragrance of her perfume blended with the scent of her desire and the sweet taste of her lips, he knew he was going to lose this battle.

The sound of the latch on the front door being turned and the door opening helped bring Jace to his senses. With more strength than he thought he possessed, he lifted his lips from hers and glanced toward the door.

Matt and two of his buddies stood in the doorway, grinning as if they'd just found gold.

"Oops. Gosh I'm sorry," Matt ventured, but didn't look sorry at all. "Forgot my wallet." He walked over to the kitchen counter and grabbed the dark leather billfold. Returning to the door, he glanced back at Jace, and then looked directly at his sister. "Click. Click." And with a chuckle, they were gone.

"Click. Click?"

"Don't ask," Kelly returned, shaking her head.

A sexy grin kicked up the corners of his mouth. "Your brother isn't sixteen. He's sixteen going on forty."

He reached out and pushed the sweater from her shoulders, and then removed the band holding back her hair. He grabbed the front of her jeans and pulled her closer, unfastening and unzipping.

"This isn't going to resolve anything," she whispered against his mouth. "But I'm tired of telling you no."

His heart rate tripled. "Then don't."

He was on fire. He didn't know how they were going to contend with the future, but at the moment, it didn't matter. It was enough to know she wanted him. As if to make sure he knew, she kissed him with a hunger he remembered so well, her hands fisting his shirt, leaving no doubt in his mind they were going to make love. He was going to take her. Right here. Right now. He was delirious with need. His blood pounded in his ears and he let out a deep growl.

Kelly was his.

He backed her against the cabin wall and kissed her, over and over, long and deep, his tongue caressing hers, making a silent demand that had her clinging to him.

He grabbed the hem of her T-shirt and quickly pulled it over her head. He took off her bra next, and sucked first one breast, then the other, while his hand alternately massaged and teased.

She began unbuttoning his shirt, but with one hard tug, Jace ripped it open, buttons flying everywhere. Her hands roamed over the smooth skin of his muscular chest, and then he felt her lips and tongue against him as she tasted him. As though she could never get enough.

He lowered one hand to between her legs. Even through her jeans, he felt the intense heat. The dampness. The scent of her desire surrounded him. She pushed against his hand and he heard a small whimper.

Without another word, Jace scooped her into his arms and carried her to the bedroom that wasn't full of sports equipment, closing the door behind him. He placed her on the soft mattress, shrugged out of his shirt and kicked off his boots. He quickly removed her jeans and then dropped his own.

The vision in front of him stole his breath. Her long blond hair draped over the pillow, her perfect breasts full and swollen, the light pink tips now hard nubs. But it was the sleepy, steamy look of want in her eyes that held him transfixed, the awareness and need clearly displayed in those blue-green eyes. Her lips, slightly open, showing brilliant white teeth, enticed him even further.

He placed one knee on the side of the bed, bending over her, his face stopping a breath away from hers. He cupped her chin, his thumb rubbing over her lower lip. Her lips closed around him and she moaned. He felt her teeth as she bit down, teasing him, sucking him deeper inside.

With a moan, he took her in a long, deep kiss. He moved to bite at her jaw, and then trailed kisses along her neck, licking, tasting, loving her down to her breasts. When he drew the hard peak of one breast into his mouth, her body surged toward his and she whimpered. He caressed the other breast in his hand, teasing, molding her. His erection throbbed with need to be inside her.

"Kelly," he growled. He could hear the animal rawness in his own voice. Using one hand, he positioned himself and pushed inside her. He stopped to allow her body time to adjust and accept his girth, and then filled her with one hard thrust. The heat and silkiness of her body was more amazing than he remembered. Hands cupping her hips, he held her up to him and filled her again and again. She called out his name as the pace became faster. Hotter. Frantic. He felt her shatter, her release pushing him over the top and beyond. It seemed to go on forever, yet it was too brief. Gasping for air, Jace dropped to his side, pulling her close, bestowing kisses on her face, her hair.

For long moments Jace held her in the darkness, her head resting on his chest, her spicy fragrance filling the air around him. Kelly was his. Every cell in his body screamed it.

There had to be a way for them to be together. He had to find a way.

He must have fallen asleep, because when he opened his eyes, there was faint sunlight coming in through the window. The sun was barely creeping over the far horizon when he awoke. Kelly was still in his arms, her head on his chest and one arm resting across his abdomen. He kissed the top of her head, his hands playing in the long tendrils of her hair. She stretched, raised her head and opened her eyes. The gleam in those blue-green depths was mesmerizing.

"Good morning," he whispered. "Sleep well?"

"Yes." She smiled up at him. The satisfaction of their night's lovemaking clearly shone on her face. "And you?"

"I'm still dreaming." He cupped her face, pressing a soft kiss on her lips. "What time will Matt be home?"

"Noon."

"Good. Because this was billed as a double feature and I'm pretty sure it's rated triple X."

She grinned before his mouth covered hers, and once again he was lost in the magic that was Kelly.

Thirteen

By the time Kelly made it upstairs to her office on Monday, the phones were already ringing off the hook. Kelly settled the baby in the crib and hurried to her desk. The day turned fast and furious and before she knew it, Mona was calling it to an end.

At the end of this week they would all fly to Los Angeles for Mona's charity gala. Then Jace would stay in town for a series of meetings on his next film project. Kelly and Mona would return to the ranch.

On Tuesday, Jace stopped by Mona's office. Her heart went into double time, but he only asked how her weekend had been and wished both Kelly and his mom a good day. He seemed to be giving Kelly space to sort it all out, to come to grips with their renewed love affair.

He couldn't know she already had.

Downstairs that afternoon she found Jace sitting in the kitchen on one of the bar stools, an inch of printed pages in a thick blue binder open on the counter in front of him.

Jace glanced up. "You leaving for the day?"

"Yep." She switched Henry from one arm to the other. "Is that your script?"

"Yeah." Jace glanced down at the papers. "I need to read the damn thing but I'm having a hard time concentrating. Thought maybe sitting out here would help."

He pushed the script aside and reached out to touch Henry's foot. "He's growing."

"Yes, he is."

"Are you and Mom almost ready for her charity event?" he asked before she could turn away.

"I think we're right on schedule. If as many people come as have responded so far, there'll be over four hundred in attendance. Mona is ecstatic."

Jace grinned. "What about you? Are you looking forward to it?"

"*Me?* I'll enjoy seeing it all come together, but I'm not attending the actual dinner and ball."

Jace frowned. "Why not?"

"Because."

"Can you elaborate just a bit?"

"I'm an employee." Her tone said he was dumb for asking. "Mona will have a full catering staff to assist her with drinks and hors d'oeuvres. The food will be prepared on site, overseen by the chef who has assisted Mona at the ball for the past five years. I'll be there to help set up, make sure everything is going according to plan, but once the guests start arriving I'll stay in the background as a precautionary measure. Basically, by then, my job will be over."

"Does Mom know your plans?"

"We talked." She hoped Jace didn't try to muddy the water. It had taken her quite a while to convince Mona she did not want or need to be there during the actual festivities. The social class of the guests was intimidating... Senators. Congressmen. Award-winning actors and producers. The elite of the elite. Kelly didn't need to be reminded she was about as far away from their inner circles as a person could get. And she had no intention of subjecting herself or Mona to any embarrassment she might cause if she committed a faux pas at the gala.

And there was the expense of a gown. No way was she spending a thousand dollars or more on something she would wear only once. She had a hard enough time making herself buy a brand of green beans that wasn't on sale. Her frugal nature didn't allow for thousand-dollar dresses. Being a guest at Mona's ball was simply not going to happen.

"Your mom and I have it all worked out, Jace," she said with as much happy bravado as she could muster. "No worries."

No worries.

With Kelly, that usually meant there was definitely something to worry about. Jace picked up the script as she walked out of the room, heading for the back door. With a frown, he rolled the document up in his hand and headed to his mother's bedroom.

"Mom?"

"Come in, sweetheart." Mona smiled as she entered the bedroom from the adjacent powder room. "I think I may have forgotten something regarding the ball. I just can't remember what it is." She chuckled. "Do you think that really does mean it isn't important?"

Jace shook his head. "I'm afraid I couldn't help you with that one, Mother. Change of subject. I just talked to Kelly downstairs and she said she's not attending the charity event. I thought you both were going. You both went through the dress fitting."

"Yes, I know." His mother sighed. "And she balked at the idea even then. She says she'd be out of her league around the people we expect to be there. Her words, not mine. She contends she's only an employee and has no business going."

"They're not one damn bit better than she is."

"I know, Jace."

He muttered an angry curse under his breath. "Give it another try, will you, Mom?"

"Tomorrow," she promised.

Jace said good-night and headed to his room, his molars grinding in frustration. Kelly shouldn't be concerned about a bunch of blowhard politicians and a few egotistical actors. He'd counted on her being there. He wasn't sure why, other

than that she and Matt had become part of the family. Kelly
wasn't an employee. He awoke every morning looking forward to seeing her and the baby. For reasons he didn't understand, Kelly's presence calmed him. As infuriating as
she could be at times, Jace would take the frustrating with
the good anytime. Her being in his life was…right. He was
the one who was wrong for her.

Other than dealing with the constant, overwhelming need
to make love to her, his life was good. Clearly he should
have said something to her about the charity event and asked
if she would be his date. Was he ever going to get it right?

"You know, we must go shopping," Mona stated the next
day as she and Kelly ate lunch in the kitchen.

"For what?" She crumbled crackers into her bowl of soup.

"For the charity ball."

Kelly wasn't sure she understood. Everything had been
ordered down to the last flower. "Have I missed something?" She put down her spoon, mentally going over the
details of the plans for the event. "They called and confirmed they would have the ice sculpture delivered by four
on the day of the ball. The chef has said—"

"The preparations are fine. You've done an outstanding
job. I was referring to us. Surely you know I expect you to
attend the gala."

"Yes. No. I mean yes, I know I'll be going but not as a
guest. I'll work behind the scenes, stick to the kitchen area.
I'll be at the hotel Saturday afternoon to help oversee everything, but like I said before, I have no business attending the ball."

Mona looked at Kelly as if she'd grown a second head.
"And why not?"

The idea was so ridiculous. She didn't want to offend
this kind, wonderful woman, but going to an event attended
by some of the biggest names in both Hollywood and poli-

tics was not going to happen. Talk about feeling like a fish out of water.

Kelly just shook her head, refusing to discuss it further, but Mona wasn't going to let it drop.

"You listen to me, Kelly Michaels. This isn't one of Jace's red carpet extravaganzas. It's my charity ball. And as my personal assistant, you are most certainly expected to attend. And you will need a gown to wear, unless you have one already?"

Kelly closed her eyes in temporary defeat and shook her head.

"No? Then Andre will provide the gowns as I originally intended. I'll call him myself and reconfirm."

What had she gotten herself into? She was not part of their world. It was just wrong to think differently. Of course, she wanted to be there for Mona. No matter how carefully one planned, there were always last-minute details to see to. But to attend the gala dressed as one of the guests was just wrong.

The trip to Los Angeles in Jace's Gulfstream was smooth and filled with laughter as Mona recalled mishaps from her past charity events. Kelly enjoyed listening to the banter but the uneasiness hadn't left her. She should not be attending this elite event. And no amount of winks from Jace or pats on the hand from Mona was going to change that.

Arriving at the hotel the day before the event, they hit the ground running. Kelly quickly realized that when Mona Compton set her mind to do something, anyone not going in her direction had better get out of the way. This fundraiser was her passion.

Kelly did her best to keep up, but lack of experience initially left her feeling completely out of her depth. Thankfully, the hotel staff had been prepped and things were accomplished efficiently and to Mona's liking. Kelly oversaw the setup of the banquet hall. The tables, chairs and decorations were brought through the door as fast as she could place them. Meanwhile Mona met with the chef and culinary artists who would provide the special touches that made this occasion a Mona Compton event.

"I think we're done," Mona said the next day as she looked around at the vast ballroom. "The ice sculpture will be delivered at four. Where should it go?"

"I thought we'd put it in an area near the dessert buffet but with enough space in between to make it accessible on all sides." Kelly walked over to the spot. "Around here. There is even an electrical outlet. We can use fluorescent lighting to make it the focus without melting it too badly."

"Perfect. I need to make a couple of changes to the place cards, only because I know these people." She rolled her eyes. "Sometimes it's better to avoid a potentially unpleasant situation than it is to cross your fingers and hope nothing will happen. You'll learn soon enough." She laughed. "Take this card and switch it for any one on the table over there in the corner." After five additional changes, Mona deemed the seating arrangement done.

"Okay," Mona said, "now it's time for us to get ready." She glanced at her watch. "Your dress should be in your room. Let's head to the salon for hair and make-up first."

"Hair? Make-up?"

"Why, of course, dear."

Of course.

Two hours later, Kelly stepped inside her room. Immediately, she saw a large bouquet on the table next to the windows. Tossing her clipboard onto the bed, she approached the flowers. There were several different varieties and the fragrance was amazing. Kelly opened the card.

To my dearest Kelly. I couldn't have done this without you. Mona.

Kelly sat down on the striped silk-covered chair nearest the small table. With all she had to do, Mona had taken the time and the trouble to send her a beautiful and thoughtful thank-you.

Tears welled in her eyes and she fought to keep them from spilling over. This was all happening because of Jace. It was because of him she was here now. It was because of him she had a great job working for an amazing lady.

She placed a quick call to Mrs. Jenkins to check on Henry, receiving the assurance the baby was fine. Then Kelly turned toward the closet.

She unzipped the black garment bag containing her dress for the gala, refusing to speculate on how much it cost.

Her eyes grew wide. Her mouth dropped open. This couldn't be right. Removing the gown from the closet, she held it up. This wasn't the design she'd expected. Not even close. Someone had made a terrible mistake. The dress was not blue. It wasn't satin. It was exquisite black lace, from top to bottom.

A few minutes later she stood in front of the mirror, her reflection nothing like what she was used to seeing. Not by a mile. The stylist had pulled her long hair to one side, the ends curled into ringlets that fell over her shoulder and down her back. The long-sleeved black lace gown fell to her feet, with a short train at the back. The form-fitting dress highlighted every curve.

It was expensive. It was elegant. It was risqué.

It was so not her.

She couldn't go downstairs in this.

She glanced at the clock. Seven fifteen. The event started at eight. A full panic attack hit her with the velocity of an air bag deployed during an unexpected crash. Placing her hands against her temples, Kelly tried to calm her racing heart enough to think. *What was she going to do?* How could she hurt Mona by not showing up for the festivities? How could she refuse to wear a gown that must have cost thousands of dollars? Yet she couldn't wear this in front of all those people. They would stare. She would die. What had the designer been thinking? He obviously sent the wrong dress. She'd expected something like a blue prom dress and instead received an elegant black spiderweb.

Clearly, she shouldn't have let Mona and the designer make the selection. She'd just blown it off the day the man came to the ranch to take fittings. When asked if she wanted to look at styles, she'd politely refused, thinking she wouldn't be going anyway so it wouldn't matter. She couldn't have imagined that with that small action, she'd pulled the trigger and shot herself in the foot.

Fourteen

"Have you seen Kelly?" Jace asked his mom as he scanned the people entering the ballroom.

"No. I haven't seen her since we had our hair done this afternoon and... Oh dear."

"Oh dear?" Jace eyed his mother. "What?"

His mother suddenly appeared apprehensive. "You may need to go up and encourage her to come down."

"Why? I mean, I'll be glad to, but I thought it was settled that she would attend."

"It is. It was. She, uh...she might not be completely happy with her gown."

Jace frowned. "Why would you say that?"

"Oh dear. Jason, please go up to her room and see if you can talk to her. She left the dress selection up to me and I may have made the wrong decision."

His mother wrung her hands, obvious concern in every feature of her face.

What in the world did his mother consider *the wrong decision*?

He rushed up to Kelly's suite. After two raps on the door, she immediately pulled it open. Quickly she looked past him down the long hall, first one way then the other. Grabbing his arm, she yanked him inside, shutting the door behind them.

There were no words for the vision standing before him. Jace swallowed hard. His body surged to readiness. Kelly was a natural beauty, but in that dress, every man at the ball would beat a fast path straight to her. His protective instinct jumped to the fore.

"You look…incredibly beautiful."

She pushed away from the door and walked past him into the suite, her hands fidgeting at her sides. Apparently, she felt something was terribly wrong. The only thing *he* felt wrong was that a certain part of his anatomy was about to explode.

"I can't do this," she said. "I can't go downstairs."

"Why not?" He frowned.

"You're kidding, right? Wearing *this*?"

"What do you think is wrong with it?"

"There isn't enough material to make a shirt for Henry."

"Kelly, you're way overreacting."

"I am not. Oh God. Jace, you've got to help me. I can't hurt your mother."

"Why can't you go in the dress? It's amazing. You look… ravishing. Good enough to eat."

"I'm serious."

"So am I."

"Look at it."

"Believe me, I am."

"It makes me look as if I'm not wearing anything but a few scanty strips of lace."

"And you think that's a bad thing?"

"Well, it isn't *good*."

Jace ran his hand over the lower part of his face. He didn't know what to say. Kelly was beyond gorgeous and sexy and that dress just confirmed it. She would be the sensation of the ball. How could she not realize how beautiful she looked? Had she looked in a mirror?

"The dress is fine. It's beyond fine. And we need to go. Dinner will be called in about thirty minutes. We'll need to find our seats."

Her hands began to fidget again. "Maybe I'll go down later. Food is the last thing I want right now. Anyway, there's no place card for me at the any of the tables. I made sure of it. I'm only an employee, Jace, playing dress-up for the night. And your date won't appreciate it at all if you show up with me on your arm."

"I'm looking at my date for the evening."

"You… I… No. You can't."

"Why not?"

"You *know*. Anyway, I'm not ready."

"You look more than ready to me. And I assure you, there is a place card at the table, next to me. You're good. Mom's better. You look beautiful. Now get anything you want to take with you and let's go before I lock the door and help you out of the dress you don't like."

"Jace, *please*." She moved farther inside the room. "There will be reporters. It will look bad for Mona if you walk into the room with me. The gold digger from Texas."

"Kelly, tonight you're my date," he stated, stepping toward her. "A very beautiful date. In that dress, every man here will sit up and take notice."

"I feel like a sideshow freak. Did you have a stripper pole put in the ballroom?"

He inhaled deeply and rubbed the back of his neck. He knew women who didn't give full nudity a second thought. Kelly was still an innocent in so many ways. It was part of the charm he found so irresistible. He understood after the media blitz about the baby that she was also trying to protect Mona and the charity. She couldn't be more wrong. But he didn't have time for the argument she would no doubt wage. He looked from Kelly through the open door to the large bed in the room to his left.

"If you really don't want to go downstairs, I can't make you." He'd make damn sure the locks were set.

"Oh," Kelly inhaled a deep sigh of relief. "Thank you, Jace."

He slipped out of his jacket, tossed it onto a chair and

then pulled at the end of his bow tie, pulling it free from its knot.

"What are you doing?"

"If you don't go, I don't go." He walked into the bedroom and pulled back the covers on the bed. "I'll just stay here with you. I'm betting we can find something to do."

"You can't do that to Mona." Then she straightened as the light dawned about what he was doing. "This is blackmail."

He shrugged. "As they say, all's fair. Which is it going to be, Kelly? Are you going to accompany me downstairs or do we get out of these clothes and spend the night together in that bed like we both really want to do?"

"Don't do this, Jace."

"I haven't done anything. Yet."

"Jace."

He walked up to her and cupped her face in his hands. If he didn't get them out of this room fast, neither of them would ever make it to the ballroom. His mother might be a little pissed, but he was past the point of caring.

"Take me very seriously, Kelly." His eyes held her gaze. "There's nothing I want to do right now more than remove that dress, inch by inch, and carry you to the bed." He took her hand and pressed her palm against his throbbing erection. "You need to decide. Now."

As soon as they stepped off the elevators, they were surrounded. People filled every available space, in the corridor, around the elevators, in the ballroom, even filling the elegant hotel lobby. As soon as Jace was spotted, reporters came out of the woodwork. Cameras flashed while reporters stood in line for an interview. Jace held Kelly's hand, refusing to let her fade into the background. He gave interview after interview focusing on the charity. He noted his mom across the room doing the same thing. Kelly stood quietly at his side until some of the questions were directed at her.

"Ms. Michaels, are you excited about this charity ball tonight?"

"Of course." She looked into the camera, a beautiful smile on her lips. "We're all excited to be a part of this very worthy cause."

"What about the man standing next to you? Any wedding bells in the near future?"

Before Jace could open his mouth, Kelly responded to the question. "We're here tonight to raise money to help women who are abused and desperate to find a better life for themselves and their children. It's a serious concern and I would expect the media to respect that and focus on the women who so desperately need our help."

"So you're refusing to comment on any personal relationship between yourself and Jace Compton?"

"Yes. As a matter of fact, I am. This is neither the time nor the place for questions of that nature. Now, if you're willing to hand me a check for a million dollars made out to the NCAW, I might be tempted to answer."

Jace was stunned by just how easily Kelly shut the man down. It was as though she had years of experience in front of the reporters' cameras. The poor guy never had a chance. He mumbled something about not having quite that much in his pocket, the others laughed, and further questions along those lines were dropped. Jace had never been prouder of anyone in his life. Though her body trembled the entire time, she'd handled it like a pro.

After dinner, the orchestra began playing. Couples rose from their seats and headed for the dance floor. Jace stood, placed his linen napkin on the table, and held out his hand to Kelly. She gracefully accepted.

He pulled her close, taking advantage of the opportunity to have her next to him. It felt so right.

"Remember when we danced in that little hotel lounge in Calico Springs?" he murmured near her ear. "It was dark. The only light was from the candles on the tables. I could have held you like that forever. And we still fit together perfectly."

"Only because you're a great dancer."

"Dancing has nothing to do with how impeccably you fit in my arms. If you like, I can demonstrate other ways we fit together."

"Be nice."

"I'm trying. But all I seem to want to do is be naughty. Very, very naughty."

"I don't know whether to laugh or take you seriously and issue a reprimand."

"Serious works for me." He leaned down and whispered in her ear, "You can even spank me if you want."

"Jace!" He loved the delicate blush that covered her fine features.

"What?" He intentionally assumed a look of pure innocence. Then couldn't hold back the grin at the expression of reproach on her face.

"You are bad."

"Mmmm. That's not what you said a week ago."

"May I cut in?" asked a man standing next to Jace, his eyes all over Kelly.

Jace nodded and pulled a gulp of air through his nose, aware he couldn't say no.

He watched helplessly as the man stepped up and put his arms around Kelly. She gave Jace a strained smile before they disappeared into the crowd.

"Well, hello there, handsome."

Jace turned to find Lena Maxwell, her dark auburn hair soft and wispy around her bare shoulders.

"Lena. How are you?" His eyes darted from Lena to the crowd on the dance floor as he tried to keep Kelly in sight. "Thanks for coming tonight."

"The pleasure is all mine." The sultry actress gave a deep-throated laugh. "Now dance with me before I have to take another breath without your arms around me."

With a tight smile, Jace complied.

"I heard you bought a ranch. Surely you're not retiring from pictures?"

"Haven't decided. Just knew I needed a break. What about you? Still fending off the offers with a stick?"

She laughed again. Jace searched the room for Kelly.

"She got to you big-time, didn't she?"

"Who?"

"The little blonde on your arm tonight. Congratulations on fatherhood, by the way."

"Thanks." Lena was trying to dig for gossip. She loved the spotlight, and knowing something no one else knew kept her right where she wanted to be.

"Brilliant idea to bring her here tonight. It will be all over the front page by in the morning. Good for the charity. Great for your career at the same time. Rumors are going to fly. Your name will be bandied about for weeks." She gave a sultry laugh. "Now I understand why we haven't seen you for a while."

Jace clenched his teeth in an effort to keep his temper at bay. Lena was the perfect example of why Kelly had been so concerned about attending tonight. He only hoped she wouldn't see this as a setup and think he was using her exactly as Lena described.

"May I cut in?" Another woman was waiting patiently by their side.

"So much for keeping you all to myself," Lena muttered, but politely stepped away. With a quick wink at Jace she disappeared toward the refreshment bar.

"Still have to stand in line to get to the great Jace Compton." The pretty brunette stepped into his arms. "Some things will never change."

"How've you been, Audrey?"

Jace absently moved to the music, only partially listening to the woman's ongoing chatter. He'd attended dozens of these affairs but tonight, for the first time, he saw nothing even remotely enjoyable in the experience. He didn't want to make small talk. He didn't want to be on center stage. Suddenly all the phony flirting and keeping up a front turned his stomach.

He wanted the quiet of the ranch and the privacy it offered.

And right or wrong, he wanted Kelly beside him.

The next man who stepped on her foot was going to regret it, Kelly decided as yet another intoxicated, overbearing fool asked her to dance. What was with the hands? This was an upscale event to raise money for a very worthy cause, not some grab-'n'-go on the shady side of town—even if she was half-naked. The cowhands had better manners.

Mona had called it right. There had to be at least four hundred people crowded into the ballroom. More than half were men, and she speculated that the majority of those were either blitzed or well on their way.

She'd spotted Jace a couple of times, each time trying to sidestep a different woman. They flirted shamelessly with him. He smiled politely but didn't appear to encourage them. He looked extraordinarily handsome in a tuxedo. At one point, their eyes met. He didn't smile, but the look that flared in his eyes warmed her down to her toes.

When the song ended, Kelly took the opportunity to excuse herself and leave the dance floor. She made her way to the ladies' room, hoping the evening would soon end. While it wasn't as bad as she'd first imagined, her feet were aching and her facial muscles actually hurt from continuously smiling, something she'd never before experienced. Perhaps it wasn't too late to call Mrs. Jenkins and again check on Henry.

She entered the elegant powder room, passing through to get to the bathroom facilities. As she was getting ready to exit, she heard the voices of several women in the first room.

"So…what did you think of Jace's new *friend*?"

Several giggles were the reply.

"I think she's nice," one of the women said.

"Oh, honey. She is going to be his downfall. I can't believe she managed to get pregnant. My husband said Jace was not enthusiastic at all about the new film. I guarantee it's because he feels responsible for that woman and her baby."

"Surely he won't turn down the role?" another woman asked. "I heard he is going to be offered the lead."

"She will probably *let* him do it. As long as it puts more money in her bank account."

What? Grabbing the handle, Kelly wrenched open the restroom door and turned toward the women in the powder room. She'd put up with that gossipy bullshit in school. All the talk about her father. Accusing *her* of breaking up marriages. She'd be damned if she would quietly take the hits again or hide like some thief in the night and say nothing as she had before.

"Frankly, I doubt she cares one way or the other. Would you? I mean, she's got her hooks in the most eligible bachelor on this continent. But she'd better ask herself how long she can keep him toeing the line."

"Maybe we should ask her for some pointers."

"Yeah. Maybe you should," Kelly interjected, staring at the speaker and wishing her gaze could do serious damage. "It certainly couldn't hurt." She let her gaze slide from the woman's face down to her feet and back, keeping a look of disgust on her face. "But it absolutely won't help. Excuse me."

Kelly pushed her way through the little group and looked into the large floor-to-ceiling mirror. Puckering her lips, she pretended to check her lipstick and then turned her head from side to side, her hand brushing down the side of her face and neck as if looking for flaws before shrugging her shoulders as though not finding any. Turning to look at herself in profile, she sucked in her stomach, arched her back and stuck out her boobs. What little she had.

"Mmm." She muttered in a disgruntled moan. She ran her hand over her stomach then across her breasts. "There's just too much material to this dress. Don't you think?"

The three women stared, each presenting a different level of shock, resentment and indignation.

"Oh well. I guess I'll leave that up to Jacie. Maybe he likes taking it off better." *Fake smile.* "You girls know what I mean." *Fade to frown.* "Oh. Or maybe you don't." *Uncaring shrug.* "Pity."

"Don't you live on a *farm*?"

One of the women, the oldest, apparently decided she had what it took to bring Kelly down a peg or two. *Bring it on, bitch.* These women were nothing compared to the kids at Calico Springs High.

Pointing finger. Surprised tone. "You're Celesta Mason!" *Aha look.* "I *thought* I recognized you." *Big smile.* "*Your* husband is the one who was caught humping one of the cooks in the kitchen two years ago. Naughty, naughty boy. But then…" *Conspiratorial tone.* "…can anyone really blame him?"

The gasps from all three could have sucked the plaster off the walls. Thank God for Mona's idle chitchat while they were placing the name cards earlier today. With a last glare in Kelly's direction, Celesta stomped toward the door, her face getting redder with each step. Her friends followed close behind.

"Bye-bye," Kelly called in her sweetest voice before the heavy door closed. *And good riddance.* She was gaining a much clearer picture of the way this game was played. Take away the million-dollar entitlements and these people were no different from the wannabes in Calico Springs.

She walked out of the ladies' room intending to check in with Mona and return to her suite. Her feet were killing her. Four hours in five-inch heels was not her thing. Before she could take three steps, she felt an arm slip around her shoulders.

"I was afraid I'd missed you, sweetheart." A man she didn't know smiled down at her. "I've waited long enough. Let's dance."

Oh, brother. He took her hand and pulled her into the ballroom, holding her far too close. He reeked of alcohol. His eyes looked cloudy; his pupils were dilated, making her wonder if he was high on booze or drugs. Probably both. He leaned forward, placing a kiss on her shoulder.

"Don't." Kelly was beyond disgusted. She'd had enough.

"You staying here at the hotel?"

She ignored his question, trying to think of a way out of this situation without making a scene.

"Come on, baby," he persisted, "what say you and me get out of here? I can think of a lot better things to do."

"I don't think so." She tried to push away, but he held her firmly in his arms.

"Don't be a fool." His voice suddenly sounded malicious. "If you think you and your kid are enough to make Jace leave the industry, you're sadly mistaken." He laughed harshly. "Yeah, I saw the way you looked at him across the room. But he's too into Lena Maxwell to care about anyone else. It's been that way for years. If you're smart, you'll let it go."

"You seem to know an awful lot about Jace Compton."

"We go way back. Sorry babe, maybe I should have introduced myself. Most people know me on sight. I'm Bret Goldman."

Bret Goldman. The man she'd spoken to when she'd called to tell Jace about the baby. So this was the jackass in person.

"It's okay, sweetheart. You're new. You'll learn."

"What will I learn?" She pushed back from him enough to look at his face. He was handsome enough, but his arrogance overshadowed any attraction someone might feel. Plus, he had some serious graying at the temples, and he carried the general look of one who overindulged. In everything, apparently.

"Who to be nice to and who doesn't matter. I matter."

"Really? To whom?"

His eyes narrowed. She needed to get away from this guy. Making a scene was becoming less and less important. Elite gala or not, he was about to be on the receiving end of an easily understood no.

He laughed contemptuously. "Be very careful, honey. Some people you don't say no to. I'm one of them."

Kelly could only gape at his arrogance. She tried her best to stifle a laugh, but the giggle broke free in an uncontainable snort. Suffice it to say it did not go over well with Mr. Full-of-Himself.

The man glared and seized her wrist. "Let's see if I can give you a better understanding upstairs." He began to pull her out of the room toward the elevators. The conceited jerk was serious. This had gone too far.

"Remove your hand. Now."

"A little wildcat. I love it."

"I don't think Ms. Michaels wants to party, Bret."

Bret stopped and Kelly looked behind her into Jace's strong face. He was clearly holding his anger in check. To someone passing it would appear they were all just having a nice conversation. But Jace had a deadly look in his beautiful green eyes. Anyone with any common sense at all would know to back off. Immediately.

"She's a little tease. We'll get past that upstairs."

Kelly struggled to remember...was she stronger with her left knee or her right?

"Let her go, Bret."

"Or what?" the man challenged.

There were no more words as Jace's fist shot out, landing squarely against the man's nose with a force that would have made Rocky Balboa proud. Bret released her arm as he crashed to the floor, taking out a waiter carrying a tray full of dirty plates in the process.

With a few muttered curses, Bret got to his feet. He

brushed at the trickle of blood running from his nose and the sight of it seemed to set him off. He lunged at Jace and grabbed his arm and swung him around, his fist flying toward Jace's face. With a quick, easy move, Jace avoided any contact and sent the man flying across the room and crashing into the wall with a roundhouse kick. Jace made it look easy. Bret attempted to keep his balance and actually came at Jace again.

This time Jace let go with a right uppercut to the head that once again sent the man flying from one side of the room to the other. When his body made contact with the opposite wall he slid to the floor like a sack of rotten potatoes.

The sight was unreal. Camera flashes filled the room. Jace's face was wrought with rage, his nostrils flaring, his mind and body not yet receiving the message it was over as he walked over to Bret, his fists clenched in anger. Jace was still in fight mode as two men stepped between him and his now unconscious—and no doubt soon to be former—manager. Their voices were low as they talked Jace down, assuring him it was over.

There was a moan and Bret struggled to sit up. Someone handed him a handkerchief and he held the cloth against his nose, not yet realizing that blood had soaked the front of his shirt.

Jace's eyes cut to Kelly. In that moment, he seemed to visibly calm down before a look of remorse and dismay flooded his features. He shrugged out of the men's hold and glanced at Bret, still lying on the floor, and then back at Kelly.

A moment passed between them before Jace turned and walked out of the room.

Fifteen

Jace entered his suite, letting the door close behind him. Shrugging out of his jacket, he tossed it onto a nearby chair, pulled off the tie and ripped open the dress shirt, sending the buttons flying. At the en suite bar he poured a triple and threw it down his throat. Bracing his arms against the countertop he stared at the image in the mirror. The contorted face that stared back, partially concealed by shadows, was not Jace Compton. It was a man with deadly eyes and a cold, menacing stare. The mouth was a thin straight line with deep grooves of leftover rage on either side. The white shirt hung open, bearing traces of Goldman's blood. Jace clenched his jaw as he stared at the face of George Compton in the mirror. His father had rematerialized and displayed all the trademark brutality and cruelty of Jace's childhood.

The beast had come out. Right in front of Kelly.

Jace poured another shot, downed it the same way and headed for the bathroom. Turning on the shower, he shucked the remaining clothes and stepped under the warm spray. He was still angry. He knew Bret was a pompous ass, knew he screwed around on his wife, knew his reputation in Hollywood circles was that of a ruthless, pushy, conniving, hard-nosed son of a bitch. But Jace had never witnessed him in full assault mode before tonight. It made it a thousand times worse that he'd set his sights on Kelly. She'd been so hesitant to attend the ball, and then to be accosted by a degenerate like Bret had Jace wishing he'd pounded the guy harder than he did.

But what churned in his gut was the knowledge that Kelly had witnessed everything. The shocked look on her face when he'd met her gaze before he turned and walked from the room would haunt him forever. Her eyes had been as wide as saucers, her hands clenched tightly in front of her as if in fright. She'd looked away from him to stare at the man lying on the floor, his face blotchy, his white dress shirt covered in blood. Jace couldn't be sure if it was shock or disbelief that froze her delicate features and made her skin lose some of its healthy color.

If there had ever been any hope he could keep Kelly in his life, hope that he wouldn't turn into his old man, he now knew with absolute certainty he could toss that dream into the trash. Someday it might be Kelly on the floor, her face bruised and bloodied. Just the thought made him physically sick.

Trudging out of the shower, he wrapped a towel around his waist, walked toward the en suite bar and poured himself another.

"Hi, baby." The sultry voice came from the general location of the bedroom. "We meet again so soon."

Jace froze. Flipping on the lights, he walked to the doorway of the bedroom and glared at the partially clothed woman in his bed, her long red hair covering her bare shoulders.

"Lena. *Goddammit.* What in the hell are you doing in here? Who let you in?" But Jace knew it wasn't the first time Lena had charmed her way into his private space, convincing an innocent employee it was her room. She and Bret, the two schemers, should get together. Or maybe they already had.

"Ah…come on, baby, don't be mad." The sound of her voice made him cold inside.

"This is not happening. You need to leave."

He grabbed her clothes from the chair and tossed them in

her direction. A contrived pout formed on her full lips as her brown eyes beseeched him to let her stay. Quite the actress.

"I can't believe you're going to throw me out. Why spend the night all by yourself?"

"Whether I do or don't is none of your goddamn business. What happened to Jack? Weren't you all into him?"

"Jack didn't work out." She sat up, not bothering to cover her bare chest. "I made a mistake, Jace. Can't you forgive one little mistake?"

"I don't care one way or the other, Lena." He settled his hands on his waist. "Whatever we had, if anything, ended a long time ago. I told you two years ago when you came up with that insane idea of pretending to be married, that was it for me. No more. Get dressed. Now. Then get out."

The pout still on her face, she grabbed her clothes and began to get dressed.

There was a persistent knocking at his door. *What now?* He glared at Lena. "If that's the press, Lena, so help me…"

She shook her head, her hands palms up. "No. At least it's nothing I had anything to do with." Standing, she pulled on her gown and began to fasten the buttons that ran the full length of the sparkling black evening dress and headed into the bathroom.

Jace took in a deep breath and clenched his hands into fists, wanting badly to reshape a wall.

Looking through the peephole in the door, he all but cringed. It wasn't reporters standing outside. It was Kelly. Running his hand over his face, he hesitated. He knew what she would think when she saw Lena. But after what she'd witnessed downstairs did it really make any difference? Swinging open the door, he stood back and she stepped inside the room.

"I just wanted to make sure you were okay."

"Yeah. I'm good." It was a sheer miracle he wasn't sitting in a jail cell. Again. "Kelly, there's something I need to tell you—"

"Jace, give me a call the next time you're—"

He heard Kelly's intake of breath as Lena walked back into the room, still buttoning her dress as she rounded the corner. The two women stared at each other.

"I'm...I'm sorry." Kelly bolted for the door. Luckily, Jace got there first.

"No. This is not what you think."

Lena smiled, her eyes sparkling in humorless amusement as she glided slowly toward the pair. "It never is." She leaned over casually and picked up her clutch, and then tossed her hair back over her shoulders in a practiced manner.

"This must be Kelly." She looked at Jace. "She is beautiful." She turned to Kelly. "Don't look so shocked, honey. Remember who you're with. This is Jace Compton's world. Better get used to it."

Firmly holding Kelly's wrist, he opened the door and Lena walked through it without a backward glance.

"Kelly, I did not invite her into this room. In fact, I'm not sure how the hell she got in."

"It's not really my business although you both being undressed was...convenient. Her timing is very good."

She glanced around the room, as though looking for a secret portal that would transport her magically far away from this place.

"Kelly?"

She tilted her head and her eyes found his. "I believe you, Jace. But Lena was right. I appreciate the glimpse into Hollywood's inner circles, but if it's all the same, I think I'd better stick with the small-town country bumpkins. Your ranch hands have better manners than most of the people here tonight." She shook her head as if in sad defeat. "There's so much more to life than...this." She attempted a small laugh that fell flat. "Is this usually the way your parties end? A few drinks, slugging it out, then a little bed-hopping with...whoever?"

Jace felt as if his heart had been hit by a meteorite. He'd

probably frightened her so badly that even coming to his room had taken every grain of intestinal fortitude she possessed. But what brought him to his knees was the knowledge almost everything she said was true.

"No, not always. Sometimes the police get involved and jail cells are added to the mix. I'm sorry you had to see what happened downstairs."

Jace didn't know what else to say. There was nothing he *could* say.

And only one thing would make this right with Kelly.

He had to end this. Now. Before he hurt her.

Bile rose in the back of his throat and his entire body tightened. He closed his eyes, dropped his head and grimaced in pure self-disgust.

What an idiot he'd been to even think of a future with Kelly. She wouldn't travel the globe with a newborn son. And she wasn't one to stay at home for months at a time waiting for him to return. And even if she was willing, he wouldn't ask that of her.

It would be an understatement to say she wouldn't be comfortable with the droves of media that would surround and follow her. Kelly would not sit back and ignore the ridiculous headlines claiming he'd had yet another affair. It would cause her to relive what her own father had done and the consequences they'd all suffered.

But all that aside, even if he walked away from films, all she would have was the beast inside him and no way of knowing what would set it off. Or when. The same monster she'd gotten only a small glimpse of tonight. It was a no-win scenario.

The very last thing she needed was mistreatment by an abusive man. God, he wanted to be part of her life, to make her, Henry and Matt part of his. He wanted Kelly until his mind and heart threatened to explode and sparks of desperation lit the darkness. But he knew, in this moment, it could never happen. He had no right to pursue her with his father's DNA running rampant through his veins.

"You were right. This is no life for you. It's no life for Henry."

He watched her. It was past time she knew the truth.

He caught her gaze and held it. His nostrils flared with the pain of what he was about to say. "What you saw tonight is who I am."

She stood in the doorway, the overhead lights making her an ethereal vision. He stepped back to the bar and poured another drink. It wouldn't be his last before the sun rose tomorrow.

"Jace? I don't understand."

"I'm trying to tell you I can't stop living this way because of who I am inside. I can't change it." He threw the amber liquid down his throat and turned to face her. "What I do for a living and all that goes with it provides an outlet. An escape from my own sick reality. It lets me drink myself into oblivion—" he held up the glass "—and the media just report a party. It lets me pound somebody—usually a professional but not always, like tonight—and release some of the rage. Makes for good headlines." He gave a false laugh at the ridiculousness of it. "Hell, they even pay me to do it. The travel, the new film locations, memorizing scripts, it keeps me from thinking. From remembering what I am inside. It helps prevent me from doing what you saw me do tonight. It's the only way I have to get through another day.

"I can't offer you the man you want, Kelly. I can't give you forever. I can't provide the home and the life you and Henry need. I can't be the husband you deserve. Ever." He clenched his jaw, determined to make her leave while she could. "I'm not even sure I can love you."

He watched her flinch as though she'd been shot. He stood helplessly as shock, then anguish, played across her fine features. Kelly bravely blinked back the tears that filled her eyes. He'd hurt her deeply, but she would be better off in the long run. Better off without him.

"After spending time with you, getting to really know you, any fool could see…" He clenched his jaw with a force that should have cracked teeth.

"See what, Jace?" Her voice was unsteady, barely a whisper. Her face had lost all of its color.

"That you don't belong here. You don't belong with me."

Kelly was a person who lived life from the heart. She was a woman who would fight to the death to protect her son, who got back on her feet every time life knocked her down, who made a home for her brother when there was no one else and kept his dreams of a future alive even at the cost of her own. A stubborn, tenacious woman who scorned pity and would rather chop off her nose than accept what she though was charity. A beautiful woman who needed to be loved and cherished—not abused. "You were right that first night, Kelly. The night we talked outside your house. I should have left then. I just didn't want to accept the inevitable."

Kelly nodded. She miraculously managed a smile without allowing even one tear to fall even though they filled her eyes, a tribute to her strength.

A brittle stillness filled the space around them, so rigid and taut with emotion the slightest movement would cause it to crack and bring the walls surrounding them tumbling down.

She turned to leave and paused when he said, "I wish things could have been different."

Without turning to face him she opened the door and walked out.

A rage filled Jace. A rage beyond anything he'd ever felt before and all directed inward, at himself. All hope turned to hopelessness. The monster had won. With a silent scream, he hurled the glass across the room into the mirror, shattering it into a million pieces. Like his heart.

* * *

A week later Jace sat in the meeting, wishing he were a thousand miles away. Anywhere would do. He absently twirled a pen in his fingers as producer Doug Hamrick went over the plans for filming his next big-budget blockbuster. Around the expansive conference table sat the director, assistant directors, five other actors, scriptwriters, technical advisers, and the attorneys and agents representing them all. Only Bret Goldman was noticeably absent. Jace had made sure of that, firing him before he'd ever left the ballroom.

Filming would last six to seven months with postproduction another four. The locations were some of the most exotic in the world. Hard as hell to reach, a challenge to film, but the ambiance couldn't be beat.

In front of Jace on the shiny mahogany table was the contract awarding him the leading role. It would afford him the opportunity for another best actor nomination along with the possibility of best picture of the year.

The mood in the room was jovial, the excitement and anticipation obvious in the faces of everyone who sat around the table. But as Jace idly listened to the questions and answers, his thoughts were of Kelly. Seven months was a long time to be away. It had never seemed so long before. But what in the hell else did he have to do? Kelly and his mom had flown back to Texas the day after the ball. He'd stayed over in LA for this meeting, hiding out at his house in Malibu, wondering how long Kelly would stay at the ranch.

The rolling surf that used to calm him couldn't touch the panic and utter devastation that festered inside. His mind scrambled to find a solution—*any* solution—that could keep Kelly in his life. But the same scenario bumped along, around and around, like a flat tire on a car going downhill, preventing him from catching a glimpse of hope.

He remembered the first time he ever saw Kelly, arguing with the guy in the feed store over the cost of a bag of oats. She'd won. No surprise there. Jace had carried the horse feed out to her truck, determined to find out her name and get a phone number before she disappeared. He remembered how her face radiated tenderness and natural beauty in the glow of the little candle on the table in the café later that evening.

Days later, when he'd taken her to the small motel, he'd immediately realized her inexperience. He'd been determined to show her what making love was really about, and that night would go down in the history books. She'd stripped him of every ounce of control he could find and made him wish for a lot more. She was so damn sexy yet so innocent in the ways of the world, so trusting of him, so eager to please. He was left speechless, shaken to his core and totally and completely enthralled.

And by the next morning, using a condom never entered his mind.

He'd asked her to dinner the following night. Partly to ensure she was okay and partly because she was so damned amazing he had to prove to himself she was for real. She accepted. And that night, after they'd eaten, he had taken her straight home to her grandfather's ranch even though it was the last thing he wanted to do.

Later that night, he'd been awakened by a light tapping on his guest cabin door. He'd opened it to find Kelly standing on the other side. Neither said a word. Both knew why she was there. The attraction worked both ways; one was not whole without the other. He pulled her into his arms and they didn't leave the hotel room for the next three days.

Later he'd secured the loan of two horses and together they roamed the hills and valleys of north Texas. They'd talked and laughed the day away, her naturally golden curls falling loose from the old brown hat she'd plopped on her head. They'd splashed in a pond surrounded by grass and cattails, fed each other olives they'd found tucked in one of the saddle bags, and made love under the shade of a willow tree on an old red blanket cushioned by thick native grasses. The memories were permanently etched in his mind.

It was in those moments when time hung suspended and his crazy world faded to nothing that he'd fallen in love with Kelly Michaels.

Kelly's charm went beyond physical beauty. It was the sparkle in her eyes when she laughed. It was in the way she held their son with such love and tenderness. It was the praise she heaped on her brother, always keeping alive the promise of a bright future. It was the soft, melodic sound of her voice and her inner strength and fortitude. It was the sparks that shot from her eyes when she was angry. Her intelligence and quick wit that kept Jace on his toes. She made him glad to be alive. No one else had ever done that.

His entire life had been built around the fear that he would become like his father. Despite his lifelong determination to remain detached, Kelly had found a way into his heart. She'd given him a child. A son. And he was still totally and completely in love with the mother of that child. But the reason they were not together—and never could be together—hadn't changed.

The vibration of his cell phone jerked him out of his reflections. Looking at the screen, he saw it was his mother. His mom knew he had this meeting. She wouldn't call unless it was important.

Jace excused himself from the conference room and stepped outside into the hall.

"Mom?"

"Jason." He could hear the quiet anguish in that one word. He had his answer. "Kelly's gone."

It was dark by the time Jace walked into the house. His mom was sitting at the kitchen bar, a cup of coffee in one hand, a well-used tissue in the other. Her eyes red-rimmed, her nose pink from crying.

"When did she leave?"

"Around three." His mother's voice was hoarse from the many tears she'd shed.

"Do you know where she went?"

"She went back to her house." Mona shook her head. "She promised she would stay in touch."

Jace could only nod. He'd pursued her. He'd taken advantage of her feelings for him and taken her to his bed all the while knowing he could give her no promises. Then he'd figuratively slapped her in the face, possibly broken her heart and stood three feet away, presenting the appearance of a cold unfeeling bastard, while she crumbled and bravely tried to hold on to her emotions, her self-respect. It was because of him and the son of a bitch who fathered him that she was gone now. He'd wanted her to walk away, to hate him if it helped her, and never look back.

He'd done his job well.

He walked to the bar, grabbed a bottle of whiskey, then proceeded to his office where he closed and locked the door. He'd drink a toast to the old man. Hell, why not?

He'd become just like him.

Sixteen

Jace entered the house, needing more coffee. His mother joined him in the kitchen. He knew she was worried. About him. About Kelly. About the situation. He looked like something dredged up from the pits of hell. Bloodshot eyes. Beard stubble. Maybe a little weight loss as well, but he didn't give a damn.

"Jason, talk to me."

He shrugged. "About what?"

"It's been over a month since Kelly left. Maybe it's time you talked to her."

"Let it go, Mom." He poured the fresh coffee into his mug.

She shook her head in frustration. "Jason—"

"Just drop it, okay? It's over. It's done. It's too late to go back. And I don't want to talk about it."

Jace had done what he'd had to do when he made Kelly leave. Out of respect he'd eventually have to give his mom some kind of explanation, but it wasn't going to happen today.

"Nothing is ever too late, Jason," she said softly. "Not as long as your heart is still beating."

With a polite nod, Jace stepped around her and headed back to the barn. The anguish of losing Kelly never let up. The pain had become a permanent extension of his body and mind. And always, with every breath, he questioned if he'd done the right thing. He'd finally stopped telling himself to let it go. He couldn't. He knew he never would.

The what-ifs plagued him. Night and day. What if his

love for her was enough to quiet the beast? In normal circumstances Kelly made happiness swell inside him. Even when those turquoise eyes shot bolts of fire in his direction because of something stupid he'd said, he felt the love for her that went to the marrow.

What if he'd done the wrong thing? What if they *could* have a life together? What if ten years from now it became apparent he'd thrown away something special for no good reason, something he would never find again? It was making him crazy.

Dammit to hell. During the day he barked at every hand on the ranch, throwing out threats that had them scrambling, the frustration and internal anger refusing to be contained. Two men had already quit. There would be more if he didn't get a handle on this. But he couldn't make himself give a damn. At night, he lay staring into the darkness. Only then did he let himself imagine going to her, holding her. Only then in the obscurity of a dream did he feel alive.

Shouts broke the silence. Glancing ahead, just outside the corral, his ranch hands circled two of their fellow cowboys who appeared determined to take each other out one punch at a time. Their faces were red, their anger obvious. These were not stuntmen rehearsing a future scene. These were men he employed, and he would not tolerate this kind of behavior.

Gritting his teeth, Jace hurried forward. The foreman stood steps away from the brawling men. "Somebody grab Decker. I'll get Colby."

Jace never slowed his stride. Before anyone moved forward per Sam's orders, Jace walked between the two men, grabbing one by the arm, slinging him to the ground. The other suffered a similar fate.

Jace continued to stand between them. "What in the hell is going on?" This was all he needed. The whole damn world was falling apart. "You have less than two seconds to explain or you're both out of here." His gaze shot from one to the other. The cowboys not involved in the fight stood quietly, waiting to see what Jace would do.

One of the men rubbed at the trickle of blood under his nose with the back of his hand. "He's been making passes at my wife."

Jace could hear the fury, the pain in the man's voice. "Is that true, Decker?"

Decker glared. "So what if I have? It wasn't like she gave me the cold shoulder."

"You son of a bitch," Colby growled and went for Decker again. Jace quickly halted his forward motion.

"That's it, Decker. Get your stuff and get off my property. Sam will tag along just to make sure you find your way." Jace turned his attention back to Colby, who still struggled to get free of Jace's hold. "Colby, let it go." He called to a couple of the cowboys. "Take him and stay with him until he cools off."

As the men hurried to follow his orders, Jace rubbed the back of his neck. Had everyone gone crazy? He had to sympathize. He knew exactly what Colby was feeling. Maybe his wife egged him on. Maybe she didn't. But Colby had a right to defend what was his. Normally a decent, hardworking man, he'd let his love for his wife blind him to everything but the need to protect her.

The breath died in Jace's throat. Is that what he'd been doing when he took out Bret? The epiphany almost blinded him. Why in the hell hadn't he seen it before? He hadn't lost himself in a mindless fit of rage. He'd done what he needed to do to stop Bret from hurting Kelly. To protect the woman he loved. There was a difference. A big difference.

Stunned from the belated realization, Jace was equally elated and afraid.

Had the realization come too late?

The television blared with the intended purpose of ensuring Kelly didn't have a chance to think. It wasn't working.

Regardless of what she did to try to keep her mind from dwelling on Jace, nothing worked. She grabbed the remote and switched it off.

Returning to the kitchen, she turned on the oven and finished stirring the homemade dressing. It was her offering to Gerri's family for her mother's birthday.

The last thing Kelly wanted was to be around people but Gerri insisted she was part of the family and refused to take no for an answer. Kelly had finally given in to her friend since second grade. It seemed the least she could do to repay Gerri for her many kindnesses and concern since Kelly left the ranch.

Gerri had asked if she could take the baby, reminding her how much her mother wanted to see him. When Gerri's brother stopped to pick her up, Kelly agreed, saying she would finish the dressing and follow in Gerri's car. At least that was the plan.

She spooned the mix into the baking pan, shoved it into the oven and set the timer. After washing the bowl and utensils, she ventured into the small living room and plopped down on a chair. Tomorrow she would call Mona. She wanted to hear her voice. She needed to hear Jace's voice, too, and feel his arms around her, but that was not going to happen. Ever.

Picking up a magazine, she idly paged through it. If she dwelled one more second on Jace she would go crazy. She didn't want to go to Gerri's mother's birthday party with her eyes red and puffy. Since that night at the hotel in LA, she couldn't seem to stop crying. Trying to make sense out of what had happened left her even more confused. The pain never ended.

The timer on the oven began to ding. She pushed herself out of the chair and walked to the kitchen and removed the dressing from the oven before turning it off. What had made Jace go from a person who had worked to rebuild her trust and made her think he loved her to suddenly assuring her she didn't belong in his life? Apparently she was good enough while they were isolated at the ranch but not good enough to fit into his life in Hollywood. She'd known she didn't belong, but he'd insisted she was wrong. Why? Why had he even bothered? She had so many questions that would never be answered.

A knock on the apartment door broke into her thoughts. Frowning, she walked back to the living room. She opened the door and the shock that hit her was like the blow of a baseball bat to the solar plexus.

Jace stood on the doorstep. He wasn't smiling. His green eyes carried a haunted look, as though he wasn't sure he should be here. But his clenched jaw established his determination; he wasn't going anywhere. "Can we talk?"

Her mind tried to grasp the realization he was here. "I think you've already said everything there is to say."

"No, I haven't. Will you invite me in? Or are we going to argue out on the sidewalk?"

"*I'm* not going to argue at all."

"That might be a first." His attempt at humor fell flat. He forced a smile that didn't reach his eyes.

Glaring, she turned away but left the door open. If he wanted to come in she wouldn't try to stop him, but she wasn't going to invite him. Her heart pounded so hard it was difficult to breathe.

Why is he here?

Kelly moved to the center of the room, wrapping her arms tightly around herself in an effort to control the storm of emotions raging through her. She wanted him to go. She wanted to put her arms around him and never let him go. His presence caused the blood to race through her veins while her mouth went dry and tears stung the back of her eyes. She'd been an emotional wreck for weeks. She couldn't sleep. She didn't want food. She only wanted to scream and pound on his chest and demand that he explain *why*. Now was her chance and she couldn't look at him. She was down two strikes and already out. She couldn't survive a third.

Jace stood in front of her as though waiting for something. Finally she glanced at him. He held her gaze and didn't let go. He bore the same haunted look she saw when she looked in the mirror.

"I just have one question."

"Really? I have about a hundred."

"Do you love me, Kelly?"

"What?" By her reaction, he clearly knew she thought he was crazy.

"If I had a regular job, say…as a ranch hand. Would you give me a second chance?"

She struggled to hold back the tears. She loved him with all of her heart. But what was the point of these questions? "You're not a ranch hand. I think we've sufficiently cleared up that little misunderstanding."

He stepped up to her. "Are you in love with me?" He repeated the question, his voice a rough demand. "After what I did…is it even possible?"

It was hard to answer a pointless question.

"Kelly?"

"What's the reason for this, Jace? Did you come all this way, go to all this trouble just to catch me off guard and knock me down again?" She was furious. She hated him. She loved him. "I don't get it. I really don't. Is this what you do? You just play with people? Play with their emotions?"

"I guess I'll take that as a no."

"What in the hell do you expect me to say? You…you made it clear you couldn't love me. You said I didn't belong in your life. I'm not good enough and I never will be. At least for once you were honest."

"That's not what I meant," he bellowed. He was getting angry. *Well, bring it on, babycakes.* He had a long way to go to equal what she was feeling.

"Then a month later you show up here, asking if I love

you? You're a jackass, Compton. Worse, you're...you're... deranged."

"I guess that really is a no." He nodded his acceptance and turned to leave.

"Most of the attendees at Mona's ball would say the answer to your question is a resounding no. I don't love you. Apparently, I got my hooks in deep enough to haul in some big bucks without letting my heart get involved."

He spun around and gripped her shoulders. "Kelly, do you love me?"

She could sense he wanted to shake her, but he merely held her instead.

"Are you in love with me?" This time his voice was soft, almost a plea.

"Yes." It was only a whisper, the best she could do, but he heard her. "Are you happy now? What...did this win some kind of bet? Do I get an award for the biggest fool of the year?"

At her confession, he closed his eyes and seemed to relax. "Thank God."

"Why?"

"Because I'm in love with you."

"Oh, please."

"You're the only woman I've ever said that to. I've never been in love before, Kelly."

"Jace..." She shook her head. "You're not in love now. I appreciate the sentiments, I guess. But this is not love. Let me clue you in. Treating someone like you treated me in LA is not love. Not even close."

He took a deep breath and blew it out, his hand wiping the lower portion of his face.

"I said some really stupid things, but for a good reason. I was trying to protect you that night at the hotel."

"Do I honestly have to tell you how ridiculous you sound?"

"My own father was bad news, Kelly. He was in and out of prison most of my life. And he was a mean son of a bitch.

He beat Mom. She left him so many times, she had him arrested, tried to find a place we could hide. But he found us. And it was bad. She fought back, but he was so much bigger than she was. When I tried to stop it, he turned on me. I was twelve when he broke my jaw. Thirteen when he busted six ribs. He didn't give a damn. He just wanted those around him to hurt as much as he did. To pay for his mistakes. He screwed up his life and he wasn't man enough to admit it."

Jace let out a breath. "I've lived with the very real possibility that someday I'll become just like him. It's in my genes. I didn't want you or Henry anywhere around when that day came. I was afraid if you loved me, if I didn't make you leave, you'd stay."

She frowned. He was serious. "You will never be like that, Jace."

"In the past month, I finally realized it came down to a choice. Beg you to stay in my life and run the risk I might someday become…abusive. Or go on with my life as it has been—empty, lonely, wanting the things most men take for granted. I'm a selfish bastard, Kelly. I need you. I can't live the rest of my life knowing I gave up the best thing that ever came into it. And if you'll give me a chance, I'll fight with every breath I take each and every day to keep the monster at bay. I will not hurt you, Kelly. Ever."

His eyes beseeched her. "Come back to the ranch with me. Marry me. Marry me for no reason other than I want you to be my wife. Because I love you."

Kelly didn't know how to take all this in. Was he telling her the truth? Did he actually believe he would hurt her?

"I've quit acting, Kelly," he said. "I never signed the contract for the new film. I walked out. It took me a while to get it through my thick head and understand what you were saying. You and Henry are so much more important than making films."

She looked up into his eyes and the tears brimmed in hers. She clamped her hand over her mouth. *What had she done?* "Jace, no. No. I didn't have the right to demand you change your life if you wanted to be part of Henry's. Oh God. That was wrong. You're leaving your career, what you love, for the wrong reason. Eventually you'll hate me for it. Don't you see? Don't do it, Jace. You can see your son whenever you want. Please don't pity me and think giving up your career will make anything right."

A look of dark humor settled into his handsome features. "*Pity?* You are the most stubborn, hardheaded female I have ever run across in my life. Where in the hell do you get these crazy ideas? I don't pity you, Kelly. I respect the hell out of you. What…you think I would pity you for making a home for Matt and Henry by working your ass off when you had no one else? You think I pity you for coming to the ranch even though you hated me, because it was a safer place for Henry? Take pity out of your vocabulary because there is no pity. Not for you. But there is respect. A lot of respect.

"I gave up the film career because I'm tired of it." Jace watched her closely, as though she might bolt and run. "I'm tired of the travel, the media circus, keeping up appearances, the lies…all of it. You were right when you said there was so much more to life. If I had any doubts I needed to get out, those were wiped clean the night of Mom's charity event. I saw everything, the people, the bullshit, all of it through your eyes. When Bret attacked you… When you walked into my room and saw Lena. I never want to relive any of that again."

"I knew you were telling the truth about Lena. I told you I believed you. As far as that creep, that wasn't cruelty, Jace. It wasn't a monster inside you. You were protecting me." She reached out to him. "I've never had anyone… No one has ever done that for me."

"Kelly, I want a home and a family." He pulled her closer. "I want to raise horses. And all of it has to include you. It's the reason I bought that ranch."

"What?"

"I could have purchased land anywhere. But you were here." Jace reached out and touched her face. "Be my wife, Kelly. Be the mother of my children. You showed me how good life could be. Don't take that dream away. Please give us another chance."

He was an award-winning actor. But she knew he spoke from his heart. She closed her eyes, the reality almost too much to take in. The only man she'd ever loved was offering her more than she'd ever dared to dream.

"If you love me, we can make this work. I haven't been with another woman since Henry was conceived. I just… there was no one… I don't *want* anyone else, Kelly, and I've had a year to think about that. I can't change what your father did, but I'm not him. I can never undo all you've been through because of me. All I can do is promise, if you'll have me, I'll spend the rest of my life making the rest of your life as good as I possibly can."

His hand went under her chin, gently raising her lips to his. In that moment, she gave him her heart, her trust, her love, returning his kiss with everything she had.

"I love you, Jace." She fell into his arms and the tears of joy fell down her face. He kissed her deeply, passionately, letting his hunger for her free, holding her tightly as though he would never let her go, as though he couldn't get close enough. And Kelly kissed him back with every ounce of love she had for this incredible, amazing, complex man. Her hands slipped up his chest.

"You're still a moron," she whispered against his lips.

"What?"

"What in the hell took you so long?"

He laughed. "Woman, you make me crazy." Then all humor left his voice and was replaced with earnest desperation. "Marry me. Now. Today. As soon as we can arrange it. Say yes. I need to wake up next to you every morning. Make love to you every night. I want a family. I want kids. I hope you do."

She chewed her lower lip as she enthusiastically nodded in agreement. He cupped her face in his hands. "There is nothing I want more than to make you pregnant again." His deep voice made her shiver. "But this time I want to look into those amazing blue eyes when we conceive our next child. I want to know the instant it happens. I want to know you see the love in my face. But you're going to have a ring on your finger when I do."

"Jace… Yes. I love y—"

Jace's mouth covered hers, with a passion she hoped would last forever. No longer would she have to gaze up at the night sky. She had found her star, and in his arms was exactly where she needed to be.

* * * * *

PUBLIC ENEMY NUMBER TWO

Anthony Horowitz is a popular and prolific children's writer whose books now sell in more than a dozen countries around the world. He has won numerous prizes for his children's books which include two more stories about the Diamond Brothers – *The Falcon's Malteser*, which was filmed as *Just Ask for Diamond*, and *South by South East* (which he dramatized in six parts for TV). Among his other titles are *The Switch, Stormbreaker, Granny, The Devil and his Boy, Groosham Grange* and its sequel *The Unholy Grail*.

Anthony also writes extensively for TV, with credits including the hit series *Midsomer Murders*, as well as *Poirot, Crime Traveller* and *Murder Most Horrid*. He is married with two sons, Nicholas and Cassian, and a dog. He lives in north London.

Books by the same author

The Devil and his Boy
The Falcon's Malteser
Granny
Groosham Grange
South by South East
Stormbreaker
The Switch
The Unholy Grail